CAST LONG SHADOWS

Cat Hellisen

Text 2022 © Cat Hellisen
Cover 2022 © Tara Bush
Editorial Team: Shona Kinsella & Francesca T Barbini

First published by Luna Press Publishing, Edinburgh, 2022

A CIP catalogue record is available from the British Library

www.lunapresspublishing.com

ISBN-13: 978-1-913387-71-6

For all the sisters and friends,
mothers and daughters.

Contents

Part One

Part One

The Penitent's Tower

From the outside, the Penitent's Tower is squat and imposing; black stone and a bear pelt of mosses in orange and green. It stands alone on its nub of hillside and looks down on fallow fields. I first saw it at age sixteen as the caravan of coaches and horses and treasure brought me to your rolling lands. I was a replacement bride, an unexpected sister. I was in mourning fierce and wrathful, determined to hate this bittergreen country.

I would love you, I told myself. And nothing else. I would save you from a fate like mine.

I didn't even know you and already I thought I could set you free.

The coaches had travelled hundreds of miles along the roads that webbed and divided the eight duchies of Vestiarik. I had come all the way from Petrell, far to the north east where the world was half underwater, where forest rose out of frozen lakes and where old gods still walked under old wood. The duchy of Jurie was warmer, greener, and the trees fluttered welcome, the lamb-lands sweet and grassy. The cities and villages we passed were bright as painted toys, rain-washed, smelling like rising loaves. My father took us through them all, burdening his wagons with trinkets and books. At night we would eat in the houses of farmlords and borderlords and riverlords, and we were welcomed. Everyone knew who I was going to be when I grew up.

I think you understand that much. We never had a choice. There was no chance for us to find out what we would become. We were bred and moulded and bartered. My sister was going to be your stepmother, and I was held in reserve, ready to be neatly tied to whichever family my father believed would best benefit the Petrells. I was never meant to come to you dressed in engagement gowns, sitting on a wagonload of gifts for your father. I was still weeping, I was still filled with guilt. And the closer we drew to your castle, the more I realised how out of place I was. The deep forests were gone here, the bears and wolves eradicated.

This was never my story.

It was the Penitent's Tower that held me and made me hope I would find my own place. In all that gilded splendour it was the one thing that stood out, raw and rotten. I remember asking my lady-in-waiting what it was, and she told me that it was the tower where traitors were sent before they were executed. So, you see, you are not so civilized after all.

The tower is different on the inside. I am right at the top in the rooms below the conical roof, and though the windows are too small to slip through, I can see the whole of Jurie spread out around me like a map. It is so very beautiful, even now. There, to the north, the violet ridges of the mountains, their caps permanently white, their robes of aspen and apple falling down to their ankles, trimmed in gold and saffron. The seasons are changing fast, the nights crack with frost. It can get very cold up here.

I don't suppose I shall have to worry long about that.

For the most part I try to look to the horizon and the distant forested mountains where I wanted to escape to. Better than to look down, dizzy, and see what is waiting for me. Below is the square, and the scaffolds and wood that the men are bringing hour by hour. The ground is silver wet in the morning and the faggots must be damp and black and soft as autumn earth. Perhaps that is a mercy. Is it yours? Do you want me to breathe in smoke and die unconscious, never feeling the flames? It would be like you to show mercy. But not so likely when you have Lilika whispering in your ear. I wonder what she tells you about me. Some of it is probably true, but there has never been a cat so good at snarling up the truth as your friend Lilika. How does she look to you, I wonder, through that blinded eye of yours? Do you see what she is?

There is someone knocking at my door. It's amusing, these little pretences. Whoever it is, they will curtsy and call me pretty names even while they make my pyre ready. I can't open my own door, but I can draw myself straighter and wear my duchess mantle and tell them, "Enter."

"My lady," the woman says, and she sinks so low I think she means to be mocking. But she looks scared enough. After all the rumours that fly through the Jurie palace, perhaps she truly believes I could change her into a toad or cast an ill-wish on her just by staring. It's all ridiculous. I have never had any real magic of my own. Just little stolen trinkets that belonged to ghosts, and nothing more than the stitchery women have passed down from mother to daughter for hundreds of years.

The serving woman has brought me food and wine. I'm still not certain why they bother, but because this is my last meal inside the Tower, tradition dictates I be well fed. It is a way of erasing guilt. She sets out my lonely feast and pours me a glass of apple-pale wine while a guard watches from the doorway. "Is there anything I can bring you?" she asks. She doesn't actually mean *anything*, naturally. But it is a gesture, and I will take it. After all, this is my last night to explain myself.

"There is a bundle of shirts in my room," I tell her. "The Lady Genivia will know which I mean. And my sewing kit." My lady-in-waiting Genivia was helping me make shirts for the poor before I was arrested. It's not that I am particularly generous or kind, but I am well-trained. My mother sewed shirts for the men of our lands, and on the day of the dancing girl she would hand them out herself. It's a fine tradition. It keeps my hands busy. "I will finish some, before—" I pause. Before what? There is no point. My hands tremble and I put them in the folds of my skirts so that this woman cannot report to you how scared I am. She will not stand in front of Lilika and tell her how the witch shook as the men dragged broken branches from elder trees into the courtyard below.

"And paper," I say, my voice firm and calm. "And ink and a pen." I will be allowed that. I gave no confession. There was nothing to confess. But it's as traditional for the condemned to write out their final words as it is for them to be given a feast, as though tomorrow brings a wedding instead of a funeral. I have had my share of weddings. I'm done with the farce.

The woman nods and curtsies again before leaving me to my meal. Though my stomach is shrunken, and I don't feel hunger much these days, I pick at the spread before me.

She returns with a small basket filled with these last requests of mine and moves to clear away the remnants of my meal.

"Wait." I stop her with an outstretched hand, and she backs away from me, eyes wide, her breath coming in shivery little rasps. I would laugh. "Please," I tell her, "Leave it for now. I may grow hungry in the night."

She stares at me in disbelief. I can see her mind working and wondering what kind of callous bitch I must be to fear nothing, not even my own end. Lilika has told everyone that I have no heart. That I seduced men and used them, that I tried to kill you and left you blinded in one eye, that I murdered my own son. I like that part especially — how she condemns me for his death, and then in the next breath will tell her rapt audience that my son was proof of my witchery. "He was an abomination," she whispered. "The duchess must have gone on all fours for dogs and bears to have birthed such a monster." She who never saw him. My little wolf-child.

And now here's the proof of every lie she tells about me. I will eat heartily and drink like a slattern, and in the morning I will go to my fire reeling and fatted.

"You may leave," I tell the servant, and then, finally, I am alone. None too soon. Just thinking of that day my son died was enough to almost undo me. And I have sworn I will never weep in front of any of Lilika's spies and lackeys.

It takes me a few moments to breathe through the cold wash of sadness. I never really let myself mourn him, and I probably never will. He didn't live long enough to name and, if we pretend hard enough, we can all end up believing he never existed. No one will mark his name in any histories of the Jurie line. He will be erased. My own name will be a footnote. The second wife of Duke Calvai Jurie. Two dates. No Issue.

Lilika can wear widow's whites. I think it will suit her.

Quickly, I take the topmost shirt, the one nearest to completion, and fold the leftover bread, cheese and fruit into it and knot it closed, making the sleeves into a loop I can sling over my shoulder. My hands shake as I fumble with the knots. I don't even know why I'm doing this. A part of me that I have never been able to kill has always made sure I prepared myself for both the best and the worst. It is a very practical side of Marjeta Petrell Jurie, and I suppose I should have listened to that aspect of myself more often. If I had, there's always a chance I wouldn't be here now, hoping for some last-minute reprieve, or for the door to fall open and all the guards to drop into sleep. I could do with magic now.

A harsh call startles me, and I turn to see a magpie sitting on the ledge of the narrow window. His charcoal head is tilted, and he watches me with one clever dark eye. The candle reflects a tiny sun.

"Come for food, have you?" I ask him softly, and he hops along the ledge, wary, but not yet frightened. I suppose I am not a very frightening figure. What could I do to him? "Ah well," I tell the magpie. "It's not as though I have much use for it now." I move like the passing of years, slowly unknotting the sleeves of the shirt to retrieve a crust of bread. I have no chance of escaping. Even if I could squeeze through these slitted windows, what would I do then? Unlike my little beggar-friend, I cannot fly. "Here." I tear scraps for him and toss them to the stones. The magpie flutters down and begins to peck.

Undeterred by my presence, he finishes his meal, then flaps up to the table to begin searching for more scraps. A second magpie appears at my window, and within moments has joined his fellow. A third, emboldened by their squabbling, perhaps, flies in through the window and onto the table. They pull apart my shirt, spilling the pilfered food like the entrails of some fabulous beast. I wonder if they once belonged to you or your grandmother, if they remember being captives. The three magpies ignore me in order to fight among themselves for the food, and when they have consumed everything, they turn to the rest of the shirts, determined to find some new stock.

There is no more food under the shirts. I could have told them that, but I have never spoken the language of birds. The disappointed magpies tear at the pile of shirts, revealing only my little wooden sewing kit, with my silk threads and my needles, and below that, a single parchment and a tiny, stoppered bottle of deep blue ink.

I chase them off and rescue the last of my belongings. The magpies go only as far as the window ledge, and they watch me intently in case I should reveal hitherto unnoticed mounds of grain and fruits.

"You can't eat paper and ink," I tell them. "Greedy little monsters."

The magpies cry once in unison, and fly away, leaving me alone with the scraps of my life. It is suddenly very cold and lonely here. I did not realise I ached so for the company of anyone, anything. I brush my eyes with my palms. Foolish. Tears are useless in the face of death, and I made my choice. I could have left you. Perhaps I should have. I could have run. Perhaps I should have.

I did neither, and I knew the price.

The pen and nib are heart-achingly familiar. They were a gift from you on my wedding day. I smile at the wooden kit. Genivia must have packed it. I can imagine her arguing with the servant, her words hooked and sharp. Why give a woman in the traitor's tower an entire embroidery set when all she means to do is stitch a peasant's shirt? I slip the kit into the deep pocket of my skirt and take the writing equipment to the table.

Once I've cleared myself a little space, moving aside the empty dishes, and refilled my wine for courage, I write your name.

Silviana.

I cannot call you dearest, as I think we have moved beyond meaningless rituals. But perhaps I should. Perhaps I should tell you that you were always meant to be My Dearest Silviana, and that it took many harsh twists to change the thread of our love to hate.

And I wanted to love you. It seems unlikely, given what has come between us, but that day I arrived at your father's castle, I was determined to be something to you. A friend, if not a sister. Never a mother. The thought was too ridiculous.

I was six the day you were born. After a year of mourning, your father made plans for a new wife, and my own father — always quick to take any deal that worked to his favour — offered up my sister as a bride.

It was a deal quickly done. Despite my family's reputation for certain unsavoury practices, there was no doubt that tying his duchy to my father's was in Duke Calvai's best interest. We held back the east. Useful in times of war. Useful if you planned to make yourself a King.

To my sister and I, still girls, and still in that strange land that only girls can occupy, the upcoming wedding was barely real. It would be years before my sister left to join your father in his far-away turrets and become the stepmother to a girl we knew only as a motherless, nameless babe. You were not a person to us, and I doubt you, as a mewling child, cared much.

You accuse me of witchcraft, Silviana, but it was no craft of mine that killed your mother or my sister. No spell that tied my family to yours. The words of men chose this day for us.

If there were spells that could have raised the dead, do you not think I would have called my sister back from the dark? I wanted her. Not you.

I never wanted you as my sister, but you were all I was given.

The last of the light is going, and I have only one candle to see me through this final night. This letter that was meant to be something of an apology that apologised for nothing; it will have to do as it is. Your forgiveness will not change what is done. I must work quickly. Though the autumn nights are long, it will be morning long before I am ready.

The sewing kit wood is satiny under my fingers, and the little latch opens soundless. There are skeins of silken thread and a tiny, enamelled box of amber beads each no bigger than a pill louse. And there, beneath the beads is a bear. It is also amber, but it is old and worn, the tiny sharp face blunted, the rough lines dimmed. I stole this when I was barely old enough to talk, and I have never given it up. Behind the bear's head is a hole wide enough to take a thin leather cord. Bears are our omens, the symbol of my mother's family and the guardians of women. Thousands of years ago some girl wore this as an amulet. Perhaps she was a priestess, or a queen. Or perhaps she was nothing.

It doesn't matter who she was, it matters only that she was. I close my fist about the little bear, warming it until I can feel the fine threads waking under my skin. Clever Genni, to bring me this trinket in my darkest, loneliest hour. It belonged to my sister and it is all I have left of her.

A God for Gods

The chapel of Furis at the palace of Duke Calvai Jurie still smelled of new earth and fresh plaster. The holy brothers, under the instruction of Brother Milos, had built it in the old style of the Three. But where the ancient temples were grown slow with their roots deep, from bent saplings turned to arched trees, Furis' temple sprouted seemingly overnight, a mushroom in the shadows of the vast sprawling summer palace of Jurie.

The palace itself was imposing, the façade in the modern style of vast windows and staircases and slender towers and tiny balconies. It had grown like an unchecked cancer from the old castle. Furis' temple was hidden at the back where the windows were slits and the stairwells narrow spirals, so as not to ruin the lines of the palace nor interrupt its view over the parklands and forests and the little knoll where the Penitent's Tower stood like a folly from the past.

When the brothers had built the chapel, they'd copied the shape of the bowed branches and the arched entrances, but the bones were stone and dead wood. Above Lilika's head, the roof curved heavenward, the thick wooden beams dark with oil. The scent of it was rich and deep, competing with the burning incense.

Lilika Satvika knelt on the dark blue slate. She was alone in the little temple. Only the image of Furis painted into the damp plaster, albumen-glossy, could see her here. The artists had made him look almost human but for the great bull head and the empty raw hole in his chest where his heart had been removed. Lilika made note of every finely painted hair and fold of cloth, the way the blood pooling in his chest cavity looked real, newly-spilled. At any moment that blood would go running down Furis's gleaming chest. He was bullock-brown, his black eyes glinting against the darkness of his bull head, his sweeping black horns ready to pull free from the white wall.

She could almost smell that barnyard stink, ripe effluent from the kine packed into their winter corrals feeding off the stores of musty grains and hays. How was one supposed to pray to Furis? She'd never done it before. He was a new god brought westward to supplant the Three. The maiden bears whose time had come and gone. Maiden witches, who shed their skins and wore furs, who worked spells and cast evil on all they touched. With them it was easy — offerings of bread and oil, ritual prayers. With Furis, things were different. Brother Milos said that all the righteous had to do was speak to Furis as a friend, and he would know their heart. Would speak back to them.

"It was an accident," she whispered.

The stone was cold under her knees and from far away the bells were ringing and ringing. Death peals. Her stomach clenched. It had been a year since Duchess Belind's death. Lilika had turned her sheets to a sea of red, drowned the duchess in her own weakness. And now the last bells were sounding to announce the end of the duke's period of mourning.

"What am I supposed to do?" Lilika asked the figure on the wall. She'd started praying to him the day after Belind's death, but Furis had never answered her. Sometimes Lilika thought it better that way. The problem with the Three was that they had tended to answer, and no good ever seemed to come of what they said. You could ask them for favours, but everything had its price. As Lilika had found out when she asked for the one small thing she had wanted.

"I was nineteen," she said. "I had no idea." She came to beg forgiveness, and while Furis offered none, at least he also didn't offer any judgement. The Three would have mocked her, laughed and told her she should have known that all pleasures must be paid for in full. It didn't seem fair. At the very least the Three could have warned her that asking for Calvai's attention would have turned out ill.

Perhaps it would have been bearable if the price were one Lilika herself had to pay, but the Three had always been capricious bitches.

Lilika had not known that it would be Belind who would pay for her silly little wishes. She had loved the woman despite who she was, drawn to her sun just like the rest of the court butterflies. "I don't know what to do," she said softly. The candles against the wall flickered steadily, and though the chapel was new and uncertain, and the image of Furis foreign, Lilika felt a little peace. Perhaps just by speaking aloud of her sins she could unburden herself. She glanced quickly over her shoulder, but the round room was still empty. "I made a girl motherless," she said, "and I know that I will carry that sin to my grave. But if there is a way to make the burden lighter, I will do it, whatever it takes."

Protection. The word slithered through her head, and the candles guttered.

Lilika scrambled back, one hand clutching at the little protection amulet around her neck. "What—"

Listen. Protect. The voice grew closer, deeper, booming through her skull. Lilika pressed her hands to her ears and rocked, but the voice could not be drowned out. *You stole a mother, you must do the work she would have done. You must balance the world against your own sins. You must mould and guide her daughter in her place.*

Slowly, Lilika lowered her hands. The figure on the wall stared down at her, and now his eyes didn't look hard and black as stones, but compassionate, the warmth of kine in the byres, the tenderness of cows to stagger-legged calves. "I already..." She did what — nursed the little infant? Milk wasn't mothering. She would have done that anyway. While the duchess stayed beautiful and untouched, Lilika would have been wet-nurse to a child that was not her own. She'd been convenient. An unmarried girl of nineteen, her baby born early, still and small and blue and breathless.

"You come here to pray?"

The sudden interruption of a male voice made Lilika's heart snap against her ribs. She turned and pressed her face to the floor.

"Come now, none of that. I'm not exactly the emperor beyond the ocean," Calvai said.

Lilika stilled the rataplan rush of her heart and raised her head. "My lord, I come here every morning."

"Ah," Calvai said. He walked the circle of the room, like a dog circling a rabbit. "I confess I have not prayed as much as I should."

She kept her head bowed and said nothing. One hand stayed pressed to the chain at her neck, the little catch pricking into her fingers. The clasp loosened, and the amulet fell to the ground. The last symbol of her connection to the Three, broken.

"Do you judge me for it, Lee?"

"Never." She dared to look up, to stare him in the face. It was one thing to look a duke in the eye when the bed made them almost equals, but another when she was simply the wet-nurse to a child too small to know the difference between one breast or another. "It is not my place to judge the actions of my duke."

Calvai laughed bitterly. "But you can, and you do. You'll just keep it sewn up in here." He tapped her forehead, but Lilika did not flinch.

"No, sir," she said, and it was truth. Of all people, she was the last to have the right to judge anyone.

The peace of the chapel was broken and there was no chance Lilika would be able to return to her prayers now. "My Lord, do you need me for something?"

The duke shook his head. "No. Advice, perhaps."

"You have many good advisers."

"None of them are you."

She bowed her head again and waited.

"The year is ended," he said, and sighed. "I have finalized the arrangements with Duke Petrell for the hand of his second daughter."

Lilika felt as though the duke had kicked her through the face. She swallowed, tried to make the words come out right. "I — I see. That is good." The word tasted like sick in her mouth.

Calvai narrowed his eyes. "She's fourteen." He snorted. "A child. This is simply an engagement. I have four years still to see through, and many things may change in four years."

"You think a better prospect may present itself?"

"Perhaps." Calvai held out his hand. "But I will not renege

on an agreement. And I need the eastern borders. The Letters of Engagement will be here within the week, signed and witnessed and sealed. Still, as I say, four years is an eternity in some worlds."

"You are not happy about this marriage?" Lilika allowed herself to be helped to her feet. Standing, she came only to Calvai's shoulder. She had always been a small woman, delicate and fine-boned. The midwives had told her it was probably why her own baby had faltered. Too small and weak to live.

"The line of Petrell has many secrets," Calvai said. "Or rather, the line of Petrell has been tainted. There is talk of witchcraft, that some of the women of that bloodline are devils and hags, that they cast spells over fields, curse their enemies."

Lilika feared Calvai would feel her hand freezing in his and question her, but he did not seem to notice. He kept talking. "Brother Milos suspects that there was such witchcraft behind the death of my wife."

"You cannot believe—" the words were choked, hard to push out.

"Of course not." Calvai dropped her hand. "It's the kind of thing old women say, gossip and sly idiocy, I told Milos that I would not have men of Furis demean themselves by prattling like crones. I heard no more of it."

Lilika swallowed. "But you worry?" she said softly.

He nodded.

"I will watch over Lady Silviana," Lilika said. "When this girl from Petrell comes to our lands, I will watch her, and I will keep Silviana safe from any witch's tricks. If the Petrells mean harm, we will see to it that they can do none. Furis will protect us." There, there, she would save the girl she'd made motherless, protect her the way a mother would. This witch-girl from Petrell would never hurt Calvai's daughter. Not while Lilika still drew breath. She glanced at the image of Furis, and nodded once, minutely. The message had come, her atonement told.

"You've dropped something," Calvai told her, and pointed at the little amulet lying on the slate. A tiny ivory face stared blindly up at them.

"No." Lilika shook her head. "That is not mine."

"Someone must have left it here" Calvai crouched to examine it. "Ah, one of the maids who clean the chapel, I suppose. We should return it to them." He made to pick it up but Lilika put her leather boot over the face.

"No," she said again. "Are we not a civilized country? You should not encourage the worship of these little gods."

Calvai looked up and frowned. "I suppose. I have never seen myself as the kind of ruler who tells his people what they must believe in."

"But the Three are the gods of witches," Lilika pointed out. "Is it not better if they are forgotten?" Under the ball of her foot, she felt the slight pulse of heat as the protection amulet flared. "Perhaps the one who dropped this did so on purpose. A renunciation of an old and barbarian religion?"

"Perhaps you are right." Calvai stood. "Brother Milos would agree with you."

"He would." Lilika smiled and dared to brush one hand gently down her duke's arm. "I must get back to Lady Silviana," she said. "Will you need to see me later?"

The duke looked to the wide chapel door, still closed against the winter chill, and dropped a quick kiss to Lilika's brow. "Always," he said. "You bring me comfort when I thought I would never have comfort again."

Lilika crushed the little face under her boot.

Moon and Mirror

Marjeta Petrell was strung between sleeping and waking. She stumbled up the stairs of the old, pointed turret toward the cold wash of moonlight between broken roof tiles. Her older sister Valerija had dragged her from their bed a few minutes ago and her mind was still cloudy with half-remembered dreams. She pulled her embroidered cloak tighter about herself and stamped her feet in fur boots, while just ahead bare heels flashed as Valerija danced up the abandoned stairwell. Valerija's voice rose high and clear as she sang magic in place, warming the air around her and casting the servants in their wing into drowsy stupors.

Neither of the girls were allowed in this section of the family palace. It was ancient and unstable, long left to mice and moss, ivy and choughs. Even in Petrell the old things had been left to crumble — old towers, old ways, old magics — all slowly fading. But there was no danger of being caught here while Valerija sang snatches of their mother's favourite song, twisting it into a new shape to suit herself. The sound echoed down the spiral of stone.

Marjeta began to hum tunelessly along under her breath, more to keep herself warm than anything else. It was the song about the golden bear who had come out of the woods to marry the milk-maid fair; a leaping tune that blew sunshine and summer under the bridges of her ribs.

The dance ended, and Valerija paused to glance back, the air around her glittering brighter. "You're so slow, Mari."

Valerija's magic sparked against Marjeta's face; little stinging kisses of warmth that threaded heat under her bear furs and velvets, right down to her toes until they were as warm as roasted chestnuts. It was enough to draw Marjeta fully out of the last tattered fragments of dreams. She snatched at the magic with her mind as though she could steal her sister's power for herself, but the threads only passed over and through her.

"I'm coming," she puffed. Though Marjeta was near ten, at fourteen Valerija was long legs and coltish grace, and try as she might, Marjeta never seemed to be able to keep up with her sister. She took the last few steps double, until she reached Valerija in the turret room.

Wind whistled through the crumbling stone and the luminous moon stared down at them from a high window. There was one more small set of steps to climb before they could be on the wide wall high above the lakes and cold black forests of Petrell. In the crisp night air where Val insisted her ritual had to be performed. Even with the magic keeping her warm, Marjeta thought longingly of the bed she and Valerija shared. The duck down covers were thick, and there were glowing embers in the bedroom hearth. It was not the kind of place one left willingly in the middle of a night where the winter stars were cold and bright as seed pearls on indigo linen. Only Valerija would think it a good idea to climb a forgotten tower and call down the moon just to see what it would say. Marjeta rubbed the crust of sleep from the corners of her eyes. "Val. Are you sure this will work?"

"Of course it will." Valerija cradled a silver mirror in her arms, gentle as a new niece. It was mantled in white silk but Marjeta knew the swirls of patterns engraved around the frame. Birds and beasts and leaves and vines intertwined in a riot of curves and curls. In the centre, the mirror was slightly dulled, and the reflection it showed was always hazy and indistinct. It wasn't meant to be used like that, for simple acts of vanity.

The mirror had been a gift to Valerija on her ninth birthday. It was too fine a gift for a child, even one born to a duke and duchess of one of the eight duchies of Vestiarik, but Valerija had magic, and their mother — who had bright threads of witchery in her veins — had passed the treasure on secretly. It did not do to speak too loudly of witchcraft and power, not when the world was changing and the old bear gods were sleeping, replaced by the heartless, horned Furis. The mirror had once belonged to Oma Zoli, the grandmother Marjeta did not remember. Oma had died before Marjeta or Valerija had been born, but they had both heard plenty of tales about her at their mother's feet. According to family stories she was the grandest, most beautiful woman who had ever lived, at once stern enough to stop snow from melting, and joyful enough to bring the spring if she laughed too loudly.

But Oma Zoli was gone, and Mama was barely a witch at all and Marjeta even less.

Valerija was all witch; down to her shadow-hair and snow-skin, her mouth like the promise of war and her eyes black as emperor hornets. So Valerija had been given Oma Zoli's mirror, the gleaming eye that saw what was meant to be seen. It saw truth, and, if you were lucky, it saw futures. Tonight, Valerija planned to invoke the oldest spells, ones meant to call down the moon and trap its truths in the mirror's surface. To ask for visions and portents.

The idea of it made Marjeta feel sticky-strange. No one ever said outright that magic wasn't allowed, but they still knew it in their bones. If Father were to hear of this... Marjeta danced from foot to foot, the cold stones eating through even the thick fur of her boots, and the wind sharp against her cheeks and hands. She pulled her trimmed cloak tighter about her shoulders. Valerija had embroidered this one for her, stitched it heavy with spellwork, she'd said. Marjeta had never been able to tell if it worked, or even what it was supposed to do. "Do you really think the moon will answer you?"

"It will," Val said. The last of the spiral of steps came to an end, the rotten doorway opening at Valerija's command and vomiting them up to the empty tower wall. The moon seemed even more enormous from here, like a great blue agate stitched to the finery of a queen. Valerija turned, surveying her lands, a smile playing at the corner of her mouth. She seemed satisfied with whatever magics she could feel in the air. "But perhaps you will be lucky enough to hear what the moon says."

It was the sort of answer Marjeta had come to expect from her sister, so she sighed, and sat herself cross-legged on the grime-dark stone. It was bound to be a long night, and she was at least going to be comfortable.

Valerija carefully set the package before her and sat opposite. With slow movements, she unwrapped the swaddling silk. The mirror was murky, the edges milky with crackled ice. "There," Valerija said. The moonlight turned the surface silver-white. "Now, to speak to the moon, you must feed her, Mama says."

"Feed her what?" Marjeta asked hurriedly, her teeth chattering together. She was certain that her sister loved her, but she also loved magic and probably wouldn't see any downside to feeding her magicless sister to the moon. She stared balefully at the mirror — perhaps Valerija would merely want a toe. There was a knight in their father's service who had a wooden toe, and who sometimes took it off to terrify the children of the court. Perhaps he had a sister who was magical too. With a quick breath, Marjeta looked away from the mirror and out over the edge of the low wall instead. Far below the fort was ringed with ice and snow and scatterings of farms, and beyond them, the pine forests, and further still, the great frozen lakes that ringed their world.

A wolf howled, was answered by its pack, and Marjeta trembled, her marrow freezing.

"We need blood," Valerija said matter-of-factly. She drew a long embroidery needle from where she'd pinned it to her maroon woollen cloak and held it before her, point up.

"Oh." That was better than a toe, at least.

"Mama says the magic is strongest with heart blood—" Valerija grinned. "Don't look so rabbit faced, Mari. I'm not planning on murdering you for a spell, you know."

"Oh, good."

Valerija shook her head. "You should never be afraid of witches. Mama says that it's men we should fear."

"Can men not be witches too?" She was curious. It seemed to Marjeta that though her father and her elder brother were considered of greatest importance, it was Valerija and Oma who had been truly powerful. But perhaps men didn't notice their kind of power, or if they did, thought it just tricks and traps. At least, the way they spoke of magic, when they spoke of it at all, was to mock it and call it evil and treacherous.

"Men are never witches." Valerija sniffed. "Never." She stared at the needle's point, her teeth small and dull under the silver light. "The next strongest magic is moonblood, but we can skip that, I think. We will make do with plain old boring embroidery blood. Give me your thumb, Marjeta." She held out her free hand, waiting for Marjeta to obey.

"Are you going to cut it off?" A missing toe she could at least hide in slippers and boots, but a thumb that had mysteriously disappeared was bound to be noticed. Mama would ask questions, and Marjeta doubted that even her perfect sister would get away with nothing more than a scolding for the amputation of a limb. Probably. She could never be sure exactly how Mama would deal with the things Valerija did.

"Oh, Mari, pet. I only mean to prick it. Look," Valerija said, and curled her hand into a fist. "I'll do mine first so you can see." She pressed the needle point fiercely into the pad of her thumb, and when she withdrew it, a bright dark bead of blood welled up. She pressed her thumb and let the blood drip onto the mirror surface, where it sank in, as though it fell into a bowl full of water. The blood coiled in a cloud of black serpents. "Now you," Valerija said, and sucked her thumb quickly. "That way it will be stronger."

It was easier to let Valerija do it, to stab that bright point into her thumb and squeeze. The pain was both unexpected and familiar. Marjeta had very little skill with needlework, and while Val could embroider neat and quick as a stork stabbing frogs, Marjeta's fingers and thumbs were all pocked with little bites from her needle. This time, though, the needle went deep and the blood would not stop welling, even after she'd dripped her share into the magic mirror. Marjeta sat with her thumb in her mouth and sucked the blood away. It tasted of spear points.

Valerija's attention was all caught back up in the mirror and the little cloud of blood that hung suspended in its icy heart. She had no time now for her sister. "Moon," she whispered.

Marjeta popped her thumb out of her mouth for a moment. It went instantly cold in the night air and throbbed like a stolen heart. "Do you need to do a special chant?"

"Yes, you need to ask. The power's all in the words, and the silver and blood."

"And you," Marjeta pointed out.

"And me, of course. But you also have witch blood, Mar." Valerija rubbed her white hands together. "Moon," she said, louder this time. "We call you down with silver, with ice, and needle blood, with warm life and cold death—" She drew back, her face gone sickly pale, an empty mask. "Did you hear that?" she half-shrieked in a delighted whisper.

"No." There'd been nothing to hear, just the howling wolves as they moved away from the fort, and the whisperings of the distant pines. Marjeta was growing colder, her shoulders hunched up and shaking; Valerija's burst of magical warmth was fading now.

"It answered me — the moon answered me."

"I heard nothing." Marjeta couldn't quite keep the trace of sulkiness out of her voice. It lay under her words like a waiting adder.

"Hush, pet, of course you didn't. I should have suspected as much."

Marjeta went hot, the flush spread across her face like a wave of illness. She pressed her thumb against her teeth and really concentrated. It wasn't fair that Valerija could hear the moon speak and all she got was trees and stupid wolves. It grew so quiet she could hear the faint rustle her clothes made with each breath. But no moon.

Valerija leaned over the bowl so that her breath misted the mirror's surface. "Moon, answer me truthfully." She sat up and looked sharply at Marjeta. "Quickly, what's your question?"

"Oh." Marjeta hadn't thought of one, and she blurted out the thing that had been uppermost on her mind ever since it had been announced that their brother Josef was going to marry, and had been presented with a beautiful new roan mare by his future wife's family, "Will I get Josef's pony Dust? It's just that she's much too small for him, really, and she likes me best and I know Mama thinks that she's too much of a handful for me, but truly she isn't and besides—"

Valerija held up a hand, "Enough, let me listen, or I'll miss it."
Silence fell. The wind hushed about the tower, and the wolves
were gone. Even so, Marjeta heard nothing. Val sat with her eyes
closed and nodded beatifically. "Yes," she said, and opened her
bright eyes, sharp as stings. "The moon says yes."

"Did she say when?" Marjeta asked eagerly, though she was
a little suspicious of the deal. After all, Valerija was definitely a
witch, but she was also still a sister, and prone to tricks and jokes.

"No," Valerija snapped. "You didn't ask. Now, shh." She pressed
her finger against her lips.

"It's getting too cold."

"Well, the sooner you're quiet the sooner we'll be done and can
go back to bed."

Marjeta closed her eyes and settled into thinking of Dust, the
iron grey hunting mare, fleet as a hare and sleek as an otter, with
her fine dished face and her tail that she kept raised like a duke's
banner. Dust would listen to no one but Josef, or so everyone
thought, but Marjeta had bribed the little mare with stolen yellow
apples and black crusts of bread and had told her again and again
how wonderful she was. And Marjeta was a fine rider, better than
Valerija, who pretended to hate riding because of it. She'd learned
to ride almost as soon as she could walk. Of course, she would get
Dust — Josef had to see that she alone would be able to handle
his old mare. And one day her father would give her one of his
wolfhounds, and they would go hunting, her and Dust and the
lean hound, and bring down a stag, or a white deer, or a wolf like
a ghost.

Valerija was whispering again, and Marjeta cracked open
one eye. The moonlight bathed Val's face, making it glow in an
unearthly way, and her whispers sounded like the edges of bat
wings, softly-scary. "Moon, tell me true. Am I the greatest of all
witches, and will my power reach from sea to sea?"

Marjeta sighed quietly. Valerija could be the best of people,
and also the worst. She was always thinking up games for them
to play, and stealing cakes filled with honey for them to share,
sticky-fingered in hidden rooms, or leading them off to thickets
filled with magic so that they could play catch and chase with the

earth people and tree people, and the spirits of stone and water, but she always had to be best at everything. She had to embroider the best coifs, or wear the newest dresses, and she wanted always to know from Mama if she was as powerful — or more so — than old Oma Zoli had been. Marjeta hoped that whatever the moon said, it wouldn't leave Valerija in a temper. Probably, she thought, if her sister wasn't the most powerful, it would be in the moon's best interest to lie. Just a little.

Valerija frowned.

The moon must be speaking. Marjeta huddled deeper into her cloak. This time she thought she could hear a hiss on the very edge of sound, just like when the baby salamander in their hearth was woken from his fiery sleep.

The wind picked up, and a ragged shadow curtain of cloud was thrown across the moon. The light faded, and Valerija stood, hurriedly wrapping Oma Zoli's mirror back up in its swaddling silks.

Shaking fiercely now from the cold, Marjeta scrambled to her feet. At least it was over, and she was probably getting Josef's pony, which seemed a good trade for a night of lost sleep and a thimbleful of blood. "What did the moon say?"

"I don't know."

It was a strange, curt answer, and Valerija's face was flushed with emotion; her dark hair a jaggy tangle of thorn points and shadows; black eyes and blooded mouth. For a moment she looked like a mad witch crone full of seething power rather than a fourteen-year-old girl.

Marjeta decided to simply keep quiet and follow her back down. What could the moon have said to her sister to manage to change her entire mood around. She didn't seem angry, but it had been something she perhaps didn't want to hear. Curiosity gnawed at Marjeta, though she knew better than to say anything. They rushed down the stairs, through the passages and back to their shared room where the vast bed waited as warm as a loaf of new bread.

The warmth seemed to thaw Valerija's expression somewhat, and the dying embers made her look less wild and strange. It was time to prod her, Marjeta thought. "Val? The moon?"

Valerija stared at her, eyes narrowed, mouth thin, and threw her cloak on the end of the bed.

"It did answer you though?" Marjeta whispered, when they had stripped off their outer clothes and were curled together like cats under their down filled blankets and their fur covers. "It said something?"

"It did." Valerija sounded sulky, so Marjeta guessed she'd definitely been told she was not the greatest witch in all the land and resolved to stop the questions before her sister turned bear grumpy. She had better things to think about than her sister's smashed ambition, like a pony that could gallop swift across the earth, hooves flying, breath misting the air.

When Marjeta was half-asleep, her head thick with the feeling of galloping Dust through the forest, the wolfhounds like a sea of hairy ghosts seething around them, Valerija spoke. "It told me nothing I could understand."

"Mnnm?" said Marjeta. She could feel Dust's hot flanks, hear the thunder of the mare's shod hooves, the bellows of her lungs, what did it matter what the moon had said about her sister's witchcraft?

"It told me that I am the greatest."

"That's good right?" mumbled Marjeta. How silly for her to be upset at hearing exactly what she wanted to hear. Marjeta snuggled deeper under her covers and tried to grab the reins of her fleeting dream again.

"I suppose," said Valerija, and if she said anything else after that, Marjeta did not hear her.

*

That morning Marjeta was dull and sleepy, enveloped in a haze of half remembered magic and moonlight. It left her feeling out of sorts and ill stitched in her own skin. Like it or not, there were no excuses to be made when it came to the sister's studies, and a grumbling Marjeta was dragged from her bed and sent to her lessons. Valerija had separate tutors, and Marjeta studied her grammars, her songs, histories and geographies with a small group of other noble bred children.

"You're slow today," her tutor snapped, when she could not remember the names of the current rulers of the eight duchies of Vestiarik, and their principal allies and alliances.

"The Duke Calvai," she said. It was easy to remember the Duchy of Jurie, he and his dead wife and motherless child. But of the others, only neighbouring Farugh and Coriast truly meant anything to her. "What does it matter who rules them?" she whined. Her forehead was damp, sweat plastering unruly tendrils of fly-away hair to her temples. "By the time I'm old enough to care, it will probably all be different."

Different indeed, when her own sister would be the Duchess of Jurie, a stepmother at eighteen to a child neither girl had ever met. She pulled a face.

"Your mother will not be best pleased," her tutor warned. "She would like it if I attempt to fill your head with something other than ponies and dogs."

"Horses and hounds are more interesting than dukes and dead people," Marjeta returned. She hated indoor days. Dull lessons, dull interminable lessons. Her hand was cramped. It was meant for drawing a bow or guiding a horse at rein. She closed her printed copy of Spensir's Histories of The Vestiariken. Her father had bought several of them from his last trip to the far away port town of Branly in Sevari. There was another name to give her tutor. She brightened. Sevari always had the newest things from the west and had even begun to build print horses and train lettermen.

"You say that only because you are a child," the tutor said. "Your decad will be here soon, and you will have to step out of childish things. You have spent ten years running about like a wild thing; the time comes for you to take your duties more seriously."

Marjeta shrugged. She was too tired to argue. Stupid Valerija, dragging her out in the freezing cold last night — and for what? A mess of nothing. In the distance, the three bells had begun to chime the hour from the new temple. The men of Furis did so like to keep time, even if the time made no sense. The bells meant her mother would be expecting her to join the women in her solarium where the women's court caught the last of the afternoon sun, their fingers working bright needles. She felt a momentary flash of jealousy as the others left, free to go do what they wanted. As the daughter of the duchess, Marjeta wasn't given such freedoms. She and Valerija would be expected to take their places in the women's court.

Part of their education, Mama always said, though Marjeta learned nothing except that embroidery was the most boring of the womanly arts, and that her mother's court was made up of wool-witted saps. She took a deep breath and trudged from the children's library and down the short passage that took her to the solarium where everyone was already gathered.

Despite the weak sun filtering through the walls of mullioned glass, the semi-circular room had to be heated. Servants kept the hearths burning, and tipped sweet herbs onto the flames, scenting the room with incenses and herbs. Marjeta coughed as she drew up a seat alongside her mother, who nodded at her, but carried on her conversation with her ladies-in-waiting.

Fresh air would be better, Marjeta thought, and looked longingly out the windows to where the gardens had turned golden white with frost. She'd prefer to be out there and cold, than in here and forced to do more needlework.

"It's not torture," Valerija said, leaning closer and whispering. The room was full of the lilting prosody of women talking across each other, laughing, or sometimes singing in time with Mama's musician. "Anyone would look at your face and think you've been sentenced to death."

"It's hot in here," Marjeta said, and loosened the laces at her neck. "And stuffy, and smelly."

"It's not smelly. A barnyard is smelly."

"It smells like women," Marjeta said. "And wine." She looked at her basket, where her current embroidery project sat in a hopeless, dull reminder of how much she loathed this part of her day. It made her stomach churn. Or was that the stink from the fires? "Why did you have to drag me out last night?" she muttered. "I feel terrible."

"Don't be such a baby, Mari." Valerija's fingers danced, her needle threading stitch by stitch. "It could be worse. Mama could make you recite all your lessons from today."

"Did she do that to you?"

"Yes." Valerija pulled a face. "And made me sing. It was awful."

"In front of everyone?"

"Just so."

Even embroidery sounded better than that. Somewhere their mother had come by the idea that the daughters of dukes should be like little show mares, able to perform prettily on command. Their eldest sister Nadija had not minded this at all, had even excelled under the rapt attention of their mother's court. Neither Marjeta or Valerija could match her, nor wanted to.

Marjeta sighed and tried to unsnarl her embroidery thread. Her feet and hands seemed too numb and bulky to hold her needle right, her head too heavy to listen to the conversations of the clutch of women around her. The consonants clattered against her skull in little showers of hailstones and melted away without meaning. Marjeta could focus on only the misery of embroidery. Her thumb ached with each little stab. She glanced over at her sister's flying fingers, the flash of the needle bright.

Val was working a design in green silk onto the sleeves and neck of a linen undershirt. She was frowning slightly in concentration, but there was no sign of last night's little adventure on the armoury roof. Her skin was clear, her eyes dark and shining like new coals. Under her fingers, ferns unfurled. It was its own kind of magic. One that Marjeta also had no mastery over. She could add it to her list of failures. Or Mama would, at any rate. She despaired of her, Marjeta knew.

Marjeta, whose stitches were wide and sloppy, had been relegated to working on a simple cross-stitched edging on a riding shirt for Josef. She jabbed the needle in and drew the white thread through on a loop, which then got caught on a knot and tangled up into a mess. This was a waste of time. She lowered her eyelids and daydreamed about Dust, letting the chatter of the stitching women sound about her like bird calls in a forest. A blanket of heat settled on her skin sun warm and thick with the promise of a thunderstorm. The fire crackling turned to the crack of twigs underfoot, the winter snap to a late summer day, almost too hot to move. It was just her and Dust, sweaty with the day's ride. Marjeta dreamily lifted one hand to push a damp curl of hair away from her forehead. Her hand was icy against her cheek. So hot here, sticky and ready to rain.

Valerija prodded her when she began snoring, bending slow as a drooping lily over her embroidery. "Wake up, pet," she hissed through her teeth, soft enough that their mother could not hear.

The fires were high and the air rank and humid from the breath of women. Marjeta lifted her face and pressed one hand against her flushed cheek.

"I wasn't sleeping," she whispered back, but around her the room had become too bright and fast, and the laughter of her mother and her ladies too much like the shrieking of foxes. Her chest was tight, the air thin. Why was it so hard to breathe, to focus? The room swam into a sludge of colours, the faces of the ladies smearing together into a monstrous many-eyed beast.

She was tired, that was all. "I'm perfectly awake," Marjeta said. She looked down at the riding shirt. It was dyed indigo, and she'd been working in a neat and simple block design with white thread along the cuffs — something that even she would normally be able to do, but her stitches marched this way and that, in haphazard rows. "I'm going to have to do this all over." The needle dropped from her fingers and hung on the end of its spider thread like a condemned man.

The floor, covered in thick carpets, loomed closer, and Marjeta tumbled forward out of her stool. She made a soft thump as she landed and pricked her wrist against her needle. The pain was bright and small, and then it was gone.

Dream and Fever

Marjeta woke in dark and cold and drowning-wet, her mind swimming through a black sea. Ghostly fish moved in the currents around her, their silver skins pale enough that she could see their stomachs. Luminous sea-nettles drifted past, pulsing, their streamers of stingers dragging beneath them. Marjeta had only ever seen dead ones before, washed up half rotting in the black lakes. The sea-nettles were floating to a surface far from this crushing darkness and Marjeta followed them up, kicking for the light and away from the nightmare world.

She woke in her bed, the only dampness her sweat soaked skin. Her bones had turned to rods of ice that rattled and cracked against each other with each shiver. She ached, the cold spilling up from her marrow and freezing her flesh. Every joint from her neck to her toes felt as though mountain dwarves had taken to them with stone hammers, pounding her skeleton to splinters. From the smell around her, familiar and musky sweet as a foal's head, she knew she was in her rooms, in her bed. But underlying it was another sour sharp scent. Illness. Like the way Old Magda had smelled before the pall bearers had shrouded her face and carried her away.

Heavy weights settled on her and Marjeta shivered and shuddered. Shrouds scented with herbs, bitter and pungent, and slightly rancid like lanolin. She twisted under the woollen drifts of blankets. Her mother's voice, distant and soft, calling for candles, and for the effigies of the Three to be brought into the room and set up to watch over her. The bear gods of Sky and Sea and Earth, carved of stone and wood, fired from clay. Marjeta burrowed deeper under the blankets as though she could escape their dead eyes. Her mother's gods scared her with their raw, hungry faces, their wooden trencher of offerings. She preferred the bull-headed god her father's new priest had brought from the south. He was stern and fearsome looking, and as far as Marjeta could tell, an impotent figure. But at least he didn't feed on fat and bones and whispers. She preferred gods who were useless.

"There, Marjeta." A cool hand pressed against Marjeta's brow. Her mother's hand, like the underside of a rose petal, gentle and as fragrant. Her mother was a distant woman taken to ignoring her other children in favour of writing long letters to her oldest daughter Nadija who had married a prince in the far west, and who was alone in a court full of vipers who spoke a language of hisses and thorns. When she did have time for Marjeta, she seemed always fondly exasperated. Even now. "Sick, I wonder that it's not from playing out all hours in the snow when you know you have work to do."

The hand withdrew. "Sit up, little love, and drink this."

Marjeta was lifted, an arm under her back to support her. Her old wet nurse Olaga, whose onion and juniper smell was as familiar to Marjeta as her own. She let the warmth of her nurse cradle her, and drank from the little bone cup her mother held to her lips. Honey heated and thinned with boiling water and spiced with dried dill. The sips warmed her a little, and for a moment the ice in her bones melted enough for her to stop shaking.

She let the hands lay her down again, tuck herb pockets under pillow, and cover her. Waves of black stormed into her vision, their edges crackling with heat and cold. It was as though her body could not know which way to turn, whether it would walk through the fury to life, or drift easily out to death. She sobbed and turned, shucking the blankets from her sweating skin. Hands drew them back over her, wiped her brow.

You cannot sleep forever.

In her dreams, Marjeta turned. She was underwater again, in the black, in the drowning, and the light she'd thought she'd reached had turned out to be a window of glass, green and silver and blue, matted with the rotting debris of twigs and little dead fish that had been trapped under the lake's winter skin. She battered at the ice with her fists, though they were cold enough that she was sure her bones were shattering with each blow, and she could see the air leaving her lungs in aching trails of fine bubbles.

You must strike harder.

The voice was familiar, and yet Marjeta was certain she had never heard it before. It came from above, from outside the ice.

Strike again.

She did, her fists hammering, her body buoyed by the hard jelly of the drifting sea-nettles, their stings cutting her skin, lashing her on with poison whips. The ice shivered but did not crack. Finally, the last of her air gone, Marjeta curled in on herself, her hands weeping icy blood into icy water.

You cannot give up, said the voice. It was rough as bark, a hard, wild voice. Above Marjeta, a shadow passed over the ice, and something large and powerful hit the surface.

Marjeta blinked as a crack spread black branches through the murky window.

Again.

Water filled Marjeta's lungs as she slammed her fists against the crack.

For a moment, she tasted air, saw the winter sky bright and blue as the back of a river kingfisher, saw a bear looking down at her, golden furred, eyes dark behind the long, dark muzzle, before the ice filmed over again.

So the days went. Marjeta slept in shivering fits and starts, and her life was reduced to the rattle of the chamber pot and the sips of broth or honeyed water. Between that was blackness and cold and heat, bears and ice, blue skies and drowning pain.

*

"You missed the wedding." Val's voice was a clear slice across the fog of dreams and illness.

Marjeta opened her eyes to the dull grey of mid-afternoon light coming through the far window. She was in a new, unknown room instead of the one she and Valerija had shared. Her sister was sitting cross legged at the end of the bed, her dark hair falling loosely over her shoulders, a small sewing kit open in front of her. She was dressed in pine green velvet trimmed with cream lace, and against the green and black her pale skin and red mouth seemed to stand out even more.

The sound of cracking ice lingered in Marjeta's head, the cold creeping still under her skin. Carefully, she pulled her hands free from under the covers and looked at them. They were dry, pink with warmth. She made them into fists and breathed in fire warmed air, the smell of herbs. "Wedding," Marjeta said groggily. The words raked the inside of her throat, and her chest ached. Every breath tasted coppery and sour. She felt thin and brittle like a leaf after a wildfire. All bones and no skin.

There was a ribbon tied loosely about her neck, with a small pouch threaded on it. She coughed, feeling it tighten against her throat.

"Josef's," Valerija said.

"But that was a long way away." With clumsy fingers Marjeta undid the bow and pulled the charm free. It was roughly in the shape of a hare and stitched in large uneven black thread. Mama had made this.

Valerija was quiet, head bowed as she threaded a needle. "It's my fault you grew so ill." She pulled a collection of material scraps out from the kit. "Oh, Mari, I should never have made you go to the tower with me, not at night like that." Her voice was choked and soft, gone small with guilt.

"I could have said no," Marjeta said.

"Could you really have?" Valerija's smile was thin, angry.

Josef was married. She'd been sick for weeks then, caught in fever and sleep and the strangeness of dreams. When Mama and Papa were gone to the black forests beyond the end of the world, Josef and his bride would hold the Duchy of Petrell. Duke Josef, Marjeta thought. It scared her — the idea that her parents could age and die. Her fingers pulled at the crude stitches on the hare charm, snapping them. It spilled open like a mouth with too many secrets to keep. Inside were spices and herbs — black peppercorns, dried rosemary, juniper leaves. She dropped the charm on the bed. Hares were the charms desperate mothers sewed for their dying children.

So ill. So ill she might have died, and Val thought it was her fault for begging Marjeta to come with her to the tower. "It — it doesn't matter," Marjeta said, though she'd missed out on dancing and music, and all the cakes and pastries and meats. The last of winter would have thawed away, and though the air would still be crisp as frost, snowdrops would start sending pale sprouts toward the sun.

Spring had begun while Marjeta had been caught in an underwater nightmare, drowning far from water. And the world had turned. No wonder she felt so thin-pressed and weak. Her head ached, her neck stiff and sore. She smelled of sweat and that sour, bone deep rot of illness.

"Mama says it will take you a long time to recover." Valerija plucked fabric together, comparing shades. They were scraps she held, not even big enough to use for slippers, but the materials were fine; wine red velvets and purple silks, linens dyed in the softest of spring shades like new buds and duck eggs and yellow trefoil. Satisfied with her selection, she began to snip at them with her small pair of scissors.

"How long?" Marjeta didn't want to be in bed all through the spring — not when there were leverets to hunt through the meadows and dogs to run alongside, when the shidders were lambing and calving and dropping litters, all kinds of new and growing things to put between her teeth and taste soursweet. Another cough rattled her ribs. She tasted ice water, pond weed, stings and poison.

Valerija looked up and snapped a thread between her teeth. "I'm sorry," she said again. "I wanted to use magic to make you better faster, but Mama said it doesn't work like that." She began to stitch, her fingers darting.

"It doesn't?"

"Mama says healing magic is a trade — I could heal you, but then I'd come out sick myself. She put out the Three instead and asked them to spare you."

Marjeta couldn't help but glance at the three idols set up on a long low table. Their offering trencher sat before them. Mama would have fed them with sweet olive oil and cubes of dense black bread in the day, and at night on cracked bones and cubes of mutton fat. There was no sign of any offering now, but small sooty tracks showed that the hearth salamander had come out during the night while the fire was low and helped himself to the gods' meal. She was a little sad to have not seen him — Tarkis was skittish and shy. "I will have to give my thanks," Marjeta said dully. A warding charm and offerings to the gods — Mama must have been worried.

Valerija pulled a face. "I'll tell Mama you've already thanked them, otherwise she'll make you pray all day." She selected two tiny snippets of pink silk and pinched one neatly into shape, then stitched it in place, and did the same with the other. "Papa's Lili has whelped," she said. "Five pups, two of them bitches."

Lili was Papa's favourite wolfhound. Her fur like cream silk, her nose and legs and tail so long and thin. She was sweet as a kitten when it came to the girls, laying her head on their laps and looking up at them dolefully, and yet, Marjeta knew she could tear out the throat of a wolf — had done so many times. And now she'd had her puppies, and Marjeta had missed their birth. Far worse than a missed marriage. Her heart constricted in her chest. "What colours?" Marjeta craned her head, leaning forward to get a better look at what Valerija was working on.

"They're all sables, but one of the girls is more golden, and her face has no mask, and her tail is kinked. Papa wanted to drown her, but Mama said that killing her while you were ill would be a bad omen. The gods told her so."

Mama's gods were good for some things. Marjeta pictured the puppy, so awkward and thin, like a strange long-muzzled lamb with wolf's teeth. Perhaps Papa would forget to kill it or keep it safe as a thank you to the gods for sparing her. She could hope.

Valerija tossed the thing on which she'd been working into Marjeta's lap. "There."

It was a finger puppet, a little hare with a tail of bound wool, and tiny onyx beads for eyes and nose. "Oh!" Marjeta slipped it onto her index finger and made it bow experimentally. While her sister stitched more hares, Marjeta played with this one, nosing it about her covers, peering it over the ridged hills of the furs, its velvet ears like flags.

"Tell me a story," Marjeta said.

"About what?"

She shrugged and made the little hare dance and bow. "About when I was little."

"About Urshke, you mean?" Val's head was bowed over her work, and her hand moved like a bird pecking for grain. The silver needle flashed. There might even be magic in her stitches, small and sweet, little spells for care and protection. It would be like her to stitch magic into everything she made, whether she thought of it or not.

Marjeta wrinkled her nose. "Who's Urshke?"

"Oh really?" Val paused and looked up at her, half smiling. "You don't remember? It wasn't that long ago."

"No." She frowned. Perhaps it was the haze of sickness that had left her body weak and turned her mind into a bland mess of rubbery porridge, but Marjeta had no recollection of the name. "Who was she?"

"Wouldn't I like to know." Val began stabbing at the material again. "You must have been, oh, three, I suppose, and Mama had given me an amber bear for a gift." She raised a hand, still holding the needle, and measured out a space between forefinger and thumb. "About so big. It was a simple thing, but I loved it. It was old, from one of the treasure heaps men sometimes find in the forests, where the ruins are hidden."

This time Marjeta nodded. She had no particular memory of this bear, but she'd seen similar. They were found only rarely and came from a time when magic was stronger. A gift of one was a small treasure — they were used for protection, for keeping a loved one safe. Amber always was strongest in protection charms, and the fact that the carving was old and of a bear would have made it even stronger. She glanced furtively at the three idols. "I've not seen it," she said.

"Well, you have," Val stuck out her tongue, "and that's half the problem. You see, after Mama gave it to me, you wanted it for yourself. I kept finding it in your fat little hand." She laughed. "You always managed to get it all sticky and dirty, and once I found you trying to eat it."

Marjeta felt feverish again, not sure if it was from the illness or some residual shame and guilt. "What happened to it?" She assumed she must have lost it somewhere, or ruined it.

"It vanished." She sighed and held out her work critically, squinting at it before setting to work again. "It wasn't a very good story, was it?"

"Not really." Marjeta settled back. "So, who was Urshke?"

"Ah, that's the thing. After my bear went missing for the hundredth time, we had a very good idea of who the culprit might be, so Mama and I went to you and demanded you return it."

"And?"

"And you told us that you hadn't taken it, that someone called Urshke had. It was hard to follow, you were still mostly a baby then, but you said it over and over 'Urshke take, Urshke take back,' and we could find no trace of it." Val snapped a thread with her teeth and paused to look for a different coloured spool of thread. "And we never did. No bear, no Urshke, whoever she was."

Urshke. Not a common name in these parts. It was considered ignorant to name a child in a way that might offend the Three. And Urshke — the little bear. Marjeta's stomach began to hurt and sweat beaded along her brow. There was no trace of the confrontation in her head, but how was she to remember something that happened half a lifetime ago? She'd been, as Val said, little more than a baby. There were sometimes fleeting images from her youngest years that flickered through her dreams, but they were snatches and snippets, nothing solid.

And no Urshke. A little bear who stole a little bear. "I don't like that story," she said. "Tell me something else instead."

They talked of the things Marjeta had missed — the dancing, and the wedding feast food, Sir Bojan taking off his boot so that he could remove his false toe because the dancing had pained it, the puppies, the first of the early lambs, Josef's recent hunt and the rumour of a golden wolf in the Salvey forest — until all three hares had been completed and Valerija had placed them on her own fingers — two on one hand and the one on the other. They bowed to Marjeta each in turn, and Val spoke in high little hare voices so that each could declare his name. "Oddment."

And "Endment."

And "Threadment."

Marjeta snorted. "Those are not proper names."

"Oh," said Valerija in a hushed aside. "They are very proper names, for hares. You should never mock something because you don't understand it."

"How do you do," said Marjeta, smiling at her sister, and bowing her head back at the three hares. "A pleasure to make your acquaintance."

"Naturally," said Oddment. "We are the brothers Leverin, and we have come to your great Duchy of Bed Room, in the hunt for a most fiendish beast — as big as a cat—"

"A cat!" squealed Endment and Threadment, and Valerija made them hop and pop all over the bedclothes in alarm, so that Marjeta could not help laughing, even though it made her cough, and her chest ache.

"—a cat, but in shape like unto a lizard, all gowden in colour—"

"The salamander!" Marjeta said and clapped her hands.

"Indeed," Oddment replied gravely. "Do you know where we would find this fearsome creature?"

She nodded. "Tarkis lives in the hearth, but why — what do you want with him?"

"We are on a quest."

Marjeta fell back on her pillows. "Always quests, while I have to stay here in bed. It is all very vexing."

"You are very vexing," snapped Oddment, just before Valerija pulled him off her finger and dropped him. She removed the other two and bundled them altogether. "They're yours," she said, holding them out. "To say sorry."

"Sorry for the tower?" Marjeta shook her head. "Don't be silly, I could have caught ill anywhere."

"But you didn't, and anyway, all that came from that was stupid nonsense."

"I thought the moon told you that you were the greatest witch in the whole land."

"It did." Valerija stood and gathered all her remaining scraps and silks, putting them neatly in her basket. "Olaga will be here soon with more broth," she said. "Don't let her know I've been, I'm supposed to stay away in case I get sick too." She went to the door, then paused to look back, her face white and troubled. "Pet? I didn't tell you all of it."

"Hmm?" The hares were soft to the touch, their empty skins like little promises. Marjeta tucked them under her pillow and encountered the silky hard curve of a clove of garlic. Mama again. She sighed and twisted onto her side to get a better look at her sister. There was something to her expression that Marjeta didn't like — fear, perhaps. What had Valerija to be scared of? Her wedding to the Duke of Calvai was still years off, and Marjeta could think of nothing else that would scare her witch sister.

"On the tower that night — the moon said that no one would ever know."

"No one would ever know what?"

"How great I am. It said, 'Valerija Petrell, you are the greatest witch in all the land, and it will be your suffering that no one should ever know it.' What do you think it meant?"

"That one day you will learn to be less proud and not tell every man and woman and bee and flower you meet how wonderful you are?" Marjeta coughed again, her eyes streaming from the racking pain.

Valerija stuck out her tongue. "Hush you. And get better fast, that Nina is boring me to tears, always whining about everything. I miss having my little lamb at my heels."

"You miss bossing me around."

"That too," Valerija said, just before she closed the door.

When she was gone, Marjeta slipped her hand under her pillow and held her three little hare puppets tight, closed her eyes, and coughed herself back to sleep.

Birthday Gifts

The day of her decad dawned in swirls of pinks and oranges, and Marjeta watched them all from her bedroom window. Now that she was well again and no longer coughing like a plague victim, she was once again back in her and Valerija's shared rooms. At fourteen, Val would soon be given rooms of her own, but until then Marjeta clung to their little nest. This was the place that made her happy. At her sister's side. Being ten didn't make up for what she would lose. In four more years, she would be where Valerija was now, but Valerija would be gone.

She would never catch up.

Marjeta breathed on the window and misted a circle. In it she drew a simple bear shape. A talisman. It was the bear who had broken the ice of her illness and brought her gasping to the lake side. She frowned and quickly rubbed the bear shape away, her sleeve squeaking against the thick glass.

"Awake already?" Val said. Her voice was croaked with sleep.

Marjeta turned away from the view of the meadows and farmlands green with life and looked at her sister.

Val was sitting up, rubbing gunk for her eyes and yawning. She was mussed and crumpled still with dreams, all sleep-sticky. She looked almost as young as Marjeta for a moment, with all the weight of their mother's expectations lifted from her.

"I've been up for ages. Being ten." The pride bubbled in Marjeta's chest. Her decad meant she was old enough to have people start taking her seriously. It always felt as though her mother would baby her for longer, knowing that she was the last of the nestlings.

Now perhaps Marjeta would be treated like Val was, with nods of deference and have people listen instead of pretending attention while thinking of something else.

Valerija sighed, and ran her fingers through her hair, unknotting the night's thoughts and shaking them free. "Too eager. It's the same as being nine, you know."

"It's not."

"It is, I have more experience in these matters, so hush." Valerija left her grooming and rummaged under her pillow to produce a small gift wrapped carefully in a pouch of embroidered velvet. It was only slightly bigger than her hand, flat and squarish in shape. She held it out. "Happy day to you."

"What is it?" Marjeta made no move to come from the window. Olaga would be here soon to dress them with the help of her maid girls, and she wanted to enjoy this time with Val.

"A gift, pet. Stop being dull and come get it, you do want it, I promise you."

Her first gift of the day. A shiver passed along Marjeta's spine followed by a prickling wave of heat. It felt like excitement and terror and fever mixed together and ground like fresh herbs. Val could read her down to her bones, even the things she hoped she kept secret. Any gift Val gave her was going to reflect all she wanted.

Marjeta left the window view, slipped across the flagstones and sat down next to her sister. Before she took the offered present, she hugged Val tight enough to make her laugh breathlessly. She breathed in the scent of her sister's hair, like dark icy currents and black figs and incense.

"You're crushing me, you mad thing." But Val hugged back, just as fierce. There were some things that didn't need words or magic. After a long moment, Marjeta released her, though she snuggled up closer to her sister's side with her feet tucked under her thighs, before she took the velvet package. The pouch moved slippery over the hard cold thing inside it and Marjeta wondered if it could be a book. She wasn't a huge reader like Nadija and Val, but she did enjoy tales. Perhaps it was even a book of simple spell workings — something she could do with practice. She loosened the ribbon and slid the velvet down in soft creases.

It was a silver mirror, delicately edged with roses and thorns and set with tiny gems of red and green and blue. Even if she had not seen it that night on the castle wall, Marjeta would have known it from the way the magic coiled under her palm, like whispers against skin.

The mirror surface was no bigger than the palm of her hand, and Marjeta could make out only a part of her face — a wide brown eye, liquid as a lamb's; the arch of an eyebrow, the line and flare of her thin nose. "You can't," she said.

"Of course I can. Oma passed it to me, so it belongs to me and I can do with it whatever I wish." Val snatched it out of her hands and grinned so that all her small white teeth showed. She had a toothless space on the lower left side, but that was nothing to the double gap Marjeta sported right at the very front of her smile. "And I do wish for you to have it."

Magic. Marjeta's heart swelled, scared and thrilled. Real magic. A priceless gift — and Val was never free with her little collection of magical artefacts. "Mama gave it to you," she argued. "Not Oma Zoli—"

"I know. Don't let her know you have it. I'll show you how it works." Val held the mirror up to her face and breathed on it, misting the mirror surface just as Marjeta had done to the window. "You remember to give it blood, right? Though sometimes it will work with just breath — but you need to work fast for that." Val took Marjeta's hand and closed it around the mirror's handle. It was cold enough to burn, like holding onto an icicle. "Once you've done that, you say, 'Mirror, mirror, take my soul, show me the thing that makes me whole.'"

Marjeta said nothing and watched her sister's breath fade.

"Marjeta?"

"It's lovely." And it would not work. Maybe the mirror was made of pure magic and would work even for someone like her, but Marjeta did not want to find out that it wasn't. It was better to have it like this. Something to keep always in the back of her mind like a promise made, and almost kept. Potential.

"Well..." Val frowned. "I'm glad you like it. Maybe you can't call the moon with it, but you should be able to do basic finding spells.

That's what it was made for — it's meant to help you find lost things." She put her hand over Marjeta's. "Best put it away before Mama sees it." Her smile was back, bright and wicked and red.

Quickly, Marjeta wrapped the mirror again and hid it in their shared closet under a book and scraps of folded material meant for one of Val's endless sewing projects.

They'd returned to the bed, where Val was brushing and braiding Marjeta's hair, when Mama arrived with Olaga and breakfast. "A blessing on your decad," Mama said, though to Marjeta it seemed she barely noticed that Marjeta was actually in the room, as all communication seemed to be directed toward the three statuettes and their offering trencher.

Marjeta glanced down at the fireplace, where the coals were being scraped and stirred by the maid, new logs ready to burn. Tarkis had scuttled into one corner, annoyed by the maid's daily intrusion, and Marjeta clicked her fingers softly.

The salamander slithered across the floor and crawled up under the girls' blankets, his warm head burning against Marjeta's thigh.

The room filled with stern silence, with the echoes of her mother's religion. The salamander's excursions remained unnoticed as Mama began burning a wrapped bundle of sage sprigs in a copper bowl, silently frowning as she watched the leaves smoulder, before she turned to her youngest daughter.

Marjeta accepted her birthday blessings, and let Mama anoint her head with olive oil infused with rosemary. The clean smell of the herb lifted Marjeta's spirits. Mama always relied on ritual to take her through the days, her hours divided into prayers and blessings, offerings and gatherings, wards and charms. Olaga said she'd not always been like this.

"I've brought you a gift," Mama said in her drifting far away voice, once she'd dotted Marjeta's forehead and eyelids with the oil. She motioned for Olaga to step forward so she could take from her a heavy case, about as long as her forearm, that tapered to a rounded point. She handed this solemnly to Marjeta, who took it with equal solemnity. Decads meant adulthood, and here was the first sign of that. It felt too heavy for its small size, the beading rough against her fingers.

The outside of the narrow case had been brocaded and beaded with a fine hand, a bright pattern of flowers and hares, and the four narrow handles visible at the top were gilded iron. A travel set of cutlery.

Mama was preparing her. Val had received a set like this, hers patterned with stags and hounds, for her own decad. There were four implements: a skewer, a wide spoon, a two-pronged fork and a sharp little knife. Marjeta didn't even have to remove them to know that they would be beautiful. "Thank you, Mother," she said, even though her heart was clenched and her eyes watering. "This is a treasure." They were all going to leave one day. That's what the cutlery meant. One day the daughters would travel out from their castle, going to other stone fortresses far from family and friends. There they would survive or die.

"A treasure is only as good as the way in which it is used," Mama said in return, though she managed a smile. "I am glad you like it, Marjeta."

Rain started to fall; the summer morning swept away by a sudden rolling grey bank of clouds. It looked as though Marjeta's decad feast would be a wet one. Hardly surprising for mid spring, but it still made Marjeta's heart leaden.

"Drink this." Mama handed her wine sweetened with honey. "And then Olaga will see to it that you are ready. Your father has a great many gifts for you."

Even that thought couldn't cheer her. The wine was heavy and sour under the sweetness and left an aftertaste that she could not swallow away. Marjeta stared glumly at the set of travel cutlery, and wished she was small again and running free as foxes from swale to shore.

*

When Marjeta and Valerija made their entrance to the hall, the rain was still battering down like a jeweller's round hammer on tin. In honour of Marjeta's decad, the hall had been decorated with garlands of ribbons and spring flowers, scented with pine boughs. Tables were laid and set for feasts, and men and women had been hired to dance and sing and perform acrobatics. It was not a formal feast, Marjeta being the fourth child — and a daughter — but it was excuse enough to set the kitchens to work, and to celebrate a spring day.

And now that day had turned its back on the revellers, they felt the impetus to drink hard and laugh louder, to sing and make merry as if to spite the weather. They sang to drown out the storm.

Marjeta had packed away her earlier gifts in her room; the mirror from Val, Mama's travel cutlery, an ivory thimble from Olaga, a package of silks and threads sent from Nadija earlier in the year and saved for her; and all the assorted little gifts from maids-in-waiting and the women who crowded around her mother.

No one really paid much attention to Marjeta. She was an excuse. She moved among the crowd like a mouse between stems of meadow hay, watching the conversations spill and splash from one face to another. When it came time to feast, she was seated next to Val, to the left of her mother, and watched the duke, her father, eat and drink. He was a distant ogre, a man she hardly knew. She'd never felt close to him. He'd fathered her, and he knew her name, but it always felt to Marjeta that she might as well have burst fully formed from her mother's forehead for all the attention he gave her.

Today was a little different. Once the meat and pastries and soups had been mostly consumed, and the wine had been emptied from many carafes, her father turned to her, leaning across the table. Just past him sat Josef, who was staring dull eyed at his plate as though he were a man whose soul had long since fled. Usually, it was Josef who was the centre of her father's attention, and Marjeta squirmed as Papa's dark gaze settled on her. Like Mama, his hair was the colour of the last withered leaves of autumn, and his eyes were slanted and black, but that was the only resemblance. He had a mouth a little too full of teeth — a condition Marjeta was sure she was inheriting from the way a new tooth was pushing out high on her gum — and a pointed jaw where Mama's ended in a flat, stubborn line like the chopped end of an antler. He kept his reddish beard trimmed close to his jaw line, not quite committed to shave it all away.

"Ten," he said, as though his solemn pronouncement made it so.

"Yes, Papa." Marjeta bowed her head and scraped the end of her knife blade across the gravy, leaving a wavy line like a river. She wanted to go to the river, catch fish, find if her secret oak still stood. Anything but be sitting here and wondering what sentence this man would pronounce over her. She'd wanted his attention, she knew, and now she had it she wanted it taken away.

"You girls seem to grow faster than reeds in summer." He glanced past Josef to where his important guest sat. A man, younger than Papa, with hair that curled dark, a clean-shaven face like he was a penitent. "Soon your sister will be going to Duke Calvai Jurie."

Why was everyone trying to remind her of this? It must be a punishment for some sin she'd committed without realising. Marjeta managed a feeble smile in Duke Jurie's direction, though the man barely seemed to notice it.

The Duke Jurie was not here to congratulate some nobody child on turning ten, but to see the girl who had been presented as his replacement wife. Val. Papa had made the engagements almost as soon as the duchess's blood had been rung from the birthing sheets.

"Yes, Papa," Marjeta mumbled.

"Don't look so sad, you'll have other things to keep you occupied." He allowed himself a little conspiratorial twist of a smile. "Like Josef here, he has something for you."

At the sound of his name, Josef jerked in his seat and swung his bowed head to look at Marjeta. He was pale, sad, and Marjeta wondered at that. His new wife was not in attendance. Too sick, had been the rumour, but it was said in a way that made it sound a lie. "Ah," said Josef, and licked his lips nervously. They were dry and cracked. "I've a present for you. Don't think I forgot."

"Thank you." Marjeta could see no sign of any gift, and Josef made no move to reveal one now. "That is very kind of you." She wanted to pull at her own hair to stop herself from hoping, to kick herself until she was bruised. Just because the moon made promises, and just because she wanted it.

"Mama says you are very fond of my old pony, Dust—"

Marjeta couldn't contain her shriek. The hall went quiet for a moment to stare, but when all she did was bounce in her seat with her hands clapped over her mouth, they soon returned to their drink and food.

Even Josef was smiling. "Ah," he said. "Seems I can make one woman happy at least, even if it's a little woman. Dust is yours, and may she bring you as much joy as she brought me."

Her brother had barely finished talking before Marjeta had breathlessly thanked him, over and over, her words almost incoherent.

Papa was leaning back, an eyebrow raised, while at his side Mama was looking pinched and brittle, her smile forced in place. "And a new bow," Papa said as he raised one hand lazily. "You're stronger now, and a better shot, your instructor says."

A servant came forward at his gesture, carrying a bow, still unstrung, but made of nutwood and horn, curved like the antlers of an ox. Another servant brought her arm- and finger-guards of tooled leather. Marjeta's heart was pounding. These were the kind of gifts she wanted—a horse, a beautiful weapon. Not thimbles and mirrors and cutlery. The moon had seen the future and told the truth. The moon had given her what she needed. She grinned hard enough to make her face ache. Who cared for magic mirrors she couldn't use, or thimbles when she hated to stitch? Who cared for the gifts of women? These men — Papa and Josef — they understood her, they knew she was like them. Marjeta stirred a fire of resolve in her chest. She would make them proud, make them see how good she was, how much she deserved these gifts. Perhaps they would take her hunting with them, astounded that some little girl could ride and shoot as well as they.

The night had improved, and the storm shuddered, half forgotten, drumming in time with the musicians and the dancing feet.

It was almost morning when she was taken to bed, her nurse Olaga leading her as she stumbled and yawned, heart as bright as a newly lit oil lamp. A strange whimpering noise came from behind the thick door, and Marjeta paused, suddenly afraid. The sound cut through the night's excitement and made her think of loss, off the terrible womanly screams of foxes. Something was in pain behind those doors, something terrified and lonely.

"Hush, lamb," said Olaga at the look on her face. "It's your last gift." She swung the door wide, the hinges silent and red with fresh oil.

At the foot of Marjeta's bed, curled up in a woven willow basket lined with hemp, shivering and crying, was a golden-dark wolfhound pup, all long legs and nose, and a tail that kinked as though it had been broken. "Sasha," Marjeta whispered, naming the creature that was to become her own wild heart for the next four years.

Spiralling Out

Sasha's low grating growl reverberated against the stone walls of Marjeta's bedroom. Immediately alert, Marjeta sat bolt upright, wary and wide eyed, watching the shadows. It had been a long time since Marjeta and Valerija had shared a room, and Marjeta no longer walked sleepy-headed to Val in the dark. The only breaths that stirred Marjeta's room in the night were her own and those of the wolf hound and the kitten-small salamander that had followed her to a new hearth.

Sasha had outgrown the little willow basket at the foot of her bed. Now the adult wolfhound stretched out across the entire bottom half of the bed, a protector and friend.

The wolfhound was a huge, hunched shape, snarling at the door. Marjeta slid one hand under her pillow to retrieve the little knife she kept there. It was one part of the travel cutlery set her mother had given her for her decad. She was nearing fourteen now, but she kept the little gift close still. She had no other weapons to hand. The horn-curved bow had been a gift from Papa, not one that even Mama could confiscate, but a bow in such close quarters was little good.

Her fingers closed tightly around the long handle of the travel knife, she slipped out of the bed, and waited. No one would come to her rooms at night. Olaga was gone on to rear more small children, and Mama and her ladies would not be wandering this section of the castle. Marjeta frowned. There was no reason for anyone to sneak along as though they had something to hide. What if something had happened — someone had been hurt or died — a messenger in the night come to tell them that Nadija was gone, or that some foreign eastern prince had finally declared open war?

Sweat dampened Marjeta's forehead, and she shifted her weight, tightening her slipping grip. Another rumbling growl thrummed Sasha's ribs. Whatever Sasha was growling at, Marjeta would be ready. Between the wolfhound's ragged teeth and her little knife, they wouldn't stand a chance.

A faint squeal as the handle was pulled slowly down. Marjeta held her breath even as Sasha tensed, and dropped into a crouch, ready to attack. The door opened a crack, spilling in the faintest blue light from the lit corridor.

Marjeta drew in a cold breath, felt her heart tremble with sudden fear, eclipsing the wave of nerve-jangling expectation.

"Marjeta?" It was Val's voice, timid and low.

With a sharp sigh, Marjeta lowered her weapon and stopped crouching. "Hush, Sasha," she said, and the wolfhound fell instantly silent. The dog leapt off the bed to stand alongside her mistress, and to push her cold damp nose against Marjeta's ear. It was not like Val to come to her at night. Not for years and years. Something must be wrong. "Valerija?"

Val pushed the door wider. She'd used magic to send all the guards to sleep. Of course. But why come here? Val had her own life to live now, a flurry of preparation as she was groomed and primped and trained for her marriage to the Duke Calvai of Jurie. She was eighteen, being spun into a chrysalis, ready to go underground and wait as the world rearranged her to suit itself, until she could emerge as something for the courts to admire and point out to each other. And if Val's life was brief after that, who was to care besides herself and their mother? She would have married well, and been pretty, and well-read enough to not embarrass her husband, which seemed to be all that the world wanted or expected of its million wives. And if Valerija were to be the butterfly, then Marjeta was some kind of fat grub, something to be ignored until it changed. Or was squashed.

The sisters had barely spoken to each other since spring, and already summer was falling into smoke and fire and gold and red and harvest chant. Marjeta had become a better rider, could shoot her bow from horseback and had even had the honour of riding with Papa's hunt, albeit right at the back, while Valerija had worked summer wool on the loom and helped Mama and the ladies weave fine tapestries for the halls and chambers.

They had nothing in common.

Not anymore.

"What are you doing here?" Marjeta said to her sister.

"I miss you," said Valerija, and closed the door behind her. "Is that so strange?"

And it wasn't, except that Val was going to leave within the year. It was time for her to take her place as Duke Jurie's replacement wife and mother his soft little daughter in far away Calvai. Already their father was preparing the wedding kists; filling them with bridal treasures, silks and golden cups, and heirloom tapestries that court women had woven in wools dyed with fantastical colours. It was harder to pretend that everything was to stay the same when Valerija's bride price was ready to be loaded on the caravans.

It was too soon.

And Marjeta didn't want to hurt, she didn't want to care. It was better that they grew apart like two saplings on opposite sides of a farmer's gate. This way each would have room to grow, space to cast their own shadows instead of living in the darkness of the other's. Mama and Papa had made sure of it.

But despite that, Marjeta couldn't help hurting. As much as she replaced her sister with the woods and the wilds, she knew underneath that it would never be enough. And it wasn't strange that Val missed her as much. They were still sisters. They had slept in each other's arms, played games all through childhood. Made magic.

Marjeta slid the knife back under her pillow. "I've been busy doing all sorts of things. Besides, you see me when we're tutored." And there was that, at least. The realm of texts and histories, where Val seemed to be free as a house martin, swooping from meaning to meaning, while Marjeta approached each new thing like a horse shying at a too high jump.

"But we don't talk." Val walked past the bed, giving Sasha a wide berth, and made her way to the hearth. No fire had been lit that evening, but the time would soon come when the serving maids would lay out wood each night. "I brought some bread for your salamander," she said.

"They sleep a lot through summer," Marjeta said, then relented. "Give it to Sasha, though."

The hound took the proffered bread only when Marjeta gave the word to eat.

Valerija brushed her hands and sat on the edge of the bed. "You've trained her well."

With a shrug, Marjeta sat down cross legged on her bed, her bare feet tucked under her knees. The night air had a sparked feeling, like the moment before a storm. Perhaps it was simply Val's presence, all full of witchery and spells. "Papa said I had to, or I didn't deserve her."

"And Mama lets her sleep in your room?"

"Mama has to do as Papa says, and he allows it."

"Ah." Valerija folded her hands in her lap, and sat on the covers, opposite her sister, mirroring her pose. "I should like a dog too, I think. A valiant protector."

"You don't hunt, what's there for you to be protected from?"

The laugh that Valerija forced sounded adult and harsh. "The whole of my future, Marjeta, that's all." Her face showed no sign of humour, her cheeks too sallow and sunken, and dark circles were pounded into the thin skin around her eyes.

"Why did you come here tonight?" Perhaps she'd had some nightmare like she used to when they were still small, and when it had been easy for the two of them to snuggle up against each other, rabbit soft and warm.

"I called to the moon again," Val admitted.

Ah, there was the heart of it, then. Why she was here, looking for comfort and protection. It wasn't like her sister to ever look miserable or troubled. She was the one who took delight in her own wit, in the little magics she could do. Before they started sleeping apart, she would entertain Marjeta at night by dancing their dolls across the room or making the great heavy gowns swirl along the floor like the emptied skins of dancers. She would play puppets with Oddment, Endment and Threadment, set them to little hare knight adventures that she narrated for Marjeta.

That was how her sister was supposed to be, how she should have stayed. Full of stories and magic. But she was growing older and even witches have to leave magic behind when they are caught in the snares of men. Marjeta hated watching what her sister was becoming. Like Mama, a little threaded puppet that smiled and curtseyed on command and kept all her secrets behind her eyes and never let her truth show.

Was Val still wanting to know if she was the greatest witch in all the counties, or had she grown out of that too? Marjeta sighed and leaned forward a little. She could smell her sister faintly; juniper and night sweat, and dried roses and ice. "Did you ask it about your future again?"

Val shook her head. "I tried, but it was as though the words wouldn't come, like they'd got caught in my throat like a sheep in brambles. Maybe you can only ask a question once? Mama wouldn't know, and I can hardly ask Oma Zoli."

"Well, don't worry yourself about it." Marjeta was tired and she wanted to go back to sleep, whereas it seemed her sister had decided that now was the time for them to begin sharing secrets again and to pretend that they were both little children. There was no point in staying awake worrying over questions that couldn't be asked, and riddles told by moons.

But maybe Val was lonely. She had no Dust, no Sasha — just ladies' maids and ribbons and needles. And sooner than soon, she would be gone far away from even that. Marjeta's heart ached in sudden painful sadness. It felt almost like a rush of fear, that same feeling when as a little child she would be convinced that some rasping beast lay in wait beneath her bed, biding its time for dark and its chance to pull her down and chew the flesh from her bones. She shuddered and reached out her hand to Val's knee. Her sister felt hot, almost feverish, despite that snowy bite of magic that prickled all around her.

"I tell you what," Marjeta said. "Sleep, forget about your moons and mirrors, and we can slip out early in the morning and I'll show you my secret oak. We can steal cakes from the kitchens and take Sasha and the horses down. I'll show you a secret route that only rabbits and deer know." As she spoke the plan sounded even better. After all, with Valerija's magic, going out into the woods without being surrounded by idiot servants was going to be easy as blowing seeds off a dandelion.

"I have work—"

"Who cares about stupid old embroidery? Listening to Mama and the looms going clack clack?"

"I learn things from them."

"So? I learn things from the leaves and the grass." Marjeta grabbed her sister's hand. It had grown longer and thinner in the last months, pale fingers like starved dancers. "Forget the moon." She held tight, squeezing hard enough to make Val wince. *Forget Jurie and the future*, she wanted to say but the words stayed down like swallowed pips. "Now. Go to sleep."

It was a comforting invitation. A brief return to something safe, and when the sisters woke before the dawn, their limbs were tangled, their faces sweaty. It was Sasha who roused them, nosing her cold hard snout against their cheeks and whining to be let out. The girls were both tumble haired, and for a minute Valerija was no longer on the point of turning thin and tall, and Marjeta wasn't following just behind. They were toddler pudgy, pot-bellied and fat-thighed and round-cheeked, drowsy with dreams, unmarred by adulthood.

The moment faded, and Valerija was a girl witch, cold as a broom handle, and her eyes sparked. Marjeta was wiry, ropey muscles that wrapped the bones of her arms, her thighs thin and hard, her chest flat, her face brown as a fallen hazelnut. Without words, the sisters dressed each other in riding skirts and blouses and short jackets and covered each with fur lined capes against the autumnal chill.

*

"I will keep anyone near us asleep, but you will have to see to the horses and the hounds," Valerija said as they ran down the corridors, their soft leather heels soundless against the chilled stone. "I've no talent for beasts." The sisters raced with hand held in hand, fingers clasped tight as knots, down the spiral stairs, past knights and guards and servants, magic trailing them like a skein of new wool. Sasha loped ahead; their gallant knight protector armed with ivory teeth and wolfish pride, her tail a battle pennant.

No one stirred. Even by the stables where the grooms had already begun their morning work before the sun had paled the sky, they met no one. Partly it was Marjeta, who knew how to fox slip through the dark and back alleys, and partly it was Valerija, who twined her magic around them both, hiding steps and skin and scent and shadow. Valerija knit herself and her sister into darkness, made their footfalls ermine soft. She covered them with cloaks threaded with magic, the shadows stitched into their borders.

As close as they used to be, they ran to the end of the stables. It took Marjeta only a few moments to saddle Dust, and Hare, her sister's little brown palfrey that was as placid — and slow – as a ruminating cow, and it was only when they had ridden far from the fortress, down until the wooden bricks gave way to soft black sand, that Valerija dropped her skein of magic.

Sound came rushing back, crisp and unmuffled, and the slight wavery indistinctness of their surroundings sharpened, as though a telescope lens had been twisted into focus. The last of the starlight unfurled around them, and the sisters breathed deep at the same time, filling their lungs with freedom.

Marjeta tightened her thighs, nudging Dust just the slightest with her heels, and the pony responded with a leap. A salmon-spring of joy just before flattening out into a gallop, her neck extended, pale mane waving into Marjeta's face. The air was silver bright, waiting for the dawn, and the two girls shrieked as their mounts pummelled the earth. It was like screaming at a birth, a wild unfettered joy at the simple rightness of being alive, of being beholden to no one. Beneath the ponies' thundering hooves, the ground smeared into a rain of damp dark earth. Wind slapped their sides, their faces, cracking their cloaks behind them.

Finally, the girls slowed their mounts. Marjeta mainly because she felt a little sorry for Hare, who was as un-hare-like as she was bovine. The fat round chestnut huffed into a slow walk, sweat already darkening her fur.

"Where are we going?" Valerija pushed her loosened hair back from her face. "You said you would show me something?"

"The secret oak. You'll like it." Going all the way to the oak meant having to follow the road out past the farmlands, and along to where the Greyling river flowed out of the forest. There was a no man's land between the last of the farm estate meadows and the forest proper; a scraggly wild world of sapling and bush and hardy oak. If you knew the right path to take, you could cut through and come to a little glade that was raised on a small hilly outcropping. There a lone oak stood surrounded by a ragged circle of beeches, like handmaids to a high priestess. From there, if you climbed right to the highest branches, you could see the slow black glint of the river as it curled through the forest. Could see the lines of silvery lakes and marches that soaked the Petrell lands.

"It's very quiet," Valerija said when they reached the standing tree. "I'm so used to travelling with Mama and the others." When Valerija did ride she was always part of a group going out to picnic, or to play games of catch and chase. Even though she could use her magic to sneak out whenever she liked, she'd never seemed to want to be far from the other women. Where Marjeta preferred silence and the loneliness of her own skin, Valerija had always looked more at home when she was with others. Perhaps it was a flaw, or perhaps she knew some secret that Marjeta couldn't quite catch.

"It's better this way. In the quiet." Marjeta swung herself off Dust's back and unbuckled the bridle and saddle. She could trust her pony to come back at the click of a tongue. And Hare would stick close to Dust and not wander. With the tack hung safely out of the way, Marjeta stripped out of her heavy overskirt and jackets.

"What are you doing?" Valerija sounded more curious than upset at the idea of stripping here, far from prying eyes.

Marjeta paused to kick off her boots and pull off her hose. "We're going to climb," she said. "Come on, you can't go up a tree in all that."

Valerija looked to where Marjeta had set her bow and quiver down on her spread-out riding cloak. "What if something comes?"

"Like what? No one ever comes here, and it's too early in the season for wolves."

"Bears?"

Marjeta thought of the bear who watched her, in shadows and dreams. She was a figment, barely real. "There are no bears here — not for miles and miles. And, besides, we'll be up a tree."

"Yes, pet, but for how long? I don't feel like being trapped up an oak tree in my undergarments because you want to show me a view."

"You're getting old," Marjeta said as she went to the oak and grabbed the lowest branch and set one foot against the trunk. "And boring." She felt free, her feet numb and pale with cold, her arms tingling from the feel of the forest breeze. Every hair on her body seemed to be more alive, more sensitive to the world. Her feelings had become too big, too strange to have a name.

"I have to, it's not as though I have a say in the matter." But even as she argued, Valerija followed her, bough after bough, her fingers curled white like bones. "I know it makes you angry, but I have to do as Mama says, and I have to marry as Papa says. I don't get to choose."

Marjeta did not answer until she was almost at the top. "You can so. Look at me. I choose not to sit in a room full of women carding wool and spinning and sewing and making pretty things." She pushed a branch out of her face and looked down. She could hear her sister puffing, grunting softly as she clambered from dew damp branch to dew damp branch. The smell of crumbling lichen and broken leaves followed her.

"You think that makes you better than me?" Valerija paused, still a few handholds below. Her voice was bitter and hurt. "You think 'making pretty things' is beneath you?"

"Of course it is." Marjeta gazed out over the unfolded forest, a rustling quilt of greens and golds under a near blue heaven. Here and there the waters glinted like broken mirrors scattered through the trees. "I hunt and shoot. I ride better than my riding master. I have a wolfhound of my very own. Papa loves me. I'm like him and he will not send me away. He likes me because I chose to be like him instead of like you or Mama."

There was a long silence — made longer by the eerie threading of the wind through the topmost leaves. When Valerija finally spoke, each word fell out of her mouth like a spat pellet of well chewed mint. "Oh, Marjeta." She snorted softly. "You think because of dogs and horses and little pretend weapons that Papa sees you as a son — some boy child born without a prick?" Her voice rose. "He laughs at you. The girl who wants to be a favourite son. Josef gave you Dusk, not Papa—"

"So what," Marjeta snapped. "He gave me Sasha."

"Mama gave you Sasha, you stupid child! She begged Papa to give you the whelp — he was going to drown it for the kink in its tail. He only gave you that dog because it was worthless to him. And a little bow that would be fit only for a boy child or a woman — who else was he going to give it to?" She was half screaming now. "We gave you things that he cannot and will not think of, because he does not see you, Marjeta. You are an amusement to him, when to us you are sister and daughter and friend. We give you the things we hope will help you in the future that is coming, and you don't even see it! Instead, you take the discards Papa throws at you and think that is love." She fell quiet, her words swallowed back up, though her face looked like she had more thoughts she could not bring herself to say.

Silence rattled into the emptiness that Valerija's voice had left. When Marjeta's heart had stopped hammering, she took a deep breath.

The zephyr had turned, coming now from the settlements and farms, and she tasted bonfires and loam and the golden-brown bite of the coming autumn weather. It tasted the way Valerija's words felt, like the changing of truths. It was a lie. Mama had never even asked after Sasha — how could she have thought to tell Papa to give her the puppy. If she had, surely she would have said something. No, Valerija was just trying to make her feel bad because she was jealous of not being noticed by the people who truly mattered. "You're wrong," she said finally. The words were weak and dusty. Cobweb words. "I know what presents you chose for me. You and Mama. You gave me things meant to make me feel stupid and small — magic I couldn't use. Or things to remind me that I am nothing — thimbles and forks. If Papa's love is so terrible and yours so fine, how come he knows me better than you do?"

Valerija sighed. Her grip tightened on the branch before she bowed her head and began to slowly make her way back down the tree. "We are not you enemies," she said, her voice a soft curl of mist, damp and barely there. "But you will not see it."

The view had turned sour. The morning had curdled all its beauty into cold, and the wind was rising from the north, bringing the nip of frost down and setting the leaves to shiver and curl. With a snarl, Marjeta began furiously clambering down, pushing past her sister and dropping the last seven feet to land crouched in the dying bracken. Her knees and the balls of her feet felt bruised, and there were long scratches down her arms and legs and face, but Marjeta gritted her teeth and dressed in silence. By the time she was pulling on her leather boots, Valerija had sunk down next to her, white and pale with sadness and exhaustion.

The sisters did not speak until both had saddled and bridled their horses and were sitting astride, ready to return the fort and whatever punishment might be meted out for their disappearance.

Marjeta whistled sharply for Sasha, but the wolfhound was nowhere to be seen. She waited, whistled again, but there was no answering bark, near or distant.

"Leave her."

Marjeta twisted in her saddle, her face red and ugly. "Oh, that would suit you, wouldn't it, to discard the gift you say was discarded first?"

"I don't mean it like that." Valerija clicked at Hare, nudging her pony into a reluctant ambling walk. "She's a dog, and she knows her way home. Probably she's caught wind of a deer or rabbit and is chasing it merrily. We, on the other hand, have no merriness waiting for us. The sooner we get back home, the better." The sun had risen almost beyond the tips of the trees, and Valerija was right — their absence would have been noticed, and men might already be assembled to come looking for them. Something that would annoy their father and worry their mother.

Marjeta set her fingers back to her mouth and gave another

whistle sharp enough to cut glass, but there was not even the faint
answering bark that would let her know that Sasha had heard her.
"She's lost—"

"She's hunting." Valerija had already ridden some way down
the narrow little path that wove between the boles of the birches
and oaks. "You trained her, you know she loves you, then trust that
she will return home. Has she never run off before?"

With a vicious and uncharacteristic kick, Marjeta set Dusk
after her sister's pony. "Once."

"And she returned, of course?"

"Of course."

Valerija looked over her shoulder, her black eyes glittering.
"There then. Stop worrying."

There was nothing to say to her. The mood of the day was
shattered. It was too late for them to pick up the pieces and slide
them neatly back into place. They returned to the fortress in teeth-
clenched silence, with only the jangle of bit and bridle, and the
steady soft clump of horse hooves against thick loam to let them
know that they did not each return alone.

Marjeta's anger was stoked and tended, she blew on it, running
over the words the two of them had thrown at one another like
handfuls of pebbles, all the way to the fortress gates, where men
waited for them, stern faced and unforgiving.

"Well, they don't look understanding at all," Valerija said, her
voice thick and hoarse as though she had been crying.

"Who cares what they think," muttered Marjeta, but a deep
black feeling had opened up in her belly. It was one thing to
pretend to be free and run wild when they were still small, but now
that they were well past their decads, they had become valuable.
Too valuable to be allowed to do as they pleased. There was bound
to be a punishment for this. She tightened her fingers around the
warm leather of her reins, and Dust shifted beneath her, picking
her hooves a little higher, her ears flicking back in worry. "Hush,
now," she murmured. "They'll do nothing to you."

The men parted, and there stood Mama, surrounded by a knot
of grim-faced women. They were all minor nobles, the daughters
of country lords sent to learn pretty manners at the duke's court

and gathered to Mama's bosom like a spider rolling up flies in silk. Witches and spinners. The deep empty feeling yawned wider.

"Marjeta." Their mother's voice rang clear and loud. "I expect this from you.' There dismissed in an instant, "But Valerija, you disappoint me."

"We didn't go far—" Marjeta began, but Val hushed her with a stern look and quick shake of her head.

"I am sorry, Mama," she said. "I meant only to spend some time with Marjeta, and we intended only to ride a little way. It is my own fault — I asked to see a particular tree she had mentioned—"

Mama held up one hand, silencing them. It would not do to have her daughters argue with her in public, Marjeta knew. She sighed. They would be schooled behind closed doors, their humiliation their own to savour.

"Get inside," Mama said, and the girls dismounted, grooms stepping forward to gather their mounts from them.

The sisters trailed their mother and her ladies-in-waiting through the corridors, casting silent looks at each other.

Valerija was right about one thing. They were punished most severely for their little moment of running wild. But it was not Mama who meted out the judgement, but Papa, furious at them both for risking his precious Valerija, so soon to be married. Even Marjeta who had grown used to her long leash, was surprised to find that she was punished alike; sent to her room and the door bolted, and no food for the day, and no company.

And no Sasha.

Bloodsports

Marjeta was good at being by herself, but to not even have the familiar whine and long face of her beloved Sasha was uncommon. Her stomach ached, a low dragging pain that seemed to want to pull her down to the ground and let the hells of her mother's gods swallow her. Marjeta pressed her fists against the pain. "Go away," she whispered. Hunger, probably. And if she let that hunger hurt her, then they would have won.

She paced the room, the feeling of confinement worsening with each step. She did not like this cold stone cage. She wanted mud and decay underfoot, the pine sharp air, the jaggy tear of brambles and nettles against her sides. She wanted the clear blue and the fading gold. She played games with her ignored collection of poppets and little wooden horses and hounds that she had collected over the years, but they left dust on her fingers, and the games felt forced. Finally, in a fit of directionless anger, she threw them to the ground where the front leg of one of the horses snapped off.

Marjeta stared at the broken toy. She couldn't even remember who had given her these things, gifts that she'd considered childish already when she'd received them. She'd had a real horse and hound — what did she need little wooden maquettes for?

Perhaps whoever had given them had hoped to tempt her away from the outdoors, back to the safety of behind-walls, where Mama and Olaga and Valerija and the ladies could see her, could always be sure they knew where she was. They wanted to make her like them.

Not adult enough to have her own way, and not child enough

to be lost in a world where she was queen. Marjeta closed her eyes and curled up tightly on her bed, rocking herself. She would not be what they wanted. The pain was deeper now, biting into her back and low into her stomach, leaving her dizzy.

Not hunger. She felt like she'd pissed herself, hot and shameful, but she was well versed in the bodies of women — in ladies and sisters and mothers. Whatever they thought of her — an ignorant child who thought she was a prickless boy, she'd always known better, deep inside. Always Marjeta had been outrunning her body. She had ridden as fast and far as she could on Dust, the sound of hooves her song of escape.

But they'd caught her, those witches, like they always did. The blood spread like a final kick in the face. Humiliation and betrayal. Her own body pointing at her inadequacies and making them obvious to the world with this hot sticky staining of undergarments. This pain. This is what you are, it said. You are nothing.

She was not a child any more. Not really. At thirteen she had taken the first steps outside of the kingdom of her imagination and set foot in the dull and thorny fairy land of adulthood. She stood between promise and truth, and it was as painful and unwelcome as the first bleeding of womanhood.

*

She dreamed of a world where her mother and sister bowed their heads to her, where she was queen, and even her father had to take to his knees. She was more than a duke's wife, greater than her sister, married away to Jurie and his orphan daughter. Pennants flew behind her, and her armies rode iron-grey horses from the east, with dished faces and high tails, their legs fine as filigree. Packs of hounds seethed at her feet, and her cowl was made from wolf skins. The dream told no stories, only truths.

"What's this?" Areya, the new lady-in-waiting, was shaking Marjeta's shoulder gently. Her voice broke into Marjeta's dreams of magic, blood-stained water, the future spread out before her in an intricate embroidery, her face picked out in jewel tones against snow white linen.

"Lady Marjeta?"

The power faded, and the world returned. Marjeta woke to Areya's hand on her shoulder, gently shaking, to the concern in her voice.

"There's blood all over your sheets."

Marjeta struggled up. She had wadded some lengths of material between her legs, and they were enough to catch the worst of it, but blood had seeped out the sides, blackly red like something already rotting, and left its marks in dull brown splotches.

"You should have called for me." Areya straightened with a sigh. "Poor thing."

"I was punished. Told not to come out."

Areya cocked her hip and rested one firm hand on the jutting mound. "Punishing yourself, were you? You knew as well as any that if you'd called and told us what was happening, we would have helped you. This is women's business and women understand. Some places even a duke's word is powerless, though no woman would let him know that." She reached out and tenderly pushed a matted snarl of unbrushed hair off Marjeta's face. "There, it's hard to think straight like this sometimes. Your lady-mother gets the worst of it, she does — such headaches and pains and fevers and ill moods. You'll be luckier if you take after your sister, Nadija. A hobbling bit of pain for one day, and a mood that barely shifts from sun to shade."

Marjeta had the feeling that she was not going to be like Nadija, or like Valerija. Who even in the most ignominious of feminine vices, seemed to be blessed, suffering without complaint or mood swings.

But Areya was already calling servants to bring the copper bath and to fill it with heated water. To strip away soiled filth and set out new clean undergarments. Marjeta let her dignity be pulled from her. When the small tub was filled, aromatic with herbs for pain and herbs to bring ease, she let herself be guided in, her skin sluiced.

"Has Sasha come back?" Marjeta allowed another jug of water to stream over her hair, closing her eyes against the sting. Areya had put soured wine in this one, to bring out the red in her hair, she said.

"No. I did wonder where she'd gone. Thought perhaps your father had kennelled her to punish you."

Sasha was still missing. Alone in the forests, far from pack and family. Her protector. A flicker of the dream swam through her head. A hundred dogs, with their long thin noses, their ragged teeth and plumed tails. All hers. No. A stupid dream. She was not a witch, to see auguries in sleep. Marjeta took a deep shivering breath and felt the tears rattling inside her head, filling up behind her eyes like scores of falling hailstones in a sudden storm. She would not give in to them. Not now. Not today. Sasha was out there. She would come back.

Her dog loved her.

Unless.

Unless nothing. Even if Sasha were injured, she would drag herself home. She was a wolfhound, and the wolves were deep in the forest. It was too early in the season for them to come so close to farm and meadow, and the oak tree in its clearing was not past the borders into the deep old forest where they lived. No. Sasha was coming back.

She was alive, and she was coming back.

"Now, stand and I'll dry you, and we've new rags for you, and warm bedclothes, and we'll wrap you up tight as a little baby, and see, your bed is heated with stones and there's tea for you for the pain." Areya was talking to her in a lulling singsong voice, as though this sudden and unexpected onset of womanhood had not catapulted her further into the awful land of adults but had somehow clawed her back to a kind of dismal infancy, where her brain had rotted to mush.

Marjeta wanted to protest. To scream that she was not a child, that she was a duke's daughter, and a fine rider, and an excellent archer. That she had shot green wood doves on the wing, that she could jump fallen logs and cross chasms with a single leap. Instead, she cried bitterly and did not understand why.

*

It took only five days for the bleeding to stop.

"You're lucky," said Valerija. "Mama's go on for weeks at a time."

Privately, Marjeta thought this explained much about Mama and her swift changing tempers. "And what about you?" Though this had never been something that had remotely interested her, Marjeta felt that she'd been inducted back into her sister's circle of friendship — that once again they were alike. Their fight from the previous week had been washed away by this new blood-bond. Marjeta remembered the night they had asked the moon together, asked about their future with embroidery blood, needle pricked fingers. What futures would Valerija hear if she asked now. Would the answers be better than the ones she'd had before?

Valerija took a long time answering, and Marjeta thought perhaps her sister had not heard her. Again, she said "What about you?" because her sister never complained of aches and cramps, or had that distant snappishness that Mama had.

Finally, Valerija shrugged. "I'm still waiting. Olaga says some girls are slow to start."

"Oh." She hadn't expected that. Valerija was the elder, the first in everything, and she had always assumed that was the way of the world. It felt awkward to be thrust ahead of her, to be somehow, in this most feminine way — more of an adult. She'd lost her childhood before Valerija, in truth. The thought sat sticky in her head, feverish and unwelcome.

A smile was skewered uncertainly on Valerija's face. "I have to go now — the new tutor is waiting for me. I am to learn everything about Duke Jurie's lands and holdings. Papa says it will be soon, and I need to — I need to..." She stood up and smoothed her hands down her dress. "I'll be back soon, and I'll bring you something sweet, I promise it."

As soon as her sister was out the room, and silence had fallen in spidery sheets, Marjeta went to her carved and painted closet and drew out a small kist at the bottom. It wasn't locked, but it held treasures that had been pressed on her through the years by well-meaning ladies of the court. Little treasures like brightly dyed threads and thimbles carved from horn and bone or blown from glass. Bent embroidery hoops and beads of glass. And, wrapped in a skein of white muslin, the tiny silver hand mirror that had once belonged to Oma Zoli. Valerija's birthday gift. The one that had always felt like mockery instead of the kindness she was sure Valerija had meant.

Carefully, her fingers trembling, Marjeta unwrapped the soft material, revealing the mirror one writhing vine at a time. The air was still and heavy, and from far below came the distant sounds of the fortress, and ever further, the harvest songs. A hawk skreed somewhere above.

Something died in the moment between one heart beat and the next: a leveret perhaps, or a late duckling.

Marjeta dropped the last of the muslin and held Oma's mirror at distance. She looked at herself with a sense of studious detachment, like a scholar-priest studying an insect under bent glass. Her eyes. Her nose. The corner of her mouth. Marjeta in pieces and never whole. She closed her eyes and remembered Val's voice, singsong and dripping with magic: 'Mirror, mirror, take my soul, show me the thing that makes me whole.'

It would never work, not for her. Like Mama, she had only a thread of power. That was why Mama turned to the gods, to beg them to be her power instead. But Marjeta hated those gods with their crude old faces. Their nightmare eyes. And maybe now, blooded and older than Valerija, she had gained a kind of womanly magic, something fierce and strange and uninnocent, something older than men's power. She brought the mirror closer to her lips. She would try. For Sasha, she would risk bitter disappointment. Even now, her dog could be lying in agony, wondering why her loyal mistress had left her. Marjeta breathed, let moist exhalations blossom on the cold surface of her grandmother's magic.

Her face slowly obscured, and all that was left was the misted surface, showing nothing. It was time. Marjeta called upon that frail silk line of her family's magic inside her, so thin and red that it seemed like nothing more than a spider's anchoring line cast in the setting sun, and spoke: "Mirror, mirror, take my soul, show me the thing that makes me whole."

Her words hit the breath, marking themselves in glistening

lines, like tear drops spelling out a sentence. In a moment, the words had vanished, and the surface of the mirror was left slickly wet, as though it were an eye sheened with tears. The reflection was no longer of Marjeta's face, her eye or nose or corner of her mouth. She breathed in sharply, and a fine slicing pain shot through her belly, deep as a hatchet strike. Magic. Power.

Instead, it showed her an oak tree, her queen oak with its circle of dancers. The view spun rapidly away from the crown of the hill, rolling down, down, down, fast as a hare through brambles, down to where the river curled golden and brown in the last of the sun, and lying on the bank, bedraggled and bloody, her muzzle a mess of scabbing and flies, was Sasha.

Her sides were heaving painfully, dried blood matted the once beautiful feathering on her legs and tail. It was obvious she was in pain, in distress. Alone, and dying.

Marjeta shrieked before throwing the mirror to her bed. She stood some distance from the silvered mirror, her heart hammering, arms wrapped tightly around herself. After a few moments, she calmed her breathing and stepped close to her bedside to peer at the images again.

Two thoughts consumed her: the first, that she had done it — she had done magic.

The second, far more terrible, was that Sasha was dead, or would be soon. And that she could do nothing.

No. Not nothing. Marjeta grabbed the mirror's handle. The image had dissolved now, and all it reflected was her face. Quickly, she wrapped it up tightly in its muslin strips and buried it back at the bottom of her kist. Then, fumbling in her haste, she dressed herself in riding skirt, in shirt and over dress and jacket, in hip quiver rattling with arrows, and finally, in her riding cloak of golden brown, rich and regal as the last leaf to fall from the plane tree.

She'd just strung her bow when the door swung open and Valerija stood there, a narrow fury, slit eyed as a tree-spirit. "Where are you going?" she said.

Marjeta swung her bow across her shoulder. "What makes you think I'm going anywhere?"

"Besides the way you're dressed." Valerija blocked the doorway, hands on hips. "I know you, Marjeta Petrell. I know you better than you know yourself. You have been too quiet." She dropped her hands and sighed. "And I felt you use the mirror."

"You spied on me?" Marjeta wanted to shove her sister, to push her out of the way and have her fall to the ground, tangled up in skirts and stupid, stupid, lying, spying magic.

"I didn't spy." Valerija held up one hand and placed it on Marjeta's chest, across the buckle of her leather strap that held her bow in place. "Not like that. Not intentionally. I just know when magic happens. I can't help it." Her palm was barely touching Marjeta, yet Marjeta could feel her sister's pulse through her skin like a second heartbeat, a counterpoint rhythm. "You have lost the thing that makes you whole."

"Yes." Marjeta shrugged off her sister's touch. "And now I'm going to find it, and you can't stop me."

"Who said anything about stopping?" Valerija smiled. "I'm coming with you."

Hound and Heart

Valerija's magic was a boon. Without it Marjeta was unsure how she would have sneaked out of the fortress in broad daylight, saddled and bridled her pony without a groom noticing, and left the grounds down the roads and past the farms and village. Not a soul turned to watch them pass, shrouded up like ghosts in Valerija's silken soft magic. Marjeta wore the childhood cloak her sister had made for her, the wool falling over her shoulders like a cape, the embroidery whispering with spells.

The two sisters rode without speaking. Marjeta glanced back at her sister. Val's face was grim with concentration, her magic sparking against the air and her skin gone unearthly white. Marjeta was also grim; with worry, and with fear. Would she be too late? Would she be punished again, and more severely and this time over nothing but bones, and the end of her childhood? In her mind she could see only the image from the mirror. Sasha on the ground, blood and raw flesh, like a broken puppet made from wires and lank handfuls of fur. She tightened her heels against Dust's flanks, urging the pony faster, even though the ground here was rotten with rabbit warrens and mole runs.

They reached the clearing with the sun high above them. Marjeta followed the mirror's vision toward the distant curve of the river. Cold river water chattered and burbled to itself, and under their ponies' hooves the undergrowth of furled leaves and tiny flowers released the bruised scent of summer. She breathed in deep enough to make her ribs ache, and even so the air seemed too thin, too weak. She could taste the end of her childhood complete under her tongue, like a bitter herb.

The smell of river water and damp earth grew stronger, and under it — a death smell — sweet, putrescent. They were too late. Marjeta tightened her hands on the leather reins, feeling the edges bite dully into her palms.

The trees had thinned, the little deer path widened. The bank was spread out before them, the grass bright and green, pocked with the litter and debris of waterfowl and fallen leaves.

Lying on her side, her ribs heaving, fur rough and staring, Sasha shifted, lifting her head to growl feebly. She was trembling all over, exhausted and hungry. Still alive, still there to be saved. Marjeta's heart double thumped against her ribs, hard enough to hurt, and she slipped down from Dust's back. The pony whickered nervously, her ears flattened, tail swishing hard enough for the ends to whip at Marjeta's arm like a warning blow from a hair switch.

"Don't—" said Valerija. She sounded uncertain.

Marjeta paused, one hand still on Dust's rein to calm the spooked pony. "Don't what? She's hurt."

"I know. I can see that. She's been in a fight with something — not a bear, I think, or she'd be dead. A fox, maybe?"

Marjeta shook her head. The fox would have come off worse in any fight with Sasha. It was something big — big enough to rake sharp claws down the side of a wolfhound, to half tear its entrails out, to leave tooth marks in its jaw. The blood along the bank had mostly been washed away, and the ground was too torn up to reveal a clear print. Something big.

Wolf perhaps, but a pack would have destroyed her, and one alone could not have taken the hound. Lynx. No. They didn't come out this close to man. She looked for some sign of Sasha's attacker. Had Sasha killed it, or had it fled, ripped and torn, back to the dark? Marjeta glanced nervously this way and that, but there was no sign of another beast. It had long since fled. She pulled her bow free, and nocked an arrow loosely, just in case.

Valerija had dismounted and was knotting the reins of both ponies to a low sturdy branch. The beasts were rolling their eyes, stamping. Even Marjeta was infected by their fear. Cautiously, she approached Sasha, almost sidling up to her for fear of startling the poor hound more than her heart could take. Hot, angry tears were already filling Marjeta's eyes. It was too late after all. She could see the snapped bone, the fly thick coil of intestine. That Sasha still lived was a nightmare. A painful joke. She wanted to drop to her knees, to scream and bat at the ground and rail against the cruelty of the world. Instead, she tried to keep steady as she drew closer, whispering. "Oh, my girl," she said, and her voice was choked, rough. "My poor, poor girl, everything will be well now, shhh, everything..."

The dog had raised her head and was peering intently about her now, ropes of bloodied saliva hanging from her ruined and blackened jaw. She whined, and her broken tail thumped weakly on the rutted ground.

Marjeta lowered her bow and slipped the arrow back into its quiver. She would use it, yes. She'd have to, it would be cruel to not, but first she wanted to say goodbye. Carefully, she approached her dog, her beautiful hound who had grown up alongside her, her puppy with the awkward spindly legs and kinked tail, who had grown huge as a child's first pony, who had turned from ungainly to graceful, with a long, pointed head filled with killing teeth. Intelligent and fiercely loyal. The flies swarmed around her, their angry buzz a funereal dirge.

It hadn't been just words. Marjeta had lost her soul when Sasha had not returned. Sasha was her freedom, her power, and here was all that was left of it. The tears were running down her face and Marjeta didn't care that Val could see. She walked closer, then knelt, hand outstretched.

Sasha made a sound between a growl and a whine. An ugly sound full of pain and fear.

"No!" The shout cracked through the air, a whip bite.

Before Marjeta could react, Valerija had lunged forward and knocked her sideways, just out of reach of the trapjaw snap of Sasha's teeth.

The world froze.

Valerija, pale as a snow maiden, Marjeta on her back in the dirt. Sasha's teeth buried in the white flesh of Valerija's wrist, the blood running and red bright as youngberry wine. The movement had torn more of the dog's inners out, and a cloud of blue green flies buzzed drunk as kings though the sullen air. White maggots writhed on the ground, dropping from Sasha's body.

Valerija did not scream, she held still as a god statue, her wrist caught.

Marjeta scrambled back, getting to her feet and readying her bow almost without thinking.

No. No. I can't do this. A wave of blackness swept down and crushed the air from her lungs. There was her sister, in pain, bitten by a dog that should already be dead. And there was Sasha. Shooting her now would be a kindness. She swallowed hard, and the point of her arrow wavered, her draw loosening. She couldn't. Not even now.

But you can. The voice was in her head, but it sounded to Marjeta that it came from all around her, from the roots of the great oaks, from the rich earth crawling with beetles and worms, from the leaves and the stretched and tattered clouds. The voice was blood and bone and stem and sap, it was the shiver of a leaf and the flick of a wren's wing.

Her grip on the string steadied, and the muscles in her back and shoulders grew solid and strong as wood. She drew cleanly, powerfully, and her vision sharpened.

Only when the point of the arrow was trained on Sasha's chest, her squinted vision focused on nothing more than this thing of fur and bone that had become an enemy, did a single, fleeting moment of regret punch through the implacable calm. And then it was gone, submerged beneath the necessity of death. She eased her fingers' grip, letting the string go with an almost loving regret.

The arrow flew home with a thrum and a solid, meaty thud.

Sasha collapsed, her jaw loosening, and Valerija stumbled back, clutching the bite on her arm. Blood dripped everywhere, a spray of brightness. Marjeta dropped her bow and began pulling her undershirt free so she could tear off the lower end. She would have to hide this.

Thoughts clicked through her mind, bright and separate and useless as the beads on an abacus: *hide the shirt when we get home. Cover Sasha's corpse. Bind Val's wound. Break the bow. Break the arrows. Break Oma Zoli's stupid, stupid mirror.*

Break everything.

Hound and Maiden

Marjeta did not crack her arrows one by one or break her bow over her knee. Nor did she smash Oma Zoli's mirror into a million tiny shards. She didn't have to. Inside her, something as fine and taut as a sinew had snapped, leaving her half a girl. Half a person. The space it left behind was black and raging, sucking every scrap of light and happiness into it, consuming it with its endless empty hunger. She did not cry, though she wanted very badly to. It was difficult, trying to force those tears to come. Like drawing nothing from an empty well and wishing each time there would be water to drink.

And Val — she hid her hurt so carefully, even from her own maids and ladies, that there might as well have been no wound at all. Only now and again when she thought no one was watching, she would scratch at her sleeve, as if wanting to tear out the wound that lay buried beneath it. Unseen, it festered and heated. She could have gone to Areya, or one of the ladies' maids, but there would have been too many questions. Instead, each night Marjeta helped her clean it out with heated water, packed the herbs they knew from their mother's teachings, and waited for the pain to die. Other than that, Val tried to pretend the bite mark wasn't there. A figment of a nightmare.

It was as though their flight into the woods to save Sasha had never happened. It was simply accepted that there was no hound. Not even that the dog had not returned—but that it simply had never been. The place at the end of Marjeta's bed lost its fine covering of shed fur, and the warmth never came back. The basket that had been unused for so many years disappeared into the kennels, the pottery bowls for water and bones gathered dust under the bed. Sasha's name was forgotten, the sound of it lost.

Only once had their father in idle curiosity asked, "What happened to that dog of yours?" and Marjeta had shrugged, and said, "It ran off."

It ran off. A lie that not only disgraced Sasha's memory, but Marjeta's too — that made her into the kind of owner a hound would run from and never return to. That was another dagger, sharp and cruel. Only Marjeta and Valerija knew that it was not true. The dog lay mouldering under branch and stone, flesh pecked away by crows, bones pulled apart by ferrets and rats and badgers. An ignoble ending.

With Sasha's death the sisters had become closer than ever, bound together in their secrecy. Bound too, in the knowledge that Val's final birthday feast in the Duchy of Petrell was coming, and that after that she would be torn from her family and remade.

"You shouldn't give up archery altogether," Val said. They were sitting in a fire-heated parlour, the young ladies of the fort with them, all presided over by Mama and her women. The nights had grown colder already, autumn curling around the stone walls like an old orange tomcat, battle scarred and hoary. Val was not whispering, but talking low, her voice just another meaningless burble in the hum of women's chatter.

A musician was playing for them. He was young and dark-haired and he made his violin weep sweet. Marjeta had heard rumours about him — that he was more than simply her mother's pet fiddle-player — that he used his bow and strings in other ways, that he had other talents.

It was the first time she'd become aware of rumours; how they flitted down the stone passageways and hid behind tapestries, how their bright eyes saw everything real and unreal, and their bright mouths whispered stories as fast as a woman could spin wool. She wondered if her father had heard these scatterling secrets. If Mama had.

And like all who heard, she wondered if there was any truth. Marjeta had begun to realise that the world of adults was a spidery castle of untruths and half lies. Not because of any cruelty, but simply because these thin webs were easier to bear than the truths that lay like ice hearts beneath them. It did not do to show the world the truth of your suffering. It was ... undignified. Childish. She glanced over at the fiddle player, at his pale bony wrists and his thin long fingers.

He was beautiful. And he was talented. Marjeta sighed. She didn't even know his name, he did not matter, and Val was still talking.

"I will shoot again when I feel like it," Marjeta said, more to shut her sister up than because it was true.

"You did what you had to," Val said.

"I did nothing." It was the truth, though Marjeta knew it sounded like nothing except petulant childishness. Val would listen, she would understand, but Marjeta couldn't make the words come out. Marjeta hated thinking of her bow, of her slim, straight arrows with their deathly tips. They meant loss and they meant lies. Marjeta pushed them away and bowed to other slender needle tips instead. She was working on a far more complicated piece than she usually tried. Mama had finally decided that the simple monochrome work of tiny squares was enough, and that it was time for Marjeta to accomplish bigger and better things. Her needle jabbed, pulling the leaf-green silk in neat rows. She tried to remember the blessings that went with this stitch. New green leaves for new green life, for awakenings and the growing strength of things. She whispered the blessing as she worked, stitching the magic as deep as she could. And while she was not powerful, she could feel something take, even if it was faint and distant.

Inside, she growled at wasting her time on spells that were no more than words and threads. But Marjeta bowed her head against her own voice, concentrating only on the jab, jab, jab of needle point and the slither of emerald thread through neat holes.

She had become better. When that thing inside her had snapped it had leached everything wild and free out of her bones, and all that had been left behind was a dreary neatness. She stitched tight and small, wrote tight and small. Took tight small steps and felt her voice dwindle in a throat that had grown closed. Under her deft fingers the silk and needle grew a curl of leaves, the calyx of a blossom, the edge of a wing.

The musician began a new song, jauntier than the one before. A marriage stamp and swirl. Marjeta's needle stilled, and she glanced up to see the musician grinning, his eyes watchful under the dark curls of his fringe. He played for Mama, and Marjeta knew it. Knew that rumours held truths.

"It's so hot in here," Val said, determined to start a conversation.

"It's not hot." It was a little warm, because of the bodies and the fire, but outside autumn winds had brought cold rain and mist. A little fire was good against that.

"It is." Val set down her needlework and poured herself wine from a decanter. She sipped at it, mouth twisted. "Even cold wine makes no difference. I feel like I could drown myself in snow and I'd still feel like someone set fire to me from the inside."

"Maybe you're getting the sickness I had." Marjeta said and snapped a thread between her teeth. It was time for a deeper shade, a blue. Indigo shadows.

When Val didn't answer, Marjeta looked up. Her sister was frowning. Perhaps that had been unkind. After all the sickness had near killed Marjeta, and Val had never forgiven herself for the role she believed she'd played. Marjeta remembered walking up to the armoury tower so long ago. They'd been children. Proper children, not half-grown maidens. They'd called down the moon. Or, more truthfully, Val had called the moon, pricking her finger and using embroidery blood to seal her magic. Marjeta had worn a cloak of shadows and magic. Or at least, it had seemed that at the time. It was just wool and fur trim and whispers made with silk. She had worn it too when she went hunting for Sasha.

Somewhere, that cloak was folded away, gone with all childish things now. And Marjeta had no desire to accompany her sister on anything involving magic. Magic was painful and full of trickery. It was better to stab, stab, stab her life into neat and ordered stitches, to be careful and precise, than to be magical.

Marjeta did not want to talk about illness, or anything else. She wanted to finish this overdress, the one that she was embroidering for Val's leaving. It would be thick with stitches when she was done, the golden velvet lost under a thousand flickering leaves and wings. It would be the most beautiful thing she'd ever made, and it would be goodbye.

It was too early and too late for goodbyes now, and neither sister ever spoke of Val's looming birthday. Marjeta did not want to talk at all. What she wanted was to sit alongside her sister and pray to the gods of sky and sea and earth that she would never lose Val the way she had lost the dog whose name she could not say.

*

In her room that night, after she had been dressed and tucked in her bed, Marjeta shook off her covers and stood. The lady Areya had her own small space just off from Marjeta's, and the room was empty but for the sound of her own breathing, and the furtive scuttle of Tarkis as the salamander rooted about in the hearth, pushing cinders between his claws. For a moment, Marjeta missed the downy snore of the woman who had nursed her through childhood, now a mother to some other children, far from this room.

Olaga had long ago been sent back to the village, another loss of womanhood. Mama had told her that she was far too old for a nursemaid now, that she needed women around her of breeding, whose virtues would force her own from empty dirt, bring them to bloom. Olaga had been replaced with the far younger Areya, and Marjeta had decided to hate the woman for the simple act of existing.

So much for fair Olaga, who had been a better mother in every way. Banished back to her croft, to the grave of her own infant child not even named.

It had left Marjeta feeling ever more hollowed out. Her childhood was being scooped from her, leaving only a thin sausage casing. Bit by bit the women stuffed her with bright thread and glass baubles and dried herbs, until it felt to her that she was a life-sized poppet. Some kind of replacement child for the wild thing that had been Marjeta Petrell.

She shuffled to the little idols on the worship table along one wall of her room. These were new mannikins, carved at her request from oak and golden sandstone and white clay. Their trench was a long flat dish of ivory. Ever since Sasha's death, Marjeta had decided that the old gods were all that she would have left. They had saved her, after all. Perhaps if she'd prayed to them for Sasha, they would have saved the hound too. They were old and powerful. Or they had been once. Perhaps one day they would be strong again.

Marjeta knew all the rituals. She had watched her mother dip her head before their graven faces a thousand times. She knew it was bread in the day, and herbed fat at night. But she also read her histories now, and she knew that these were new sacrifices. Replacements for older and darker ones. She had no stillborn scrap or slaughtered enemy, though. Marjeta did not feed them with fruit sweet oil or hearth baked bread. Instead, she pricked her thumb with her needle, and bled for them. And always, every night for two weeks, she had begged the same thing.

Do not let me lose my sister. Never let her leave me.

In the drowsing hearth, the salamander shifted and growled. Tarkis snapped his head out of the coals, and Marjeta shooed him away irritably. The salamander hissed. He was too used to taking the offerings. Marjeta sighed. "I'll bring you something, I promise. Not this, little lizard. This is for them."

A sound of footsteps in the passage, and Marjeta wiped the fallen blood away with a rag of dark cloth before anyone could see. It was better if no one saw this. The maids chattered among themselves, and even the most innocent gossip could touch the ears of a duke and bring him to temper. Women's gods, women's faith. They were meant to worship Furis now, like the dukes in the west, like Calvai Jurie who was rallying the duchies together against their common enemies, uniting them under his new religion.

Resentment stirred. Father didn't care about her or Sasha. Her sister had been right.

The door blew open, bringing with it a flurry of sparks. Her sister stood in the frame, still prickly with magic.

Marjeta sighed. "I might have known." She peered past Val. "What now, have you cursed the whole wing to unnatural sleep?"

"Mari, you must come," said Val, ignoring her, breathless, her cheeks red with exertion, eyes bright as candles. "You'll never believe it!"

"Believe what?" Marjeta took her sister's proffered hand, sweaty and hot, and let herself be dragged out into the passage. Flames guttered along the walls, lamps against the things the dark would bring.

"There!" Val pointed with her free hand, her voice rising in triumph. "There, at first I didn't believe it myself, but then I saw her again, and I knew it was her, so I came to fetch you." She turned her triumphant face to Marjeta's, her smile wide and innocent.

"Saw who?"

"Look, can't you see she's come back?"

Marjeta went cold, doused in fear as thoroughly as though someone had tipped a bucket of ice water over her head. There was nothing at the end of the passage: no woman. Not Olaga, certainly, who would have been as hard to hide as a rabbit in a mouse nest, not Mama or Nadija or anyone else she could think of. The passage was a dark maw, toothless, empty. "Who, Val? Who is back?"

"Why?" Val's voice was confused and bright. "Can't you see? It's Sasha. Sasha! She's come back to you."

Marjeta's fingers tightened around her sister's. The passage stayed as empty and black as it had always been, though she squinted, desperate to see the hound, to see her form spring out of the flickering shadows. Val's fingers trembled, the shiver racing under her skin. Marjeta turned to look closely at her under the guttering flame light. Her sister was bright with fever, her eyes glazed and her cheeks high points of colour in skin that was otherwise as blue-white as icicles.

"Val," she said softly, tugging her sister's slick hand. "Come, you need to get to bed. I need to call Mama."|

"No!" Val pulled her hand free. "Look, Marjeta. Look! You don't understand. I raised her for you. With magic, I called her back and now she's here."

The words flayed her cold skin. Val had gone fever mad, or strange with magic, perhaps. It wasn't unheard of for witches to get lost inside their own heads. But this — the worst was that Marjeta wanted so badly for it to be real. She wanted her sister's vision, even as she hated her for having it. It didn't matter what she hoped for. There was nothing, and the sparking magic fell like dying ash and turned to dust and the voices rose in the passageways as the women woke, bleary eyed, their hair wrapped in sleep silks.

"What's all the shouting?" the nearest woman asked, her face wrinkled and raw under her snood. "She's making sound enough to wake the dead."

"She's—" Marjeta began, but she had nothing to say — *mad, sick*? "Seeing things that aren't there," she said in a half whisper, but already hands were drawing Val away, were plucking at her cheeks and her wrist, feeling the heat of her, the damp soaked into her gown. Marjeta was suddenly aware of that sharp, sweet undertaste of illness in the air. The stink of sickness in the body's humours that hung in a miasma around her sister.

Before she could understand what was happening, the maids and ladies had taken Val from her, herding her back to her room, calling for heated wine and for herbs. For the priestesses of the gods and even for Papa's narrow little priest. For the god Furis to come watch over his child.

*

"I want to see her." Marjeta had never raised her voice against Mama, not even at her angriest. All the neat little threads were coming unravelled inside her, and that wildness was spilling back. Perhaps Sasha had returned, in a way.

"You cannot, lamb." Mama was implacable. "She is ill." Her face was drawn and sallow, too lined, her robes buttoned skew by panicked maids, her hair still in its sleeping coif. "Very ill. She's hidden some bite from us. A wild animal perhaps."

Not wild.

"No," said Marjeta. "She's just caught a chill, like I did—"

"It is graver than that." And when Mama's voice skipped and choked, Marjeta knew that it was. She let them lock the door against her, let the kind and sheep-like maids lead her gentle as an eweless lamb back to her own bed. They warmed her bedding, stoked the fire for her.

"Here." Areya made her sit down and held a wine glass to her mouth. "Drink this."

Marjeta turned her head so that the rim of the glass pressed against her cheek. "I do not want wine," she said. "I want my sister."

The lady-in-waiting remained implacable. "Drink this, my lady. It will help calm you."

"And why do you think I need calming?" Marjeta pulled her head away, but Areya merely held the wine glass out again. "Do you think I will run shrieking through the castle, seeing monsters?"

"No." Areya set the glass on a small side table. "You wish to help your sister."

"Of course!"

"You will be no help to her in the state you are in. You must think, and you cannot think when your temper is raised like this."

"And your wine will help me—" Marjeta spat.

"It will." Areya managed to sound utterly unmoved, calm as a mountain in the face of a storm. "I will not force you. You are not a child. I will talk to you, as one lady to another, the wine will soothe, and give you a clear space in your mind."

Marjeta shot a glance at the wine. It was dark and cloudy, and faintly within were tiny lights. She blinked. And the lights were gone. She reached out and took the wine, the stem clutched awkwardly in her hand to prevent her trembling from spilling the contents across the bedding.

Areya smiled, one faint twitch in the corner of her mouth. "Good," she said. "Drink, and let the maids sing."

The wine was bitter, and the maids sang old folk tunes to her, their voices chiming in and out like bells in a garden of brittle flowers, until Marjeta pretended to sleep, and they finally left. Even silently-watching Areya, who had given her a final cool-eyed stare before closing the door softly behind her.

Alone in her room, Marjeta took out from her box of treasures the little scrap of material that had once been the hare charm Mama had made for her when she'd caught ill those many years ago. The material was stiff beneath her fingers, and the herbs had grown dry and brittle. She crushed the mess between her fingers, releasing the smell of rosemary and juniper leaves into the room. The peppercorns cracked, turned to a gritty dust. Her head reeled. The wine had been laced with soothing drugs, and it took a gargantuan effort for her to stay awake.

Very carefully, Marjeta spilled the old herbs back into the hare's body, and with a crimson thread, she stitched the broken charm together. This was women's magic, and it was old and dusty, but Marjeta would take any hope she could. Once the hare was fixed, she went to the door and called for Areya.

"What's this then?" Areya asked, as she cupped the little hare in her palm. "You want me to take it to the lady Valerija?"

"I want you to place it under her pillow," Marjeta said. "Please. Mama won't let me see her—"

Areya curled her hand closed around the charm. "You made her a blessing," she said thoughtfully, "but the magic in it isn't yours."

"Who cares who the magic belonged to," Marjeta snapped. It had been her mother's, thin and weak, old and dry with the years, but it had still been more magic than Marjeta could make herself. And it had brought her back, after all. "Just take it—"

"Hush," Areya said. "I'll take it, but you must promise to sleep now. You'll do your mother and sister no good fretting like this."

"I will, I will, I promise, just please take it to her, tell her I need her to be well, and when she's feeling better, I'll bring the finger puppets, and tell her that Sasha was never her fault and—"

"Shh, now." Areya frowned. "I said I'll do it, but I'm not moving till I see you in that bed. It won't do for you to fall ill likewise."

Obediently, Marjeta crawled under the covers, and lay her head down. She kept her eyes open long enough for Areya to nod and close the door firmly behind her.

Marjeta breathed out a shivery sob. A moment later, something warm nudged at her hand, and for one glorious second, she half believed that Sasha had returned. but the head was too hot, too small and hard. She ran her fingers over the delicate scales, and let the salamander curl up next to her. It wasn't often that Tarkis came out the fireplace for anything more than to steal the sacrifices from the idols.

Marjeta sniffed. "Don't go," she whispered.

Tarkis rumbled throatily and pushed himself against Marjeta, curling up alongside her. After a moment, he began to lick at Marjeta's fingers with his narrow rough tongue. The feeling was strange and soothing, gently lulling Marjeta closer to sleep.

When she woke, the bells were ringing. Not the maiden's voice silver and glass in the night, but the old black tongue of the temple bell, iron and heavy as a dragon. Marjeta scrambled from her bed, tripping over the sheets and nightshift that tangled up her legs, bruising her knees against the carpeted stone.

The bells.

The bells that rang a dolorous refrain, a message from field to turret that a member of the House of Petrell had walked into another world. Marjeta's stomach roiled as though she had drunk dirty slush straight from the ground, a mess of mud and filth and frozen water. She wanted to throw up. She wanted someone to tell her she was dreaming.

The salamander was gone, returned to the safety of the hearth. All that was left was that long mournful clanging that drowned out every other sound in Marjeta's head.

You killed her. The thought rose clean and clear as crystal. "I didn't, I didn't," Marjeta whispered softly to herself. "I never shot Sasha, never." With a mindless fury Marjeta dug out and unwrapped Oma Zoli's mirror, breathed on it hot and tearful and said faster than wildfire, "Mirror, mirror, take my soul, show me the thing that makes me whole."

The mirror ran wet, the breath melting away, but all it showed Marjeta was a slice of her own face.

The Three Faces of Women

When the first wife had died, Lilika had been able to believe it was her own fault, but when the second died before she'd even had the chance to be a wife, Lilika had turned to Furis, to her prayers again.

While the first death had been a curse, she wanted to believe the second was a blessing.

She'd gone to the temple, and to Brother Milos, who had come from Verrin to replace the old priest of Furis. She did not liked this man, he was sour and cold, and he looked at her with eyes filled with disdain. He looked at Lilika like she was cow shit trampled into a fine woollen carpet. But he'd made the sign of the horns over her and had listened to her.

"The duke's bride-to-be is dead," she'd told him.

"I am well aware of it, and it is no concern of yours. Your duties lie in looking after the girl and making certain that she will live long enough to marry the Sevari heir."

"Did Furis do this?"

"Furis does all things," Brother Milos had sneered, before turning away from her. "I must prepare the temple for service." It had been a dismissal, but Lilika had not gone. She'd settled down to pray for visions that never came.

Now she stood in the same place, though there was no Brother Milos to look down on her. An old woman was on her knees polishing the wooden floor so that it gleamed under the green-glass rays of light from the leaf-patterned windows. But other than her, and her sweeping silence, the temple was still.

Lilika went to the far end of the temple where the great painting of Furis dominated the back wall. The bull-headed man stared down at her, and the hollow of his heart was an empty promise. Lilika wanted to scream. There was supposed to have been a change after the Petrell witch girl had died. Calvai would see Lilika as a fit bride and keep her. She would be mother, wife, duchess.

The old woman got to her feet, gathered her rags and bucket, and gave Lilika a respectful nod before leaving.

Finally alone, Lilika walked up to the wall, stepping onto the raised stage below it, where no woman was ever supposed to go. She reached up to touch Furis' empty heart. The painted wall was cool under her fingers, but after a few moments the wall began to warm, and faintly under her palm she could feel the *thrum, thrum, thrum* of a distant heartbeat, as though Furis' heart echoed from wherever he had hidden it. "I thought," she whispered, but the words choked. She tried again, swallowing away the bitter taste of despair. "I thought my penance passed," she said. "I thought you would reward me."

Furis laughed, but it was a gentle comforting sound. It shook the walls and the wooden floors, but only Lilika felt it. She listened as he told her what to do.

The new bride was coming, Furis said, and it was through her that he would make Silviana a queen. It was the first time he had mentioned Silviana's future, and the words made Lilika tremble. She had not asked for that. She'd wanted only that Silviana would be loved, would never know that it was Lilika's greed that had taken her mother from her. She'd made no bargains about queens. A world like this one did not like a queen. It dragged them through blood and pain.

Lilika pressed her forehead to the wall, her shoulders shaking. One more. One more bride to live past, and then the world would swing her way once more. Perhaps this witch girl would teach Calvai that he needed Lilika more than he needed a Petrell bride, or a Jurie son. "Please," she whispered to the wall. "Not a queen, just keep her safe. It's all I've ever asked."

I will crown Silviana with holly, Furis said. *I will give her an applewood sceptre and a robe of fire. I will take her limited human vision and bless her with mine.*

She stumbled back from the wall, and Furis stared down at her, his bull head blurring and shifting, until it looked almost as though he were no longer a man, but a giant bear standing on its hind legs, grinning yellow ivory.

"*Get out!*" Lilika screamed. This was not Furis, perhaps she'd never been praying to him at all. She made the sign of the horn, and the bear only laughed again before it faded away.

Shaking still, Lilika stepped back to the wall, now once again the familiar image of Furis. How had the Three crawled their way into this sacred place? It was not forest grown. It was built by men with stone and stripped and polished wood. It was a human invention. She knelt down to the bright floor, her fingers brushing at a dark knot in the floorboards, almost like a staring eye. From it sprouted a single tiny green twig, the bud of a leaf tight and small at the tip. Lilika snapped the twig from the dead board. It was not possible. The Three had been cast from this duchy. The hymns sang were all in Furis' name, and the priests had replaced the woods women.

Was this a sign of the coming witch bride? A portent? Lilika scrambled to her feet. She must protect Silviana, and most especially from this invader, this worm, this foreign salamander.

Furis would not want a queen, and Lilika would make sure that no such danger ever befell her charge. She would have the new bride removed, one way or another.

*

It was not often that Lilika left her realm and went to the high old parts of the palace where the dowager duchess held court. Six years had passed since Silviana's birth and Lilika could count on her fingers the number of times she has met with the girl's grandmother. The woman would not call her, pretended perhaps that Lilika did not exist. But the dowager duchess also knew that if she wanted news on her grandchild she would have to either make the journey to Silviana's rooms — a humiliating and painful experience for her, where she was carried down stairs and up, along twisting routes, and then subjected to Milos' purity rituals — or she would summon Lilika and question her.

Neither happened with any frequency, but change was coming. Perhaps Sannette also trembled in her rooms, not knowing what this new bride-to-be would bring. Sannette had been old when she married, lost too many infants, sickly and small or stillborn, before she'd had her surviving son and daughter. Child after child born limbless, or twisted, eyeless, cursed. The deaths had aged her and ailed her. Her husband's death had seemed to only hasten her illness.

"What is that?" Silviana's voice was piping clear, cutting through the muted stillness of the sealed rooms. People here worked in whispers. The mood was sedate and quiet, as though too much noise might trigger an evil curse. That if they whispered, Silviana would not turn out like her grandmother.

Lilika curled the note in her fingers, coiling it back into a tiny scroll. Silviana knew, of course she did. There was only one person who sent their notes as though they had been fastened to the legs of homing pigeons. "Your grandmother summons me."

Silviana shrugged, and turned back to her game of cards, sliding the cards across the carpet with one finger. "And what will you tell her?"

The warmth in the room grew oppressive, as though the fires had been built to blazing levels, hot enough to burn a witch.

"She will ask how you are doing, and I will tell her the truth."

Silviana did not look up from her cards, but moved them into a new sequence, one that Lilika could see meant she would soon have won her solitary game. Then the girl laughed. It did not sound like the joy of a small child, but bitter and cynical. The girl; friendless, siblingless, surrounded by women scared that any harm that came to her would be blamed on them, was neither child nor adult. She had the experience and wisdom of neither. "What truth would that be?"

"I suppose it will depend on what questions she asks," Lilika said. She pictured the girl grown, tall and strong, her hair like a dark cloak about her shoulders, her eyes storms, her hand holding an apple tree sceptre, while at her feet the bodies lay pecked by crows. The dark green of holly crowning her head with bright points, berry emeralds mirroring the blood on her hem. She shook her head, and the girl was a girl again. Not a queen. Not a creature to be shaped by the intervention of some intruder goddess. "It will not happen," she whispered to herself. "I will not let it."

"What's that, Lee-lee — speak up?"

Lilika blinked and cleared her throat. "I said only that I do not know what your grandmother wishes to know." She unrolled the note again to peer at the brief missive. "It is blunter than usual, perhaps she means to make preparations before your father's new ... woman arrives."

"It's ages still before she gets here." Silviana dismissed the approach of her future stepmother with a flick of a card. "And what does it matter. She's some mud dweller from Petrell, she has no power. My father will control her."

When the listening women shuddered slightly, Silviana appeared not to notice. "Look," she said, glancing up at Lilika, her smile bright and sweet. "I've won again."

*

The Dowager Duchess Sannette was not a woman to be trifled with, even now with her illness, her twisted legs. She might not have been able to walk, or even speak the language of her husband's people with much fluency, but Lilika knew it was a fool who thought the old woman simple. She saw much. Or rather, she saw little, but her women saw much. They were the shadows in the corners, the old women twisting wool into yarn, counting the silver, polishing the mirrors, doing a million small and seemingly inconsequential things, but always flitting back to their duchess, to whisper in her ears. To tell tales.

Little birds.

Lilika snarled at the door, then composed herself. It would be the usual queries after Silviana's health — always an important part of any conversation regarding the girl. Calvai and his mother both seemed convinced that Silviana would break the moment she caught a chill, or breathed air that was not the palace's own.

There were days Lilika was convinced that Silviana would only be allowed free after the old woman died.

It would come, sooner or later. Already her spies thinned in number. Winter always took a few. And now there was only the Secretariat Elsa, who was as angry and thin as her mistress, and the handful of women who groaned at every cold snap, whose bones were like glass, whose skins could not keep them warm.

They were not dead yet, however. Lilika dipped her head as she was beckoned into the rooms by the Secretariat.

The rooms smelled.

Like old women, yes, urine and powder and that faint sweet scent of decay. But also of shit. A pungent sharp aroma of bird droppings, and millet, feathers and hearts.

While the dowager duchess might not have been able to leave her rooms with any ease, she had loved birds as a girl. Had gone bird watching with her husband and drawn many ink sketches. Some of which were even preserved in Caneth's library stacks. But now they brought the birds to her. Every hunter who could, brought her back some chaffinch or tit, a robin or wren or magpie. It did not matter. If they were alive, Sannette wanted them.

The birds lined the walls, their cages stacked into intricate wire palaces. They called and screamed and sang, and the noise beat at Lilika's head. A cacophony of meaningless sounds. Lilika hated them.

It took a while for her intrusion to become accepted, and for the birds to settle down into a somewhat quieter confusion of notes.

"Ah," Sannette said. "The wetnurse." She was bundled up with blankets, seated in her wheeled chair. It made her look tiny, rumpled.

Lilika dropped a slightly too brief curtsy and bowed her head. She had not been a wetnurse for many years.

"Come closer. I can't shout."

Lilika stepped over the drapes that lay scattered on the floor. They were used to cover the cages at night, and perhaps the only time that the denizens of this room were quiet was when the drapes were over them.

"The girl is dead," Sannette said. "Good."

There was no answer to that, so Lilika merely nodded.

"My son, he is a good man, sometimes, but like his father, also a fool."

Lilika kept perfectly still. It was dangerous to acknowledge any truth in the old woman's words. She had foreign gods, foreign ways and curses.

Sannette waved a papery hand. It trembled under the weight of the simple action. And Lilika wondered how many years the dowager duchess had left. Would she even live to see Silviana's decad? "Witch girls, the Petrells. But pretty, and a good border against the emperor, yes?"

"Yes," Lilika said, when she realised the dowager duchess was waiting for an answer. "The East has been quiet for a good many years, but the duke does not trust the Empire. Having Petrell—"

"I don't need a history lesson, idiot." Sannette smiled, showing the remaining pegs of her teeth. She had once been beautiful, according to the portraits. "The Petrells have a spare."

"They do."

"Talk my son out of marrying her."

"I—" Lilika shut her mouth with a snap. The old woman knew. She knew everything. What little bird had seen her go to Calvai's rooms and had twittered in Sannette's ears.

"He won't listen to me," Sannette continued, "but you, you have his ear when no one else does."

Lilika swallowed thickly. Calvai might lie with her, but he would not take her meddling in his affairs, and certainly not in his potential alliance with the Petrells. "I will pray, your Grace," she said. "I will pray that he does not marry the spare. It will be in Furis' hands. We have years yet before she is of age."

"Useless," the old woman said. "What good is a snatch if you don't use it? Prayers," she shook her head. "Prayers are lies we tell ourselves when we are too weak to change the world."

The Secretariat hummed softly. "If the wetnurse is useless, my Grace, we shall look into other protections. We do not need her."

"Yes, yes." Sannette nodded. "You are dismissed," she said to Lilika. "You and your prayers."

Part Two

Part Two

The Tower Letter

The shadows are long as memories, and as black. The cold seeps into this tower of mine, filling up the space around me until all I wish for is furs and fires, and deep inside me the bear-girl stirs. She has always been there, watching over me, keeping me wild at my heart.

Poor Silviana could have done with a voice deep inside that fought for her and her alone. The truth is that everyone who took Silviana's side did so in guilt, in selfishness. I am not exempt from this condemnation. Indeed, I hold myself the worst of them.

I could have simply stayed quiet and done what the world required of me. I could have been regal in my self-defeat and bowed my neck to Calvai and sewn and embroidered and thrown parties as routinely as the seasons turned. It would have been a dull life, one lived already dead, but don't many women already do so? Why did I think myself better than that?

Who was I to presume?

I was myself. Always. First and Last. And I deserved all I wanted and did. That's what it means to be alive. Men don't always see it that way, and they don't understand that we have other strengths and other weaknesses, that we must be more than stepping stones, mattresses, lambing ewes and servant girls. And too often we keep ourselves quiet. Our mothers and sisters and aunts trained us that way. They gave us the power then told us not to use it.

And I? I had no power. And I would not let that stop me.

The room is cold. The room is cold. The room is cold, and they will not let me light a fire. Perhaps they think I can use it somehow, that they know the salamander, symbol of my family line, can walk through hearth to hearth. Or perhaps they think it a kindness that I will not look into the black hearts of flames and wonder what it will be like to die.

The shirts, half finished, are in a pile and I wrap one over my shoulders as a shawl. It helps only a little but does not stop my fingers shaking, the cold air so cold it bites into my finger bones and turns the tears on my face to frost.

The letter sits accusing. It would be best to finish it, to explain everything. To offer you forgiveness for your own part in your destruction, just as I offer forgiveness to myself. We were too much the people we were trained to be. We did our best to walk new paths, and yet and yet, we were moulded before we were born. Our bones learned the shapes we were meant to be from the songs our mothers sang us while they pricked their fingers and stained white quilts red. With a sigh of clouds, I lean forward to pick up the letter, to redip my nib in rimed ink.

I never wanted you as my sister, but you were all I was given.

I stopped there, unable to go on, but I must, I must before the moonlight goes, before all the broken pieces reform and my reflection calls me. And while it's true I never wanted Silviana when I should have had Valerija, it didn't matter which of them died. Sisters, we are made to be torn apart, the soft webbing of our flesh meant to be rent.

My tongue was never my best asset. I could think things but when I tried to say them, they came out tangled and wrong, the meaning not so much lost as totally rearranged. I sewed as well as I spoke, in knots and snarls and lost needles. But hand me a pen and an inkwell and I find a voice. Perhaps, if ever there was something that was truly me then it is this moment when I press my shivering nib to the rough nap of the paper, and the ink flows shiny.

If there was witchcraft in our lives, it was not some hidden desire to harm but a frustrated attempt to protect. I wove spells. There, you have it — your confession. Brother Milos could not beat it out of me, but there it is, nonetheless. Freely given.

Witchcraft wove you, Silviana. It is the blessing and curse that knitted you together, bone by slender bone. Witchcraft gave you that skin of snow and the raven wing of hair. It gave you the war red mouth and the black eyes of winter storms. Anyone could see that. My sister was like you. Made in magic, forged in a womb that bled the blood of witches. But where my sister had teachers and an army of women who could guide her spells and power, train her to hide it and use it, what did you have?

You had Lilika. You had me.

You should have had witches all around you, Silviana. You should have been like my sister and free to learn all that there was for you to learn.

Don't throw this letter away. Your hand trembles. Rage. I have seen you draw a line fine and narrow, the brush poised just so, I have seen you dance, every movement precise and perfect. You do not shake, you have an economy of grace that serves you well. But right now, you're reading with one good eye, and you're thinking that if I weren't already damned, you'd damn me yourself, again. That I am a liar who twists words to her own ends. Lilika has warned you over and over again, that every act or word that originates from me is not to be trusted.

Be angry. Make this paper tremble. Curse, if you must. Invoke the name of a god you cannot trust and who hates everything about you, if it makes you feel better.

But don't be angry with me.

I will tell you, now, the truth. You will grow angrier, crumple the pages, throw them away. But you will not throw them in the fire, and after a while, when the stars have fallen and the snows have hushed the world asleep, you will pick up this ruined letter and smooth it open, and you will read.

It's all a story. I have made it up; filled in the ways the world turned, the conversations and the details. But for all the trim I have pulled out of thin air to stitch to this empty silk, the tale I tell you will still be true. It will be true because you will read it and you will know in your bones that everything I tell you now, you already knew. In some secret storehouse of matrilineal memory, you will see the story unfold exactly as I have spilled it.

I give you the witchcraft you should have had and tell you how you began.

There are five sheets of paper left for me to write on. Obviously, the powers that brought me here thought if I ever felt moved to confess my evil, and the spells I cast in the hopes of killing Silviana, or how I went to the forests and consorted with wild animals, all the men I lifted my skirts for, then I would need plenty of space in which to detail my crimes.

My fingers are frozen stiff, and I take a break from writing to huff on the chapped skin and rub my hands roughly together. From far below comes the eerie singing of the wolves that have returned to the lands with Calvai's death, and further, the stray scream of a vixen, like a woman condemned. When my hands are warm again, or as warm as I will ever get them on this night, I slip my little box of thread and needles from my skirt pocket. The magic near sings under my skin. It is strange to think that once I could barely do more than sense magic, and now it calls to me, begs me to use it.

It was Valerija who went to secret tutoring. Of course, we all learned to stitch and embroider, but men pay no attention to what goes on in the banal chatter of women, and it is easy to teach magic thread under thread. While we all sat at our chairs and worked on cuffs and collars, I merely made a mess while Valerija learned to pull power with a needle. If I'd realised that, one day, I would be able to twist this power myself, perhaps I would have paid more attention.

Even so, I know enough to let my senses guide me, my hand hovering over the narrow loops of threads, the colours a meadow of flowers grown under glass. With some surprise, I settle on a green of winter rivers, a green of moss on ancient rocks, a green of shadowed leaves. Three greens where I had expected suns or fires or blood red carmines.

Still, it does not do to argue with magic. I braid them together, cut them with my teeth, spit wet the ends to take the amber beads. I breathe on them, warm and wake them. The bear sits watching me blindly, but even from my chair I can sense three giddy spirals of magic unfurling from it. There is always a bear watching, somewhere. In my head, Urshke laughs in her barking growl, and I smile back, thin and tiredly amused.

With the newly made thread coiled on the desk, I turn back to my pages. I should finish the story before I finish the magic.

Or start the story. Beginnings are always hardest. How far back does one go? What words to set the tone? How much must I explain, will I say too much or too little?

A deep breath.

I will start where all stories start, with a wish and a dreamer.

Once there lived in the duchy of Calvai a woman like the sun, married to a man like the moon. She was brightness and joy, and all who saw her loved her. She wove happiness with her hands, and all she saw she loved. Even the moon grew warmer when he was with her. But for all their joy, all their love, this sun woman had one secret pain that she carried deep inside her. A wound that would not heal.

*

For try as she might, the Duchess Belind could not conceive, and every month her grief was renewed.

Her husband came to her and said, "Why is it that you do not give me a child? Your sisters have many children, your own mother too — what curse lies on you that all our love cannot bring one life into this world?"

"Oh, husband," she cried. "I do not know. I have prayed, and tonight I will pray again."

When he left her, the woman like the sun stared out her window at the wide white fields and felt her heart dimmed. She went back to work, sewing at shirts for her duke, the linen as white as the snow that blanketed the world outside.

Perhaps it was the smoke of the fires or the blur in her eyes from unshed tears, but the woman like the sun, who was normally so quick and careful and precise in her stitchery, pricked herself with a needle, biting deep into her thumb.

The blood welled bright, dripping all over the shirt.

"Cursed, " she said, and sucked her thumb, tasting the copper and salt. The rooms in her tower were warmth and safety, but perhaps it was warmth and safety that cursed her. She opened the great window and crawled up into the seat and stared down at the winter below her. The gardens stark and stripped, the sentinels of distant mountains uniformed in grey and silver. Far away the rush of water where the linn emptied into the wishing pools, the clash of it only a faint echo. There were black-barked trees tied with ribbons, the woman knew, though she had never tied her own ribbons there. That was for the old, for those who still thought bears answered wishes. No bears lived in Jurie now.

She leaned further, fingers clasping the icy ledge and as she leaned, a single bright garnet fell to the snow, and another and another, until she brought her bleeding thumb back to her mouth.

Below her, the three stains spread.

Oh. The woman like the sun made ribbons of her thoughts and tied them to the west wind. *Can I have not even one child? One small thing that is mine alone.* She gave herself over to dreaming. *A girl with skin as pale as these winter drifts; her eyes and hair black as the dead trees; her mouth like these three blossoms below me, a mouth of salt and copper. A winter girl.*

Of Witches

"It's time for another mother already?" Silviana looked up from her game, her hand tight around the throat of a lifeless hare. At nine years of age, the girl had slipped into the liminal space where she grew coltish and lean, but babyfat still clung to her cheeks, her rounded belly. Her games were childish, but her thoughts had turned redder and darker.

Lilika broke off her conversation with the court ladies and higher servants and stared at her with bug eyes. Lilika had always looked delicate and quivery as a field mouse, but now her dark eyes bulged so that the comparison was even more apparent, and Silviana laughed.

"It's hardly funny," Lilika said. "And you shouldn't eavesdrop."

"Not laughing at that," Silviana said. Not at all. Why would she laugh over the idea that in a month or so, she would have a new mother? One to replace another she did not remember, and another she had never met. "And I don't eavesdrop. You talk."

Silviana had been sitting on the thick rugs of her playroom floor, making a small articulated hare covered in real fur, with terrible staring glass eyes, do battle with a lead soldier. The hare was winning, but only for the moment. Silviana had been at war since morning and the floor was littered with the discarded corpses of dolls and toy animals. The women of her father's court tended to treat her as though she were a fire, rather than a person. They crowded around her as though she were important, but never actually directed any conversation toward her in particular. Mostly, she treated them to the same level of erasure, but now the talk had turned to her new step mother, and her father's upcoming marriage. "So, it is to be soon, then." She dropped the hare, where it sprawled broken-backed in the thick pile of the autumn rug. "A mother."

"That is so," Lilika said. "But not truly a mother. She will be a wife to your father, but that does not make her someone who will care for you."

"I'm nine," Silviana said. "Not an idiot."

Lilika gave her a small, secret smile. "I never said you were, my darling mouse." She put down the knitting she was working at, her polished needles smooth from years of clicking. "But when this chit arrives, she will want to get you on her side, mother or not."

There was a murmur of hissing disapproval from the gathered women for Lilika to share such secrets with a child, but Silviana scooted closer to Lilika, and cocked her head. "On her side?"

"Women like her do not marry for love," Lilika said. "They cannot. They must marry to make good alliances, and she will need to knot the marriage firm. Her father and duke will expect nothing more. And by making herself mother to a motherless child, she will tighten those bonds."

Silviana digested this. It was not that she had no idea how the marriages of the women of the nobility worked. She had studied enough history under Caneth to know exactly what was expected of the dukes and their families. Her own betrothal to her cousin had been formalised almost as soon as the last earth had covered her mother's coffin. It was how the families kept ties and checks, strengthened trade, kept borders safe. She was also aware that her new stepmother-to-be was far younger than her father. Younger than her own mother the Duchess Belind had been when she had died.

It was a strange thought, as though the world had kept a wife in stasis for her father, just waiting until he was ready to wed again. The world had carried on and grown older; the wife had not.

Lady Valerija Petrell had gone to her grave before she had gone to her wedding bed and Silviana had seen her only as a portrait miniature, too young to be anything but a wide eyed, black eyed, storm eyed girl, like an older sister made of snow and war. And now another Petrell was to be finally sent in her place. "Is there a litter of Petrell daughters to pick from?"

She looked to the scattered toys on the gold and copper and red rug and thought of dead mothers she'd never met. "Who is my father going to marry this time?"

"The youngest," Lilika said. "Marjeta Petrell."

The name told her nothing. Not the age — though it would be less than her sister — not what she looked like, or how she behaved. There was only a frame of letters, and an empty space within. Silviana picked up her hare again, though the battle lust had drained from her blood. "I suppose it does not matter which one comes here."

"Indeed," said Lilika softly. "But perhaps it will be better this way. I heard too many rumours about the other." Her voice had dropped low, conspiratorial. "About both, to be sure."

Somewhere, Silviana once remembered reading that it was bad luck to speak ill of those who had walked from one world to another, but her curiosity was piqued. "What kind of rumours?"

"Well." Lilika lifted the lead soldier, and made it spar with its tiny longsword against the hare. "I can't say truly that it was not lies and evil gossip, but people do say the line of Petrell breeds witchery."

"Oh, I don't believe in witches, Lee," Silviana said. " I believe in Furis, just like Father."

"That's not all I heard," Lilika drew ever closer, her voice lower still.

"What else?"

"You must be careful, my little mouse."

Silviana's heart grew cold, her skin tingling with a sudden sweep of fear. There was a note in Lilika's voice that was not born of idle gossip and recounted tales, but of actual, marrow deep terror. "What is it?"

"Be careful, because the mills have brought stranger stories to me, and there is one I do not like." Lilika paused, heightening the moment of anticipation. "They say that this Marjeta was hungry for power. That both women were witches and they battled since childhood, always at each other's throats with curses and spells. That she poisoned her own sister so that she could marry your father in her place. That she could hold power over the Duchy of Jurie instead."

The words were ice shards, biting deep into unprotected skin. Silviana shuddered and drew her hare from where he lay, cradling it to her chest instead, as though it were warm and alive and could bring her some measure of comfort. In her mind's eye she saw this Marjeta Petrell, wild haired, her eyes dagger glinting, her mouth cruel and sharp. A witch and a murderess. "Father would not truly marry her if that were so," she whispered.

Lilika shook her head. "Of course not. As I said, it is merely rumour. People say the strangest things in times of mourning."

"But Father needs to marry someone," she said. "And if she casts a spell on him—"

"Hush now!" Lilika laughed, then lunged forward to cuddle her. "I have told you stupid stories, meant only to entertain you. Of course she's no witch. I did not mean to scare you, my sweetling thing."

"So, she's not a witch?" Silviana broke free of the embrace. "You're certain."

Lilika gave her an odd look, then glanced over her head to where the ranks of serving ladies and ladies in waiting had stilled their needles to watch. "Of course," she said. "Doesn't Brother Milos tell us that no witch can walk on the stones that Furis has blessed?"

Silviana nodded.

"And has Brother Milos not cleansed this castle, every inch of it, and consecrated it in Furis's name?"

She nodded again, more certainly this time. It was an act she could remember. The one time she'd been allowed out of her rooms and into the entry chamber, so that the suite could be free of female impurity while Brother Milos worked.

"Well, there you have it." Lilika grinned. "Even if this poor girl is a witch," she laughed, "she will never be able to walk into the castle."

"Furis would strike her dead," Silviana said. "As soon as she crossed onto the castle grounds, he would strike her with lightning, burn her up on the spot."

"Exactly." Lilika smiled and sat back. "Exactly. And whether she be witch or not, I will always be here to protect you from anyone who would even think of hurting you. I swore it to Furis Himself."

"I know that," Silviana said. "I'm hungry — when shall we eat?"

Choose Carefully

The Duchy of Jurie was far to the north. From the maps, Marjeta knew that the land was dark and ragged, threaded with forests and studded with craggy mountains and little dimples of farmland. But she saw none of it. She travelled in a wagon pulled by four immense shaggy horses and kept the heavy velvet curtains closed against the thin light of the sun. The interior of the wagon was thick with cushions and goose-down filled blankets and woollen comforters. Beneath the seats were all her treasures: some for her, but most destined for Duke Calvai Jurie.

It wasn't even her dowry really, but Val's. Packed away after her death, and now, three years later, drawn out again to be handed over to the duke, along with Marjeta.

Val, who would not need a dowry to cross the green river and walk the shadowlands. Val, who was the greatest witch in all the land, in all the eight duchies, and who would be forgotten while her bones turned brittle and black under the cold earth.

Marjeta clenched her fists and drove them into the pit of her stomach, churning her dress, twisting it until she was certain her clothes would tear.

"My lady?" Her lady-in-waiting Areya was nervous, her frown half troubled, half distasteful. Still, she reached out one hand to still Marjeta's continual twisting. Her palm was warm, soft, and the lace cuff wreathed her wrist in silken webs. Marjeta shrugged off her lady's touch. She didn't want pity or concern, or any bile-sour imitation of either. Even after so long, she wanted her sister. Alive.

The shriek of axles, the rattle of iron-rimmed wheels, and the steady slow hammer of shod hooves on gravel and hard packed dirt. The women did not travel alone, of course. Her father went with them, though Mama had stayed behind. Val was well buried, and all the new marriage plans were drawn up, but it seemed that Val's death had taken more out of Mama than she could stand. She had lost Nadija to marriage, Val to a dog bite, and now Marjeta was whisked away too.

It didn't seem right to trade in his last daughter as a replacement after her sister's untimely death, but Papa wanted her in Duke Jurie's castle — far from the ghosts of wolfhounds and witch girls. Perhaps he thought she was cursed. That she would rub off on Josef and his bride and any babies they might quicken, like dark marks that could not be erased.

Maybe she was ill luck, Marjeta thought. She took a deep breath and forced her fingers to let go of her dress, to straighten. "When will we stop?"

Areya bowed her head. "I am not sure, your Ladyship. Your father wanted us to ride as close to the edge of day as possible."

Marjeta looked at the situation objectively, as though she'd stepped outside her own body, and watched her family's drama unfold like a puppet playlet in the twilight. Her father raced because he wanted them to reach Calvai's fortress before he was tainted by Marjeta's evil. He wanted to spend as little time as he could near her. Fear for his kin was a scourge that drove him. Did he look at Marjeta and see only a curse? Perhaps he thought her a byblow, a wife's treachery. Devil spawned, god spawned. What difference would it make? Let Jurie have her. It made no matter if her luck infected him. The duke had already lost his first wife and been left with a squalling infant girl. And he'd lost a bride before she'd been bedded, and now he was getting this replacement child instead. Dead brides and a motherless infant. Marjeta sniffed back sudden tears, her grasp on her objectivity faltering.

Hardly an infant now. The girl would be nine, at the least.

And what would this child be like, growing up with no mother in the cold northern reaches of the Duchy of Calvai? A thin and sickly thing, more ghost than girl. And the duke? Marjeta buried her head in her hands and swallowed down a tearing sob. Val's husband. Together they'd laughed about him; so old and serious, with his trimmed beard and moustache ("To hide a weak chin, of course," Val had said), with his muddy grey eyes ("winter puddles") and his thin mouth ("Died in childbirth? Hah! Of boredom more like — there's a man who never smiled once in his life.")

All said with vicious humour, the kind that masks a desperate fear of the inevitable. But they had pretended, and Marjeta recalled they hadn't minded his hair. The duke had thick chestnut hair that went wavy at the edges. Val had called it a mane, but she'd said it with some glint of genuine laughter. He was a grown man, but at least he wasn't bald and fat and older than sin.

The wagon shuddered and juddered along the road, and outside the voices of the men rose. They were calling a halt. Tents to be raised, fires to be started, food to be prepared. The women who travelled with the retinue would be set to work, as would the men, but Marjeta would sit in her wagon, in her dark rancid womb, waiting for the night. She would not see the sun. After nightfall she would sleep in a tent lined with carpets and curtains, with a bed made for her, she would eat well and simply, and sleep under guard.

There was no riding her pony at the head with her father, no regal march into Calvai under the flag of Petrell, the white salamander curling across the green. She was being brought to him in a wagon full of gold and silver, with wooden kists of fabulous gifts, ensuring their friendships. Not even the right girl but a substitute wife.

She sat straighter. Enough of this, she was her mother's daughter too, and witch blood ran in her veins, fine as silver threads. Maybe too fine to use, but it still made her stronger, metal in her body. She would act it. She would make the witches of her line as proud as they could be over a girl who could barely raise an image from a scrying mirror. She didn't have magic, perhaps, but she had her mother's gods, old as witchery themselves. And in a small iron chest, curled in sleep, the salamander from her hearth.

Areya took up her embroidery hoop as the wagon came to a stop. "It will be a while before your tent is ready," she said. "Perhaps you'd like it if I told you a tale?" Areya was the daughter of a count who controlled one of Petrell's border forts. She was twenty-three, and one of seven girls. There was little more for her to do than become the glorified servant of a sixteen-year-old girl pretending to be world-wise and emotionless.

"A tale?" Marjeta looked at her: a thin-faced woman with wide eyes set far apart, and a mouth that was very small like the start of a kiss. "No." She followed the pin and stitch of Areya's fingers. "I want to pray. Set out the gods for me, and fetch wine and bread and oil."

She waited impatiently and unmoving until Areya returned with a basket of victuals and had unwrapped the gods from their travel case and placed them in a row. The woman seemed to want to handle them as little as possible, her fingertips barely touching the little statues, her face twisting. She withdrew as soon as she could, and Marjeta was left alone with her mother's gods. Her gods now. Where before she'd found her father's horned god less of a threat, now she wondered just how much the god of men truly looked out for mothers and daughters. A useless god, a foreign god. That was why The Three no longer listened. Too many men like her father and his little priest gave sacrifice and worship to the wrong god.

The sound of shouts and instructions faded away, leaving Marjeta in a bubble of silence. She moved mechanically and stiff as a clockwork poppet from the east, dribbling the oil, the wine, breaking the bread into three small pieces.

"Bring me back my sister," she said. No salutation. Even these gods were enemies. They had not brought her mother happiness, they had not saved anyone. Marjeta clenched her jaw and breathed in through her nose, until her chest felt stretched out, her ribs like steel around a wooden barrel. Finally, she let the breath loose across the faces of the gods, and inside her that thin red thread of magic twitched. "Bring me back my sister."

She smashed her hand into the offering trencher, into the oil and wine, pulping the bread into a soggy mess, before smearing it across the faces of the manikins. "Bring me back my sister."

The gods said nothing and Marjeta stared at them dully, at the mess on her hands, until Areya returned.

The lady-in-waiting took one silent looked, then withdrew again, only to return a few moments later with a bowl of heated water. She remained silent as she cleaned Marjeta's hands, finger by finger, her head bowed.

"Do you laugh at me?" Marjeta asked, dully.

Areya paused in her ministrations, then tilted her head to look up. "No," she said. "I find there is little to laugh at in the situation." She sighed and got to her feet to set about righting the mess Marjeta had made. She paused for a moment while straightening the gods. "I think it is a cruelty to send you in your sister's place."

"Couldn't waste a spare daughter," Marjeta said to her clasped hands. They looked nothing like her own. Cold, white, smooth. She twitched them, and they moved. Definitely hers.

"I suppose they could not," Areya said with a long sigh. "We'll be moving again soon. The captain says we will see the great palace soon. They built a place far from the town, and the lands around it for fifty miles are given over to parkland and some small forests, that the duke may hunt."

"And be far from the stink of his own citizens," Marjeta said.

"It does seem like that, doesn't it?" Areya turned to face her. "There." Outside the noise of the caravan had grown louder, shouts and clamours, and the sound of animals re-hitched to wagons. Their own shifted and jerked, and Areya held out one hand to the coach roof so that she would not stumble. "I believe we're on our way."

A shout from ahead, a bugle blast, and the loaded coach strained forward, then began to roll smoothly on again. With every revolution of the iron rimmed wheels, Marjeta was dragged closer to her new home, and further away from her sister's grave.

She took the small glass of wine Areya poured for her and drank it. She was dry eyed now, feeling scoured out, as though sand had scraped her insides clean. What use were gods that answered no one.

"Do you believe in them?" she asked, nodding toward the three figurines.

Areya cocked her head. "What else would you have me believe in, my lady?"

"Furis, perhaps." She said it without any real meaning but Areya laughed once, scornfully.

"You would have me worship a god who hates us?"

That got Marjeta's attention. She thought of the temple and the new priests her father had installed, and how sheep faced and pathetic they seemed against the wildness of the three's tree-grown temples, the songs of the wild. "Hates us?" Certainly, Furis seemed to have little time for women in his stories, but Marjeta had dismissed it as the idiocy of a foreign religion.

"He hates magic, any magic but his own, and he especially does not like it when women use magic," Areya said.

"You talk as though he were just a man."

Areya sat down and looked at her, careful, her brow furrowed. "All gods are just men, or women. We make them into something greater because we fear the empty space that would be left without them. And we hand them power, piece by piece. I trust The Three because they have had a very long time to build their power and they are not scared of wild things, of magic and women. But this Furis, he's new, and new gods bring blood into temples. He will evirate all the wild beasts and bring them gentled to the altar."

A disquieting thought. "Mother says the Duchy of Jurie follows Furis, that only a handful of people still follow The Three."

Areya nodded. "You go to a place that will not welcome you. You should know that now."

It only compounded her sense of dread and loss. It wasn't that Marjeta wanted to cling to her mother's faith, her stupid gods, but they were still hers and she didn't want them torn away either.

"In public," Areya said, "you must be dutiful, and follow your husband's faith. You will have to choose your god, but I tell you to choose carefully. You must be the perfect duchess whenever anyone sees you."

Marjeta clenched her hands. "And when no one sees me?"

Areya smiled, and leaned forward, put one hand over Marjeta's white-knuckled fists. "I will see you, and with me you can be yourself and worship as you want." She rubbed her hand softly up and down Marjeta's wrist. "Do not think you have been abandoned. The Three watch over those who watch over them. They are women, and they understand when women have to hide their true selves."

"I hate it here," Marjeta said, her voice small enough to disappear. "I'm not even here yet, and I hate it."

Areya got up to pull open one of the thick curtains that shielded them from the outside world. Marjeta blinked and drew back from the sudden spill of unwanted light. It seemed to highlight her patheticness, her sorrow and impotence. She wanted to stay in the musty, velvety dark and pretend there was no world outside.

"It seems pleasant enough," Areya said. "You should look out, see the land, at least. You've always loved the growing things. Perhaps you will love them here too."

"Perhaps."

Areya held out her free hand, the other still keeping the curtain pulled back. "Come, my lady, 'for there are flowers even in the fields of our enemies'."

"Don't quote histories at me."

"I will until you give in."

Marjeta sighed and shifted so that she could peer out the window. She could smell the herbs and dust trapped in the velvets, the warm saltiness of Areya's skin, even the smell of her hair, fennel sharp and faintly musky at the same time. Cold air seeped through the glass, and outside the land gleamed frost edged, green under white, the hills and stones almost black against a clear blue sky.

"What's that?" She pointed to a large turret building, round and stark, on a distant hill. It looked menacing and forgotten in equal measure. Like a rotten tooth that had been pulled and discarded.

"That's the Penitent's Tower, where the old kings would imprison traitors before they killed them." Areya pulled a sour face. "Most often those traitors were their own family, and one can never tell from histories who were actually the traitors, and who were the just. Histories, after all, are written by those who have already won all the battles and hung the witnesses and paid the scribes."

The tower made Marjeta feel sick, the thought of those who

had died there or waited for death in its cold lonely embrace. How many hundreds of years past? At least she would be in somewhat more comforting accommodation. She watched the turret grow smaller, then disappear from view behind a rise. "The palace will be an improvement on this carriage," she said. But it felt like a platitude. Meaningless, meant only to convince herself. "I hate it," she said again, fiercer, softer.

Areya was pulling some of the smaller kists free from under the benches, and checking their contents were in order before redoing the buckles. "I suppose you'll just have to suffer through it as best you can."

"I don't mean the place," Marjeta said.

"I know you didn't." Areya's face appeared in front of her. She poked Marjeta's nose as though she were a small child. "Be careful, Lady. While it doesn't do to trust every fool who dances into your path, it would be a grave mistake to make enemies of strangers. Be nice to all you meet, give them chances before you decide where they belong on the board. You will need friends in this place."

"I thought that's why my mother sent you," Marjeta said dully.

"Hardly." Areya had ducked down again, though she returned a moment later to set a small iron chest next to Marjeta's side. "That's why she sent this." She flipped open the lid to reveal Tarkis, curled up on himself and twitching in his dreams.

The salamander, warm still and hibernating in his carry case, brought a rush of warmth to Marjeta's heart, as though her chest were overflowing with summer floods. Here was something real, something that was home. And the bedding he lay on was equally familiar. She reached out one hand and stroked it, following the familiar pattern of embroidery. A cloak, one she'd worn as a child, one still prickly faint with her sister's magic, stitched deep and held there, preserved beyond death. Marjeta felt one corner of her mouth pull upward. She might be on her way to a castle of strangers, friendless, but there was Areya from her mother's court, a childhood cloak of shadows, and her salamander from her own hearth. Little pieces of home. "We should light a fire for him as soon as we arrive," she said, as she twisted on to one side and examined the sleeping salamander, curled and golden, his sides gently rising and falling. Fine wisps of smoke curled from his tiny delicate nostrils, and she could see the movement of the eyes under the thin pale eyelids. "And feed Tarkis. He'll be hungry after all this travelling."

Areya nodded and pulled at the curtain again.

Marjeta closed the lid.

"Look."

This time Marjeta put up no fuss, and there in the distance, the pale stone of the castle of the Duke of Jurie rose from a sea of green and ice lawns, like a small, delicate mountain. Marjeta pushed one hand against her stomach, and thought of fire, and fur, and darkness.

All Works

The girl usurper would soon be at the gates. Messengers had brought word from border scouts who had seen the Duke Petrell's caravan snaking through the thousand valleys, past the Penitent's Tower and into the vast palace grounds. Lilika stood uncertainly, her hands filled with folded sheets. She liked to spend time near the laundry rooms, for they were set close to the kitchens, and to where a small courtyard was often used by messengers to sit and take some small beer and apple pasties for their troubles.

Lilika's duty lay with the care of Silviana, but she was so much a fixture of the palace and so often by the duke's side that no thought was given to her increasing duties or the way even soldiers would follow her commands. She never phrased them as such, of course. That would be a fool's route, all braggadocio and swagger. She would only suggest, or ask, or say, "I heard the duke mention..." And now, within an hour, the woman who would take all that from her would be in the palace, set up in her suite of rooms like a crab in a periwinkle shell. And once she'd outgrown that, she would move on to the suite of chambers reserved for the duchess of Jurie. "She's just a girl," Lilika chided herself, and pressed the sheets harder against her chest.

"Your pardon, Lady Lilika?" said the messenger who had brought her the news of the caravan's imminent arrival. He was sitting near the open door, on a stone bench, his legs stretched out in the sun.

She shook her head, startled. "The poor thing," she said. "The duke's betrothed. She's still only a girl. So young."

The messenger finished his pastry and flicked the crumbs from his jacket. "And not quite ready for court, is what I heard," he said. "Bit wild. running about at all times, playing at hunting and what not."

Lilika blinked. "Is that so? Well, truly, she may be even younger than I had supposed. How old is she meant to be?" she asked, though she knew the girl's date of birth. "Twelve? Thirteen?"

"Sixteen, as I heard it," said the messenger. He winked over his mug. "Gives the duke a little breathing space, at any road. He'll have another two year's grace before he has to be finally done with his mourning."

"Come now, we must not speak of our duke so. A man has a right to mourn. He loved the Duchess Belind dearly."

"A mite too dearly if you ask me. Nine years already it's been, and that's nine years wasted without no proper heir. As lovely as she might be, Lady Silviana is no duke. No," he puffed himself up. "About time enough to take a new wife, even if she is a witch."

"Hush," Lilika said. "We'll have no such talk. These rumours serve no one well. The girl is not a witch. It was an unfortunate accident that her sister took ill and died. The two might not have been close, but that does not give us leave to spread talk of poison and spellcraft and whatever other nonsense these gossips have been breeding under their tongues." She clucked. "Just a poor girl. And we shall do well by her."

"Not meaning to offend," the messenger said. "Just telling it as it was told to me. Poison, you say?" He squinted. "I heard she laid a curse, sacrificed a hunting dog as part of a ritual—"

"Thank you," Lilika snapped, "for your conversation. But since our future duchess is nearly arrived, I must finish making her rooms ready, and prepare to greet her." She raised the folded sheets as if to prove that she had merely been down to collect the linens. It was almost true. She could have sent servants to gather the sheets, and as soon as she returned, she would give orders for the final touches to be put on the girl's rooms. Hearths made ready, final dustings and clearings, the Book of Furis lovingly arranged on its sacred table.

She was just surveying the waiting rooms when the secretariat maid to the dowager duchess came to her. The two women looked at each other uneasily. The Secretariat Elsa and her lady had never shown overly much interest in Lilika, each enjoying the fiction that the woman was merely a wet-nurse who had stayed on past her time. The dowager duchess knew exactly what Lilika was to her son, but everyone pretended otherwise. Elsa drew herself up to her full six foot and sniffed through her narrow nose. "The Dowager Duchess Sannette requests your presence."

A sudden black and empty fear gripped Lilika, shook her right to her bones. Silviana's grandmother was not an easy woman; her grasp on the language of her husband and son was rudimentary, and after her husband's death at war, she had retired from palace life. She lived on almost as an afterthought or a ghost, but every now and again she had to reach out her wrinkled claws and disturb the palace calm. Trust her to do it now when everything was already in disarray. Lilika curtsied. "Immediately," she said. It was not a request, and both knew it. They had spoken before of the coming of a Petrell bride, but that altercation had not gone well.

Lilika pressed her mounting nerves and irritation down and followed Elsa from the main palace building, past the great halls and open courtyards filled with blinking windows, to the Pavilion rooms, where the Lady Sannette had made her rival home. It was a mini palace, staffed with its own loyal servants and footmen, maids and bakers and scullery girls and butlers. But with each year, there were fewer servants in the dowager duchess's house, and her rule faltered. All that were left these days were the birds, and even they grew fewer.

She was old and frail. She had been old when she'd been married to Duke Frederik, old when her husband died.

Lilika paused outside the lady's grand receiving chambers. The floor was carpeted in deep rose wool stitched with golden hares and deer, the edges a tangle of vines and leaves and wrens. Great banks of windows let in the early afternoon sun, but despite the glassed-in heat and the roaring fireplace, the dowager duchess was wrapped in a fur lined quilted jacket, her withered legs covered with plaid wool.

The wire cages were filled with watchful eyes, pointed beaks, clipped wings.

"Girl," Sannette said, her black eyes sharp in their net of wrinkles. Her face was pointed, and had once been delicate and neat, but now the flesh had fallen away, and age had whittled her down to bones and hollows. Only her black eyes were still alive. She stank of roses and illness, perfume and powder.

Smiling, Lilika curtsied deeply. "My lady, you wished to see me?"

"I did. How is my granddaughter?"

"She is well, she is in good health."

"And is she happy?" The claw hands fiddled with something in the woman's blanketed lap, and Lilika suppressed a shudder. She was like a crow digging through entrails.

"Most happy, My lady. She would love it if you were to vis—"

Sannette held up a wrinkled hand, "Stop, no. I think she would like it not as much as you say. Old people, yes." She smiled, showing the gaps in her teeth. "They frighten the young. Show them the future. They do not like this."

It was best not to argue. The dowager duchess may have little power in truth, but she still had influence in her own crabbed way. Her son paid her no more attention than he would any old woman, but sometimes, for the sake of propriety, he would pretend.

"Come closer." The old woman beckoned with a finger and Lilika found herself moving reluctantly forward. Despite her husband's conversion to Furis, and her son's continued support of the new religion, Sannette came from Southern Ageri, and she'd made no attempt to follow in the men's footsteps. She did not worship Furis, but nor did she follow The Three. Lilika had no idea what the old woman prayed to, if she even did.

"This girl, the one who comes to marry my son?"

Lilika nodded.

"She's a witch girl, yes? You could not stop it. They come like snakes, or like hares, and I cannot tell." She fumbled again with the thing in her lap, then jerked her hand forward. "Give this to my granddaughter," she commanded. "Perhaps it works better than your prayers."

Lilika reached out hesitantly to take the dangling amulet. It looked ancient, malformed, and as her fingers closed around it, she realised what it was, and what it meant. Protection. Even the old woman cared, alone in her fake palace, forbidden in unspoken ways from seeing the granddaughter her son loved and coddled so.

"I will tell her you sent her this," Lilika said, as she curtsied deeply. It was not something she could ever pass to the girl in front of Brother Milos or any of his people, but perhaps the little trinket could do what Furis could not, and truly keep Silviana safe from the machinations of witches. She turned on her heel, heading quickly back to her rooms near the Lady Silviana's quarters. One hand slid into the pocket of her skirt, where it closed fast around a rough grey stone with a hole pierced right through the heart of it. A hagstone wound with red and yellow embroidery thread; barbaric and ancient. Protection did not come from stones and rituals and the correct coloured threads to bind the magic. That was the work of the Three, and she had left such evil behind her. What she should do was throw the dowager duchess's little stone far away and never mention it to Silviana.

Instead, she held it tighter, felt the pulse of it against her palm like a thrush's heartbeat. Perhaps Furis knew that Lilika would need every tool at her disposal to keep her charge safe, and it was he who had given this to her. Had made Sannette pass it on talon to talon, all in order to keep Silviana from evil.

Brother Milos would not have agreed, but then, he was a man, and one bound tightly in rules. He was blinded by them and Lilika was not. She would pray for guidance and a vision of the future, and she would know whether or not to pass on Sannette's gift.

*

Nine years ago, Lilika's rooms had been almost bare. Functional, clean and furnished only with the most basic necessities of her position as the guardian-carer of the young Lady Silviana. Back then the duke's daughter had been nothing more than a squalling, pinch face infant, her head squeezed out of shape, her skin greasy with vernix. Lilika had seen newborn infants before, and she was well aware of how hideously disfigured they looked on entering the world, but some part of her had half expected this child to be born cleaner, prettier, as though magic and death would have elevated her.

The rooms were filled now. Years of slowly accumulated goods. Gifts of status, wardrobes built up from the remnants of the duchess's old clothes. Lilika had bought herself trinkets from the Fair of the Goat that came every year through the mountains, had slowly filled her meagre shelves with actual books. She'd never been stupid, even when she'd been near illiterate. And Lilika had always been quick to learn new things.

"I was never content," Lilika said to the tapestried walls, and shivered. "I wanted too much, and it was my downfall." It was true. She should have been satisfied with what she had. Plucked from the throng of women who served the duke and duchess, elevated beyond all understanding to the side of a woman who had shone like the sun on the face of the great forests

And over time, a confidant to one.

And over time, a mistress to the other.

She had stood between the sun and the moon.

Lilika took a soft tasselled pillow of faded velvet and placed it on the floor so that she could kneel before the glazed picture of Furis. It had cost her near a year's wages and there was nothing in the room that was worth more. All her belongings together, books included — did not cover the cost of this one thing. The painting had been her first true purchase with the money she'd earned in the duke's employ.

She swallowed and covered her eyes with the palms of her hands, as though scared to look on the portrait and see it looking back at her, equal measures of pity and contempt. "Forgive me," she whispered, then stood rapidly and placed a fine white veil over the painting, over Furis' bull head, his black stare.

Working quickly, as though afraid that the god would appear in her rooms in person just to find out what she was doing, Lilika drew a small brass mirror out from under her bed and spat a pearly gobbet of froth which she smeared quickly over the surface with one finger. She whispered as she worked, a hurried incantation that she'd last used before Silviana had even been born. The years hadn't dimmed her memory, the spell too tangled up in the pathways of her mind, sharp as brambles. She pricked her thumb and squeezed a few drops onto the mirror's surface. The hazy reflection of her face was gone, replaced by a shimmering swirl of crimson and silver that moved in a way that blood and saliva never should.

The spell hooked itself into her, pulling at the long untouched magic in her veins. She had sworn never to use witchcraft again, never to turn to The Three. She had given herself over to Furis in penance for her guilt in Belind's death. Lilika's heart hammered painfully against her ribs. It felt like something that no longer belonged to her. "Show me," she whispered. "Quickly. I need to know."

When she'd been little more than a girl come up from the nearby village to work in the palace citadel, she'd been desperate to know what her future would bring her, though scrying was a notoriously vague practice. People tended to misread their futures, try to find ways to change them. She'd used the mirror then, as her mother had taught her, and her mother's mother, and all the ancient women of the village knew.

It wasn't about changing things, Lilika thought. It was simply about knowing them. If she knew what was coming for her at least she would be able to face it. Not knowing was paralysing.

She sucked in her breath. An image of a black tower was forming from the swirls and patterns. Lilika was familiar enough with the Penitent's Tower. A sudden ache pierced her side. The tower? Was that how she was going to end? The new duchess would find her out for a traitor, discover her place by the duke's side and do her best to destroy her.

"No," Lilika hissed. "I will not let—" but the picture was drawing her in as though she were a crow flying to the high turret window, to see herself in penitent rags, ready for burning.

The figure that coalesced before her was not her own.

Lilika leaned back and smiled. There on her knees and wearing the white of court traitors was a woman she did not know. She'd seen the dead sister's portrait, of course. This woman was not that shining raven and milk beauty, but it was easy enough to see the similarities in the line of the jaw, the long, proud slope of the

Petrell nose. Where Valerija Petrell had been sleek, this one was wild and rough haired, eyes amber brown instead of black. The woman in the mirror was no girlish slip of sixteen, so this day was still years to come.

But come it would.

The mirror woman went to the table where the remnants of her last meal waited for her. She ignored these and picked up a quill, carefully uncapping a small pot of ink, as she set to writing. Her confession, most likely. Or a will. There was no walking out of the tower and back into life. Wearing the whites meant she was ready for burning.

The image hazed as the spell reached the end of its course, and the vision of the future duchess's ignoble end turned to smeared spit and blood on a scratched and ancient hand mirror. Lilika wiped the mirror clean and wrapped it back in its cloth before drawing back the veil on Furis' face.

The god glared down at her, impassive, but Lilika's heart had lightened. True, for a moment she had wavered and gone back to the ways of her old gods, her old life, but surely Furis would understand why. "I exist only to serve you," she said, once she was back on her knees on the little prayer pillow. She covered her eyes again. "All I do, I do in your name, for your will. You will show me how to serve you." As he had once before, when he'd given her the duke's child and then taken it from her before it was old enough to be born. When he'd made sure she would be a perfect nurse to the duke's legitimate daughter when his wife had died. Always, Furis had given her exactly what she needed even when it seemed he took away. His vision was greater. Hers simple and small. She had to trust him. He had sent the hagstone to her through the dowager duchess, that much she was sure of now.

If Furis was angered by her use of the old magic, she would be punished, beaten and brought back into line like a wayward beast. But wasn't it Brother Milos who said that all men served Furis with their talents? That the woodworker's skill was praise and servitude as much as the peasant's labour, or the scribe's. It stood to reason that the works of women served him too. Needlework and drudgery and magic. And if Furis disapproved of her works, he would strike her down.

Lilika lowered her hands and bowed her head. "I will do all as you will it, and only as you will it," she said, lightened in spirit. She would either be praised or punished now, but whichever happened, she would know what she was meant to do. Furis would guide her. If he was pleased, then that would be her permission to use women's magic against the witch.

It was time to meet the future wife of her duke. She would stand between her and the young lady Silviana and offer the girl what protection she could from this interloper. This traitor. And if she must arm herself with strange weapons to do it, so it would have to be.

The future was, after all, a strange land.

Teeth

The first Jurien person to greet Marjeta to her face, to name her and offer her a smile, was a rose dark woman hardly taller than Marjeta herself, though she was a good many years older. Old enough to have had a baby and lost it. Old enough to be a wetnurse when the duke's daughter had been born.

"You must be tired," the woman said, and her brown eyes were acorns still on the trees, her hands warm, her teeth little white beans. "You've travelled far." She ignored Areya as though the lady-in-waiting did not even exist. "My name is Lilika. I'm nurse-guardian to the Lady Silviana."

Silviana. Duke Jurie's only daughter, and — in a matter of years — Marjeta's stepdaughter. The thought made her shoulders tense, her back ache. Instead of letting her fear show, Marjeta pushed herself to dip her head, to keep imperious. She was the future duchess, and who had come to greet her but a servant. No duke, no honour guard. Her father had arrived a few hours before, and, surely, he would have been met by the Duke Calvai. Perhaps the men were already engaged in rumours of war and sharing of battle stories. Her father had a new cannon at the Petrell castle, and every day he trained new men in using the modern lightweight wooden and iron rifles they had procured from their eastern neighbours.

"Where is my father?" she asked, though something about the woman's touch despite her gentle smile made Marjeta shudder almost imperceptibly. She felt like blood and magic, distant and deadly.

Lilika removed her hand from Marjeta's shoulder with a jerk, frowning. "Are you ill?"

"No." Marjeta turned from the woman and snapped her fingers at her maid Areya and the servants with her. "I am never ill." She gestured for them to bring her private kists — the rest were to be left to Calvai. Her father would hand them over, but he would not get the chance to pass her on like one of them. "Show me my rooms."

A shadow passed over Lilika's face, a flitted darkness that hinted at disgust and irritation, and then it was gone, and her smile was back. She curtsied low and deep, her head bowed. "Of course, if the Lady Marjeta Alis Petrell would follow me, we have a suite of rooms prepared for you. The duke hopes that it will be to your satisfaction."

Marjeta said nothing. How could anything be satisfying here? It was colder than the touch of a drowned ghost girl, the stones black, the glass windows black with the reflections of storms, the sky blacker still. Even the huge twin hearth of the Jurie high hall — big enough to drive two chariots in side by side and roaring with huge fires — did nothing to cut the chill of the air. She followed the nursemaid Lilika's back, gaze fastened on her gown of forest brown stitched with golden leaves of oak and trimmed with white rabbit fur. A decent set of dresses. Perhaps a bit too fine for a servant, even one whose charge was the duke's only heir. Marjeta scowled.

At least in Petrell she had known her place. She'd had to do her duties as a Petrell heir, of course, but she'd also had freedom that she'd understood. She could run and scavenge in the wild forests and play along the lake and river shores. She could steal bread from the kitchen cooks, who would only wink and shoo her on kindly, and she could light fires in the forests and burn rabbit meat and eat with her fingers if she so cared, as long as she'd been dressed in the right clothes at the right time, she'd had space of her own to carve out in her own manner. Now all that was gone, and she was in a world where she no longer knew the paths. She'd been a last daughter, a salamander in a house of magic and mirrors. Here, she was both a Duchess and Not, an ill-made replacement part.

Stop it. Marjeta drew herself straighter and walked with careful determination, her head very high. Her appearance was her only armour. There was nothing else to defend her here. *You are not afraid.*

Duke Calvai Jurie's great bear symbol was everywhere from the rearing black silhouette on the flags to the bear skins that seemed to cover every surface she looked at. There was even the immense head of a monstrous beast of a bear hanging above the fires in the great hall. A bear so big that it must have stood as high as a dragon when it lived. They were all reminders that she was an outsider.

A salamander in a bear's den. But the Three sometimes took the form of bears, and Marjeta let that thought warm her, even if it was only the smallest trace of safety and familiarity. She tried to pay attention to the layout of the citadel as much as she could, but either it was built in a series of mazing twists and dead ends and curious turns especially to confuse invaders, or Lilika was purposefully leading her along some incomprehensible path. The servants carrying her things had begun to huff softly by the time Lilika drew up outside a wide wooden door trimmed with gold plated hinges and latticework.

"This will be yours, my lady." Lilika dropped a curtsy before unlocking the door with a great iron key she wore hooked at her belt. She pushed the door open and ushered Marjeta to step into her new living area.

Trembling a little with a mixture of travel exhaustion and the strangeness of her new surroundings, Marjeta brushed past Lilika and entered the darkness.

It took Lilika only a moment to light the candles in their sconces, and for the room to be revealed in a flickering of gold and yellow. The air smelled faintly of dust and mould, and over that, of rushes and sweet herbs. It was obviously a place long deserted, newly cleaned out for her arrival.

Inside was a revelation. Not one room, with its space only for the four-poster bed and the wardrobe and little tables, but a suite of rooms. One after the other, the walls lavishly decorated, each with its own vast hearth. The floors were thick with woollen carpets, tufted to look like grass and starred with woven flowers like chamomile. Marjeta was used to her single chamber. Large spaces in the Petrell castle had been reserved for her mother and the ladies to work in. Here, she had a set of rooms that could fit the women of the Petrell court easily. Not just one table to work at, but desks for writing, desks for eating at, desks for playing games, a long empty table, carved and gilded and painted. The bed itself was near twice the size of the childhood bed that she and Val had shared. It was thick with rich indigo covers, deep enough to drown in. On the floor next to the bed was the ubiquitous bear skin, but this one taken from a bear of reddish gold, its back and head fur frosted almost white at the tips.

There were chairs for sitting, chairs for reading, long velvet-cushioned chairs to stretch out on and nap. The whole air was one of ridiculous waste, of the kind of sumptuousness that was completely at odds with the bitter cold, the black woods, and the austerity outside. While beyond the thick stone walls the winds raged and the clouds gathered snow in their bellies, here everything was softened and warm and thick and safe. A bear's den. A duchess's den.

One thing was missing, however. Or three, to be precise. The house idols and their altar were nowhere to be seen. Instead, one of the tables held a small white plinth, on which rested a single book. Marjeta recognized it as the holy book of Furis. It was disconcerting to see that held in high esteem, with no place for The Three. The reality was more unsettling than she'd expected.

Marjeta turned round and round, taking in the suite's surprising excess. Was this because she was to be Calvai's wife one day? It didn't seem right that any mere guest would be treated to such luxury. What of her father's guest rooms — would they be the equal of this? Somehow, Marjeta doubted it. These were rooms meant to coddle a kept wife.

"There is food and wine for you, Lady Marjeta. I will leave you to rest, and have the servants prepare you a bath—"

"A bath — yes, please, that would be most welcome." Marjeta trailed one hand against the furs at the end of her bed. Soft and white, winter stoat, stitched into one immense covering. Her heart beat faster. What was Petrell to this? She'd had no idea of how poor her father's Duchy was in comparison. "Where is the Lady Silviana Jurie? I would like to meet her."

Lilika smiled too sweetly. "That will come in time. There are preparations to be made." She stepped aside as the last of the men hauled Marjeta's kists and travel chests inside. "The duke will want to see you tonight at the welcoming feast. I'll have servants bring you warm water and something to eat." She dipped in another little curtsy. "We welcome you, Lady Marjeta. This is your home, and we are your people. We will do everything we can to ease your heart and body after such a long journey."

"Thank you," Marjeta said, remembering something of the wariness her mother had drilled into her. Sixteen or not, her new place in this household was that of the future bride of the duke. It was in her best interests to remember this always. These people, kind as they might be, were not hers. "Your thoughtfulness is welcome. I will see Lady Silviana in due time, I am sure."

She smiled at Lilika until the woman left, then dropped all pretence and fell back on the great bed. Above, her ceiling was an endless knotwork of intricate carvings and panels, the high walls muraled with a history of the Jurie line. "I feel like a mouse," she said to the vast bedroom.

"You don't look like one," Areya retorted. She was already sorting kists, unpacking the gowns and clothes into the long, panelled cupboards, and stowing various trinkets and goods in the hinged benches that filled the deep recesses below the mullioned windows.

When the fires had been stoked and the food placed in readiness for her, Marjeta got up to go pour wine for the two of them. It trilled against the gold swirled glass. "Look at this — even mother doesn't have glass as fine, not even on feast days. A mouse," she repeated, staring at the fire sparking in the depths of her wine. Perhaps if she drank enough of this, she would feel warm and full inside. The wine could replace the black emptiness that seemed to have taken the place of her innards.

"And this makes you a mouse, how?" Areya accepted her wine with a dipped curtsy as though it were usual for her to be served by her Lady, instead of the other way around.

"Once," Marjeta said, "one of Mama's cats caught a field mouse and was playing with it under my bed."

"Not that unusual an occurrence." Areya said. The Duchess Petrell had a fondness for cats that had bordered on excessive, and they had colonized the Petrell castle with their claws and striped furs. The cracking of tiny bones was a common enough nighttime sound.

"No." Marjeta shook her head. "But I don't know why, that time, something stirred in me, pity perhaps. The thing wasn't dead, and the cat was batting it about, letting it run a little, then catching it again. Finally, I intervened and caught the mouse in one of my sister's handkerchiefs."

"She must have been best pleased."

Marjeta laughed hollowly. "I never told her. But this mouse. It was so tiny and fragile, and I could feel its heart vibrating against my palm. It was terrified. And I could not release it because then the cat would simply go on with his game. So, I put it in one the wicker cages that Josef used for finches."

"It could have gnawed its way out, sooner or later." Areya sipped at her wine, then packed away another armful of gowns.

"But it didn't. It simply sat there, unmoving. I left it water and a crust of bread and a piece of fruit, but in the morning it was dead."

"I see," said Areya. She waved a hand at the table "And you, you have been left fruit and bread and water, and you could walk out your wicker cage, if you wanted."

"I suppose," Marjeta sipped at her wine. It was rich, too heady and bright. She was used to her wine watered down, the sharpness cut.

"And you think one day someone will open the cage and the mouse will be curled stiff in a corner."

"I can't leave," Marjeta said. "Where would I go? My family's honour would be shredded."

Areya shrugged. "You don't stay for that, do you?"

Marjeta stared at her. It wasn't because of her family's name that Marjeta would marry and do her duty. It was to honour her sister's memory, and even Areya could see that. She cleared her throat. "Don't presume to understand me."

"I presume nothing. Drink your wine, my lady."

"And that will help?" she sneered.

Areya cocked her head. "Perhaps. After all, you did not leave your little wild mouse a thimble of wine, did you? It might have made all the difference."

Despite her fear and helpless anger, the comment startled a laugh out of Marjeta, which turned quickly to a cough.

"Come, drink deep, and I will help you freshen up and dress you for the feast."

"Like a goose," Marjeta said glumly, though she complied by draining her glass.

"Goose or mouse." Areya shrugged. "Best make up your mind which you want to be, my lady."

Marjeta stuck her tongue out and was ignored. While Areya arranged heated water and fresh clothes, Marjeta opened her salamander's kist and nudged it awake. "Out with you," she said. "I think you will approve of the hearths, at least."

Tarkis yawned wide, his needle fangs glinting, before he uncoiled himself and chirruped in pleasure at the sight of the huge open hearths, banked with marble and heaped with burning logs. He skittered into the nearest and disappeared among the flames, scales turning to gold and black and red.

"Well, one of us suits this place," Marjeta said. "If there are hearths like this all through Calvai's palace, Tarkis will be happy as a pig in mud."

At least she had this much. Areya, who was almost a friend, in her own older, distant way, and Tarkis, who had been with her since she was barely able to walk. Home, and the salamander the symbol of the Petrell House. Marjeta allowed herself a small triumphant smile. It pleased her to know that the sign of her own house would live here.

And Jurie's symbol was a bear. That too was its own shade of auspiciousness. For wasn't it a bear who had saved her from fever and led her from the black lake and back to life? Marjeta considered this new idea and glanced down at her jumble of kists again. "We should do one thing first," she said slowly. "Take down that." She nodded to the Book of Furis on its pedestal, "and set out the gods. It is past time for an offering."

"You're certain?"

Marjeta nodded. She pointed at the long table, the one with its curved and gilded scrollwork, the surface painted in blues and greens and golds. It was as though it had been left there as a sign —beautiful, and long enough to take the gods and their offering trencher. "There," she said. "We must never forget where we came from and who we are."

In a few hours she would be expected to be at the feast. It seemed only natural that Petrell and Jurie would all celebrate this new unlikely union, at least while Marjeta's father was still a guest in Duke Calvai's summer palace. Not that there was going to be any marriage or wedding feast for years to come.

They would celebrate their engagement instead, call Marjeta sister and friend and wife-to-be.

Marjeta shivered. These people were strangers, and their words would be as empty as her own. All the promises they would make to each other... Marjeta knew that this was part of court life — Mama had taught her this, whether she liked it or not. The last few months as her sixteenth birthday approached had been an accelerated lesson in how to survive in her sister's place. She'd been like a plant hastily grown indoors so that it would be strong enough to be transplanted into cold soil early in spring. All the things Val was supposed to do — wind her way into the life of Duke Calvai Jurie's castle while still keeping her threads to home secret and strong — now these were for Marjeta to do, and she felt utterly small and inadequate. She might have been only a handful of years younger than her sister, but life had grown them differently. Perhaps having her home gods here to watch over her would help. She didn't have to believe in them, just keep them as reminders.

"Eat something." Areya pressed an apple against Marjeta's closed hands. "And we'll need to bring something decent back from the feast." She nodded to the hearth fire where Tarkis had vanished. "Yonder worm is not going to be happy with apple cores, you know."

Marjeta took a bite of the apple. It was a bright golden fruit, larger than any she'd ever seen back home, and the flesh was crisp and pale and delicately sweet. It crunched between her teeth.

"Which dress was it that you wanted to wear tonight?"

"I don't care." Marjeta sighed. "This is the sort of thing I never understood. But I'll have to, whether I like it or not." She needed to stake out her territory, show a little iron under the embroidery. Just a glimpse. Not enough to let Duke Jurie know she was his enemy, but enough to let him respect her. For a little while.

"Better late than never, I suppose," Areya said. "The dress is armour, and a signal of intent. I can help you choose, but I need to know what you want to say to this duke and his court."

"I hardly know that myself," Marjeta admitted. She felt a sudden rush of relief that Mama, distant as she had been all through Marjeta's life, had known to send Areya with her. The woman was a good few years older, but she was easy and friendly with an iron core of competence.

"What about the green?" Areya held out the hem of one dress. It was a very beautiful piece of work. Val herself had embroidered it, sprigging it with tiny wildflowers in palest reds and blues and golds, their tracery of feathered leaves like shadows on the dyed linen.

"It would make me look like a child," Marjeta said. "Innocent and sweet."

"And you'd prefer what?" Areya arched a heavy brow. "Would you like hunting leathers and a sword and bow?"

Marjeta huffed in amusement. "I don't want to scare him just yet."

Areya conjured a dry smile in return.

"But I want him to know I'm not some cade lamb, desperate for love from whoever gives me milk and kindness."

"Oh, that you've never been," Areya said. "Your Olaga loved you dear, and she told me to look out for you, to keep you safe when she couldn't, but she knew you well, and she made sure I knew too."

"You knew Olaga?"

"Some. I spoke with her more once we realised your mother wanted me to take over from Olaga when you left your child-time." Areya released the hem and smoothed the dress back into its place. "I'm not your enemy, my lady. I'm not your friend neither, but you get to choose which side you want me on. That's part of what leaving childhood means. It means finally paying attention to the things around you whether you care for them or not. In this, every person you meet is a teacher."

"But you're the one my mother thought I could learn from fastest."

Areya inclined her head and winked. "See, you're not quite a fool."

Marjeta contemplated the compliment, barbed as sharp as an insult. She shook her head in dry amusement. "Call me Marjeta, that's better than my lady, and definitely better than not quite a fool. So. What dress would you choose — if I were to want to appear meek, but hint at teeth."

"The yellow." Areya turned to search for it, drawing the overdress out with a flourish.

Marjeta frowned. "Yellow?" It was much like the green; the embroidery of flowers and leaves, hinting at spring and youth and joy. Again, it looked like a child's dress. And even with the underskirts and fitted jacket, the low bodice and starry net of the head covering, it would make Marjeta look like she was still just sixteen. "Yellow is a priestess's colour. It seems no better than the last."

"Priestesses are just witches with book learning, Marjeta. You really should pay more attention to the things women talk about," Areya said. "It is also well known that the previous duchess came from the county of Ester and that she always wore something yellow to represent her people. Yellow means something in this land, just as it does in Petrell. It shows the court that the woman who wears it does not belong to this land's master. And it is a reminder of death."

"Oh," Marjeta said with sour amusement. "Teeth indeed."

*

Marjeta was ready when the servant Lilika came to fetch her. The woman said nothing at the yellow dress, though a flicker passed across her face, a tremor of grass blades as a snake moves through a meadow, but Marjeta was not quick enough to catch it by the tail. It could have been disgust, suspicion, anger — or perhaps most likely — a twinge of gas.

Servants had lit candles along the most used passageways and these lights flickered in pale welcome, though the rest of the rooms were dark, doors closed and forbidding. Lilika led Marjeta back through the network of tapestried tunnels and Marjeta let herself become immersed in the pull and warp of the building. While the palace and linked castle buildings were far larger than her own home had been and had been slowly added to throughout the centuries, Marjeta had a way with directions that came from years of hunting through the forests with Sasha at her side. She winced at the memory of the hound, at her death and Val's. It didn't matter. All this was past, and now she could choose to mourn what had happened or learn from it.

I will learn from it, she thought fiercely, and let the shape of the paths soak into her as though she were tracking hare in her old forests.

She could hear the feast hall before they arrived: a familiar sound. Marjeta glanced at her companion, and Areya rolled her eyes, her mouth twitching. The barrage of chatter and boasts and the clank and thump of drinking mugs and trenchers and boots. The men there would all be loyal to their duke. The strangers in the midst would be Marjeta and her father and their retinue.

The hall didn't fall to silence when the women entered, though a few men paused in chewing to leer speculatively at them. Marjeta was certain the looks were for Areya or Lilika, and certainly not for herself. Next to them she was a pointed stick. The older women were ripe, beautiful, and they wore their plain gowns with a kind of swishing artistry that Marjeta didn't even attempt to emulate. There would be years enough for that, she realised grimly. Years that stretched out ahead of her like a prison sentence.

She kept her head high as she marched to the high table where her father was sitting to the right of Duke Calvai Jurie. Here was the man she was to marry, and her heart stuttered at the reality of it. It crashed down on her, making her stumble. A gentle nudge from Areya had her walking forward again, even as her lady-in-waiting made her way to the lower ranks of tables reserved for minor house nobles.

Marjeta put foot before foot, and though the walk to the high table seemed endless, eventually she was standing before the raised table and the family she was supposed to embrace now as her own.

She dropped a deep curtsy. "My Lord Duke," she said, and kept all traces of trembling from her voice, pitching herself low, decorous. "May Furis bless your House." The words tasted wrong, the shape of them awkward against her tongue. She wanted to spit them far from her.

The duke nodded when she rose from the curtsy and indicated for her to take the empty seat on his left. Throat closed and tight, Marjeta bowed her head and walked around the table to take her place, shivering with awareness that all in this high hall were watching her. A great fire was lit behind the high table, and the heat of it poured onto the backs of the noble family, bathing them in fire and red light.

There were men and women all down the high table, so many faces that they tumbled through her head, a whirling snowstorm of little flakes, all apparently different, and yet all blurring into an indistinguishable mass. Marjeta found herself seated between her future husband, with his luxurious hair and weak chin, and a young man who was awkward and gangly as a six-month-old lurcher, with feet too big and limbs too long and thin.

The duke looked down at her. His mouth was curved in a nervous snarl that reminded Marjeta of a dog uncertain of whether it should bite or not. She thought of Sasha again and her stomach clenched. *Learn from it. There were ways to deal with hounds like this. Firm, gentle, and show yourself to be no threat.* "Good evening, my Lord Duke."

"And to you," Calvai replied, briskly, and abruptly. "You are welcome at my table." Of the yellow dress, he said nothing, but as soon as he had greeted her, Calvai turned back to talking to Marjeta's father, leaving her in a well of silence, a lonely cell in the wall of chatter around her.

The young man to her left leaned closer to her and said cheerfully. "It's not you, by the way. He talks little to anyone. This is the first time I've seen him speak to someone for so long." He nodded to the conversation Calvai and her father were having, their voices low and earnest. "Probably already discussing the finer points of war to the east and peace to the west."

"Is that so?" Marjeta had no idea what to say to him. She was separated from even the friendliness and guidance of Areya, who was at a lower table with other maids of the court. This she had to negotiate on her own. Marjeta had never really had to talk to anyone who she hadn't grown up with before. She tried to pretend this youth was Josef, but they looked nothing alike. Where Josef was dark and handsome, the man next to her was russet, a gangrel creature, freckled and with wide large features. The only beautiful thing about him, as far as Marjeta could tell, were his eyes. They were soulful and deep brown. Sasha eyes. "War is a pressing concern here so far from the borderlands?"

"Probably," said the youth as he grabbed a piece of bread and sopped through the remains of his meal. "I've never cared much for that type of thing. More's the pity, as Uncle Calvai says. I'm Devan."

"Marjeta."

"Rather guessed that," he said cheerily. "I'm from the south, my mother is Calvai's sister, but she seems to think I'm growing up all soft down there, so she packed me off to my uncle. It's the sort of thing you can do with a youngest son and not feel badly about. I think it's meant to make a man of me," he whispered, then winked.

"Is it working?"

"Not sure." He took another hunk of bread and pronged a section of roasted pheasant. He appeared to have the appetite of a winter starved bear. "They've made sure I do a lot of hunting, which helps. People here get very excited when you bring in a dead wolf."

"Wolves are dangerous, that's why. They take sheep, children, even grown men and horses."

"I suppose," Devan said. "I'd really rather be sailing. I'm good at that. Eckstad's on the ocean, you see." He paused to stare glumly at the remains of his haul. "We're about as far from the ocean here as possible."

Marjeta grabbed her own food, though she tried to be less savage about it. She had to look like a duke's daughter and future wife, her mother had impressed that much on her at least. "You don't like hunting? I love it."

Whether it was her sudden enthusiasm or something else entirely, Devan smiled. "I don't hate it at all," he countered. "I like anything that gets me out of this palace. I'd prefer to sail, obviously, but a horse is good, and the feel of the wind and the sun. I could almost pretend to be back home."

She understood the sentiment. With her new duties as future duchess there would be little chance for riding unaccompanied, but she could still take her horse out with a retinue, ride under crossed boughs, hooves crushing pine needles, rabbits and foxes skittering through the undergrowth, birds calling in warning, the sun falling in butterfly dapples where it could. She breathed deep, as though she would take in lungfuls of forest air rather than the thick close must of beer, wine, and smoke and meat and men inside the duke's hall.

"Perhaps we shall go hunting together," Marjeta said. It was a little forward, or it would be if she was just some unmarried chit, but this was an engagement feast, she was already someone else's property in all but name. Innocent property, who thought that a hunt wouldn't matter. Hunts meant many people, hounds and horses and noise. There was nothing improper there.

Devan paused to consider the invitation, glancing up at his uncle before smiling lopsidedly. "Perhaps," he said. "Though I suspect it would make a better show if you were to spend your time with my cousin."

The Lady Silviana Jurie. Marjeta's stomach tightened as though she'd taken a floury bite of unripe pear. Neither the duke's daughter nor his aged mother were in attendance, as if they were monstrosities he wanted hidden away. "I thought I'd see her here," she said, swallowing to cover away the strange taste in her mouth. "This ... future daughter of mine." She tried to make it sound like a joke, but she knew as soon as she said it how ridiculous it must sound. Her, sixteen and dressed up in the yellow of another woman's country, pretending that she was anything more than a traded substitute.

Silviana was a child, for sure, but so was she. The engagement was simply a formal sealing of intent. Marjeta would live in the summer palace with the same status as another foster child. Much like Devan himself. After two years, when she reached marriageable age, there would be a wedding and feast, and by then the deal would be done. She would go from child to wife, with no moment inbetween where she would have the space to invent herself. "What is she like?"

"She's..." Devan frowned and made a little sound that seemed almost a sigh—not annoyance, but something else. "She can be sickly, and weak. Uncle's been very protective of her since her mother died. He keeps her far from crowds, after the priest told him that her mother died because of tiny demons that leap from one host to another." He shrugged with one shoulder and ate a strip of meat, chewing and swallowing with a wolfish hunger. "Anyone who wants to see her first has to be cleansed by Brother Milos."

That sounded like a tall story, Marjeta thought. Demons and cleansings. Typical foreign nonsense. Everyone knew the safest way to ensure one didn't get ill was to ward with spells and protection amulets, and to embroider the twenty-three pleas of protection as delicate sigils into the hems and cuffs of your clothing. That was part of why the stitchery had to be so precise. A stitch wrong, or missing, and the wardings were useless. And why the women of her mother's court spent their evenings in embroidery. It might not have been witchcraft like Val could do, but it was its own kind of magic.

"Uncle will want you to meet her as soon as possible though," Devan said through a mouth stuffed with food. "He's keen for the two of you to make friends." He swallowed and bobbed his head. "Silvi's lonely, poor thing. That much even I know."

As if she had overheard the conversation, Lilika arrived at Marjeta's elbow as soon as the last of the platters were cleared away, whispering for her to join her, that it was time for her attend the Lady Silviana.

"It was a pleasure speaking with you," Marjeta said, and curtsied formally to Devan, and repeated the dip toward the duke and her father, neither of whom noticed.

"And to you," said Devan. "Don't keep Lee waiting," he said, half smiling. He was drunker than he should be, sprawling down in his chair, limbs floppy with wine and ale. "She can nag like any mother hen, never stops. Cluck, cluck, cluck," he raised his voice, but Lilika only ignored him, gesturing for Marjeta to follow her

They walked together through the hall, and Areya rose quickly when she saw them pass, her cheeks red, and her hair wispy and undone.

The Daughter of the Sun and Moon

It was not the first feast Silviana had missed, nor would it be the last. She was used to it. Her world was this: a suite of interconnected rooms that began with the small entrance hall, where Brother Milos or one of his priests performed the rites of cleansing that kept her safe from any harm or sickness, and culminated in the tiny room just off her bedroom.

Silviana was in the third room from the entrance, a glorified playroom filled with all manner of objects to entertain her. The lamps and candles were all lit, and the walls danced with painted animals, stags and foxes and bears that leaped between the windows and over the tapestries. She was not alone. A servant tended the room, and one of Lilika's small coterie played harp to fill the air with music instead of loneliness. Silviana sat crosslegged on a large thick bear fur in the centre of the room, surrounded by chairs and couches, books and gifts from her father and her father's court. There were poppets from the south, with their jointed limbs and tangled strings, fine clockwork engines faintly imbued with magic from the east. Not true eastern clockwork — those were fiercely guarded and never left the cities — but little miracles nonetheless. Animals of wool and wood with staring glass eyes, leaded soldiers and kings and a painted castle for them to siege, and a huge wooden horse on rockers, delicately painted, and maned and tailed with real horse hair. This was her favourite, and she'd named him Dragon. For the moment though, Silviana did not ride on Dragon and pretend she was fierce and wild, hunting through the estate forests, or travelling to great adventure. She was growing too big even for this giant rocking horse, her legs long enough now that her feet skimmed the carpet as she rocked.

Spread before her was a game of cards, each card not printed on the new machines, or from woodcuts, but hand painted and lettered by the castle librarian, Caneth. He'd made them as a gift for her mother, back when his eyes were less clouded and his hand steadier. While the cards had once been her mother's, it was Lilika who had taught her all the games and showed her not just how to play and win against others, but how to do so against herself.

She sighed and flipped over a hare card and tucked it neatly in the row of discards. There were only a handful of cards left to turn, and no way to win this round. She had lost. Her mind was unsettled.

Down below and across the central court, the high hall was filled with men and women feasting in welcome of her new future stepmother. A witch girl from the east, a serpent, a Petrell.

"I will hate her," Silviana said fiercely.

The gentle stream of music faltered. "My lady?"

"Have you seen her, Genivia?" Silviana gathered her cards and folded them in silk and returned them to their box. There was no need to be more precise. Today there was only one her worth mentioning.

"Only from a distance," Genivia replied. She returned her hands to the strings but did not move them, waiting for Silviana's permission to continue.

Silviana shook her head. "What did she look like?"

"A girl." Genivia shrugged. "Younger than sixteen, skinny and hard. She looked like she'd been sucking on a lemon rind. A face that would curdle milk."

"She's ugly?" The thought of this heartened Silviana for reasons she could not quite understand. Here was this usurper, this stealer of future affections, this thief of rightful places, and she was a brattish scrawny child. The idea pleased her.

"Not hideous." Genivia laughed. "She has the kind of face that needs growing into, all angles and flatness, and hair that needs better braiding." She touched her fingers lightly to the harp and brought out a gentle trickle of music. "But she is no sun."

"What is she then?"

"I suppose we shall see. You're not to worry about her."

"I'm not worried." Silviana stood with a huff. She was annoyed. She understood that her father and grandmother meant only to protect her and that Lilika was the same. They cared for her, loved her fiercely. Nothing would be allowed to harm her as long as they lived. Certainly not this skinny witch-thing. Lilika had sworn as much to her, had got down on her knees and held Silviana's hands in her own and told her that no matter what rumours she might hear about her new future stepmother, that Lilika would watch over her. That Furis himself had made her guardian and it was by his power that she was protected.

Silviana's right hand went to her neck, to the braid of blue and silver thread that Lilika had knotted there, the grey stone heavy against her breastbone. It was a hagstone. Lilika had given it to her late that afternoon, just before she had gone down to join the feast preparations. It felt awkward and rough against her skin, scraping a raw mark. She scratched at the graze, wondering how something so silly as a stone would keep her safe. Lee had said it was a gift from her Grandmother, which only made Silviana itch to take it off. The old woman frightened her, she was too close to death to be reassuring. She mumbled her words and mashed her food with her remaining teeth. She smelled of urine and roses, and Silviana hated the few times she would deign to be wheeled into Silviana's rooms and touch her cheeks and whisper with her foreigner's tongue.

"What's that?" Genivia asked. "A new necklace?"

Silviana started and dropped her hand. "Just a silly little thing," she said. "A toy." She breathed deeply and looked to the Book of Furis open on the small octagonal book table inlaid with mother of pearl and veins of gold. The book had been her mother's. It came from the east, written in the prayer-flag script that Silviana had only just begun to learn. She wandered over to the book and touched the gilded capital gently. Though she could not quite read what was written there, she knew from the illustrations that it was from the story of the crippled maid who had brought Furis well water to drink in the heat of the day, and how he had blessed her and made her withered legs strong again. If he could do that, then caring for the safety of one girl was nothing. "I am protected," Silviana said. "Furis watches over me."

Genivia narrowed her eyes and said nothing, but her music grew louder, filling up all the spaces in the rooms, coaxing the flames in the hearth to leap higher and burn brighter.

The hours were going so slowly. Surely, they must be done feasting now, Silviana thought. She had been served her own meal, had eaten, and drunk milk sweetened with honey. On a normal night she would have been undressed already, her maids having bathed her and dressed her in her nightgowns, warmed her bed and let the fires in the main rooms slowly burn themselves out. But, tonight, she was to meet the interloper, and she was still in the formal gowns Lilika had chosen. They were stiff and uncomfortable, and all Silviana wanted to do was be out of them, be warm and safe, and half asleep.

"How much longer do you think?" she said and yawned widely. She was done with card games, too restless and bored to play with her toys. But she was even at nine, aware that she would have to play her own part in the performance, that the witch must see only what her father's court wanted her to see. And that meant being presentable and distant.

"I shouldn't think that long." Genivia left off playing. "She will come here soon. Lilika said she'd bring her. Here, sit by me and I will brush and braid your hair."

"It's already braided." Silviana frowned.

"Yes. But it will give us both something to do."

"It will give you something to do," Silviana pointed out. "I'll just have to sit there."

"Think of it as a lesson, then." Genivia gathered the wooden brush and settled in on a low stool just behind Silviana. Her fingers were quick, playing and picking at Silviana's braids as though she were just another harp, and this was music.

"A lesson in what?"

"In sitting still and thinking." Genivia gave one loosened lock a gentle tug. "Do not fret, Lilika will be here with you."

"I know that." Silviana pressed a hand against the hagstone

hidden under her dress. "I am not afraid." she sneered the last word. "Don't ever think I'm afraid, Genny."

"No. Of course not."

"She's nobody," Silviana said. "I'm the daughter of the sun and the moon."

"Just so."

From beyond came the soft flow of voices, and Silviana sat up straighter, pulling her hair free from Genivia's touch. "They're here," she said and got up off the floor. She would not meet this monster while sitting on a rug and having her hair braided like a little child.

Instead, she took her seat on the white chair that was reserved for her, even though she barely used it. It stood at the head of the room, the fur at its feet, the hearth behind her like a frame for a portrait. She settled onto the velvet cushion and stared straight ahead of her, watching the side door through which her guest would have to enter.

She could hear just faintly Brother Milos's slow sonorous voice as he intoned the blessing of cleansing and imagined that she could also hear the faintest lap of water as he washed their hands clean of impurities, as he prayed for their flame souls to burn out all evil thoughts.

Would it be enough to make the witch girl safe? She shook her head. Lilika had said that it was just petty rumours, that no one could be sure the girl had indeed killed her sister for the chance of Jurie's throne.

Silviana clutched at the hagstone through the layers of material, then released it and breathed in deeply to calm the clenching of her stomach and settled her hands on the slender arms of her chair like a queen about to meet an enemy. "Furis watch over me," she whispered.

Hare And Foxes

Marjeta wanted to hate her, this wide-eyed girl with her hair dark as the water at the bottom of a winter lake, her snow skin and spilt-blood mouth. She wanted to find her annoying, a simpleton, a brat.

She wanted her to be everything but a reminder of the sister she had lost.

Marjeta thought of the three gods set out on the long, painted table in her new rooms, and hated them instead. *Bring me back my sister*, she had begged, and they had answered. Awful mocking irony.

The rooms where Silviana lived were so lush and gilt as to put even Marjeta's suite to shame. She blinked at the sheer ostentation of it, the scale of wealth and power. But there were iron grills fixed into the stonework windows, and no amount of coloured glass could hide that. Marjeta stopped looking at the finery and focused on what it tried to hide instead. This was no little girl's room, but a lady's cage. There were beloved toys and kindly nurses as decoration for this vault ceilinged aviary, and in the centre of it, perched on a white chair carved from ivorywood and upholstered in emerald velvets, sat a child, her legs swinging under her ornate robes.

"You may approach," she said softly, as though she were a diminutive empress, and Marjeta some ambassador sent to curry favour, beg gifts and armies.

Marjeta took a deep breath, glanced to Areya, and nodded. Her lady gave her the smallest twitch of a supportive smile. What was she afraid of, Marjeta thought? After all, this was just a little girl — the age she'd been that night she'd climbed the tower with Val and her silver mirror. There was nothing this girl could do to her that hadn't already been done. It was best to make this child her friend, let her know that she didn't have to be alone in her gilded cage.

She stepped closer to the throne-like chair, her toes resting against the edge of a large bear skin that stood covered the carpet there, and curtsied. "It's good to finally meet you, Lady Silviana," she said. "My name is Marjeta—"

"I know who you are," the girl said. She sounded small and soft. "Father said you would come here." Strip away the finery, replace them with the normal plain shifts and wools of a small girl, and that was all Silviana was. Wide eyed, hesitant. She reminded Marjeta of nothing so much as a small kitten. One day it would be a hunter, perhaps, but to start it was fluff and wide eyes, and teeth and claws so small they were not weapons, but toys.

Marjeta stood straight, channelling all the regal poise she could remember from her mother. She couldn't let herself forget what this girl could grow up to become. Under current laws she could not be the inheristix, but laws changed and until such time as Marjeta could give the duke a son, she could become heir to Calvai lands, and Marjeta was just a political wife, passed along to make sure that Petrell and Jurie stayed allies. She had to carve herself a place and defend it or be pecked to pieces. "I'm sure your father wants us to be friends. I was hoping that we could get to know one another better," Marjeta said. "I've brought you a gift."

"You have?" For the first time, Silviana's expression changed, and a hint of smile showed. It made her look even more her age. Marjeta had to get that part of Silviana to like her, to make sure the girl was on her side.

"It belonged to me," Marjeta said. "My mother made it for me when I was young." The toy was one Marjeta had brought with her not out of any emotional attachment, but to use as a lure for this girl. She glanced back at Areya, who hurried forward with the small wooden chest. It was plain, but polished to a high sheen, and the hinges moved easily. Marjeta raised the lid and drew out the gift.

In truth, she remembered being given it when she was barely six years old, and the creature had been well loved. It had been stitched together from scraps of silks and linens, a multicoloured patchwork of tiny scales, with beads for eyes and claws, and for the thin ridge along its back. The salamander was no longer than a child's arm, but it had been made with love and skill. The material was soft under her fingers, and Marjeta ran one fingertip along the beaded spinal ridge, listening for the faint clack. She'd abandoned this toy in favour of her bows and play-swords, not realizing at the time how much of her mother's care and love had been poured into its making. There were faint traceries of embroidery across the patchwork scales, binding it stronger. "These symbols," she said, moving closer to Silviana so that she could show her, "are protection emblems. My mother sewed them in place to ward against diseases, against enemies, against all ill wishes. See?" Marjeta held the salamander out to the girl.

"Why would she do that?"

"Because she cared," said Marjeta. It occurred to her rather belatedly that the child might see the gift as a cruel reminder of her own lack. She swallowed and tried to spin a better tale. "And its why I am giving it to you. I will not make you one, because I will not presume to replace your mother. But I can share what I have with you, in the name of friendship." There, that sounded plausible enough, and Marjeta thought gratefully that at least some of Mama's lessons must have sunk in, whether Marjeta had meant to listen or not.

Silviana took the toy salamander hesitantly, and spent a moment examining it, before she carefully placed it behind her, and hopped down from her chair. "You're not very old," Silviana said, and sat down crosslegged on the bear skin rug and began pulling at the tufts of fur, stroking them between her fingers like she was petting a live animal.

"No." Marjeta looked to the watchful figure of Lilika, who was smiling thinly. The nurse-guardian took a seat on a narrow chair near the wall. She seemed to slide out of sight, small and unobtrusive. She hadn't liked that gift, Marjeta could tell, hadn't liked the idea of someone else holding any kind of power over her diminutive charge. "I'm not. But I'm older than you."

The girl shrugged. "Everyone is older than me." She paused in her stroking. "You're not the one Father wanted."

"No." Her stomach went cold and tight, and for a moment Marjeta thought she was going to throw up right there, nothing but bile and snow. "He was meant to marry my sister, but she died. So here I am."

A moment of stretched out silence grew, the ends of it icy. Silviana appeared to be mulling this over, her brow creased in thought. "My mother also died," she said, finally. "People say I killed her."

"Did you?" Marjeta kept her face still. She knew what it was like to feel guilty, but the guilt was her own secret, and Val had whispered her forgiveness before she died. No one else knew about Sasha, and about the secret ride into the forest. No one had ever thought to accuse her of her sister's death — and to do that to a child. Marjeta shivered. What a pointed cruelty.

Silviana looked up from her contemplation of the rug and folded her hands in small fists. For a moment she looked so like Val that Marjeta's lungs began to ache. "Perhaps," said Silviana, and Marjeta breathed out. "I don't remember."

"It would be strange if you did." Her voice was shaky, a last leaf on an autumn bough voice, and Marjeta concentrated harder on pushing away all her thoughts of Val, on feeling nothing. This girl hadn't killed her mother. Men liked to say that because it gave them something to blame. Life was like that, full of risks and dangers, even when your battlefield was a wool coverlet and a wide bloody sheet.

"Strange." Silviana's face broke into an unexpected smile. "Brother Milos says that all the women of Petrell are witches, and that Papa shouldn't be bringing vipers like you into the castle."

There was a quick sound of indrawn breath, and Marjeta turned her head slowly to look at Areya, who had taken a seat across the room, as a mirror to Lilika. Areya's head was bowed, but Marjeta could see the dark flush of her cheeks. On the opposite side of the room, Lilika had placed a woven willow basket at her feet and was unfolding an underskirt across her lap and selecting thread. She wasn't paying attention to the talk — or so it seemed — but there was a sly smile caught just in the corner of her mouth. A barely-there twitch. Marjeta noted it and narrowed her eyes.

She needed to speak to the girl without her wolf-protector, but now was not the time. Marjeta bent down, and took a seat crosslegged by Silviana, so close to her that their knees met. She was dizzy with exhaustion from the days of travel, the newness of the castle, the wine and rich food at the feast, and now this solemn, lonely little girl — one minute vicious as an adult, and the next vicious as a child. She smoothed her hand across the bear fur and breathed in the musky faint smell. For a moment, Marjeta wished she had something to occupy her hands — wool to wind or thread to stitch. She had no interest in it, but it was mindless work and would have served as a kind of armour against the vulnerability of simply talking to Silviana.

So, the man who had washed her hands and blessed her in the entrance hall was her enemy, then? Marjeta was hardly surprised. He had seemed aloof and disdainful, as though she were an untrained cur let loose in his house to piddle in a corner. "The priests of Furis call all women witches." She was probing at a wound. Pretending idiocy to get a reaction. To see where a child's loyalties might lie, when she knew full-well they would lie where her nurse had told them to. "Sky and Earth and Sea do not need men as priests." Marjeta leaned back and let herself smile. "I don't follow the gods of men."

"Lee-lee says different." Silvi folded her arms across her chest. "She says that in Petrell you have three gods made of old rubbish, and you feed them bread and oil and the women dance naked around them and ask for blessings."

"People ask them for blessing, yes." She laughed at the idea of any of the women in her father's castle dancing naked about their house idols. "And we feed them bread and oil. But nothing more than that. I have my own set of house gods. I could show them to you some time, if you'd like."

The girl was mercurial. Her sullen expression dropped away to be replaced by one of utter delight. "I want to see them!" she said. "Are you truly a witch — can you do magic?"

Marjeta had no magic. She knew that. But so many ill things had happened that Marjeta wondered if her father had been right to send her away. Perhaps, Marjeta thought, she could do magic, but hers was broken and twisted and made everything come out wrong. It showed her death and killed the things she loved. "No," Marjeta said softly. "Of course not."

The lines had been drawn long before her arrival. The priest Brother Milos was teaching Silviana that her stepmother-to-be was a viper, and probably hissing the same to every ear that would hear him. While Duke Calvai had paid Marjeta no more attention than he would a shipment of unbleached linens, that couldn't hold forever.

In a matter of years, they would be married and Marjeta would need to bring red cheeked heirs into the bear den; squalling hairy monsters. She shuddered. What would Val have done? How would she have dealt with this? It had been her path, after all. At the time Marjeta had only been concerned that Val's wedding would take her away and that she would lose her sister and closest friend. She hadn't given much thought about what it had meant to Val. How neither of them had any say in the final decision. They might have argued their cases for or against certain lords and dukes, to be sure, but even so their choices would have been limited, and their father's word would have overruled their own.

Tears burned behind Marjeta's eyes. She kept them wide, scared that, if she blinked, they would be dislodged to run down her face. Childish. Weak. No, she was going to use this burning.

So, she was a viper? Brother Milos wanted a serpent to point at, an enemy that he could denounce. Well, Marjeta would give him one, but she wasn't going to be a viper for him. The Petrells were salamanders born in fire. She was going to rise from righteous fire, with a skin more poisonous to touch than any viper's bite could be. Marjeta held onto the heat of her unshed tears, twisting it round the little red thread of her weak and useless magic. Feeding it. She felt the pain drying up, to be replaced by something cleaner. Being scared and lonely would destroy her here. Rage she could use.

It wouldn't do to rush into this new world with no alliances. She needed Silviana on her side. It was already clear that Lilika held her in control. Now the girl was to become a pawn, tugged between the two of them. It wasn't exactly how Marjeta had planned to go about her life in the Jurie castle, but it was exactly what her mother had been trying to make her realise. She'd just been too selfish in her own unhappiness to understand what all those lessons had been for. Why Mama had made her sit and embroider. It had nothing to do with making pretty things or sewing charms. It had been so she could hear the talk of the women and broaden her education.

Marjeta smiled. Witchcraft and gods were dangerous ground, but she was sixteen, and she remembered enough of her own wishes from half a lifetime ago. "Do you know the game Hare and Foxes?"

Silviana shook her head.

"Ah. Well, all we'll need are three small white stones, and one grey one — bigger than the others. And a piece of chalk."

"Chalk?"

"To draw the markings."

"Where will we get stones?"

Marjeta frowned. "From the grounds, of course."

Lilika coughed nervously. "I'm afraid the Lady Silviana is not allowed to leave the castle under any circumstances."

Confused, Marjeta cocked her head to stare at the little nursemaid. The woman met her gaze with a barely concealed triumph. "I was told as much. I did not mean to break those rules," she said. "There are stones on the castle grounds."

"No. You see, you misunderstand. The Lady Silvi is not to leave these walls. She must stay in her rooms at all times."

Marjeta stood. "You mean to say that Silviana has never been outside?"

There was no answer. Marjeta stared at the two of them: Lilika smirking as she stabbed her needle into the underskirt, her hand played, and Silviana sitting wide eyed and forlorn on the bear skin rug at her feet. When she'd assumed Silviana was a prisoner in a pretty cage, she hadn't quite known the extent of it. Marjeta would have to gather stones herself some other time. "Oh. Well, perhaps another game," she said softly. "Is there one you can think of?"

Silviana clutched at her chest briefly, then nodded, and that was how Marjeta found herself hopping on one leg through the passageways of the rooms belonging to the little girl. It had been years since she had played this game with Val, where one had to copy the other, and the actions grew more and more ridiculous until one or the other collapsed in hysterical giggling. It was not a game you could play on your own. Marjeta was hard pressed to imagine Lilika playing this. Perhaps she did what she had to in order to have the heir on her side. Her mouth thinned. Lee-lee had definitely played silly games, and perhaps she even cared deeply for Silviana.

It was to be a very odd war, Marjeta realised. This battle for affections. And no matter what she hinted, she had no real magic like her sister's.

She would need a plan and she would need information.

*

Marjeta's father had left soon after the ceremonies and the feasting turned to sullen hangovers and roiling stomachs. They'd had a brief, emotionless goodbye, and then Marjeta was alone.

Perhaps not totally alone. It became more and more evident to her that her mother had chosen well in sending Areya with her. The lady's maid was a voice of calm and reason. And home: familiar accents, familiar sayings. Marjeta found that the days here passed much the same as they had at home. The Duke Calvai Jurie might be wealthier, but his vast lands and holdings still ran on the same seasonal clocks. Eskin, the nearest village, might be kept at a distance, its boundary marked by the Penitent's tower, but there was still the citadel that was contained within the summer palace's grounds and all it took to keep the palace community going. Sewing, and repairing, gathering and feasting, milking, churning, weaving, and the day in and out drudgery of work.

The duke had left Marjeta alone since that one brief meeting at the feast table. If he was at all troubled by her presence, Marjeta had no sense of it. He had no time for girls, even — or perhaps especially — if they were engaged to him. Soon the rhythms of castle life became comfortable and boring. Marjeta was still being tutored in all the things she was expected to know as the future wife of a duke. She had to embroider and weave and work as she always had. While it was true there were more servants here than in her family home, even a duke's future wife was expected to help where she could and Marjeta found herself following her own mother's path, sewing shirts to hand out on feast days, embroidering intricate charms into hems and collars. The people of the nearby village of Eskin and Verrin, the city of the old fort and the home of Jurie's army, would not bow their heads to her unless she made them love her. They had loved the Duchess Belind like she was their sun, and there was no way Marjeta could hope to outshine her. She could do only what her mother had trained her to do.

Marjeta soon learned that the duke's absences were to be many and long. And it was Brother Milos who held the men and women of the palace in his fierce, cold grip while the duke spent most of his time in Fort Verrin. The palace where she now lived had once been the summer home of the ruling dukes of Jurie. After Belind had expressed a desire to live there rather than at the Verrin seat, the court had been relocated. It was far from a convenience. While the summer palace was more opulent, larger, and warmer than the traditional hill fortress in Verrin, it had moved the ruling family far from the heart of trade and consequence. As a result, the Juries and their retinue lived in a pretty, gilded bubble, their only thoughts on their secluded world. In Verrin there was news of war, and grim-faced soldiers practising with their light rifles and swords, and farmers paid their taxes straight into the war coffers, but in the summer palace, hardly a breath of outside discontent entered. Instead, the palace was left isolated to stagnate in its own petty feuds and power grabs.

It was so very unlike her own upbringing in Petrell, where the castle had been a rough and ready fixture of the town, its arms wide enough to enfold the villages and markets. Here, Marjeta was distanced from reality. And that strange distancing and the duke's frequent stays in Verrin made the summer palace feel rather like a private fiefdom under the control of one man.

Brother Milos, the head of the Temple of Furis, and Duke Calvai's right hand. Everyone of rank in Jurie's court was expected to attend nightly services in the chapel hall. It was a chapel of the horned god Furis, filled with strange foreign incense from the east, and the images painted onto every wall told the life story of the foreign god, from his birth — sprouted whole from the head of a milk white bull — to the day his own horns erupted from his skull in sharp points, to his sacrifice of his bloodied heart to save his people, on to his final moments when he ascended to the sun and made it brighter.

Marjeta had never paid much attention to the horned god while in her father's court. She'd been aware of him as something that her father pretended to follow. There had been a priest at home, and a handful of lay brothers, but they'd had nowhere near the power the men of Furis had here. The celebrations and feast days that marked the year in Petrell had revolved around the Three and various minor forest and water deities. Even the Day of the High Sun, which was the most important day in Furis's worship calendar, overlapped with the midsummer celebrations that she'd grown up with. Furis's feast days had been tacked on as grudging extras. All the things Marjeta had learned about him were simply that he came from the east and he sometimes appeared to his people as a white bull. More than that he hadn't interested her.

"Why do I have to know this?" Marjeta pushed a dense roll of text away from her across the low wooden table. She was in the under-library, a stacked room filled with dust and pamphlets and codices and folios. Ancient hand written books and new printed hymnals and treatises were shelved in a haphazard order understood only by the librarian, Caneth.

He was an old man, a back bent double from hunching over his desk, and weak watery eyes that seemed to work only by candle light. He rarely ventured into the sunlight, as it gave him aches in his head so intense that he would vomit for days. Despite his strange, slightly misshapen appearance, Marjeta had found Caneth easy to talk to. He treated all men and women the same — as if they were fools, but valuable ones to be talked to with patient kindness.

"The texts of Beathis?" Caneth looked over the edges of his spectacles. "Because I was given to understand that you had little knowledge of the horned god," he said. "It is a primer text, useful to read before tackling the collected bibles of the east."

"Have you seen the horned god?" Marjeta asked.

Caneth snorted. "No more than I've seen the sun rise at midnight, but that's not to say it has never happened or that Furis himself isn't watching us now, invisible as air." He straightened a little at his desk. "One does not have to see a god to know he exists — only to see his actions."

"I can see my gods." Marjeta pointed out.

"No, you see three idols. Of which every household has a set. Hardly the same thing as frightful beings from beyond this world."

Marjeta shook her head. Could Caneth not see? Even though her mother's worship of The Three annoyed her more often than it did not, they were still more real than Furis. She had grown up with the idols in her room, had fed their tributes to the salamander in the hearth and never been struck down by some almighty power, but that didn't mean The Three were powerless. Or that the idols were nothing more than carvings. "The Three see through the eyes of every idol," she told him. It was the sort of thing her mother said, but now she felt a strange prickle under her skin, wondering at the truth of it. Did they? The thought was far more terrifying than the idea that they did not.

"Do they?" Caneth echoed her own thoughts. "How very boring for them, I should think." He shuffled through the papers on his huge, cluttered desk. The lights in the oil lamps flickered and smoked, greasy tendrils that had licked the under-library's beams black. "Regardless, you must read the texts, like it or not. The duke expects every member of his court to take part in the service and worship, and he will want you marked in the faith before he marries you."

"That's still years away."

"But the Feast of Horns is in a matter of months, and as the duke's intended, you will be expected to take part and to know the responses."

It was true there was no escaping the regiment of Furis's feast days, at least not in the near future, but Marjeta kindled a small hope that she could find a way to avoid this coming marriage. A pale, hopeless hope. She was already being moulded into what the duke wanted. After her religious readings, she would be tutored in the ways of the duchy of Jurie and after that, she would be cleansed and shepherded to Silviana's suite of rooms where she would sit with the girl and with the sour-faced Lilika, and stitch until her pricked fingers felt as though they were ready to drop off.

The only good thing would be listening to Areya hum as she worked. She kept up a constant refrain of all the songs of Marjeta's home, and if she half closed her eyes (pricked thumbs be damned!) she could pretend that the dark haired, snow girl stitching so prettily across from her was her sister Val, and Lilika could be reduced to a blur of shadows and form, a maid or mother, it didn't matter. If she let herself daydream, she could fall back into a world where after her lessons she would be free to ride Dust through the fields and woods, where Sasha loped at her side, and the world was unchanged and familiar.

Marjeta brushed her hand across her eyes and blinked. The low light here made her vision strain. She refocused on the text, on the tales of the white god with his bull horns, his bleeding wound on his chest that never healed, on the story of his heart that he kept safe, wrapped in flames and iron and buried at the bottom of the ice sea to the north. It made no more sense to her than the stories of her own gods. They were tales for children.

All she wanted was to throw the book across the room and run away. She wanted to wrap her arms around Dust's warm neck and bury her face in the mare's shaggy mane. Breathe in the familiar barn-sweet smell of her, listen to the rumblethump of her blood and heart, feel the velvet lips nibble gently at her hair. She should be free, and instead here she was buried underground with an old man and the lies of a foreign god.

A Mirror is an Empty Promise

"Lady Marjeta?" Caneth gently shook her shoulder with one wrinkled hand. "You fell asleep."

Marjeta stretched, her spine cracking loudly in the quiet of the underground room. It was still and dark. Most of the candles had been blown out, and there was no one in the stacks but Caneth and herself. Areya must have returned to Marjeta's rooms to finish her own duties. "Ah, I'm sorry." She had idea how long she'd lain asleep. She wiped surreptitiously at a damp spot on the old dark wood of the desktop. "I must have been tired."

"Or bored," Caneth replied. "A not unusual occurrence in the young." He smiled behind his beard and carefully closed the books Marjeta was meant to have been copying out. "When I was your age, I preferred to be down here, but I know most of the younger men and women find it very dull. For me, I was weak and slow, and suffered from terrible coughing fits. It was only here where it was cool and damp that I found my breathing eased. And I was fascinated by all I could learn. I became the library apprentice simply because I was here. All the time."

Marjeta sincerely hoped that he was not hoping for the same thing to happen with her. "I always liked hunting best," she admitted. "I have a pony, Dust, and I used to have a — dog," she faltered. "We would hunt together," she said. It had been such a long time since she'd left the castle walls. Without any orders, she'd become as caged as Silviana.

"Not everyone is made for the libraries, just as not everyone is made for the forest," Caneth said. "You need to know these tales, on Duke Jurie's orders, but do not forget your own skills and strengths."

It was good advice. She nodded.

"And sometimes, we must find new ones. Now." Caneth stacked the written work into a pile, though he added one of the library's precious tomes on top. "Take this one with you but bring it back in the morning. And don't worry over much," he said at her incredulous look. "There is no one who comes to read these. And I trust that you will care for the things other people find precious."

Marjeta left the library, her arms full with the heavy stack of papers and the priceless book. Her mind was busy with thoughts of riding through the woods outside the castle, on exploring her new world. She'd spent weeks fruitlessly courting Silviana. It was time to do something for herself alone.

"Ah, it's you!" The voice was male, young, and charmingly delighted, and made Marjeta trip in surprise.

She spun around to face Silviana's older cousin Devan. She'd seen little of him since the first night's feast, submerged as she was in studies and needlework and castle work.

The gangly youth was flushed from running, russet brown hair tousled and sweaty. He had dark eyes like his uncle, but they were not cold and unflinching. Not black and empty as the eyes of ravens. His were warm, like good soil, like the promise of green things waiting to grow. "I've been hoping to see you again. You've been hidden away for so long was beginning to wonder if Lilika had buried you already." His smile was broad, toothy.

"Not quite yet," Marjeta said. "She's trying her best, though. I believe she plans to shroud me with embroidery silks and paper." A flicker of apprehension and excitement moved under her ribs as Devan began to walk alongside her. He had brought the smell of good earth and pine crushed underfoot, of horses and white winds into the castle.

"Ah." Devan said. "Lilika does like to know where everyone is at all times. Gets very protective over Silvi, and I suppose now you're just an extension of that."

"I'm not her charge." Marjeta breathed in deeper, trying to

capture that scent of wildness. She'd become so used to the stale dampness of walls, of the acidic must of chicken shit and straw dust in the palace yards, of human sweat and iron industry. She'd half-forgotten what outside smelled like.

She was meant to go study further in her rooms, then meet with Silviana and her music tutors, then follow in Lilika's pious footsteps to the chapel hall so she could kneel and pray to a god she could not care less about. Marjeta shook her head. It had barely been more than a few months and she was already being reshaped into someone she was not. "Would you wait here for me?" she said to Devan.

He frowned at her.

"I mean only to leave these papers in my chambers," she said. And change into something more suitable than palace gowns. "I think that today I would rather ride horses than play with some little girl and sing hymns," Marjeta said. The next words rushed out of her, penned up for far too long, "Would you be so kind as to escort me to the stables?" He was the duke's nephew, surely it would be appropriate for him to accompany her on a ride. After all, there were rumours about roving bands of wild men and boys who made the surrounding lands their home and preyed on unwary travellers. She was not so foolish as to go riding in a strange land all alone. Even armed. *A fool, maybe. But not an idiot.*

Devan gave a slow nod, and Marjeta twisted one side of her mouth. "Good," she said. "I shan't be long, I promise." Areya would have words, for sure, but Marjeta could not spend the rest of her life in mourning for everything she had lost.

*

Marjeta's rooms were quiet. The fires had been cleaned out by an enterprising maid and stacked with new wood and coals. Tarkis lay curled on the pile of logs in the main fireplace, and raised his head and glared when Marjeta tramped in.

"Oh, hush you." She set her papers down on an empty desk. "Someone will come to light them soon enough."

The salamander growled and settled back again, his scales gone a metallic green-blue like verdigris on copper.

"Areya?" Marjeta called as she trotted through the interconnected rooms, but there was no sign of her lady-in-waiting, nor of any other servants. She sighed. It wasn't as though she could not undress herself, but things did go faster with an extra set of helping hands. Still, it was better this way. There could be no dismay at her decision to go riding with Devan, no lectures or clucking about her role and duties as the future duchess. She shimmied out of her palace robes and dumped them in a pile on her bed. She had a wide split skirt for horse-riding, in the Eastern fashion, and a form-fitting jacket and high leather boots. The split skirts were really very wide legged trousers and could be folded and tucked into the boots to be worn as regular riding trousers if one wished.

It didn't take her long to dress, but there was still no sign of Areya. Marjeta frowned. It was strange for Areya not to be here in her rooms, especially when it was the usual time for Marjeta to return from her studies and dress in preparation for her time with Silviana. A cold thought struck her — what if something had happened to Areya just as it had to Val?

The silence mocked her. The familiar bustle and smirk gone, leaving the rooms more like a gilded tomb than ever. Marjeta hesitated, then quickly dragged her small private kist out from under her bed, and dug down to the bottom, to where a familiar and untouched bundle lay wrapped in layers of protective silk. She drew it out in a state between dread and curiosity. With this, she could see what she wanted — up to a point. She could see the thing she held dear, and what here in this palace of strangers did she hold dear but a lady-in-waiting she barely knew. The only truly familiar thing about Areya was the glimmer of magic in her eyes.

"You don't have time for this," Marjeta said to the mirror that lay, still bound, upon her bed. "And it's a terrible idea," she added. The last time she had looked into the mirror it had shown her nothing good — only her dog, dying, and what had that led to but her own sister's death? It had been years since she'd unwrapped the cursed thing, and wasn't that for the best? Besides, Devan was waiting for her in the halls below, probably wondering why he had agreed to take some brainless girl out riding.

Except there was no sign of Areya, and the fear that clouded her mind was stronger than the worry over what the duke's cousin might think of her. "Let him wait," she said fiercely. The mirror made the palms of her hands itch and prickle as though it were silently begging for her to unwrap it. Perhaps mirrors also became lonely, hidden away from faces.

Quickly, before she could talk herself out of it, Marjeta pulled the one end of the wrapping, unravelling the silks from the mirror. For a moment, she saw a flash of a reflection that was not hers. She started and looked behind her but the room was empty as ever. Even Tarkis hadn't moved from his perch on the hearth logs. The walls were the same painted patterns of trees and beasts, hung with woven tapestries and gilt-framed paintings in the modern realistic style that Furis' temple had made popular. Marjeta glanced back at the mirror and saw only her own face, or a part of it. The reflection flickered and for a moment her eyes looked too round and black, her skin shadowed as though furred with a thick bear pelt, but the shadow passed, and it was just a hazy image of herself.

"Mirror, mirror, take my soul, show me the thing that makes me whole," she whispered quickly, but there was no answering call of magic, no tickle of energy shifting through her. The mirror showed her nothing but herself. "I should have known," she said, setting her mirror down in the trencher laid out before The Three, "that it would be as useful as talking to you. I could beg you for blessings or curses and receive nothing in abundance."

A sudden cough made her turn sharply. The Lady Genivia was standing at the entrance to her bed chambers. She was one of Lilika's cronies; her chief errand runner and agreeing voice. She was tall and broad, with ginger hair that she wore pulled back from her face in a way that made her look perpetually angry. Her skin would have been pale as cream, and indeed the parts that were not covered with red brown freckles were. She looked nothing like a gentle-souled musician, though she could play the harp with surprising skill.

"What is it that you want?" Marjeta snapped.

"Forgive me." Genivia dipped in a curtsy that was correct in every respect and somehow still managed to radiate disdain. "I thought you would need help preparing for your visit with the Lady Silviana."

"And why would I?" Marjeta began to nonchalantly fold the mirror back up into its ribbons of silk. "I have Areya for that."

"Begging your pardon, but Areya has been called away in great urgency. A messenger came from Petrell calling her back home for the funeral of her mother."

The blood drained from Marjeta's face. She put out a hand to the nearest bed post and used it to keep herself steady. "I had not realised," she said breathlessly.

"The messenger demanded she return with him; he was a house rider from Hanevas. There was no time to find you. It was arranged that I attend you in her absence."

"I see." Marjeta cleared her throat. "I have no need of you."

Genivia narrowed her eyes, but merely curtsied in response.

"At least not until this evening," Marjeta amended. "You may perform your duties alongside Lilika until after dinner, and then attend me thereafter."

"Do you not need assistance dressing for your audience with Lady Silviana?" Genivia stared at Marjeta's outfit, and then toward the discarded gowns. "You seem to have had some trouble choosing a suitable gown."

"I am having no such thing. You may send my apologies to Lady Silviana. I am unable to attend her this afternoon. I am feeling unwell," she said flatly, daring Genivia to contradict her.

"I see." The unwanted lady-in-waiting nodded, then dipped a perfunctory curtsy. "I shall do as you request."

Marjeta waited, her breath tight in her lungs, until Genivia left. Only once the woman had gone did she feel able to breathe easier again. Even then her chest ached. It was an unkindness to feel abandoned when Areya left because of a death in her family — of her mother — but it was lodged fast as a stone. She glanced at the grim-faced idols. "And I suppose now you expect invocations for the dead, and oil and bread to ensure their safe journey?" she said softly. Areya was not here to perform the rite. She brushed her hands down the front of her loose trouser-skirt. Had Genivia seen her whispering spells to the mirror? "Damn her. She had no right to enter my chambers." Until that moment Marjeta had felt a modicum of safety in her own rooms. There had only ever been herself and Areya and quiet servants. Now it had been invaded and her only ally whisked away.

Genivia would be in and out her rooms like a cat, careless of where she went. Marjeta packed the mirror away and shoved the kist back under bed. She would need to be more careful from now on, but she'd bought herself an afternoon's space and she had a slice of freedom waiting for her. It was time to go meet Devan and let this uneasiness be drummed under the sound of hooves.

A Stork in Swan Feathers

The ticking of the clock was overly loud in Silviana's receiving room. The clock had been a recent gift from her father just before he left to go to the old fort in Verrin for the next few weeks. It was far too lovely for a girl who had not yet reached her decad. Tall as a man, the blackwood carved with floral whirls and jagged leaves, the clock face set with ivory and gold. It came from the eastern toymakers, and the timing was unparalleled. The pendulum sounded in beetle back clicks, slicing the minutes into orderly pieces. It was the kind of gift an emperor gave a valued mistress.

Silviana hated the clock. It measured out the empty spaces between now and then, reminding her that no matter what she wanted, time passed at the same heartless beat, neither too fast nor too slow. She glared at the slender hands, willing them around the face. It was so boring in her rooms with just Lee-lee and the old women, the ones who had once served her mother. All they did was knit and sew and read boring books, and sometimes they would drink sweet wine and play card games with her, but they let her win, and Marjeta did not.

In a few minutes the Lady Marjeta would be here. She was running a little late, that was all. Perhaps Brother Milos was taking his sweet time with the cleansing ritual. She strained her ears but could hear no voices. No sign that Lady Marjeta was at her door. Silviana flicked a card over in impatience, barely registering which it was. The image blurred, fine lines erased into streaks and smudges.

Despite Lee-lee's warnings, Silviana had found herself drawn more and more to her father's future bride. Marjeta was younger than anyone else who ever came willingly to her rooms and it seemed to her they shared secrets without speaking, simply by the relative distance of their years. Once Devan had been the nearest thing to a playmate she'd had, but their friendship was bound up in the knowledge of what was to come. Their lives laid out before them by the whisperings of court advisers and her father's own grand plans.

When Marjeta had been brought before her, Silviana had been ready to hate this usurper, but instead she'd fallen half in love. Here was a girl only a handful of years her senior. A girl with no pretensions to be her mother or keeper. A girl who came bound up in the forbidden.

Silviana looked up from the game of cards she laid out in readiness, the hands all dealt. Three hands in total for herself and Lilika, and Marjeta.

The clock ticked resolutely. The summer air grew heavier and hotter as the day progressed, the mullioned windows refining the sunlight into baking glasshouse heat.

"It seems our future duchess could not bestir herself to arrive on time," Lilika said. Every now and again she reached over to pick up a light, round paper fan on a bone handle, and would wave it at her cheeks, her eyes closed. Her lap was filled with wool she'd been spinning, and the gentle clack and whirr played a soft counterpoint to the ticking clock.

Silviana wiped the sweat from her forehead with a silk handkerchief, then slowly and deliberately focused on the card she'd flipped over on the waiting pile in the middle. A Fox Prince in snow, all jagged teeth and red and grins. Snow; snow sounded like relief.

"Cheating now, are you?" Lilika asked.

"It's my deck," Silviana said. "I'll look at it if I please."

"Furis does not look kindly on cheats and gamblers," Lilika began and Silviana sighed loudly.

"It's not gambling if I have no coin." She slid the Fox Prince back into the remaining deck. "Besides, I can always pray for forgiveness after."

Lilika's face went puce, as though she had forgotten how to breathe. Silviana would have laughed but there was something too real in her suddenly terrified expression. It passed as quickly, and Lilika twisted up one corner of her mouth. "You cannot fool Furis, little heart. He watches everything you do and the price you pay for guilt might be higher than you like."

It was just one of many reasons Silviana found Furis disturbing. Lilika seemed to like the idea that her god watched her every moment of her day. Silviana found it horrifying. Did he watch even when she went to the privy, or when she picked her nose, or only pretended to read her lesson work? At night, did he really crouch over the foot of her bed and watch her breathe slow, dream her strange dreams. Silviana flushed. Dreams were not truths, she was sure, but if Furis truly did see straight into her head and heart, then she was already damned to the Empty, that cold black nothingness that waited for sinners and witches. Only the night before she had woken from a dream where she had taken Lilika apart as though she were a doll and hidden each limb in a box about her room. The woman's empty head cried softly until Silviana had filled its mouth with velvet and fruitcake.

A muted sound filtered from the entrance room, and Silviana sat up straighter before reminding herself not to appear too eager and settled back into a crosslegged slouch before her cards.

Genivia swept into the room with no sign of the Lady Marjeta at her side.

Silviana frowned. Perhaps something terrible had happened? She reached for her own fan and took a moment to flutter the hot air.

"And what delays our Lady?" Lilika asked, as Genivia dropped a hasty curtsy first at Silviana then Lilika, who really didn't deserve such a show, Silviana thought. Lilika was a village woman and Genivia came from a good family in Verrin town.

"I bring Lady Marjeta's apologies," Genivia said. "It seems the sudden departure of her lady-in-waiting has caused some shock to her frail system. She claims illness." She was wide-eyed, her usually pale cheeks pricked with high colour along the bones.

"Does she now?" Lilika set aside her wools and spindle and

gestured to the empty seat alongside her. "And what is it about our dear Lady's health that leaves you looking so pale? Surely a bout of ill temper is not catching?"

Genivia glanced about the room. "I confess I saw something most strange," she said, her voice low. "I am not sure quite what it was."

"The people of Petrell are a strange people." Lilika said. "Their ways are foreign and heathen, it is only to be expected."

"How are they strange?" Silviana asked before Genivia could begin her tale. "Is it because of their forest gods?" The fan was hardly helping. Silviana dropped it and wished instead she could throw open the windows and let in the outside, the forbidden. "Caneth says they were our gods once too."

Lilika pulled a sour face. "They were. But the people of Jurie have moved on and left the old barbaric ways to the barbarians. There is no pride in clinging to old powers simply because they are old. The customs around the Three are evil ones. They are soaked in blood and sacrifice."

"How do you know?"

Lilika laughed dryly. "My family followed the Three. It is blood and curses and revenge. The magic they use costs more than you would like to think on, my little one. It is old and cruel."

Silviana thought of her dream where Lilika's bloodless, decapitated head had spoken, over and over again. "Forgive me," it had whispered in its dry, winter voice, like the sound of bare branches against glass. "Forgive me, forgive me." Silviana hunched her shoulders as though to protect her belly against the sharp beaks of crows.

"The Three are nature forces," Lilika continued. "Bears who take the form of women, or women who take the form of bears. They are old forest creatures, and they understand only old forest languages — kill, mate, hunt and die."

"And Furis?" Silviana argued, her arms wrapped over her stomach. She hurt inside and had no idea why. "Isn't he just an animal spirit too? He is half a bull, after all." She surprised herself at her own audacity. It was not like Silviana to so openly say anything against Furis. Mostly, she accepted him as merely another aspect of her world over which she had no control. But other people in the palace followed different gods, and no storm struck them and turned them to living pyres the way Brother Furis said it would.

"It's not the same at all. Furis is a man who became a god," snapped Lilika, "not an animal spirit."

The avenue of conversation closed, and Genivia glanced sidelong at Lilika as though waiting for permission to begin her tale. At a nod, she smiled tightly. "I went to go fetch the Lady Marjeta from her chambers and to give her the news of Lady Areya's departure as you asked," she said to Lilika, "but when I approached the rooms I heard talking, which I thought strange as Areya had long since left."

"Perhaps she was talking to a servant. Or perhaps she was praying," Silviana said. "Lilika told me she attends the chapel services."

"Only because she must," Lilika said. "She keeps a house altar in her rooms. Brought her idols with her from Petrell. Go on."

"There were no servants." Genivia shot Silviana an exasperated glance. "But nor was she praying to her little manikins." She took a deep breath and lowered her voice further, dipping her head closer to Lilika's so that Silviana had to lean forward likewise to hear better. "She spoke a chant, some ritual chant, and, in her hand, she held a small mirror — one that I had never seen before."

Lilika's usually pretty face was marred by a deep ridge of lines across her forehead. "A curse? And a mirror? I have heard of mirror spells; relics of the Petrell witches and fiercely guarded. They can cause great harm if ill-used. What was the curse you heard?"

Genivia shook her head so that her gleaming curls flowed and bounced about her shoulders. "I confess I could not hear it all, but I did hear the word soul, so perhaps it was an exchange spell of some sort?"

"An exchange spell?" Silviana knee-walked closer to the women, eager to hear more, and settled herself on a low cushioned seat.

"Evil stuff," Lilika said. "To offer one's soul to a malevolent force in a witch's bargain."

"Why would anyone do that?"

Lilika smiled grimly. "They are usual in love spells, and to bring back the dead."

"Could she do that?" Silviana's heart raced. She thought of the bright woman in the portraits in her rooms, the woman in yellow who shone like the sun. By now she would be rags and bones and withered leather. All the light would be gone from her. Even if a spell could bring her back, Silviana doubted she would want her dead mother traipsing about the palace with her skin hanging in tatters from her yellowed skeleton.

"Who knows?" Lilika said. "It is enough that she is trying to cast spells of such wickedness in our very home." She shivered. "Was there anything else?"

"No." Genivia shook her head, then faltered. "Well, it is a bold lie that she is unwell, and she was dressed most oddly, in her eastern manner, and truth be told, I have heard from servants that she spends too much time primping and preening. She feeds her idols with oil and bread and talks to the fireplace as though it were a living thing that could answer her." Genivia sat back. "As you know, I do not care for idle gossip, but we must be careful around her and any influence she might have on our Lady Silviana."

"Some of the remote eastern people still worship nature spirits," Lilika mused. "It could be she is the same, uncultured as she is. Or perhaps she has called up a fire demon and commands it to her bidding."

"Or perhaps she means to trap someone's heart," Genivia said. "Whose?"

Genivia shifted in her seat. "Well, if she were to have the duke's love as well as his marriage vow..." she began.

"Hush now." Lilika smiled widely. "Come, we must not speak such nonsense." The look she gave Genivia was one that spoke volumes. They would discuss it further, Silviana knew, but not where she could hear.

"So, she's not coming, even though she said she would," Silviana said. "And she's probably a witch anyway, so it hardly matters." She paused. "Why is it so wrong for her to want my father to love her?"

The two older women looked at each other, and even the crones coughed and muttered. Finally, Lilika leaned toward Silviana and clasped her hands. "Love must grow naturally like a seed from the ground. To force it with curses will grow only ill things. In truth," she sighed and let Silviana's hands go. "I do not believe it is your father she wishes to ensnare."

The old women muttered louder, eyes feverish with gossip.

"She's young still, and her head is filled with air. She wants the men of the castle to look at her and delight."

"Like they did my mother," Silviana said.

"Like your mother." Lilika nodded. "But your mother was beautiful and generous and kind. Your father loved her as the moon loves the sun, and all those who saw her fell likewise in love. There was no magic to it. I think our little future duchess believes she can fill your mother's dancing shoes, her gowns and crowns." Lilika laughed once, harshly. "It is like a stork thinking it can be a swan. She will drown if she's not careful."

Troubled, Silviana touched the witchstone at her chest. Lilika had told her it would protect her from curses and the evil eyes of those who would do her harm. Despite her warm feelings for Marjeta, she could never trust her. Silviana wore the stone always, worried that the spells her future stepmother spun were getting to her despite its protection. She was a subtle witch, making Silviana like her with games and careless truth.

But here was the truth. Marjeta's visits to Silviana were merely a chore, part of her act as she readied herself to take Silviana's mother's place. She would throw them off without a thought if it suited her. She wanted everyone to love her as they had the Duchess Belind, and she cast evil spells, called up fire demons, and read from unholy books so that she could steal all that love. "I must be careful," Silviana said.

"What's that, my love?"

"We must watch her," Silviana said. "I confess a fondness," she said, "but now I do not know if that is part of her spells."

The women all turned their heads like snakes, to stare at each other. "Indeed," Lilika said. "It can be hard to tell. The only way to make sure is to follow the way that Furis leads you. He can see even into the hearts of witches, and if you trust him, he will guide you safely."

"Does he guide you?"

Lilika paused, then nodded slowly. "I believe he does. And I believe if you pray to him now and ask for his help that he will protect you from the witchwork that the Lady Marjeta has cast." She knelt down by the low chair and put one hand over Silviana's hand. "And if there is no spell, it can still do no harm," she said. "We would be safe, rather than sorry."

The tall clock in its shroud of wooden leaves and vines clicked out the silence, until Silviana sighed. She thought of Marjeta, who laughed without thinking and smelled like herbs and fur hoods, who played cards and board games and didn't seem to resent it, who ran through the rooms and hallways and made the old women frown. And she thought of her dream where Lilika was hidden in pieces throughout her rooms like a broken doll, and how happy the dream had made her. Perhaps it wasn't Marjeta she should beg protection from. There were things in her own head as dark and wild as the stories Genivia and Lilika shared. Were they there because of Marjeta, or had they always been there and Marjeta had only woken them?

Both options were troubling. "Yes," she said. "I suppose we should pray."

The Wild Boys

Though no magic wrapped Marjeta and her companion's footfalls in silence or turned their shadows to cloaks, no one paid her or Devan the slightest attention. Marjeta wasn't a precious daughter here, or beautiful enough to attract attention. With her plain looks and plainer gowns, she was simply some chit following a boy through the castle passages.

The moment Marjeta stepped outside the door of the crown court, the smells of the palace citadel enveloped her close as a swaddling blanket. A hunched feeling lifted that Marjeta had not even realised she'd been carrying it across her shoulders. She straightened, breathed in deep. It had been too long. A warm drizzle fell, starring the workers, silvering Marjeta's shoulders. "The stables?"

"This way." Devan beckoned her on and they crossed a wide cobbled yard, the stones slick with mud. The stables were whitewashed, straw roofed, the ground marked here and there with fresh horse dung. Marjeta could smell the familiar rich and earthy scents of the stable yard, could hear mice rustling in the weeds and the stones of the walls. She breathed in lungfuls of muggy air, tasting the world.

Curious horses peered over half doors, and there — at the far end, a familiar broad face, shaggy still with the last of her spring coat. The pony tossed her head and whickered in recognition. Poor Dust, waiting for her, sad-eyed and abandoned.

How did I let this happen? Marjeta picked up speed, half running to the end of the lane of waiting horses. If she'd been home, nothing would have stopped her from seeing Dust every day, rubbing her velvet nose, bribing her with purloined leaves and roots from the family kitchens. In just a matter of weeks she'd let herself be spun motionless into place; a fly shrouded in silk. "I'm sorry," she whispered to the pony as she rubbed the velvet soft nose and ears.

No one stopped Devan from saddling his horse, or Marjeta from doing the same. Grooms touched their forelocks when they saw him, greeted him with quiet cheerfulness and went on about their work. As far as they were concerned, Marjeta was with him, and therefore had full rights. If they recognized her as their duke's future wife, they gave no sign of it.

Hardly surprising, Marjeta thought as they trotted out past the high stone walls and onto the packed road that led through the open lands to the nearest small farming village. The sun greeted them, boiling away the layers of clouds, and Marjeta's hair dried in frizzy wisps as they left the palace grounds. A chorus of insects and birds made the sunlight hum over the farmer's fields. The day had turned languid, familiar and comforting as a childhood story before bedtime.

They were still a good thirty miles from the capital city of Verrin, and the village was much like the one that served the castle back at her own home. People worked, some in fields, some in small home gardens. Women turned the front rooms of their houses into small shops, and the familiar sounds of industry followed them as they walked the horses down the main road. The clatter of looms, the thud and smash of churns, the flap of laundry beaten against rocks in the burn.

It was achingly familiar, even if the voices around her were not ones she knew. She could pretend she was back home. Marjeta closed her eyes, felt faint spatters of rain catch on her eyelashes, run down her neck and cheeks. She could plunge herself into a past summer, imagine that a lean wolfhound paced at her side, that her bow was slung at her back, her quiver at her hip. She blinked and raised one hand to wipe her face. No. That time had passed. Even Dust felt smaller and slower, her gait slightly off. Age was wearing down her joints. Those summers were gone.

Devan quickly turned them off away from the village high street and down a smaller path. After nearly twenty minutes they had left the bustle of the rain-soaked village behind them and were heading past the high clumps of brambles and bracken, coppiced trees like clenched fists. Long sweeps of green fields fell to either side of the path, and even these were lost as the path grew narrow, edged with long-neglected hedges that grew high enough to bow overhead in places, making tunnels of underwater green light. From the boughs above came the rustling and trilling of sparrows and yellowbills, and bright jacketed magpies would flutter across now and again, bursts of jaunty energy. The air under the boughs was soft with birdsong, warm with the leaf-filtered sun.

They let their horses amble down the hollowroad, both content in the stillness far from the bustle of castle life, and in Marjeta's case, far from the expectations layered on her, far from Lilika's scowl and Silviana's sickliness, far from the reminder of all she'd had to leave behind her, and far from the parchment must of Brother Milos and his god. "Are you supposed to spend all day learning religious works too?"

Devan laughed. "I think Uncle gave up on me. He made sure I knew what to do in the rites and rituals and left it at that. I'm more use to him as a hunter. I have sword lessons, I'm drilled in court etiquette enough that I won't embarrass myself or him, but he knows I'm not a knight. I'll fight for him if I need to but give me a good fast mare and a doe to chase, and that's all he needs from me."

"And you can't captain a ship out in a forest," Marjeta said.

"Eh, I dare say if we were close to the ocean, he'd have me heading a ship of my own by now," Devan said with a shrug. "Uncle Calvai has his faults, like any man, but he'd rather put talent to use than waste it. It was my father's call to send me here."

"Why though?" Marjeta clicked her tongue, urging Dust a little faster. The mare picked up speed, shambling along in a halfhearted trot that jolted Marjeta's teeth. "Seems to me that your father gained little by sending you to a place so far from the sea."

"He had his reasons," Devan said stiffly. "And here I have some opportunities I wouldn't have had back home."

"Like?"

"A very good music teacher. I played the violin only passably terribly under my previous tutor. Uncle Calvai has a knack for choosing men and women of talent to adorn his castle. Or Duchess Belind did, once and now — oh, sorry." He cleared his throat. "My uncle keeps very good court musicians, and they've managed to beat some sense of musicality into me."

The way he said this made Marjeta suspect that Devan was a far better musician than he pretended. Certainly, better than herself. She could barely hum the notes of a hymn in tune. "And what am I then?" she asked, half to herself.

"I told you," Devan said, "If my uncle sees talent, he won't waste it."

"Is that so?" Marjeta wondered if there was a way to prove to her future husband that she would be better off riding with the hounds than copying out texts. "The ladies of the castle sometimes ride with the hunts, don't they?"

"Not on proper hunts," Devan said. "But yes, sometimes." He glanced at her, his hair curling over hazel eyes. "You'd want to join? I don't know if Uncle would risk it."

"I'm a good rider." And a better shot.

"Still and all. He's lost one wife, and one in waiting. Don't think he'd care to lose a third. And," he frowned, as though suddenly reminded that this had been a terrible idea, "it's not safe in the woods. The duke has enemies."

"So why take me riding today?" Marjeta squeezed her heels against Dust, urging her on until the pony broke into a slow canter. Devan was quick to follow; she could hear the thunder of his horse's hooves behind her, catching up.

"Because," he called, "you looked like a horse kept too long in a stable and gone nasty with it. If I'd not dragged you out the palace for your own good, you would have turned too ill-tempered to be of any use."

"Use to who?" Marjeta laughed angrily. Devan was right. Marjeta felt angry and excited at the same time, too quick to temper. If she'd been a horse, she'd have been the shifty-eyed one that kicked any groom as soon as look at them.

It would be no good to her to be so sour, especially around
Silviana and her keeper. She needed a way to be herself so that she
could keep working on her friendship with her future daughter-
in-law. She needed a way to keep her head down around Brother
Milos and not attract any of his unwelcome attention. She had to
find a way to keep herself from becoming what they wanted but
fool them into thinking she had.

The way to stay herself was to keep doing the things that
brought her joy. Marjeta had never been someone meant to sit
in a corner with needles and threads and card games. She needed
the forest and the open, she needed Dust and the smell of the real
world.

As soon as Areya returned from Petrell, and the duke from
his trip to the Verrin Fort, she would gather all her small store
of courage and face her future husband. She needed to run free
far more than she needed embroidery and worship, and the duke
would have to see that. She would find a way to make him give her
what she needed, and in a way that Brother Milos could not stop.

Marjeta gave Dust her head and urged the storm grey pony into
a gallop, her hooves thundering dully on the mulch of rich soil
and fallen leaves. Dust moved like a storm, her fine, powerful legs
eating up the ground.

Behind her, Devan kept pace on his compact, dish faced bay.
The two raced under the bought of the hedges, until finally both
horses slowed to a walk, their sides huffing and steaming. Marjeta
brought Dust's head down and clucked softly to turn her mount
back toward the palace. Running from books and priests had
cleared the heavy black fug of the castle from her mind.

"Wait." Devan had stilled his little mare, and his head was held
high, slightly canted as though he listened for something only he
could hear. He was frowning.

"And now?"

Devan held up a hand and shook his head.

Marjeta gentled Dust, bringing the dancing pony to stillness.
Around them the forest light fell in a shroud of green and silver,
the logs and trunks furry with moss and ivy. In the high hidden
tops of the elms and horse chestnuts, the green pigeons clattered

and cooed, then fell silent.

That wasn't right. There was no bird song, not rustling of lizards or mice in the jagged undergrowth, in the fallen leaves and black mould.

A whip-sound sliced the damp air, and Marjeta felt a rush of wind past her cheek, punctuated by the heavy *thock* of an arrow biting deep into wood.

Devan unfroze. "To home!" he commanded. "Now!"

Marjeta did not waste time. She was unarmed — *stupid, stupid, stupid* — and had no idea who was attacking them now, or why. Another arrow spat past her and she saw it land in a large black oak, spitting chunks of bark where it hit. No time to waste on wondering, all she could do was lean in against Dust's neck and trust to her speed, trust to the winding pathways through the forest that it would be enough to keep them both from being wounded or killed.

The next arrow caught her upper arm, slicing through the fabric and skin, but not striking true. "Go, Dust, go!" she hissed, her heels pressed tight as she felt the pony surge beneath her, fear proving a better goad than a girl's voice. There was no time to turn and see what Devan was doing. Marjeta could hear only the incessant drumming of Dust's hooves, and nothing else. She twisted her head, eyes streaming, to look back but all she saw was the army of tree trunks and the wild undergrowth, heavy with greening berries, and the churned ground.

Home, he'd said. He would meet her there, or he would not.

Marjeta pressed back a sob when a moment later, Devan's bay mare burst out from a side path, sending Dust rearing in sudden fear.

"Stay calm," Devan said. "We need to get closer to the palace grounds, and we'll be safe. They won't come as close as the village. Not in broad daylight." He urged his mare on at a canter, and Marjeta followed, her back tingling with the fear that at any moment an arrow would lodge deep between the bones of her spine, ending her.

None came, and when they finally reached the broad path and the first of the scattered village hamlets, Devan slowed them both.

"I'm sorry."

"It was not your fault." The panic had lifted, and though Marjeta's head still drummed, her breathing had returned to normal, and the shivers that had paralysed her arms and legs slowly began to ebb away. "Who were they?"

"It was my fault," he said. "I should never have led you so deep into the forest. The Old King's Wood is safer, but I thought too many would see us there and..." He shook his head. "I betrayed you, and your duke."

He's not my duke, Marjeta wanted to say. "I came to no harm," she told him instead. "All is forgotten and forgiven."

"If only it were that easy." They rode side by side though the village, and Devan kept looking warily about, his eyes hard. "You were injured."

"This?" Marjeta looked down at her arm. The arrow had cut a thin groove and torn the sleeve of her riding jacket. "It is no worse than if I'd been caught by a bramble. Perhaps I was."

He frowned and reached out across the space between them to brush the skin. It had at least not bled much, the wound already dry. "I did this to you."

"You did not," Marjeta flushed. The touch against her upper arm had been swift and gentle, but even though his hand was gone, withdrawn, it felt as though the touch had sunk into the proud flesh and flowed with the blood in her veins. She coughed. "It's a graze, and the coat easily mended." She shook her head. "Who were they?"

"The Wild Boys," Devan said. "Mention this to no one. I will talk to my uncle as soon as he returns. It's not like them to hunt so close to the palace. They grow bold, and winter will make them bolder still."

"I still want to ride again," Marjeta said after a long silence, when the village had dwindled behind them and the multifaceted palace loomed on the hillside, peering down over its stone boundary walls.

"Madness," Devan said, but he sounded less grim. Amused rather. "A Petrell, of course."

"Of course." Marjeta tossed her head. "We fear nothing." And if it was a lie, then at least it was a lie Marjeta was determined to make truth. For the first time in weeks, and despite the attack, Marjeta felt more like herself, less constrained by ghosts and rules.

The lady Silviana was not Valerija, and Marjeta couldn't wish for her to be. Any more than Marjeta could pretend to be a person she was not. As soon as the Duke Calvai Jurie returned to the summer palace she would dress herself in yellow and demand an audience with her future husband. How much worse could he be than a wild forest hunter, how much deeper could his arrows go?

Queens and Witches

It has been a long night filled with the distant calls of hunting owls. I cannot sleep, must not. I want to cling to every last second and write more of my letter to you. The tower allows for little else but prayer and explanations and I am sick of prayers.

This letter has turned on itself. When I began it, it wore confessional robes and bowed its head, but as the tale grows, she raises her head and throws back her hood. Her hair is not meekly braided and covered in silk veils. She wears a crown.

My letter is not a penitent come to you to beg forgiveness. I don't think she cares about forgiveness any more. She is just a storyteller.

A witch-queen.

She will have you listen to her tale, and she does not care whether you judge her good or evil. It matters only that you hear.

One candle left. It does no good thinking these thoughts and not setting them down. A story without a listener is not a story. It is a miscarriage. I pick up my pen and dip it in the ink. Even with the orange light from my solitary candle, I can barely see. The paper is a lighter swatch of grey against darker, and I write half-lost words. They exist in a space that is neither truth nor lie, a halfworld of halftones. The nib drags across the paper, and my life follows in lines and curves. When the candle runs out, I will write in the dark.

*

When I was sixteen and had been in your father's palace only a handful of months, Areya left to attend her mother's funeral. I cannot begrudge her that, though it was a period of bitter loneliness for me. I wonder if you recall the day when Areya returned from my homeland.

Did my face change? Did a new lilt come back to my tired repetitions of Brother Milos' forced readings from his seemingly endless collection of books? Perhaps it was too subtle a change to notice — I had to keep my face clear of all my thoughts. I played with you, I smiled and read out loud and danced the court dances when instructed. I wore my girlish dresses, and my hair was braided back by servants. I was careful every day to take the brush from them and clean it myself. I burned every stray hair.

I saw nothing of Devan beyond passing glimpses at meals. I was accompanied always by Genivia — then still a sour faced enigma — when I insisted I had to see to my pony. I held Dust as I would have held a mother, and though I did not make a sound, I dried my face against her tipped fur and breathed in the sweet smell of her. It was an anchor in a cold black lake. For all that the Duchy of Jurie was deep in the heart of summer, I was in my own personal winter nothingness. I was cold all the time, my fingers numb, and cheeks ice-burned. Only my heart burned like a banked coal.

Waiting.

I held on to the ember that when Areya came back to me, I would ask her for her help. I needed freedom, and I knew I needed to walk carefully. My freedom could not look free. It had to be a gift, a patronage, and I would have to smile and curtsy to thank for it.

Finally, Areya returned. Older and colder, her face pinched with grief. We held each other in silence, and I imagined what it would be to lose my own mother. She was almost lost to me already by then. Her voice was fading, her eyes and hands were all I remembered. I could hear her in my head when I read out her infrequent letters, but slowly her voice had begun to sound more and more like mine. When she died, would I notice? So Areya wept, and I wept with her. For her, for me, for all the deaths to come.

The duke returned a handful of days after Areya. He was

burdened with news and gifts, but none came to me. I saw only the new novels in your rooms, the fine dresses you paraded before us, the faded bloodstains on the pages when I read aloud to you, the horse meat pies that I ate at my future husband's side.

No news, only the hymns of thankfulness to Furis that Calvai Jurie was delivered safely. They did not call him king, but the word tolled under their songs, a deep and ancient bell calling for the past to march forward into the present.

While your father may not have told me anything, I kept quiet, and I listened. Women talk, men talk, servants and lordlings talk. Gossip can spread through a palace faster than illness if it touches the right tongues. So, I heard that the duke had strengthened his army at the Verrin Fort, whispers of war to the west, and to the east, that people thought Vestiarik needed a king once again.

What did all that matter to a girl who would never go to war? All I wanted was to ride my horse under the weeping boughs of the trees, to feel the sun fall on my face and the wind lift my hair from my neck.

"I want to ride again, Areya, and for that I need the duke's permission." I told Areya. I wanted to ask for her help, but the words caught themselves in the tightness of my throat and instead I asked, "You'll not stop me?" I had not told her of Devan, of our ride, and of the arrow that had grazed my arm. I did not tell her of any of these dangers. In my mind they did not matter — I was alive, and I did not plan to ride that far from the palace again. A little freedom was all I wanted. A small space to lay claim to. "I don't want your approval, though I wouldn't mind it," I said to her.

You can see I had learned little of the subtleties of diplomacy. I was sixteen, and though I thought myself an adult, I still had a child's belief in my own natural superiority to everyone else. You might say that five years have changed me little, but I assure you that in this much you are wrong, and this was the point where I turned and faced adulthood. I needed Areya's help. I needed a friend. And I needed a sister. It would be easier to go against your father if I had someone at my side.

Areya could see right through me, of course. She always had

the knack to see past my obfuscation and pathetic lies and know exactly what it was I needed from her. "You want to make the duke malleable."

"I need him to take me seriously."

"But not too seriously," Areya told me. "You need to be a sharpened dagger hidden inside a jewelled case. A killing blade where one expects a dinner fork."

Areya helped me prepare for battle. She took it on herself to armour me. Together we decided on the yellow dress that would remind him of his dead wife. I had worn it the night my father gave me to yours. You will not remember, I suppose. You weren't at the feast, but I came to you afterwards. You were so small and solemn, and all I saw was a girl who reminded me of someone already dead a span of years. So now I know how Calvai might have felt when he saw me in that dress. Was it cruel? Perhaps. But we who have no weapons must use what we can to protect ourselves.

I told Areya to braid my hair in Grace's Serpent. Even though your duchy no longer follows the old court styles, mine does — or did. Grace's Serpent meant logic and negotiation. It was an adult's code. It had history. I thought it would lend my meagre years some gravitas.

I sent for a messenger and organized a private meeting with your father. A dinner. Some strange and awkward intimacy. It felt unreal. We had barely spoken. I was supposed to be his wife one day, and yet I had to strain my mind to even think what he looked like beyond the cipher of hair and beard and duke's coronet.

"Tell me what you know of magic?" Areya said to me once I was armoured.

There. Is that word you have been waiting for? I know it shook me a little when Areya asked me that. Magic was hushed over here. It was brushed into corners, washed out with well water, it was emptied into latrine pits and buried. But it was still there, Silvi. Magic. Under your feet. In the air and the threads and the whispers of women and the reel of music. It was even in the echoes of the prayers Brother Milos intoned to his idiotic god.

You can't escape it. You never could.

"I know little enough," I admitted. "It was my sister who knew spells and charms. I understood some of the basic principles, but with no power..."

"I think you underestimate yourself," Areya said, "but perhaps you were always more suited to swords than wands. What do you know of the queens from history?"

Now, I sat with you while we studied the histories your father wished you to know, and I am well aware that they erased the queens from your books, but I learned my histories in a different land, and there, we remember. It had been years since I'd studied the Old Queens, and even then, my tutor had told me it was more myth than truth.

Which shows what he knew.

Perhaps you have since gone to Caneth's stacks and found the truths for yourself, hidden in the forgotten scripts and scrolls. Forgive me if you have. I apologize if I insult your studies, but there are always things we can learn from each other.

In the old days queens fought like warriors alongside their men and women. They wore swords and armour, and witches blessed them before battle. Perhaps if I'd lived a thousand years back, I could have been one of them, I remember telling Areya that last in bitter fury, so deep was my disappointment at being born out of time.

But Areya had never been a fool, unlike myself.

"You think that because the time of warrior queens is past, that you have no weapons?" The conversation seems so clear in my mind, as though a little play is being acted out before me. If I make the actress who plays me seem a little wiser, or prettier, you must forgive me. I have many flaws. Vanity is only a small one.

Areya stands tall in my play. She is beautiful and strong and prickly with magic. All the things I am not. When she lectures me, the words bite against my face, whiplash kisses. "It's not like you to be so eager for defeat. The Lady Marjeta I was sent to serve reminded me of those queens, and I was more than a little disappointed to see her lower her bow and her head and do as she was told without fighting." She flicks a finger lightly at this Marjeta's ear. "Not like the girl from the castle, with her arrows and her short sword and her hunting hound."

"That's not fair!" The *Marjeta I was not* claps a hand to her stinging ear. "I cannot be that person here. If I'd behaved badly, it would have reflected ill on my family, and how am I to make Lady Silvi my friend if I do not pander to this castle's little laws, and to that glorified nurse Lilika?"

"Wise decisions, but I expected more. You could make other moves, use other weapons."

Marjeta tilts her head, considering. She glances to the three idols on their patterned altar table, then at the hearth where her salamander sleeps.

"Not them, but you're looking in the right direction."

"I don't understand what it is you want me to do," Marjeta snaps.

"Come now, your sister was not the only witch at court, surely you knew that. And you also know your mother sent me with you for a reason. Any woman in her coterie could have served as an adviser, could have pinned you into pretty dresses and combed your hair just so." She snapped her fingers. "I've been waiting for you to ask me for better help than that."

See, it was always that simple. I had to ask for Areya's help. My mother could not have acted overtly. She told me what I needed to know in history lessons and the fluttering conversations and whispers of her shadow court. She expected me to stitch the snippets together and see the truth for myself, but, certainly at sixteen, I was not at my brightest point.

Your father's court was caught up in the words of men like Brother Milos, and even my own father had been swayed into pretending worship of the horned god, but that didn't mean that there were no witches in Petrell besides my sister. They had just gone about their ways quietly. They pricked their spells into the hems of dresses and shirts, seasoned the food and drink with ritual herbs, added charms to their households. Who cared, after all, if women embroidered birds on their babies' nightgowns, buried iron under the hearth and threshold, or took the first calf of spring across the river twice before returning it to its dam? These were small things, and no one noticed them.

This was the spellwork Areya would give me. I'd told myself I was never interested in magic. I hated being reminded of what I didn't have. And that had been foolish. A warrior should know every weapon that could be wielded. Yes, I'd trained in my own weapons and I was a better shot with the bow and arrow than most knights, but I'd ignored the weapons my friends and enemies could use and that was the blinkered thinking of a puffed-up fool. I had chosen wilful ignorance. My first act as an adult was realising that. My second was saying the following: "Please, Areya, teach me what I need to know."

And so, she did. First, she taught me that all magic used on another must be done with their consent. "You must ask for my help."

It confused me. If my mother was weaving her own spellwork around her husband, and countless other Petrell women were doing the same, I could not understand how. That first rule was inviolate, Areya told me. But surely my father would never have asked his wife for magical help, nor did husbands ask their wives and daughters to make the harvest rich, or to save them in battle.

She taught me many things, my darling Areya, and some lessons were more painful than others. But this, at least, was an easy one.

"There are many ways to ask, and just as many to offer. Look." Areya held up a small pendant made from fine filaments of long dark hair. I recognized them as my own. Threaded on this lock were three small chunks of amber beads. Amber for good fortune. I reached out to touch this spellwork that was designed to bless me, and only me, and I said, "Areya Hanevas, I beg for your help in my battle against the Duke Calvai Jurie."

In that moment I was a queen, and Areya my witch-guard.

*

I set down my pen. Flex my aching fingers. Is it dawn yet? The sliver of sky has turned silver and pale, but I have not heard the first of the cockerels yet. They will announce my death. I would prefer them all to be mute.

Negotiations

Duke Calvai might have agreed to her request for a meeting, but now that she stood outside his doors, Marjeta felt a little breathless and sick. Areya had braided Marjeta's hair round her crown in the complex multiweave of the Grace's Serpent, sprigging the points of braids with fine, leaf topped copper pins, so that Marjeta appeared to be wearing an intricate and delicate coronet. She'd touched black dust to Marjeta's eyelids, and red oil to her cheeks and lips, and musk oil to her wrists.

Marjeta took a deep breath and glanced at her companion, who reached out to gently tuck a stray strand of hair back into place.

"You look like a queen," Areya said.

A queen going into battle with a witch at her side. Marjeta smoothed her hands down the front of her dress, wiping the dampness from her palms, and gave a last nod to Areya just as the guardsman opened the door from the entrance chamber into the duke's private suites.

Hidden under the front of her dress, pressed against her breastbone, the pendant was warmed by skin and blood. Marjeta imagined she felt its magic spreading through her with each pulse. Perhaps it wasn't just her wish that it was. She'd never been magic sensitive, but she had enough of Oma Zoli's blood to sense a quickening of a spell, surely. She breathed deep and let the spellwork settle through her veins.

Areya put a hand to her elbow in gentle reassurance. "I'll wait for you here," she said in a low voice. "But you must get him to ask for your help before the spell can catch." The room was set up for the two guardsmen, but there was a bench there where Areya could sit and pass the time stitching.

Stitching what, exactly? Marjeta felt one corner of her mouth tremble as she tried not to laugh. All these times Areya had sat patiently in the lady Silviana's suite, stitching and weaving, and she'd been making spells, sewing protections, preparing her magic for when Marjeta would need it. It felt good to know that not only was she not alone here, but her mother had made sure she would have the help she needed most.

But what help would that be if Duke Calvai Jurie did not ask the right questions? How could she make him ask for something he didn't even know to ask for? Or perhaps she was thinking about this all wrong. After all, Areya had said that there were many ways to make a person ask for something. Perhaps, it was not so much the intent of the other's words as how the witch could interpret them.

The guard ushered Marjeta into a large room lit with smoking candles in delicate wrought iron posts. The woollen carpets were patterned in plain geometric designs of blue and gold, and a square wooden table waited in the centre of the room, already set, and lit with more yellow candles in an elegantly curled candelabra. The light flickered on the hollow-cheeked face of the man Marjeta had barely spoken to since she'd been brought to his domain.

Duke Calvai stood and gestured for her to take a seat. He managed to give her a little half bow that was balanced between welcoming and surprised. "Please," he said. "You are welcome at my table, Lady Marjeta."

Marjeta dipped him an equally informal curtsy and took her place opposite him. She knew little about Calvai except for the snatches picked up from gossiped conversation among her mother's women, and the dry reports of political advisers in her father's castle. She knew him only by his daughter, his servants, the horses he chose for his stables, the books he brought back for his libraries, his silent glances at occasional public dinners. He was old enough to have fathered her. Thirty-eight.

This was the man her sister had meant to marry.

Marjeta clenched her fists, then released them slowly, breathing out as she did so. "I apologise for the presumptuousness in asking for this meeting," she said softly. She tried to pitch her voice low, not rush the words. She wanted to sound older than she was. Wanted the duke to see her as a person worthy of his time. She wanted him inclined to support her. If he thought her nothing more than a silly child, she would have no way of staking out her place in the household, no rights except those Lilika allowed her.

"Hardly," Calvai said. "I should be apologising to you. You've been welcomed into my house as both my guest and my future bride, and I have been a terrible host. I should have made time for you sooner. The fact that you had to approach me shames me."

"It has been a busy time for us all," Marjeta said in a murmur as she made herself comfortable. While the chairs were not ornate, they were thickly cushioned and upholstered, the seats wide and the arm rests broad and padded. Calvai might not be ostentatious in his personal wealth the way he was with Silviana, but he still lacked for no creature comforts. "There is nothing to forgive."

Calvai laughed dryly. "If you say so." The first of the waiting servants moved forward to fill their wine glasses and place a stone platter holding a small loaf of dark bread rolls and a bowl of oil between them. "It would be my pleasure to break bread with you."

Marjeta inclined her head. As the host, it was the duke's position to share out the bread between them. Traditionally, a larger portion would go to the guest, and a smaller to the host, no matter who was more powerful. It was a polite lie, meant to save face for both parties. Calvai tore the bread: one large piece and one smaller, as expected. He placed the smaller on his own plate, but instead of placing the larger before Marjeta, he tore it again. The bread was now divided into three equal pieces. He placed one on Marjeta's plate.

The third he placed back on the stone platter between them.

There would be an explanation for this, and Marjeta would not beg for it. She stared at her future husband, waiting.

He glanced at her, his expression obscured by his moustache and beard. Perhaps he was laughing at her, but Marjeta did not think so. His eyes were serious and oddly grey and pale in the candle light. "There are three at this table, are there not?"

"The third?" Marjeta said, though she kept a small smile playing on her lips, as though she were mildly amused by this strange action, rather than offended.

"You bring ghosts with you," Calvai said. "They walk behind you, holding your wedding train."

A cold shiver passed through her. Marjeta fought to stop herself from raising a hand to press against the concealed charm at her breastbone. Instead, she concentrated on the feeling of warmth pulsing from it, grounding her.

But the duke seemed to be talking not to her, but to those spirits he claimed were in the room. "A dinner of brides," he said. "All three of you, and ghosts must also feed." He gestured at the lump of bread, then carefully poured a thin drizzle of oil onto it. "Do you not agree?" he asked Marjeta.

So that was it. Despite all his outward show of his faith in Brother Milos' god, the duke was still a man trained to older rituals. "Of course," she said. "We must honour our dead, always." Perhaps the old man had been driven mad by the deaths of his wife and her promised replacement. It had been a very, very long time since it had been required that the dead were honoured at feasts. Only on the high days did the head of the family perhaps pour a drop of wine in a glass to remember those who had gone, but that was the most anyone bothered to do.

Marjeta bowed her head for a moment in a gesture of respect.

"I know why you are here," Calvai said. He pointed to the bread on her plate. "Please. Eat. We will talk on full stomachs. It always makes the conversation kinder."

Marjeta picked at her portion, dipping it in the shared bowl of oil, and chewed at the dense, hard bread, watching Calvai do the same. They drained the small glasses of cold white wine in silence. When they were both done, the ritual over, the servant whisked the stone platter and the untouched third lump of bread away. "And why am I here?" Marjeta asked. She was a little dizzy. The wine was strong, not watered down like it normally was with her meals, and the strangeness of the preceding ritual had caught her off guard. She would have to tread this path very carefully, picking her route through the garden of the duke's mind. Beneath her bodice the charm warmed, sending hair thin tendrils of fire across her chest and down her arms, sparking at her fingertips. She drew Calvai's glass closer to herself, in pretext of filling it for him. This time she was certain that she could feel Areya's spun spells dancing from her skin to the blown glass vessel.

New platters were brought in, rich venisons in gravies, roasted pike, pheasants. A minor feast. Marjeta's stomach was tight with nerves, but she made herself pick at her ladled portions. Everything tasted of salt. Of fear and vinegar.

"I know you are unhappy," Duke Calvai said. "I may not have had the time to come see you, but that does not mean you have been pushed from my mind. I care greatly what happens to you and to my daughter. Lilika has told me that you are not fond of the lessons in religions, and that you chafe at what you feel is imprisonment."

Lilika. Like a little trained bird, speaking secrets in her master's ear. "I confess I am not used to being so much inside. In my father's house, I had time for outdoor pursuits."

"Your father said you were a fine one with a horse, and passable with a hunting bow. And I noticed the pony you brought with you. I was told you have a fine seat, good hands."

That was news. These were not the things her mother would have boasted of to her daughter's future husband. It stilled her that her father had thought to mention them. "I do indeed ride and shoot," Marjeta said. "And yes, I have come here to beg leave of you that I might be permitted to join the court ladies in following the hunt." Not to hunt, that would never be allowed, but if she could at least ride with the other women at a safe distance, it would be better than nothing. Perhaps asking was that simple. She merely needed to tell the duke what she wished, and he would ask her how he could make her happy.

"It is far too dangerous," Calvai said. He frowned, and his grey eyes silvered in the candlelight as he took a drink from his spell-touched wine. "I cannot permit you to ride far from the castle, and certainly not with the hunt, not even to follow it. My land is more dangerous than your father's, as you will find. He protects borders from invasion, that much is true, and we seem to be safe here in the very centre." He smiled thinly. "Not all enemies wear the armour of foreign invaders. There are packs of bandits who make the darker parts of the woods their home. It is not safe for a woman to go to these places, even with an escort." He shook his head. "No, you cannot travel far from the walls."

Marjeta waited. Perhaps the duke would merely need to drink more, or Areya's spell simply needed time to take root in his mind and change his thoughts. "I see," she said. "My safety is important to you."

A round of desserts were whisked in to replace the emptied platters. The smell of almonds and fruit and honey spicing the room.

"It is." Calvai lightened at her acceptance. "I knew you would understand. You see it with my daughter. There are some who think what I do to Silvi is cruelty, but I cannot lose another I love." He poured himself another glass, though this time Marjeta waved his offer away.

Her head was heavy and tight as though a headache had just caught its claws in her. She had no idea how the man was drinking more, and yet still seemed fine. This time as he drained his wine, the alcohol loosened something inside him, and some of the tightness around his eyes faded away. He even smiled, "I know it has been hard for you to come here," he said. "And that while I mourned the loss of a future wife, you mourned for a sister."

Under the table Marjeta clenched her hands into fists. This was not how this conversation was supposed to go. No, she thought fiercely. *You will not use my sister against me, you will not use her name and memory to tame me. My sister is not my bridle.* "Please — stop," she choked. "I cannot bear to speak of my sister. It breaks my heart."

Calvai paused. Silence pooled in the room. Marjeta could hear her own breathing, the rumble of blood in her ears. Could taste honey and saffron so thick and sweet against her teeth that it made her feel ill.

"I understand." He spoke softly, barely breaking the silence. "We have lost the ones we loved, and it leaves a hole so dark and empty we are sure it will never be filled. But perhaps we can soothe each other's pain someday. Until then, how may I hold a candle up into your darkness?"

There it was. Her heart thundered and her blood heated. *You will give me what I want, Duke Calvai Jurie, or suffer another loss.* The pendant flared then, so sudden and unexpected that Marjeta let out a small shriek and pushed back from the table, her chair catching in the thick woollen rug and half-toppling before she caught her balance.

"Marjeta!" The duke got to his feet, but the chair rocked back into place, and Marjeta felt the spell rush through her, as though it had been waiting all along for her to give it permission to work.

"I — I am fine, Lord Calvai," she said breathlessly, still reeling from the lightning spark of feeling the magic so real and powerful. She wanted to grin, but swallowed down the need and said, "I think perhaps the wine at your table is very strong, and I have no head for it."

"That is true," the duke said, "but please, you must call me Calvai, we cannot have formality growing between us."

"Calvai," she agreed. "I will do so."

"It occurs to me I am being harsh." Calvai settled himself back into his seat. "While I will not change my mind about you joining the hunt, there is perhaps something else I can offer you."

The magic hadn't been strong enough to give her exactly what she wanted. Probably because it had to work through her, Marjeta thought. If it had been Val sitting here, Calvai would be eating crumbs from her palm like a tame raven. But there was at least something more being promised. She clung to the faint glimmer of hope.

"You are stronger than I had expected. More wild perhaps than I had been led to believe, and you're no weakling content to sit on cushions and thread needles. I understand that keeping you within the palace will not be good for you," Calvai continued. "I believe I have found a solution. After all, my first wife loved to picnic in those woods, and I know how much it means to ladies to have these outings where they might play their games. At the end of every week, I will allow you time to ride. There is a secure stretch of land where you will take your horse where I know that no ill can come to you."

It had to be the enclosed piece of forest known as the Old King's Wood, a tame forest, with no creature fiercer than a fox hiding in its bushes.

Marjeta nodded. It was better than nothing. And almost better than she had hoped.

"I cannot, even then, allow you to ride alone, of course. You will be accompanied by two ladies at all times, and by my own nephew. It will be for your protection. Besides these excursions, you are never to leave the palace without me." Calvai smiled, now overtaken by his own show of genial benevolence. "Do we understand one another?"

"Of course." Marjeta bowed her head. "Thank you for kindness, and for your understanding of the needs of someone as far from yourself as I am." So, she was still to be a prisoner. But unlike Calvai's daughter she would at least have a precious few hours freedom a week. It was a glimmer of light in a world that had become dark and small, and Marjeta focused on it. It was all she could do. At her heart, the magic of the pendant faded, having done what it was meant to.

The meal had come to an end, and with it Marjeta's first tentative steps toward something almost like witchcraft. Heat drummed under her skin, blood pounded like storm waves inside her ears, making her dizzy. She barely remembered standing to leave or inclining her head in queenly gratitude. Under her feet the ground had turned to silk and clouds, and she held out a hand for balance.

Calvai caught her. His hand was steady, warm like a standing stone in summer, and Marjeta felt almost as though she could hold on to him, that her world would revolve around this moment of solidity. "The wine's gone to your head," he said, and faint laughter threaded under his words. "You should be more careful."

"Around you?" Marjeta said, bold, artless.

"Perhaps." Calvai escorted her to the door of his chambers, and out into the room where his guard and Areya waited. "Around anyone. You are lovely, and the world likes to grind beautiful things into dust."

The words were cold water against fire. Marjeta pulled back

slightly, her hand still in Calvai's. He leaned forward to follow and brushed his bearded mouth against her cheek before releasing her. "Good night."

"Yes." Marjeta's hand fluttered up, almost as though to touch where he had kissed her, before she brought her hand safely down to her side, where it could not betray her by wiping the feel of it from her skin. "And a good night to yourself," she said. "You have my gratitude."

He only laughed once in response, a dry twig snap of mirthless amusement.

Areya was already at her side, curtseying, thanking the duke, and bidding him goodnight, and before Marjeta realised it they were already out in the hallways, walking down the long high-walled corridors. A shadowed face flickered in the corridor behind them, and Marjeta paused to look back. The lamps burned, and the shadows moved only with the fire. She frowned. "Did you see—"

"See what?" Areya stopped and stared at the empty hallways behind them. "Something wrong?"

"I thought." Marjeta shook her head. "I thought I saw Lilika. No. I'm — the wine was stronger than I'm used to."

"And the magic," Areya added, grinning.

"And that..." It had felt rather like falling off a cliff and being drunk at the same time. "No, I must have imagined it. Why would Silviana's nursemaid be out here, so late at night, here of all places?" She laughed softly. "My mind likes to play tricks on me, it seems."

But Areya's smile fell away and she stared too long at the deserted corridor before finally linking her arm through Marjeta's and walking her back to their apartments. "Did you get what you wanted?"

"In a manner. I got ... something. At least, I think it worked," Marjeta glanced backward, then pulled the pendant free and drew it up over her head. The hair, once dark brown, gold touched, had been leached white. All the colour had pulled out of the strands of Marjeta's braided hair. The amber beads had paled, gone almost translucent, and as Marjeta looked at them, the first began to crack, then crumble. The others followed in a moment, leaving a mess of pale grains and greyed hair curled in the cup of Marjeta's palm. She dusted them away, the spent magic falling to the dark floor. "He has given me leave to go out once a week, in the palace's small private forest, and under supervision," she said. "I'm to go with Devan, for protection, and be escorted by two other ladies. One of them will be you, naturally, but we need to make sure the other is not Lilika or one of hers."

"So, it did work," said Areya. "Perhaps this means he's yours now."

"Perhaps." Marjeta flinched at the memory of the kiss against her cheek, the sour breath of wine. "Perhaps not."

Stories of Forests

Lilika was not herself today. Silviana watched her nurse as she paced the room, pretending to clear bits and pieces away. Sometimes she sat and worked at her embroidery hoop, but within minutes she had discarded it again, picked up a book, leafed through that, left it and turned to something else before taking up her pacing once again.

It was because Marjeta was due for her visit. The usurper's presence always seemed to needle Lilika, but now more so than ever. "What is it?" she finally asked. "You're making me dizzy."

Lilika dropped the hoop she'd just lifted and blew out a long sigh. "I have seen something," she paused and looked to the windows, away from Silviana.

"Seen what?"

"I misspoke. I have heard rumours," she said.

"About?" Silviana was meant to be reading from one of the small hymnals her father had brought her when he came back from his secret wars. This one came from a temple to the far north, where great scholars gathered to read the work copied out by ancient scribes. While it was certainly a very beautiful piece of work with its illustrations and careful lettering, the rich gold and the plummy ink, it was a burden. Hard to read, and with every touch Silviana worried that she would accidentally destroy it. She would have preferred a hymnal straight from the printing presses, and perhaps something Brother Milos had not made her read a thousand times already. She closed it carefully and set it on a small table for safekeeping. "What rumours, Lee?"

Lilika shook her head, her face pinching up. "Not ones suitable for the ears of a young lady."

Ah, definitely something about Marjeta, then. Silviana knew she could winkle it out of her servant if her pin were so sharp that Lilika never even felt the prick of it. "Brother Milos says that gossip is the evil of women put into words," she said instead, and was rewarded with a quickly hidden scowl.

Lilika might give Brother Milos her public support, but Silviana was not as stupid or blind as either seemed to think she was.

"How true," Lilika said drily. "Let us speak of something better, then."

"Yes." Silviana smiled widely. "Today Marjeta comes to visit me," she said. "I do enjoy her visits. I never expected to," she carried on, pretending to be unaware of the darkness in Lilika's eyes. "But she's taught me some strange eastern games, and she does sound so pretty when she speaks."

"She sounds like a barbarian," Lilika said. "She mangles her words."

Silviana grinned. "Not true. Sometimes she sounds like you do after a long day, and I think you sound beautiful."

There, Lilika flashed an actual glare at the door, unable to direct her rage at Silviana. "She is not like us," Lilika said. "I know you find her fascinating, but you must be careful. We do not know her heart."

"I do not know your heart either," Silviana observed. She flashed another brilliant smile. "But I know your love for me. Is that not all I need?"

A babble of voices rose from the hallway, distant, but a sign that Marjeta and her shadow approached.

Lilika gave Silviana a long, slow look as though she had just realised that her charge was no longer six years old. "Be careful," she said softly. "She will try to tame you, like a bored shepherdess tames a lamb and ties ribbons on its tail. But the lamb is still meat, ribbons or not."

"Our shepherdess approaches," Silviana said.

Marjeta had just passed from Milos' entrance hall and entered Silvi's domain. She wore her hair loose, and kept her dress simple, cultivating a childish appearance around her future step-daughter. Silviana narrowed her eyes.

"And what plans do you have today, Lady Silviana?" Marjeta took her usual seat, crosslegged on the great bear fur. It always made Lilika scowl, which Silviana was convinced was why Marjeta did it.

In a way it was fun, pressing on Lilika's rules like that. Silviana scrambled down from her chair and joined Marjeta on the floor. "That game with the stones, the one you started to teach me? I would like to play it again." Hare and foxes — they'd been playing it with wooden and amber beads borrowed from Marjeta's lady's maid. One large flat wooden disc with a hole bored through it for the hare, and a handful of misshapen amber for the foxes. Marjeta had kept the pieces aside, wrapped in a piece of scrap cloth she kept bundled in one pocket of her overskirt. She drew them out and let them tumble to the ground. They were half hidden in the thick brown fur, but the amber was easiest to spot, glowing warm and orange in the light of the candles and hearth fires.

Silviana already had a piece of chalk in hand, ready to draw the hare board on the stones by the hearth. Chalk scraped on stone as Silviana set to work. She was aware that Marjeta was watching her sketch out the winding map of squares and circles.

"It took me years to memorise all the patterns for a hare board. I always made Val — my sister — do them."

"The dead one," Silviana said. "The other wife who never was."

The servant Areya hissed under her breath, and clacked her needles louder, but Marjeta only stared at Silviana with wide, dark eyes. "Yes. I'm not even sure I remembered the board correctly. I had to go ask Areya after I showed you."

"And were you right?"

"I was." Marjeta nodded but she seemed slightly surprised at the revelation, as though it was something she'd never realised before.

"So, you never needed your sister as much as you thought." Silviana had never understood why Marjeta was so concerned with her missing sister. A sister wasn't a mother.

"Hmm," Marjeta said noncommittally as she crouched down to

get a better look at Silviana's drawing. "That's very good. Though you've missed one here." She traced another path between three others, "But it's almost perfect otherwise. It took me years to get it right, and Val showed me over and over."

"I've nothing else to do," Silviana said, "except memorise things. Brother Milos makes me learn new verses every week. To strengthen the memorising parts of my mind, he says." She sat back on her haunches. "I can recite almost the whole Book of Punishments," she added proudly.

"That's ... wonderful," said Marjeta. "There. Now, I think you can cast the hare."

The game began, and after a while Marjeta's strange stiffness began to settle, and she even appeared to enjoy herself. If the witch-wife was a shepherdess and herself the lamb, Silviana thought, she was a rather soft shepherdess, and Silviana rather a wolfish lamb.

"Come," Silviana stood and held out her hand. "I wish to play something else," and she began a fast-paced game of catch as catch can through the rooms, darting about the furniture and forcing Lilika and Areya to join them. Silviana was fast and small, and she avoided capture so many times that soon Marjeta was laughing, her hair falling in disarray about her shoulders, and her dark eyes flashing bright.

"I think that's enough for today," Lilika panted as she staggered to a stop. Her normally perfect tresses looked a little frazzled and rough, and her face was flushed. While she'd often indulged Silviana's need for games, normally she'd cut them short as soon as she'd had enough. She could have let Marjeta and Silviana play on without her, but that never happened.

Silviana bridled. Before Marjeta had arrived, she'd been all Lilika's to mould as she wanted. Lilika had been her mother in everything but name. Her wetnurse, her caretaker, her confidante. But now Lilika acted as though she owned Silviana and that Marjeta was here to steal her away. "Must we!" Silviana paused and leaned against the passage wall. "We've just barely started."

"We've been wasting far too much time on silly games," Lilika said, as she straightened Silviana's dress and skirts. "You've lessons to attend, and surely you want to spend some time with cousin

Devan? You can't ignore everyone just to play." She glanced at the other, older girl. "And I'm quite certain Lady Marjeta has plenty to occupy her before prayers. I have heard she's fallen behind in her script-work."

Marjeta only nodded, but when Silviana glanced back, she saw her pluck a strand of jet black hair from the stone wall where Silviana had rested for a moment. "Your lady is right, Silviana." Marjeta tucked her hand in her pocket. "I can't take up all your time. It isn't fair to others."

The girl felt her expression fall and hated herself for it.

"But don't fret," Marjeta added. "Tomorrow will be here soon—"

"Yes." Silviana flicked a loose strand of hair out of her face. "You must come tomorrow straight after my music training. There's someone I'd like you to meet."

Marjeta looked startled, as Silviana had wanted her to be. "I'll be sure to do that. As soon as my studies are done." She glanced across at Lilika with a small, tight smile. "After all, we know how important our education is."

"And I'd like to hear about how you grew up," Silviana said, ignoring Lilika's permanent scowl. "You've lived out there." She gestured to the windows. "It must be very different to how things are done in my father's land."

"Rather different," Marjeta conceded. "I had more," she tilted her head, "freedoms, I suppose. I was the youngest and no one much minded what I got up to." She snorted softly, her eyes hazy with memories that Silviana wished she could squeeze out of her and take for her own.

She clenched her fists, jealousy making her heart small and hard. "What did you get up to?"

"There'll be time for this later," Lilika said, but Marjeta ignored her.

"All kinds of things. I spent a lot of time in the forest. I could ride faster than any hare, and my dog would run with me..." She took a deep breath and shook her head just slightly.

"What was the forest like?" Silviana imagined it dark and full of terrors, of stalking things, of screaming things, monster-faced boys who could not wait to gut her, to hoist her up by her own entrails and leave her hanging from the cold black pines. They hated her, Lilika said. The Wild Boys hated her father, and everything about their family. The things they would do to her if ever they caught her were enough to give her nightmares, and Lilika did so relish the telling of them. Silviana thought she might prefer to hear Marjeta's stories. "Was it frightening? Were you scared?"

"Not scared, as such," said Marjeta. "Oh, I could tell you so many stories about the forest."

"But not now," Lilika snapped.

"Tomorrow, then," Silviana commanded, and Marjeta only nodded, a strange smile caught in the corner of her mouth. It seemed that she was no longer in the room with Silviana, even though she had not yet left. Her mind was far away. Perhaps she dreamed of her dead sister, and how much better a dead sister was than a live step-daughter. Silviana wished she could see into the heads of the women around her and read their thoughts. She hated not knowing what people truly thought of her. It made her feel unsteady, as though the floor was made of spider silk and she was all alone in the dark.

A Witch Worth Burning

That evening, in the sanctuary of her rooms and far from Lilika's razor words and Silviana's secretive smiles, Marjeta drew out the pocketed strands of Silviana's hair and placed them carefully on the table in front of her lady in waiting.

"Could I use this for a spell? I don't want it for me." Marjeta flushed at her own presumptuousness, then swallowed and continued. "Though I am going to be the focus." She reached up and snipped a handful of hairs from her own head with Areya's sewing scissors. Marjeta laid these out on the table, where they glinted with hints of gold and nutmeg and copper. "Can you braid Silviana's hair into this, and use the disc and beads she played with as ornaments? I want it made into a bracelet small enough to fit Silvi's wrist."

Areya frowned. "That's not how it works," she said. "You want to cast a spell over Silviana and make sure the friendship between you grows, and you need her permission. Permission should be easy enough, but you must wear the spellwork if you're the focus."

"No. I want to weave in a spell, yes, but not for friendship." She touched the strand of black hair very gently. "It's a protection charm, to keep her safe. No child asks their mother's permission for protection; the dams stitch it into their clothes and blankets, carve it into their cots." How many times had she seen her mother and the court ladies embroider protection sigils on hems and collars or cover tiny blessing-blankets for a birth? It had to be possible to transfer that kind of magic to a braided charm, surely.

"A parent does not need permission to protect their child,"

Areya said softly. "And Silviana is not your child."

Marjeta looked up. It was true enough that she'd not given birth to Silviana, but there was a marriage already announced, engagement chains worn at the throat. "But she will be, one day. And by those terms, the protection might work."

"I still can't help you," Areya said.

"Or you refuse."

"No. Nothing like that. You have to weave it yourself," Areya said. "I'll tell you the patterns and show you how it's done but for a protection spell, the parent must make it."

"You know as well as I do that I don't have any power."

"I can't promise it will work." Areya shrugged. "But your blood is still witch blood. The charm on the duke too, that was proof enough there is magic in your veins. And for a parent's protection spell, well, your mother has no magic—"

"And look how well her charms worked!" Marjeta shouted. "The baby she lost, Josef and Sonya are unhappy, Val is dead, and here I am."

"And here you are," Areya agreed. "Alive, healthy, and the future wife of a powerful duke."

"It's not much," Marjeta said, but the anger was leeching out of her. She was too tired to fight. Here she'd hoped to give Silviana something to keep her safe, and all she'd ended up doing was reminding herself of her own powerlessness. "You think my mother is happy with how her protection spells have worked out? She'd be happier if I had died, and it was Val in this castle." It was said with no sense of self-pity, but as bald fact. Valerija had been the shining evening star in the constellation of their family. Bright and beautiful, a way-sign. And Marjeta had been a dwarf star, spinning around her sister's magnet heart.

"You cannot know that." Areya's voice dropped. "I wager no parent wants to lose any child, but your mother would never wish your sister's death on you, whatever you fear." Areya sat down opposite her at the table. Her warm eyes were dark in the low light of the candles, and there was something infinitesimally softer about her, as though her bones had bowed like wax candles. When she spoke again, her low voice carried faint tenderness, a brush of feather and fur against a child's cheek. "Weave the charm, Mari. You know how to braid, you know how to put beads on a thread. It's that simple. There are no magic words — just making the charm with love. A mother infuses her love into the working of a charm, and it catches, or it doesn't."

Areya had never called her by such a familiar name before, and the smallness of it pierced her. A needle point to the heart where a sword thrust would have failed. Marjeta carefully picked up her snipped lock of hair and with trembling fingers threaded the single jet hair in the centre. It would take a long time to weave this — her skills had never leaned towards domestic crafts. Love. It wasn't as though she felt love for this girl whom she'd known only a handful of months. Or perhaps... Marjeta conjured up Silviana's face, the way her expression became so naked and happy when Marjeta paid her attention, the clever little things she said, her enthusiasm for everything. Perhaps love can catch a person quite unexpectedly.

"Use a four-strand braid," Areya said. "Or a five, if you can. Three for the gods, and one for Silviana."

"What would be the fifth one?"

"It would work your own protection in, but it's not necessary."

"But it would make it stronger?" Marjeta glanced up to see Areya nod approvingly. She would do a five strand then and work the beads into the weave in the bear-star pattern. It came back to her, unfurling like spring crocuses in the pale sun, memories of how the patterns and braids worked. All those magic things she'd never paid attention to but had soaked under skin anyway, like mist watering a field. With renewed effort, Marjeta concentrated on the way she felt around Silviana, how the girl's good cheer despite her imprisonment lifted Marjeta's own moods. She closed her eyes and breathed in deeply, conjuring the smell of Silviana's rooms, the perfume of lavender and sage, the fresh smell of a child's skin. She bowed her head and began to work, always holding on to her images of Silviana, and how she truly wanted her safe.

Safe from fear, from loss, from loneliness. Safe from finding out she barely mattered at all.

*

Marjeta woke bleary eyed. Pale light streamed in the window, and a hand was shaking her shoulder, forcing her out of a dream she could almost remember.

"Come along, sleepy. I've let you lie in far past cock crow, and now you've missed your breakfast."

Marjeta rolled onto her side and covered her head with her arms. She'd been up so late, she was sure she'd heard the servants in the castle begin their daily work by the time she'd crawled into bed. And now her head ached fiercely. The light only made it worse. A herd of wild ponies were kicking her skull in. And the dream — she'd been trapped, bound at hand and foot, gagged so she could not scream. Her mouth was filled with dirt and pieces of apples. And a man had been staring at her, his face wrapped in black silk as though he was too hideous to be seen. All Marjeta had been able to make out as he approached were his eyes, black in the darkness, deep as holes into the night, and the great black horns that had sprouted from his forehead. Bull horns.

The dream came back in a rush of unwanted clarity. He was going to cut out her heart. The knife in his hand, silver and sharp, the only thing that had caught the light.

Marjeta jumped out of bed as though to escape the source of her bad dreams. The desk where she'd been working last night had been cleared of her attempts at a protection bracelet, and a meal set in its place. "Where is it?"

"I brought you breakfast from the hall." Areya pointed to where a bowl of porridge sat waiting. It was cold, congealed.

"Not breakfast." Marjeta frowned. "And that looks ... hideous."

"Oh, this?" Areya pulled a small bracelet from her skirt pocket. "It's very nicely done, magic or not."

Marjeta snorted, but her chest fluttered in relief. She'd feared that she'd dreamed working on Silviana's gift, and that the strange whispering under her skin that she had been sure was the furtive shift of waking magic had been nothing more than wishful thinking. "I believe that's a compliment."

"You believe correctly." Areya dropped the bracelet into Mari's waiting palm. "And it was a pleasure to procure you your hideous breakfast."

Marjeta flushed. "Sorry, I didn't mean—"

"It is revolting, though," Areya said. "I thought we could feed it to Tarkis and go down and see if we can't rather snatch some bread."

"Agreed," said Marjeta, after giving the bowl of cold porridge another look and putting it down on the floor near the fireplace. Tarkis was coiled up in the grey ash and coals, and he stirred from his place and waddled out, leaving a smoky trail of dark footprints across the stones. The salamander nudged the bowl, licked the contents to test, then proceeded to eat sloppily, wide mouth smeared with flecks of beige porridge oats.

"At least you seem to enjoy it." Marjeta dressed quickly and gathered the empty bowl. The little salamander had waddled back to bed, and on the house-altar, the stone tray sat empty. "I suppose you lot want something too," she said to the Three.

"Don't mock them," Areya looked up from winding a ball of wool she'd dropped to the ground.

The cerise threads were intense and bright, and for a moment Marjeta had a vision of Areya as a priestess, binding a marriage. She shook her head. "What does it matter?" she asked. "They are no more powerful than stones."

Areya snorted in disgust and picked up her bag of wools and threads. "You've spent too much time with Brother Milos and that old man in the dungeon. You can't use magic and then pretend that half of it doesn't matter."

Marjeta bristled. She hated that the Three and magic had to go hand in hand. What good were gods? If they even cared about humanity at all, which Marjeta had little faith in. She changed the subject. "Old man? Oh, you mean Caneth." Mari looked down at the bowl as her stomach grumbled. Perhaps giving Tarkis her breakfast had been a mistake. "He's not that bad," she said. "He's one of the nicer people I've met here, and he's nothing like Brother Milos."

"Few people are, thank the Three. Between him and Lilika we have enemies enough."

"Are they, though?"

"Are they what?"

Marjeta followed Areya out into the hallways, their footsteps soft as snow, her voice low. "Our enemies. We barely gave either of them a chance before we decided they were against us."

"They are. Lilika holds on to power through the duke's daughter. And Milos is the same, and he has his god on his side. Even if either of them actually liked you, it wouldn't matter. You are the future duchess, and they need to mark their territory well, hold fast for when you have power. You are their enemy simply by existing."

"I understand that," Marjeta said. "I can see why they look at me and see trouble, but would it not make more sense for them to befriend me, rather than make any outright moves?"

Areya glanced back, and laughed once. "There was never going to be a chance of looking at you as a friend. Before you arrived, Milos had already chosen his side. You should listen harder to the things he doesn't say. The things that his god Furis doesn't say. You were, first and foremost, a woman from another god, a witch—"

"But I'm not."

"It doesn't matter to him. The Petrells and the Savenika have always been the bloodlines of witches. Any daughter from their marriage would have the mark on them, even if they had no magic themselves. You were tainted stock, as was your sister. He campaigned strongly against both unions. Said that witches were for burning, not marrying."

"I — I didn't know that." While Brother Milos had never been friendly or familiar, mostly he was a shadow she could ignore, like a stain on a serviceable dress, but she'd never thought that he might truly wish her dead. They had reached the kitchen doors, and more servants were rushing past them, the passageways a hive of activity. The smell of baking loaves was strong, and Marjeta's stomach grumbled. Perhaps making magic took as much energy as running wild through forests. All that effort for her paltry bit of power. Valerija could spin a dozen spells before breakfast and not have looked any weaker for it. But perhaps that was simply how it was — natural talent could not be ignored, but hard work could almost match it. Marjeta frowned at the thought. Could she have put as much effort into magic as she had into archery, or riding, and been a witch worthy of the name?

A witch worthy of burning. She shivered, her skin turning icy at the thought of such a terrible death. Brother Milos' thin, hollow-cheeked face rose in her head, horns sprouting like branches from his high forehead.

Areya flicked her shoulder, and Marjeta started, her half-spun ideas of magic blowing off into the morning.

"As I said, you need to listen more. Pay more attention." Areya paused and put a finger to her lips. "Time to steal a bun, I think." It was clear they were to talk no more about Lilika's and Milos's alliances and wars. Not publicly.

In the safety of her homeland Marjeta had been so busy with shooting and hunting, with Dust and Sasha, that she'd had paid scant attention to anything political. What had been the point? She'd caught snatches, for sure, but almost immediately forgotten about them. They'd been unimportant. Adult intrusion into her perfect child's world. And then — her stomach lurched — and then Val, and after. And she'd been numb and sad, brittle as an old unglazed pot. And now she played a game of hare and fox against foxes she hadn't even seen as foxes. She'd picked up on Lilika's dislike, of course, had known she'd need to have Silviana on her side as soon as possible. Brother Milos had simply been an annoyance.

And she had yet to meet the duke's ageing mother, a woman who lurked in a high tower with a court of ghosts and caged birds. From all accounts Marjeta had overheard, half the palace already thought the woman dead, and the other half assumed she was mad. Her servants spoke only to each other, and no formal invitation had been offered toward Marjeta to meet the dowager duchess in her lair.

Was she a fox too? Or did she wait silent as a snare. Or was she, like Marjeta, a foreign hare trapped in a labyrinth of carnivores?

It had never occurred to her that the game was real and if the foxes caught her, they'd put her on a spit and roast her. It was time to start paying attention. And if the dowager duchess would not offer her hand, perhaps Marjeta would have to break protocol and offer her own.

*

Since the dowager duchess had extended no invitation, and Marjeta was not yet married to the duke, the problem of an audience with her was a difficult one. Under no circumstances could she simply turn up, nor could she demand a meeting. She could invite Lady Sannette to her own rooms, of course, but the old woman would never accept the invitation, and such a blatant snub could only damage Marjeta's reputation at Jurie's court — such as it was.

"Birds," said Areya, when Marjeta put the problem to her.

"What of them?" Marjeta was fussing with a seam that had caught and come loose on her last ride, stitching it neatly back in place, and reworking the fine embroidery that had been ruined by the assault of bramble and thorn. She'd grown a little taller, barely an inch or two, since coming to these lands, but the split skirts still fitted her, and she did not want new ones made. These were hers, brought from home, worked at by Petrell fingers, the magic woven through weft and warp by the needles of her people; mother and sister and distant cousins, and women she had ignored. Because she'd been a fool. She was not one now, or at least, not so much of one. The thread hummed under her finger tips as she traced the carefully stitched outline of an oak leaf, an acorn. "The dowager duchess has many birds, that's hardly news."

"Is it likely that she will want more," Areya paused from brushing mud off the hem of a riding coat. "That is the way of the wealthy and the old and the lonely. They grasp always for more to hoard around them, as though they could build themselves a temple of things that will keep death away."

"And you think I should, what, offer her a bird?" Marjeta plucked a sap-green thread from her basket. "The court hunters do enough of that."

"Of a sort. You should send her a gift."

"I've sent her plenty of gifts," Marjeta pointed out. Her father had packed many trunks full of presents to be scattered among the Jurie court like corn before hens, and Marjeta had doled them out as Areya had instructed, but those sent to the dowager duchess had been like throwing pebbles down a cliff. She had never responded.

Her dislike for her son's choice in bride was made apparent by her silence.

"Send her one she cannot ignore," Areya said. "She is a foreigner, sent to marry a Jurie duke, like yourself. Perhaps there is something in your stories she cannot face. You should make her face it."

"Hmm." Marjeta narrowed her eyes and sat back slightly, thinking. Her gaze fell to the fireplace, where Tarkis was curled, round as a cat, his head tucked under a clawed leg. "She's from the south, Ageri, I think?"

Areya nodded. "A warmer land than this one, all goats and kingfishers and donkeys. The Southern Ageri standard is a pelican, silver on green. The women there wear long aprons and scarves."

"I remember." There had been a visit from Southern Ageri rulers when Marjeta had been barely more than a toddler, but they had looked so utterly strange, bewildering with their layers and layers of stiff clothes, the colours deep and bright as winter berries and dunnock eggs. "The dress I arrived in," Marjeta said. "It barely fits now, we shall repurpose it."

She and Areya worked on approximating the long aprons of the Ageri, and Marjeta, armed with manuscripts borrowed from Caneth's vaults, edged it with flocks of pelicans, and between them, stitched in a message, translated and copied carefully.

'We must never forget where we came from and who we are.'

Meetings

The summons had come sooner even than Marjeta had expected, and she entered the dowager duchess's receiving chambers with her heart feeling cracked and vulnerable as a hen's egg. This part of the vast, sprawling grounds had once been the summer pavilions, and the windows here were huge, letting light spill in various colours across the thick carpets, so that they were mottled and faded. It would take many fires to keep these rooms warm in the darkest heart of winter, Marjeta thought, as she walked across the rose wool, her feet sinking into the thick pile.

The air thrummed. It was filled with an avian purring and trilling, so loud that it vibrated in Marjeta's chest. It smelled of filthy hen coops; feathers and acrid, almost reptilian notes. She passed banks of cages filled with birds familiar and unfamiliar. There were magpies and little red-capped warblers, cages filled with tiny humming flocks of lilac finches. More and more of them, until Marjeta felt that she was walking through a nightmare, a thousand eyes watching her, a thousand miniscule tongues calling out her fortune. Only the empty cages felt peaceful, as though a reminder that all things had to come to an end. That birds died or flew free, and only the hollow space remained.

She came to where Lady Sannette waited; an empress in a wheeled throne, wrapped in many layers of silks and furs as though these could ward her against the cold of her husband's lands. The woman was older than Marjeta had expected, until she remembered that Sannette had been sent here at twenty-nine, her husband-to-be barely seventeen. Another alliance bought with wedding vows, and no thought given to either heart. Marjeta swallowed away her discomfort of the rooms, the birds, the black watching eyes, and curtseyed in greeting. "My Lady Sannette, greetings to you, we hope we find you in good health."

"You are a witch."

Marjeta blinked. She had not expected quite this level of directness. Mostly the Jurie court talked in half-truths and insinuations, with every meaning needing to be carefully tweezed out like splinters from raw flesh. And there were women gathered all about, listening. Though they were old, rarely seen outside these rooms. This was a separate land, and it played by different rules. "Not quite," she responded. "My sister was."

The Lady Sannette huffed, and spat on the ground. She was brittle and small as one of her birds, puffed up with furs instead of feathers, but that didn't mean she was weak, and Marjeta shuddered in sudden fear. "All of you, witch girls, like snakes, you are everywhere, under the rocks, in the walls. Egg-eaters," she hissed, and made a gesture, like a spiral over her bony chest. "You will not hurt my granddaughter."

"I don't plan to," Marjeta said. Perhaps it had not been wise to try to meet with the old woman, after all. Around her the women of the previous shadow court flocked, and whispered to each other, and to ears outside these chambers. What chatter they could spread, if they chose. If they were told to.

"She has protection," the dowager duchess told her. "My protection." With a gnarled finger, she beckoned Marjeta closer. Marjeta obliged, stepping nearer and bowing toward her, that the old woman could whisper. "I've seen you," she said. "I dream of you, witch-girl, you come to destroy everything. You are a thief, a murderer, but you wear a bridal robe and a king's crown."

Marjeta drew back. "I am neither."

"You come to steal these lands, to take its throne for yourself, you will murder all who stand in your way." The old woman's voice was rising to a crow's harsh call, her accent thickening. The court of old women and wizened men began to mutter in anger and consternation. In their gilded cages, the birds, roused by this display, shrieked and trilled and hooted; a cacophony of vitriol. "I curse you," the dowager duchess screamed, one bony finger pointed, jabbing toward Marjeta's heart. "I curse you by the goddess of Eternal Night, of Misery and Sadness. I curse you in her name that all you love will die, will suffer. Their suffering will be yours. Their deaths will be yours—" She was cut short by her ladies-in-waiting, who rushed from their myriad inconsequential tasks to soothe her, and to send Marjeta away with angry glares, flapping hands.

Marjeta walked from the Pavilion wing with her legs feeling stiff and painful, her back aching, fists clenched. What had she ever done to rouse the damn woman so? She'd expected a modicum of empathy at their similar fates, and instead the dowager duchess had cursed her. It was meaningless, of course; her gods were far from here, they had no power, no temples. Only one senile old bitch to give them offerings.

But it unsettled her. "Do not think of it," Marjeta told herself out loud. "She has no power left in this castle, and you need never see her again. Her words are nothing. Her curses are nothing." Perhaps it would be wise to give the Three extra oil and bread tonight, ask for a blessing.

She almost laughed out loud. The gods were all gone, and the old woman was no more a witch than she was. There had been no magic in her curse.

*

Her head thrumming with the day's lessons, Marjeta made her way to Silviana's suite. One hand was clenched in her pocket, holding tight to the hair and amber bracelet she'd made three evenings before. It wasn't that she didn't want to spend time with Silviana, but a combination of Brother Milos's endless pious droning, lessons with the various tutors Calvai deemed appropriate, and more time spent reading in Caneth's library seemed to suck away every available tick of the clock.

And her strange, fruitless meeting with the dowager duchess. That had been a surprise, throwing her off balance. Marjeta still wasn't sure where she would place her on the board, if she was hare or fox, or something altogether more dangerous. She was aware of a shimmering trail of whispers that had followed her after that, and she shut her ears to them, hoping it would soon die down.

The woven spell bracelet hummed against Marjeta's palm, faint flickers of energy, prickly as a hedgehog's rounded back. Magic, she knew. There was no point pretending that she hadn't done this. Small a spell as it might be, it was definitely real. It made her heart feel like a plucked bowstring, thrumming painfully against her ribs, hard enough to bruise. If only Val still lived, how proud she would have been. How delighted.

At least there was one person she could share some of her joy with. Marjeta glanced back and smiled quickly at Areya, who inclined her head just the slightest. It was communication without words, as though the meaning could flow from face to face, all Marjeta's magic flickering in her eyes. "I hope Milos doesn't make us wait forever," Marjeta said, as they drew up in front of the closed doors that led to the entrance cell before Silviana's suite. She was used now to this little pantomime of his; where he pretended himself the arbiter of goodness, cleansing the evil from the women before they could enter Lady Silviana's sanctuary.

Marjeta looked on the cleansing ceremony with a new eye. Before her realisation that the game was not really a game, she'd thought it nothing more than an idiotic bit of farce, meant to keep Brother Milos busy and make it look as though he were necessary to the functioning of the castle. After all, what use was a priest if there weren't rites to perform, prayers to be said?

It was not just a silly waste of time, but an exercise in power. It was part of Milos's gateway. If he decided that someone was too tainted to go near the Lady Silviana, he could declare them so. Milos could tell the duke that they would need to fast or do penance before the cleansing rite could work. It also served as a time delay. It forced visitors to stop and wait before reaching Silviana. Time that could be used in all manner of ways, should those with the young duchess need it.

Marjeta gave Areya a knowing look as she allowed Milos to chant his incantations, before turning back to him with her face bland and idiotic as though she were a simpleton. Perhaps not that far from the truth. Marjeta almost laughed at herself. She'd been thinking she was so clever and grown up, playing with Silviana and dining with the duke, and meanwhile she'd been too stupid to see just how dangerous the battle field was.

Sour as ever, Brother Milos fair spat the last words of the ceremony, apparently sensing some change in her, but he said nothing to stop Marjeta from entering.

"Don't play with him," Areya whispered as she gathered Marjeta's cloak from her shoulders. "Teasing stray dogs leads to festering bites."

It was good advice, and yet Marjeta felt untouchable, powerful, her veins full of magic.

"That man would like nothing better than to see you at the stake," Areya reminded her. "Don't give him a reason to drag you there."

"I'm behaving. I did nothing more than turn my gaze skyward, toward the Palace of Furis," Marjeta whispered back, just as the door opened with a crash.

Hurtling toward her, braids flying, was Silviana. Her cheeks were flushed with excitement, her war eyes shining. "Mari!" she said. "You're late! I told you there was someone I wanted you to meet!" She grabbed Marjeta's hand and dragged her forward.

There again, a name her sister had called her, so casually used. Marjeta's heart lurched, and she schooled her face into mirrored excitement as Silviana pulled her from room to room, until they came to the main parlour with its huge fireplace that took up half of one wall, the frieze of dukes and duchesses of Calvai merrily painted about the walls, as though they dangled like puppets from the ceiling.

There was Lilika, watching, yellow-eyed as a tabby pondering a mouse, and the tall grey figure of the music master. Marjeta had seen him in the duke's court before but had never been introduced. Instead, she took lessons with dour Genivia who tried her best to teach the distinctly unmusical Marjeta to learn the fundamentals of the harp. Marjeta tried to dip a greeting curtsey to the elderly gentleman, but Silviana was still pulling at her sleeves.

"Slow down there, starling," said a familiar voice. "You'll drag the poor girl off her feet."

"Lord Devan," Marjeta said, and smiled. In a flush of memory, Dust galloped beneath her, hooves thundered in pine needles, the air smelled of forests and green things instead of stone and tapestry, and the sound of women's voices were hushed by the cackle of the jackdaws and crack of dove wings. "You're the someone Silviana wanted me to meet?"

The lanky young man ran one hand through his hair. "It appears so."

"You know each other already?" Silviana sounded crestfallen. Here she thought she'd had something to show off to her newest friend, and it had turned into just another reminder that she was not truly part of castle life.

"We met the night I arrived, in the great hall," Marjeta told her. She decided not to mention that she'd already gone riding outside the castle with Silviana's beloved cousin, and that the duke had arranged that she go riding weekly with Devan as her protector. It would be too much like rubbing her freedoms in the girl's face. "I brought you a gift," Marjeta said instead.

"A gift." Silviana looked a little less devastated, but she still seemed suspicious that this was to be another let down.

"Yes." Marjeta took Silviana's hand, still tight in hers, and sat down on the bear rug. Silviana took her place opposite her. "I made it myself."

"You made me something?" The girl sounded confused. "But why? It's not my birthday."

"No. It's a — a friendship gift." Marjeta was hardly going to explain it was the sort of gift passed on from mothers to their children. "Here you go." She drew the little woven bangle from her skirt pocket. It was gold and amber, the wooden and amber beads woven firmly into place.

Silviana frowned and took it gingerly. "What is it?" A flicker of distaste crossed her face. "It — it's made of hair!"

"My hair, and yours," Mareta said. She flicked the wooden bead. "And this, and the amber are the beads we played with. It's called a protection charm, you wear it as a bracelet." She lifted the bracelet out of Silviana's fingers and slipped it over the girl's hand and on to her skinny wrist.

"Oh." Silviana glanced at Lilika who was watching them from the wall, her eyes narrowed. "Is it magic?"

One corner of Marjeta's mouth twitched upward in a ghost of a smile. "Not real magic, no. You can think of it as a good wish — like a prayer."

"But prayers are words." Silviana pushed the bangle off her wrist. "This is made from pieces of people. I don't think I can wear it," she said. "Brother Milos wouldn't like it."

"No. I suppose he would not." Marjeta's heart fell. She'd wanted to give Silviana something that showed her just how much she was loved. And it was not even about trying to replace Lilika in the girl's world, but to show her that she didn't have to be alone. It was the first bit of true magic Marjeta had made all on her own, and paltry as it was, she'd still hoped that Silviana would have taken it. "It's all right," she said, and her voice dropped. "You don't have to wear it. Keep it, perhaps it will bring you some luck."

"It hardly looks dangerous," Devan agreed. He sat down with them, one knee knocking against Marjeta's as casually as if they were children out at a picnic beneath the trees, and not three almost-adults, in training for when they would rule or be ruled. "Not like proper witchcraft at all."

"You know about witches?" Silviana's eyes widened.

"A little. They live in the woods, wild as wolves, and wear animal skins and drink blood."

Areya coughed from her place by the wall, and Marjeta couldn't help shaking her head. "And where did you get such ideas?" she asked.

"Common knowledge," Devan said, and winked broadly. "Don't fret, starling, there are no witches in Jurie. We hunted them all out."

"Did you?" Marjeta commented dryly. "And how did you manage that?"

"Oh." Devan seemed surprised by the flat tones of her voice. "It's a jest. I don't think Uncle's lands ever had witches, and we've never hunted them. Not as long as I've lived here."

Which just went to show how blind men could be sometimes, Marjeta thought. Even if the only bit of spell-crafting that went on were for minor hedge magics, there was no way that the entire duchy had never seen a witch. "The Lord Devan's correct," Marjeta said, changing the subject. "The bangle isn't magic. And it's not dangerous at all." She made herself smile. "I think we should teach your cousin hare and foxes if he likes. It's always more fun with more players."

"No." Silviana shook her head. "Devan was going to tell me the story of the wild boys of the forest."

"Wild forest boys?" Marjeta raised an eyebrow, remembering that she was never supposed to have heard of them before. Even though one had nearly pierced her with a well-placed arrow. She swallowed and rolled the lie smooth on her tongue. "Are these men made of leaves and bark? Are they real, or are they like your wild witches too — stories to scare children into behaving?"

"Wild, for sure," said Devan. He gave her a wink. "And made of flesh and bone. They bleed as surely as you would if someone cut your throat. They are real as can be, and far more deadly than some tales told to scare babies. Your father has put a price on their heads," he said to Silviana. "They're murderous, barely human. It might be that your Lady Lilika wouldn't like me telling you such bloodthirsty things." He grinned at Lilika, who merely *tched* in response and motioned for him to carry on with his nonsense.

"Better the girl knows the truth of what's out there," she said. "So she won't have cause to wonder why she must stay here and not try to leave."

"I never do," Silviana said. "The doors are locked. Where would I go?" She dismissed Lilika before she could respond, turning her attention back to Devan. "Go on, then. Tell us. You promised. And I won't be scared."

Devan laughed. "All right then. These forest boys — a pack of thieves and blackguards. Orphans mostly, we think. Or layabouts that ran off to live wild rather than do honest work."

"Ran off to live in a forest, feeding on nuts and berries?" Marjeta pulled at the fur she was sitting on. "Seems more work than living in a warm house and watching sheep or bringing in a harvest."

"Not everyone likes an honest life," said Devan. "I don't claim to know their reasons, but they're there, living in the woods and robbing anyone who gets caught in their traps. They weren't too bad last year, but this season they've started coming in and stealing from the village — eggs out of coops, cloth and tools."

Or shooting at intruders in their woods.

"You've seen them?" Marjeta wondered what they looked like, these feral forest boys. Were they small and young as Silviana, or were they as much boys as Devan, lanky and near-grown? Probably the latter. It was a hard life in the woods, and the weak and small would die first. These were not babes but vicious men.

"I haven't seen them close up," Devan said. "But they've been sighted by reliable men. And this time it's not a word of a lie. Folks say there's those among them raised by wolves, and run on all fours, and have pelts as hairy as any bear. Some of them can walk upright fair enough, but they all speak to each other in growls and barks."

Marjeta snorted. There was no need to embellish it. The Wild Boys were scary enough. It only took one feathered arrow to prove it.

"You're lying," said Silviana.

"Not a bit of it. The truth, I swear by Furis and by the ocean."

"You shouldn't say that," Silvi said. "You shouldn't make oaths by any gods, not even Furis. Brother Milos says."

"Does he now?" Devan leaned back on his palms and the movement pushed his knee more firmly against Marjeta's, a comforting nudge. She didn't flinch — half for fear of being obvious at moving away, and half because the sudden heat that flared from her knee and ran up her thigh was as sweetly compelling as the warmth that came from a spell taking hold. She swallowed. Devan was talking, and she tried to concentrate on his words.

"—sure to never do that again. I like my liver and lights all on the inside."

"You're disgusting." Silviana wrinkled her nose. "What will happen to these forest boys when winter comes? Soon it'll be freezing and snowing, and they've nowhere warm to live. They'll have no food or blankets or fires."

Just from the tone of her voice Marjeta could hear that Silviana thought of them as children like herself. That she felt a strange kinship with anyone who was not yet an adult. But the truth was that even if there were one or two near in age to Silviana, they were not soft and safe. She felt a twinge of pity. Probably they'd never had the chance to be. But that wouldn't save them from the duke's laws if they were fool enough to go near the villages and castles and forts.

"Ah well, I daresay they've lived through winters before," Devan was saying, "But it won't get to that. Uncle is organizing a hunt and we'll bring the miscreants in, and they'll serve their punishment."

The warmth from Devan's unintended touch faded suddenly. "What will happen to them?" Marjeta asked.

Devan shrugged. "Into the cages, I should think. Or in village stocks. Depends on what Uncle's feeling when we catch them, and what Brother Milos thinks a suitable punishment for thievery."

With Milos in charge of punishment the Wild Boys would probably wish they were dead, Marjeta thought darkly. His god seemed a rather vicious revengeful sort.

"Will you go along to hunt them?" Silviana asked. "With the grown men?"

Devan nudged Marjeta again with his knee. This time the movement was intentional, and entirely innocent. "As if that's even a question. The grown men, she says." He leaned closer to Silviana and tickled her, trapping her as she squealed and giggled. "Grown men? What are you saying, starling? I'll have you know I can hunt as well as any of those other men in your father's castle. And probably play sweeter music." He let her go and leaned back. "And I can definitely sail better than all of them put together."

"And make bigger boasts, it seems," Marjeta added. There was no chance the duke would allow her to join that particular hunt, and Marjeta was certain that even if he would, she'd want no part in it. Hunting half-grown boys through a forest as though they were starveling wolves was not the kind of thing she wanted to take part in. She was no stickler for blood and guts — had caught and skinned rabbits with Sasha. But hunting humans. Even criminal ones. No. She shivered.

"Cold, Lady Marjeta?" Devan asked. "The season's just turning, but it gets bitter here at night. Even in autumn. By winter you'll have ice for blood." He grinned. "Still, autumn's a favourite time for me. When the trees turn gold and red, like the branches caught fire and trapped the sun. You'll see that in the Old King's forest, not so much outside it." He jerked his chin as if to indicate some far-off primeval wasteland. "Out there's mainly pine and spruces, though you get a seam or two of aspen. It's only in the old forest that you see the autumn colours."

"Why's that?" Marjeta asked. She was relieved the talk had turned away from the feral children and the hunt that was to come.

"Ah, well, the legend goes that when the King Asger ruled the land and the duchies were united under one man, that he had a wife who was from the summer lands in the south, and every night, she cried for her homeland. So, King Asger sent a man to gather all the seeds and berries her could find from the summer land and bring them back to the castle. This castle." Devan said. "And he had the land all around the castle cleared, and planted, and grew his queen a forest from her home."

"That's..." Kind? Generous? Marjeta didn't know how to describe it. It was both, and neither. For sure, he'd done something to ease her pain, but it was just like little Silviana in her beautiful suite of rooms, filled with tapestries and rich ornaments, and toys brought from foreign lands. Both the summer queen and Silviana had been paid off with things but no one had ever thought to open the door and say, *Go, find the place that brings you happiness.* "That's interesting," she settled on, her voice trailing.

"It is." Devan grinned. "I've heard you spend enough time in the library stacks, I'm sure you'll come across some histories."

"I'm there copying out religious texts, not reading stories about men who probably never even existed."

"Oh, King Asger was real enough. Uncle reveres him, sees him as sort of standard to live up to. Get caught in a lecture from the duke on King Asger and you're liable to lose a birthday or two to the time taken." Devan stood, and bowed to Silviana, and then to Marjeta. "Speaking of — I've taken up too much of your time, ladies. And I have training. Master Gaith will have my head if I am late again."

"Well, we can't have that," Marjeta said. "It seems to me that your head is best kept on your neck." The loss of the warmth at her knee left her feeling odd, almost ill, as though she was coming down with a fever. She shook her head. "Perhaps we will see you here again." Or in the Old King's Woods, with the forest wrapped around them like a warding spell.

"Only if I invite him," said Silviana. She was looking between them, her mouth turned spiteful and teethful.

"I'm at your beck and call, Silvi," Devan said. "Always will be, little starling."

"Good." The answer seemed to have mollified her sudden bad mood somewhat, and she stood to embrace her cousin goodbye.

Marjeta did not, of course. She did stand, just like Lilika and Areya, and drop the young noble a curtsy in farewell. It was oddly formal after they'd been sitting on the floor together, talking of playing games. Marjeta felt dizzy, out of place, and she was relieved to sit down again after Devan had left.

Silviana's happiness had faded as quickly as a rainbow, and she looked more miserable than Marjeta had seen her in weeks. The child spun on her emotions like a toy, careening from joy to anger to misery. Marjeta was reminded of herself, a little, before her mother had trained her to be careful in what she showed on her face. Silviana might be tutored in everything from eastern mathematics to world history and politics, but no one had taught her to school herself. It was a dangerous thing to be so clever and yet so untamed. A girl who grew up in a cage had no opportunity to learn self-control.

"Perhaps we can play a game of Follow Me," Marjeta suggested as a distraction from Silvi's growing ill temper. "Or Areya has cards — she knows Hand of Four and Dead Man's Army — we could teach you those—"

"I don't want to play," Silviana said. "You didn't tell me you already knew my cousin."

"Oh, well, yes." Marjeta smoothed her skirt over her knees, and sighed. "As I said, we met the night I arrived here." She paused, wondering if she should go on and tell the girl the truth, and what mood that might rouse in her.

"You took all the fun out of it," Silviana told her before she could speak further. "He was mine, I was going to introduce you to him, and you took that away."

"It was still the first time I'd spoken to him properly." It was best to leave all talk of their ride through the woods outside these rooms. She felt sorry for the girl — here had been her big moment — how often did she have the chance to introduce two people to each other? To her, it must have seemed momentous. "If it hadn't been for you arranging this meeting, I would never have heard the story of King Asger and the forest." Or heard more about the hunting of the boys. "But we don't need to run about at games," Marjeta said. "I haven't heard you play." She pointed to the small harp that stood in one corner of the room. It wasn't usually there, and Marjeta assumed it must have been brought out for Silviana's lessons with the castle music master. It was smaller than the one Genivia taught her on and though Marjeta had little patience for the instrument herself, she did enjoy hearing it well played.

"I'm tired," Silviana said, in a cold voice. "I think you should go."

There was no point in arguing with a sullen child, even though Marjeta's impulse was to reach out and throttle the girl. She was proud of herself for doing nothing of the sort, and instead getting back to her feet, and curtsying goodbye. If her mother could have seen just how much she'd grown up in these past months, she'd have died of shock, Marjeta thought wryly. "Till next time."

Silviana picked up the discarded protection charm and looked at it but didn't answer.

Blood on the Floor

So, Silviana had not accepted her gift. Her protection. There was nothing Marjeta could do about that, and perhaps it had been vain and foolish to think that something as simple as a protection charm would bind them together like family. Marjeta lay in bed, the coverlets pulled up under her chin. The room was warm thanks to thick walls and thick carpets and a hearth still red with glowing coals, but it wasn't the approaching chill of the night that made her bones ache.

She was tired. She spent every day filling her head with names and numbers and rituals and histories, writing down until her hand cramped and her eyes watered. Tired from trying to balance herself between childhood and adulthood — to make a friend of Silviana, but to tread carefully so as not to cause too many ripples in the power balance. Tired from finding herself caught between acting as a wife-to-be for Calvai and being a girl who found her heart beating faster when Devan was near. Tired of being a witchblood mouthing the hymns of a foreign god.

It would be simpler if there was no marriage hanging over her head. If she'd been younger and she and Silviana had simply been paired together because they were two girls who needed suitable playmates. Instead, she swam in dark waters. What had looked like a shallow stream had turned deep and black and treacherous, and Marjeta felt herself being swept along without any real control.

"Idiot," she said fiercely to herself. "Swim."

A crackle and spit came from the fireplace as Tarkis shifted. A moment later the skitter of claws across stone, and the weight as

the salamander leaped on to the edge of the bed. Marjeta smiled
despite herself when the creature's scaled head appeared in front
of her, quirked to one side, large golden eyes blinking rapidly. The
salamander gulped, then chirruped softly.

Salamanders generally weren't overly friendly, but Tarkis had
lived in Marjeta's fireplace for as long as she could remember.
Usually, salamanders stayed near the same hearth where they
hatched, never leaving their territory. But Marjeta's mother had
packed Tarkis up as though he were a pet and sent him to this
castle with her. Another lonely outcast, and perhaps even more so.
At least there were other humans in Jurie.

"Sorry," Marjeta whispered as she scratched the salamander on
his head, behind the little ridges of bone near his ear holes. "You
must be so very lonely, so many miles from home." He rested
his solid, comforting weight on her chest, warming her with the
residue of hearth-heat.

The salamander had been no bigger than a sparrow the first
time Marjeta could remember seeing him, still pale as stirred
eggs, and toothless. Now he was larger than a wild cat. His scales
had darkened to a dull coppery gold, the edges touched with an
orange-red. In the breeding season, female salamanders turned the
blue black of fire hearts, but the males burned fierce and bright.
Mari had never seen Tarkis in breeding colours, but from his size,
the lizard was getting closer by the year. And what a miserable, sad
breeding season it would be. "Mama should never have sent you,"
she whispered.

Tarkis nudged her hand and rumbled contentedly. The sound
of nails across scales sounded crisp and dry as sand on sand.

"What is it you do all night here?" she asked as she sat up and
set the salamander down at the side of her bed. Marjeta shoved
the covers completely off and pulled a cloak over her sleep gown.
Her feet were bare. Good for silence, perhaps, but not so good for
warmth. She settled on pulling on thick woollen winter stockings.
There would be no sleep tonight. Her head was too full of thoughts.
She needed something to distract her.

"Come along." Marjeta opened the door and peered cautiously
out, looking both ways down the passage. There was no sign of

anyone out, and Areya's doorway to her own small bedroom was shut. "Let's see where it is you go, little Tarkis."

The salamander nudged past her ankle, moving low to the ground in a sinuous sideways ripple. His sharp little claws made a soft quick rasp against the stone.

Marjeta followed him down the passage, waiting when he paused to raise his head and taste the air, his soft throat gulping, pale and delicate in the darkness. The salamander ran a complicated path through the castle but kept them far from prying eyes. Every now and again he snapped at some small bug or spider in the shadows, and once chased a thimble-sized mouse down a small, narrow passage. By the time Marjeta caught up with him, she had begun to regret her impetuous decision for midnight explorations. The palace was vast, and even though she had been here a few months, there was much of it still a mystery to her.

"You better be able to get me back," she muttered.

The salamander skittered ahead, and Marjeta stopped to lean against the wall and pull a small splinter out of her one sock. It had caught just under her big toe, and she felt carefully for it in the dark

"What's this then?" The voice came from around a corner, and Marjeta froze, splinter inched between finger and thumb, balanced on one leg.

Lilika. And what was she doing roaming the palace at this hour? As far as Marjeta knew, Lilika was practically stitched to Silviana's side. It was odd that she should be here now while her precious charge lay sleeping untended. Marjeta kept very still, a million excuses bursting through her brain. At any moment Lilika would turn the corner and find her. She swallowed. Did she even need an excuse? Surely, she had the right to wander at night if she felt like it? She was not Silviana, chained to her rooms, nor was she meeting with secret lovers.

The thought made her burn. It would look like it, no matter what she said.

Tarkis growled, a low spitting noise. It was a warning, and Marjeta knew a salamander approached when it was angry could land you with an eyeful of burning venom.

A door clicked softly closed, and Tarkis's warning growl grew louder. That idiot Lilika must be approaching him. Marjeta held her breath and kept still. If Tarkis attacked, Lilika would be blinded for a moment and Marjeta would have the chance to run.

The woman hated her enough and if she caught her wandering the castle alone at night, would make all kinds of unsavoury accusations. Gossip would spread, and already there were whispers that witches were sluts who trapped men. It wouldn't take much for Lilika to imply that Marjeta was out meeting men, using her sex as a weapon and a spell, with no thought to her upcoming vows.

Unfortunately, Marjeta was not completely sure she could find the way back to her rooms alone. She'd been so intent on following Tarkis that she'd paid little attention to the route. She looked around. It was vaguely familiar — there was a painting on the wall across of a woman in reds riding a goat-like unicorn with a single sweeping backward horn. She was passing through forests of oak and aspen and beech, and all around her the painting shone with golds and reds. Marjeta thought she'd seen this painting before in a corridor near Silviana's suite of rooms. She'd circled the palace while following Tarkis. No wonder she'd almost stumbled onto Lilika.

"Come now, lizard. I'll not harm you." Lilika's voice took on a strange new timbre as though she'd grown two mouths, and each spoke at the same time. The sounds deepened, melodies flitting under her words. "You're the witch's little pet, are you not?"

Tarkis stopped growling.

"See, there, I said I'd not hurt you. Now, where were you off to?"

Marjeta slowly lowered her foot and pressed herself against the walls, deep into the shadows. There was a small alcove only a few feet down behind her in the passage. She inched back, moving as slowly and quietly as possible. In the stillness of the night-shrouded palace, every whisper of material and every tiny shift seemed to echo and bugle like war pipes. Her heartbeat was a percussive thunder, her breath roaring bellows. Finally, Marjeta felt the wall disappear behind her and she slunk quickly into the deepest corner of the recess and hid behind a statue of a stone monster threaded with cobwebs and dust. She pulled her hood and cloak close about her, and lowered her head, one finger pressed under her nose to still the itch of a dust-induced sneeze.

Lilika was still talking, using the kind of singsong voice people often did when talking to animals, her pitch higher, almost girlish. Marjeta would have found it annoying. There was something there, though. Something that prickled at her senses in a familiar way. Marjeta kept absolutely still, straining to listen.

Lilika crooned again, and there: bell echoes under the lilting cadence, the sound of spells. So like Val's voice when she had wrapped Marjeta and herself in silken ribbons of magic to hide them from view.

Marjeta's heart was a wren under a cat's paw, pressed small, cracking under the velvet pressure. There was no denying what she heard. Magic tugged at her, pulled gently, calling like to like, and though Marjeta could barely string a protection charm together, she was still witch blood, and the magic knew.

"There, my little cock, strange that the witch brought you, and stranger still she lets you roam." Lilika came into view and Marjeta tensed. She'd had years of practice seeing Val when Val had not wanted to be seen, and this was just like those times. The spell was meant to mask a human form. Val had used it often. It suggested to a casual observer to turn their head at just the right moment, for their eye to slide over the shape and carry on as though nothing were there. However, if you knew someone was there and you were concentrating on looking, the spell could be fought.

Lilika was blurry, and Marjeta struggled with the urge to turn her head and look elsewhere, but she renewed her focus, squinting at the blurred figure until her head ached.

The older woman never came clearly into focus, but she became more perceptibly real. She stood in the gloom, her brown dress shifting with greys and stones, the salamander held in her arms like a large golden baby. It wasn't struggling, but its stillness was wary rather than content. It too heard magic. There had been no indication that Lilika was a witch before. She was as pious a woman as Marjeta had ever seen, worse, perhaps than any other, with her constant sign of the horns whenever Furis's name was mentioned, her prayers, her encouragement of Lady Silviana's religious education. She seemed close to Brother Milos. And he hated witches.

Surely it was a mistake. Lilika was no more a witch than Tarkis was a winged fire-breathing dragon. As the pair stepped next to the stone monster, Tarkis struggled in Lilika's grip, keening and calling for Marjeta.

"What is it, cock?" Lilika's voice had turned sharp, almost angry. "Is someone there?" She said this louder, her voice filled with the imperative to walk forward, reveal yourself.

Tarkis twisted suddenly, turning his head to snap at Lilika's wrist.

She dropped the salamander with a muted shriek and clutched at her wrist with her other hand. Blood was streaming down her hand. The salamander had bitten deep.

"Little serpent," Lilika hissed as Tarkis scuttled off down the passage. "I'll get you for that." She paused to hold her savaged wrist closer to her face and scowled. "Damn it all." Lilika turned on her toes and headed back the way she'd come.

Marjeta gasped softly, her aching lungs finally freed. She doubled over, the last traces of Lilika's spell breaking off her like cobwebs.

Her head was buzzing. This was unexpected. Unbelievable. She had to get back to her rooms and wake Areya. Neither of them had even the slightest indication that Lilika was witch blood. Areya would know what to do. Lilika must have her own plans in plans, and her iron hold on Silviana began to make more sense. For all Marjeta knew there were bindings and spells worked deep into Lady Silviana's rooms.

Her own pathetic little bracelet would have been a charm gifted far too late.

Did the dowager duchess know? It seemed possible that she did, and that she too was caught in a web, unable to leave her rooms, sick and twisted years before her time

There was still the question of why Lilika herself was out roaming at night, cloaked in magic and hiding herself. There were ways to follow someone who wore a cloaking charm — Val had taught her the most basic, simple way to do it, one that needed just the faintest suggestion of ability. But it still involved having in your possession something that belonged to the person you wished to uncloak.

Marjeta glanced down to where the spatter of blood had already begun to dry, soaking into the stone. She knelt to run a forefinger through the dark splotch. The blood smeared, and Marjeta caught the faint tingle of the remnant of Lilika's spell.

"Show me," she whispered to the blood. "Show me Lilika." A name, and a possession. Such a simple piece of trickery that even a useless nothing like Marjeta Petrell could do it. The hook caught, a tug and prickle that Mari felt just under her fingernails. A small, annoying itch that slowly burned up inside her bones, leaving her feeling sweaty and ill. Small and simple as the trick was, it was still power.

*

There was no way she could spin a cloak of shadows and spells with which to hide herself. Marjeta was well aware of her limitations. On the other hand, Lilika would not be expecting anyone to be following her, and Marjeta could keep a decent safe distance between them. She set off, tracing the route of her prey by the pull of the spell hooked under her nails.

Now that the spell was caught, the blurred figure of Lilika was sharper than ever, and the constant push to look away was only a minor irritant. Soft as dust falling, Marjeta padded behind Lilika, her stockinged feet hushing against stone. Her heart was beating high in her chest, and she was terrified that at any moment Lilika would realise she was being followed and turn around.

But the woman was utterly preoccupied, rushing at speed down the maze of corridors and up winding staircases, following a network of rarely travelled routes through the vast cluster of buildings. Hunter and prey moved from the sprawling, cake-like edifice of the new palace to far older parts. Sections of the original fort, judging from the cold and the pervasive smell of damp stone. The very first and oldest parts.

Marjeta's eyes adjusted to the intense gloom. Judging from the heavy chill in the air and the lack of windows, the low ceiling, they were deep underground.

Lilika paused and muttered a few words, and the spell of shadows dropped from her, falling golden in leaf flutters before vanishing completely. The woman smoothed her hands over her braids, tucking a few loose strands in place. Ahead of them, a single torch guttered weakly, casting a halo of warmth around Lilika as she preened. Finally happy with her hairdo, Lilika shook out her skirts, brushing off whatever dust might have been picked up on her journey through the castle. She spent a moment examining her bitten wrist, brow furrowed in annoyance before marching forward and off down a righthand corridor just past the lit torch.

"Lady Lilika," said a deep male voice, and Marjeta froze, her heart hammering.

"Sir Provas," came the clipped response. "He's expecting me."

"As usual, my lady. Though you're running late."

"I was delayed by the rather unusual pet the witch brought with her from her mud hut."

The guard and Lilika laughed together and Marjeta bristled. Petrell was not as vast and sprawling and showy as Jurie's summer palace, but it was no mud hut, and to hear her home so sourly dismissed made her hate the duke's castle even more. It was a porridge of architecture, she told herself, gaudy where it should be strong, pretentious and overdecorated. She'd take a mud hut over this silly cake of a building, especially if it meant not marrying the chinless, ancient duke that came with it.

Lilika was still talking, and Marjeta concentrated, keeping close to the wall and deep in the shadows.

"The lizard must have escaped — children can be so careless — and I meant only to return it to her when the cursed thing bit me."

"The duke was wondering at the delay, I daresay he'll want an explanation."

Marjeta backed up, very, very slowly. The sound of her blood pulsing through her body filled up her ears, as though she were being pushed slowly under a black lake. She'd walked right into a hidden domain that the duke kept private and inviolate, and she'd followed Lilika to get there. Lilika, who was only a serving maid to a girl child. A former wetnurse kept and elevated beyond her status. And here she was going to the duke at night, and with every sign that this was a common occurrence, with a scheduled time.

Marjeta swallowed past the clamour of her own heart.

"We should hardly waste more time, then," Lilika said, and her voice was curt.

"Certainly." The sound of scraping hinges, the creak of wood, and a distant voice saying Lilika's name, then the thud of a closing door, the voices muffled.

That had been the duke's voice, Marjeta was sure. He spoke little enough to her, but she did have to speak with him at dinner and listen as he spoke to his men and soldiers. She tiptoed away from the arched entrance, and from the guarded rooms belonging to her future husband. With her throat tight and her mouth dry, she kept going until she was sure she was far from the guards, and finally stopped to take stock.

Marjeta was in an addition to the palace that was perhaps only six hundred years old. The stone was different here — not the black smooth rock from near the duke's secret quarters, but a lighter, rougher stone with a sandy texture. The corridor opened out in a hall filled with huge wide pillars supporting an intricately vaulted ceiling but which was otherwise empty. She had passed it once and inquired about why it wasn't used. No one had been happy to give her an answer, which had only made her all the more curious. Marjeta knew exactly where she stood. The Belind Hall, named for Duke Calvai's first wife; joyous, vivacious, given to parties and to surrounding herself with musicians and dancers, and women and men of the court. She'd liked beautiful things and believed in celebrating every moment given her. A golden woman, down to her love of yellows.

Her portrait hung in the hall of faces where the walls were covered with the glazed visages of dukes and duchesses and graces and princes and princesses and kings and queens, and Marjeta had gone to study this dead woman with whom she would never compare. The perfect, matchless wife who was neither witch nor child.

The Duchess Belind had been a woman of russets and gold and

honey, with skin as creamy and soft as fresh butter. Her hair had fallen to her waist in foxfur and autumn leaf curls, and her eyes were flickers of green, promises of spring. The artist might have been trying to flatter, of course, but others had whispered how she'd been a beautiful woman.

This was who she had to follow. Marjeta took a breath and stepped out into the empty hall. She could sense the traces of dead Belind's laughter and the sweep of her skirts across the stone. Echoes from a past she'd never seen. Marjeta spun in place, her thin cloak flaring around her, whispering in answer, her stockinged feet softer than embroidered dancing slippers. The only musicians that played were the ghosts, the silences and heavy years.

This had been Belind's place, and Marjeta was supposed to fill it somehow. How could she, when she was just Marjeta Petrell, dark and bony, plain faced, plain, plain, plain. A nothing girl.

She was here to replace a shining woman. One the duke had loved so much that he'd given her everything she'd wanted.

She was here to replace her magic sister, who had never even made it into the castle at all.

She was here to one day replace Lilika who knew magic but still had priests on her side.

And what was Marjeta against this? Her skills lay in the things that wouldn't help her behind castle walls. What good was a duchess who could shoot a leaf from a bough at thirty paces, when she was intended to be only a bowl in which to build a son.

She spun to stillness, and instead of screaming, Marjeta pressed her hands to her head and drew in a deep breath. Crying wasn't going to help her; she'd dried herself out with Valerija's death. And nothing had brought her sister back or changed the way the world turned. What she had to do was find a way to make a space to be herself. She'd taken a small step towards that when she'd gone to the duke and gained her rides in the Old King's forest. Perhaps that was best — to cling to the little joys she could find and keep them close to her heart like secret thorns that stirred her blood.

There was no way to become Belind. She would stop worrying about trying to keep Silviana on her side. Let the girl grow up the way she would. It wasn't Marjeta's place to esplanier her into a warped daughter, bearing fruit of familial love and good faith. Enough of this dance where she and Lilika pulled Silviana between them. She would offer the girl her hand in friendship, and nothing more.

Lilika, Silviana, the duke — even Areya — they saw her as a game piece to be moved into position, to fight to win and wear her coronet, or die trying. But who had decided that she should play? It had not been Marjeta herself — she'd merely been placed on a square and expected to follow the rules of engagement.

"And I accepted it," Marjeta said to the empty ballroom. "Just like you did." She wondered if Belind had been a little like herself under her golden beauty. Had she also smiled at secret mistresses and wished to be home, to be herself? She'd been only a handful of years older than Marjeta when she'd died; perhaps if she'd known what Silviana's birth would have cost her, the Golden Belind would have thrown off her gleaming coronet and run for the forests. Perhaps she should have. "But I'm not you, and I don't have to do what you did." Marjeta said as she turned her back on the empty room and retraced her steps.

Tomorrow she would clear the board and pack away the pieces.

The Sun's Shadow

Lilika's hand still smarted where that damnable reptile had bitten her. She'd tried to take it back to the witch girl's rooms, but it had wriggled itself free and run off into the dark. In annoyance, Lilika had pulled her spell ragged around her and slipped through the catacombs of her design, tracing and backtracking so that she would meet no unwanted servants or witnesses to her sojourn. While it was true there were those who knew that she left her own chambers some nights and made her way to the subterranean rooms that the duke reserved for their assignations, it was hardly a thing she wanted the whole castle to know.

She never went to his official rooms, only this secondary set of rooms, their purpose obvious from the moment one entered. In her heart, Lilika knew the duke saw her only as a convenience. He was a man with man's needs, but he was also noble and of a gentle persuasion, or so he had persuaded himself. He would never force himself on any woman, nor push his advances on his wife-to-be before she was secured as an adult and wedded to him with iron rings. Instead, he took the woman who stood at his side and looked after the child his first wife had given him.

Lilika smiled sourly to herself at Provos stepped aside to usher her into the mistress rooms. Officially, they existed in a half-world. Legally the duke could take mistresses, but it was wise not to flaunt his other women. Certainly not before the wedding was signed and secured, and out of respect, it was never spoken of after.

She cast aside the last traces of her spell like burrs plucked from a dog's rough coat and drew a smile onto her face. She did hold a love for the duke in her. A fondness. Once she'd been so deeply in love with him, she had hardly been able to breathe around him, lest he realise she existed and dismissed her within a space of moments. It would have broken her heart.

But that had been then, and she'd still been untempered by her time in the castle, still raw and rough as gorse hedges, prickly, her brightness sparked between dark jagged thorniness. She'd been no sun to bathe the duke's face in love and beauty and wonder. She had not been Belind, and that had been all there was to it.

Now Belind was dead — the sun sunk deep never to rise again — and her daughter saw Lilika as a mother. And Calvai saw Lilika as a wife. In the way it mattered to men.

And Lilika saw Calvai for what he was. A duke, certainly. Which was simply a title inherited, wealth passed down from throne to throne and son to son. A father. A father who kept his daughter like a nightingale in a cage of splendour. A man. A mewling thing, propped up by the lies carved into his bones, the rattle of money and sword and armour, black as shells and as empty. A man who wanted a crown and a king's throne, and the armies to gain it.

"You're late." Calvai was stretched on a chair, sprawled back, legs akimbo. In the flickering light of candle and lamp the shadows under his eyes were blacker, bruised blue as winter lakes. His face was thinner these days, the beard grew strands that were both auburn and silver and his eyes were feathered at the corners. He carried his ambition too close to him and it burned up his fat like fuel, sucked moisture from his skin.

"I was waylaid by a lizard," Lilika said, and laughed prettily. Before the duke could grow cross, she stepped lightly around him and rested her palms against the tense brackets of his shoulders. Without a word, she pressed and stroked, smoothing out his fierce fancies, his simmering and bubbling. Under her hands he began to soften.

"Ah," Calvai said. "You know me so well, not a word is needed to bring me back to myself."

"You put yourself under far too much stress."

"And if I do not, then my duchy would crumble at the edges. Bad enough that I must war with foreign men to stake my claim, but it is an insult when the attacks come from within my own lands. If I were to ignore them, my duchy would be eaten away like a feast cake by ants." He shrugged in irritation.

"These ants," Lilika said, and began to work hard, her thumbs and fingers digging into the iron muscle and melting the pain away. "Would they be the Wild Boys?"

"They are worse than ants," Calvai said. "They are fleas. Blood sucking, and always leaping out of reach. I can find no nest to burn out, no queen to kill. They are hardier than lice and gone before we even know they are there. Just today they waylaid a convoy bringing wools up from the meadowland to the dye pits."

"They must have buyers then," Lilika said thoughtfully. "Wool is not so easy and light a load to move."

"As you say." Calvai twisted around to look at her, and his face was a sick man's in a fever. It made his eyes glimmer foxfire, and Lilika shivered under her layers of skirts and shifts and stopped herself from making the sign of Furis' Horns at him. "I have enemies at my borders. And without. And those without play the tunes, and those within dance."

"What will you do?" Lilika stepped away, and unpinned her cloak, carefully draping it over a wooden stand in the corner of the room. It left her feeling like a crab peeled out of its shell. Calvai was in a mood tonight, and she liked him less when he grew like this.

"I believe I know who goes against me, and for now, I keep surety against him. He will make no open move. But I must have more weapons, better horses and horsemen to ride them."

"You raise an army," Lilika said. With her hands trembling, she undid the ties of her blouse at neck and cuff.

"I have an army," Calvai corrected. "I merely need better protection at the border forts, and that means recruiting more men."

"Duke Andrais will never believe you need more men simply because of a pack of wood-crawling brigands. And do you truly suspect your sister's husband of working against you?"

Calvai shrugged. "Karina cannot control Andrais, which is why she sent Devan to me. My own sister does not trust her husband,

and I should?" He laughed bitterly. "Of course not. But he knows better than to go openly against me, not when news comes weekly from Petrell of further border wars, and even their duke grows nervous. Him with his bears and his witches. And Furis has spoken." Calvai reached forward and drew Lilika into his lap, stroking at her belly and arms and thighs, soothing her down like a nervous mare.

"Has he?" She cocked her head, pretend playful as her stomach tightened. Furis spoke to her in signs and visions and dreams. He told her how to pay penance, to care for Silviana that she would grow up straight and true as a birch, uncorrupted by the accident of her birth. Furis showed her the path to walk and the example to set, he had guided her into Calvai's bed and told her when to whisper against the witchbride and when to stay silent. But she had never thought he spoke to her duke in the same way. "What does he tell you?"

Calvai laughed and held her tighter, his hands heavier against her skin now, as though he could remould her, stretch out her bones and make her taller, pull her hair from darkest loam to sunshine, press her face into the contours of a dead woman. "Ah, I am not so much a fool that I talk to gods," he said. "I had enough of that with my mother and father, and their priestesses. But I know the value of a good man in a place of power, and the mouthpiece of a god."

"Be wary of Brother Milos," Lilika whispered, against her own sense of safety. "He has his own motives."

"Don't think I am unaware of that." Calvai gave a deep sigh and let her go, gently pushing her to stand so that he could slip her skirts and underskirts down her hips. "I know what adders look like. But for now, he is a useful snake."

And what am I, Lilika thought distantly. Does Calvai see me as another serpent coiled about his fist — a weapon that must be used with caution, then discarded? Does he mean to stamp my head into the dirt when he is done with me? But she said nothing of her disquiet, nor did she let it show on her face, or in the lines of body. "The witch girl," she said.

"Don't worry about her," Calvai spoke softly, his voice the

murmurings of leaves against the breast of the sky.

"Wait," Lilika pushed his hands gently down, holding them loosely in her own. "You must get Petrell closer to your side." If Calvai wanted a king's throne, then he needed border lords and dukes who would rally to him when he went to war against those who would rather die than see a king take the duchies again. "A grandchild."

"In good time. I can't rush a marriage without it looking unseemly. 'Til then, I trust you to watch her. You have your ladies, your little bird eyes. They will know if she needs reigning in."

"Already," Lilika said. "You should not have allowed her to go riding with Devan."

"Ah, no harm can come of it. She will not test her freedoms if she thinks she has them."

Lilika wondered how Calvai could say this so cleanly, and yet not see the same about his own daughter, flesh of his flesh, sun of his sun. It was true that blood clouded the vision. When it came to Silviana there was no logic in Calvai's mind. He had made of her a treasure and a goddess — something to be worshipped and kept safe. He did not see a daughter. She sighed and tilted his face so that she could lean down to kiss him, his beard feather soft against her chin, her cheeks. She closed her eyes and dreamed of a god with bright black horns.

Passing and Falling

The passing months settled into a routine for Marjeta. The feast days of Furis came and went, each with their own pageantry and celebrations and chants. Marjeta did not keep the days of The Three, though she gave them stolen food from Furis's feast tables and filled their trenchers with cakes and honey. She grew the last of her inches out in measured moments. She rode Dust alongside Devan and ignored the heads of murdered boys piked as warning on the outskirts of the castles, the cages with the starving men who spat at her as she passed beneath them. She ignored the growing armies in the far away fort at Verrin.

As for the girl herself, Marjeta treated Silviana kindly, played games, learned alongside her the dances and divisions of history, let her fondness grow vast and shallow.

It did not do to get attached. Playing the game meant getting involved, exposing her heart to a bed of pins. It was better to drift vacant through the hallways, so much a ghost that at times Marjeta settled her hand on the long thin head of Sasha, padding alongside her, and felt the heat of her fur, the smooth sleek dome of her skull.

"You dream too much," Areya said. They were setting out the bread and oil before the Three, though for Marjeta it was a meaningless observance. As meaningless as the hymns she would sing later in the palace temple. Furis, the Three — she cared for none of them.

"What would you have me do instead?" Marjeta asked. Her eighteenth birthday approached, and with it the knowledge that her time as a child was passing. She would be bride and not bride to be. "Weep?"

Areya sighed. "Hardly. I am not overly fond of wiping up puddles of useless tears. But come now, I expect more from you than this."

"Than what?"

"Than drifting through your days like a thing already dead."

"Am I not?"

Areya glanced sidelong, her brows heavy. "No. And it makes me sick to hear you prattle so. Do you think you are the only girl in all of the duchies who has been bundled off to marry a stranger? Do you think that none have come before you who have lost the ones they love?"

"Of course not." Marjeta snapped, an unexpected shiver of emotion thrumming through her like a bow string released. "Sorry, I do not mean to speak so," she added, softer, slower, her eyes again losing focus. She began gathering the workmen's shirts that the maidservants had pieced together. She and Silviana and Lilika and Areya and the other women of the court would sit at Silviana's pointed little feet and embroider the cuffs and collars with birds and leaves and hares, a thick thicket of stitch and snip. Her mother had done this every year. An act of charity and goodwill when the shirts were handed out to village men at the Feast of Last Apples as a thank you for their work on the harvest, and through the year.

Dimly, Marjeta had been aware that her mother did it for no reason other than politics. It sweetened the minds toward her. It had taken little convincing to instate the same here. Silviana had loved to be seen as generous, charitable, a fount of milky-sweet protection. She wanted the people she never saw to love her.

When Marjeta had put forward the Petrell tradition, Lilika, strangely, had not argued against it. Merely looked at Marjeta shrewdly and nodded that it was a fine task for bored noblewomen's hands.

Marjeta pressed the bundled shirts to her chest, and sighed. "What is it that you want me to do, Arrie? I have pretended at being a huntress and brought down death, I have pretended at witchery and it got me nothing, now I pretend at duty. So far, it has done me no harm."

"And when it does, will you discard this mask and exchange it for another? Will you wear disguise after disguise in an attempt to run from your future?"

"Is that what you think I do?"

Areya raised an eyebrow. "Answer that yourself. You've the brain for it, use it on yourself for a change."

"We will be late," Marjeta said. "And Silviana does not like to be kept waiting."

"How strange, when Silviana is not the duchess, and will never be," Areya retorted. "After your marriage, will you still bow and scrape to a little girl?"

The word marriage struck Marjeta between the eyes, a cold stunning blow. She lifted her hand to her forehead, expecting to feel blood hot and wet under her fingers. "What would you have me do?"

"You don't have to play the game to win, but like it or not, your piece is on the board. At least play to survive," Areya said. "You must begin to model your own court, slide in people you trust, or Lilika shall have the entirety of the board and you will be removed." She paused, and her features softened. A little more kindly, she said, "You do not need to use magic or swords to win this, Mari. You need your wits, and your mother gave you those in abundance."

"And you want me to become like Lilika, with her slyness and her whispers?"

Areya shook her head. "Not at all. Whoever it was who put it into your head that being clever means being slippery-sneak did you a disservice. Being clever means finding the things you love and holding them fast. It means building places for safety, finding friends you can trust, and knowing yourself in truth."

"Find something I love," Marjeta repeated dully. "I love ... riding, and music, and shooting a bow. I love the brightness of growing things, and the skree of kestrels, and walking slowly without direction or meaning. I love stories in the darkness, and the smell of lavender soap." She wondered at that last, how much it made her think of home and her mother, of the room where she and Val had grown up, their clothes laundered always with that lavender as a blessing. It was such a familiar smell that she'd paid it no attention then. Now, here, it was as faint and foreign as the past.

"You can still go riding," Areya said. "Give me these shirts, and I'll take them to Silviana with your apologies."

Marjeta did as she was told, her heart flickering, nervous and bright. "And I am just to ... go off?"

"No. Go find Devan, go hunt in the wild woods and breathe clean air." Areya took a deep breath. "This castle breeds ill-will like a disease, it takes in through the lungs and spreads through thoughts and whispers."

"Lilika will not like it."

"I will tell her you have taken with a spell of fatigue and cramps, that it is your time of the month and you are sour company."

"Thank you." Marjeta snorted, but she was already running away inside her head, far from the gilded rooms and the packs of waiting women, all nervously watching each other. "I feel bad," she said.

"About?"

"That you will have to sit there alone, enduring those snakes for my sake."

"Ah," Areya smiled. "It's not all bad, now that you've brought in your mother's habits. The musicians were a honeyed touch — it mutes the gossip and stills the rattling sabres."

It had been one of the few changes Marjeta had made along with the charity shirts and the extra dance lessons — the installation of a trio of musicians who played at their trade while the women stitched at their own. The move had emboldened even Silviana, who had requested art lessons from her father's portraitist, and though the needles still clicked and clacked, and the threads drew blessings through fabric, there was now not only the lament of Genivia's harp, but whistle and hum, the clinging oil of linseed, the buttery tones of paint. It had changed the atmosphere of the girl's chambers, had made them something that was not wholly Marjeta's, but neither was it Lilika's territory alone.

Marjeta smiled. It had happened so slow and soft that she only realised now how she had changed the landscape of the game board. "Love," she whispered as ran down passages, her leather booted feet thudding against the stone and startling servants. How strange to think she had plucked love and brought it into Silviana's rooms, jarred and watered it. How strange to realise she had not even noted the acts herself. It had taken sharp-eyed, sharp-tongued Areya to point it out to her.

Her strength came from her loves, and she would need such armour to face a loveless future.

*

The Old King's Wood was rich with wet humus under hoof, the earth smelling like life and death and eternity. The leaves fluttered high overhead, trunks seeming to spiral up to the curve of heaven, their trunks wreathed in ivy. Wood pigeons clattered in the branches, and wrens rustled through the smaller bushes that grew here and there where the sun found space. The open ground was crisscrossed with moss-painted trunks, and Marjeta nudged Dust toward them, letting the rhythm of hooves sound a sweet familiar refrain, then the breathless whistle of silence as her pony took the jump, muscles bunching beneath her thighs and seat.

Her hair ripped loose, wind scraping her cheeks and joy rose in her, filling up her lungs and pushing all the air out. It was like being free, being Marjeta Petrell, being part of Dust, two creatures joined to make something powerful and swift and purposeful. This was magic too, even if Val had never seen it.

"Slow down a little, peregrine. Not all of us can keep up," Devan said as he drew his own horse up alongside her, their mounts hammering the ground in time, the wide avenue between the walls of trees theirs alone. It was not usual or accepted for Marjeta and Devan to ride out without Genivia's silent watchful gaze, without Areya bright as blades alongside her, but startled as Devan might have been when Marjeta had cornered him in the stable yard, he had put up little argument.

One might even think he had wished for this — a moment alone with her, no doyenne to disapprove at every fluttered look.

You dream, Marjeta chided herself. Not when Devan called her peregrine the way he called Silviana starling. All he saw of the two girls were pseudo sisters, to be nicknamed and coddled. She reigned Dust in, slowing to an ambling trot. There was no point pushing — either Dust or her chances. Dust was far from a young animal these days, and though she spent most of her time in the semi feral herd that roamed the Old King's Wood and the pastures there, the pony wouldn't take well to being run hard.

It was late summer now, the brambles in the undergrowth thick with rough tangles of thorns and reddening berries. The world seemed limitless, heady with potential. There was no place in this gloriousness to weep, to wish for things that she was never going to have. The villages and palace were already making preparations for the Festival of the Horns. After the autumn equinox it would be Silvi's twelfth birthday celebrations, and after that... She could not escape her own birthday. Marjeta swallowed away bile. After that, she would prepare herself for marriage. It did not do to think about it. Marjeta shoved the black knowledge away and forced herself into the here and now. It was still summer, just. The air smelled green and sweet and rich.

"The usual spot," she called to Devan, and he nodded. They had long since settled into a routine. Under normal weekly circumstances she and Devan would have their chance to race, to gallop through a world that seemed to have been laid out just for them, followed by a more sedate picnic where Areya and Genivia would set themselves comfortably, food and wine would be shared, and finally when the ladies were engrossed in their crafts, their books, their chatter, Devan and Marjeta would go off a little way and set up their archery, fighting for who would have the closest grouping in the shortest amount of time.

On a good day, Marjeta would win. Devan's skill as a huntsman was excellent, but at this sport Marjeta excelled. There was no way she would be able to take him in any fight involving swords or knives or staves, that was true. She had none of his training or experience, but in this at least she knew her skill was solid, borne of years of practice.

Today there would be no picnicking. No observers. Just the hard flight of feathers and horses.

She smiled at the satisfying thud of an arrow biting deep into wood. The tree they used was broad-trunked, scarred from their months of using it as a target. Devan had used a knife to dig a series of circles to serve as targets and rubbed charcoal into the raw wood. It was crude but serviceable.

"You love this too much," Devan said. "Going to have to look at something else besides arrows and horses one day."

Marjeta smiled as she drew back until the string pressed against her nose and chin. She stilled, slowed her breathing, ready to release on the slow out breath, felt her weight settle into her stomach. She loosed, and the arrow sang. "Really?" She lowered her bow and glanced across at her opponent. "You're saying that to distract me, and it's not going to work. It never has."

Devan snorted. "You've seen through me," he said. "If I can't beat you fair, I have to resort to more underhanded tactics. My pride demands I win."

"Your pride demands you concentrate more and whine less," Marjeta said.

Devan had grown even taller in the last year, and while he was still skinny, his chest had filled, and his face seemed to have settled into a more-or-less pleasing configuration. His ears, which had seemed over large, were now suited to his long face, and what had started as a too girlish pout of lips had widened, though he'd kept the curved upper bow. It gave his mouth a sensual rakishness that contrasted with the intensity of his dark gaze.

I'm studying Devan's mouth. Marjeta fumbled the arrow she was nocking — like some demented chit who watched the stable boys at work and made an idiot of herself.

She'd known Devan since the day she'd arrived at the castle. He was not a confidante, she shared little of her secrets with him, but he was a friend. He was a friend who expected nothing more of her than someone to ride with at the end of the week and to shoot targets with in a sun-drenched wood. If he even thought that much of her. Marjeta gathered her arrows and put them carefully back into her hip quiver. It was more likely that Devan saw this as a duty. After all, he trained throughout the week. What fun could he possibly have escorting a gaggle of castle ladies to their silly little picnic. He went on hunts. He rode with the duke when they went on raids against the wild boys of the forest.

This was babysitting.

"What?" Devan frowned. "You're giving up?"

"Something like that."

"It's not like you to be moody," Devan said.

And not like her to run from duty and lie and be wild. Certainly, it had not been like her to do that in many months. Marjeta had fashioned herself into some semblance of a lady and it had finally stopped chafing. The ill fit of her life had worn her numb and complacent.

"Has something happened?"

"Something never happens," Marjeta said lightly. "I do the same things every week. You should know. You see me with Silviana after every one of your music lessons, you see me when we go to worship, and you see me once a week with a bow in my hands. Nothing ever changes."

"You're like a kennelled dog," Devan said. "Even with this." He moved one hand in a wide sweep to encompass the woods, the brambles and the birds. "You're let out for your run and then brought back in on a rope."

"Even dogs have packs," Marjeta said. It slipped out of her, unexpected and bitter. She had Areya, of course, but one servant with her own life hardly made a family.

"You have Silvi," Devan said, and then more uncertainly. "And me."

"You know nothing about me," Marjeta laughed once. "Do you know I keep a dragon?"

"What?"

"Not actually." Marjeta crooked her bow against the sawn off stump they used for unstringing their weapons, and pulled back on the upper limb. "I have a salamander in my fire place, though. They're distantly related to dragons." She folded the bowstring carefully and wrapped it in leather.

"You have a magical creature," Devan said slowly. "In your hearth?" He shook his head. "You truly are in a strange mood today, peregrine."

A sudden impulse tore through Marjeta. "When you see me," she said softly, "what is it you see? A little girl from some pitiful duchy; lonely, stupid? A little girl who pretends to be something she's not? Who rides and shoots but isn't allowed to hunt? A falcon with clipped wings?" Her voice rose. "You call me peregrine as though it's a joke, but all you do is remind me every time that I cannot fly." She snapped her mouth shut and flushed.

"No," Devan said. "I see ... I see you."

"An easy answer."

"Is it? It's a safe answer, anyway," he said. "The truth is I see Marjeta Petrell, who looks like a warrior maid from the stories my mother used to tell me." His whole face turned an alarming beet. "I should see nothing," he said, in a whisper almost too low to be heard. "And I tell myself over and over that I should see nothing."

Marjeta's throat felt swollen inside as though she'd bitten into a pear. Her eyes watered, her skin itched. "I think," she said breathlessly. "I think I'm ill. We should go back."

Devan nodded, his dark hair falling over his face. "Wouldn't want you taking ill," he said, and cleared his throat and made a show of glancing up at the high tree boughs. The sun had greyed, clouds passing over head, dimming the forest further. "It's going to rain soon," he added.

As if that were any deterrent to being outside. There was always rain in Jurie. At least in summer it passed in quick squalls or was little more than a soft drizzle that barely penetrated the latticework of forest boughs. And Marjeta always travelled with a thick woollen riding cloak rolled up until needed. The threat of rain was simply an excuse to remove themselves from this uncomfortable new territory.

"Yes." Heat rippling up from the soles of Marjeta's feet, crawling under skin, melting through the fine connections of bones, and muscles, sparking so hard in her chest that breathing became a struggle. It was immense, like no feeling she'd had before. Like being ill, yes, but not. Like drowning and falling and waking from a nightmare all at the same time. At any moment she would open her eyes under ice and see the grinning bear face of her dreams and nightmares staring down at her, teeth ivory yellow, black eyes older than the earth.

The words were impossible to squeeze out, her brain seemingly incapable of finding a thing to say that didn't sound idiotic, mundane, pointless. "We should," she managed, finally. As though needing an excuse, the sky had knitted the clouds darker. Even as she gathered her own light pack and went to where Dusk was tethered, the first deep, distant rumble sounded.

"And not too soon," said Devan. "I should have known a storm was coming. Your Dust has been edgy, she always is."

"Animals sense the changes in the air," Marjeta agreed, as though they were having a normal conversation, and that the strange interaction from moments ago had never happened. It was better that way, she thought. Because anything else would only be a travesty. A cruel and pointless endeavour. And dangerous.

The Duchess's Cloak

Evening had fallen blue and black and Marjeta was exhausted. She was looking forward to a good meal and a sound sleep, for her mind to fall to silence and be wiped clear of all thoughts of Devan, and what she'd felt in the woods. At the moment her suite seemed to be too full of people. Maid servants clearing away the detritus of the day, lighting fires in the grand hearths, setting warming pans in her bed, filling the table with an array of food. The sound of them was giving Marjeta a headache, and she breathed a sigh of relief when the last left, curtsying quickly as she closed the door.

Areya gave her a knowing look that made Marjeta feel like a glass blown wrong, cracking along the flaws. "How was Silviana, and did our dear Lilika accept my illness?" She smiled, tried to keep her tone light and gentle.

"They weren't overly concerned about your absence," Areya said.

"Oh?" Marjeta idly set the trencher with The Three's uneaten sacrifices down in front of the hearth, and Tarkis appeared a moment later, head thrust from the flames, grinning. "How strange."

"They had other things to occupy them." Areya was setting out the supper dishes that a servant had brought in, arranging food just so, and pouring wine for her mistress and herself. They had long since given up any pretence at formality between them when they were alone. "The Lady Silviana is unwell."

Marjeta's stomach lurched. Her mouth flooded with gall. Unwell was such a small word, and yet. She cleared her throat, swallowing away the strange bitter aftertaste. "She's caught some cold, no doubt." She took her place at the table, and Areya did the same. "Even the duke cannot cage her from every small sniffle."

At the hearth, Tarkis was scraping the empty trencher across the stones, as though he could find every last grain of food and drop of oil in the threads of space in the pattern of the wood. "Pig," Marjeta muttered, and tossed a thin cut of the roasted beef in his direction. "If only the world knew that magical beasts didn't live on starlight and ashes, but steal scraps and gorge themselves on leftovers, they'd think less of you then, you monster."

Tarkis growled in an ecstasy of joy and hauled his prize back to the fire and disappeared.

"It's no cold," Areya said. "She runs a fever. She sweats and paws at her eyes like a dog. I gave her a tonic of elder and mint, but the girl looks too pale."

A stone weight filled Marjeta's stomach. "She gets no sun." Marjeta stabbed at her vegetables. "And children have fevers. I had—" she coughed, dropped her fork. "I was fine."

Areya sighed, and changed the topic "And how was your time with Devan?"

A sudden flush caught Marjeta unaware, and she stumbled over her words. "I — It was f-fine. Cut short by the rain, of course. And I beat him at archery." She swallowed hard, not certain why she felt this sense of shame. She had done nothing. She might as well have had a chaperone watching over her, so proper was her behaviour. And his. They had done nothing, she reminded herself.

"Hmm." Areya leaned back on her chair, her gaze thoughtful. "Don't do anything foolish, my little hen."

"I am not — what do you mean?" She bent her head to her meal, only half aware of cutting her food into mouthfuls, of raising her fork and chewing on flesh and roots that tasted of ash and slime.

"Look at me."

Unwillingly, Marjeta raised her head and stared into Areya's pale, almond eyes. She focused. *We did nothing.*

"You're becoming more and more beautiful every day," Areya said, and Marjeta drew back, confused. "No, listen. You don't see it because you don't look like Valerija. I'm not a fool, and I can see the way your mind works. You think that beauty is in long dark hair and buttermilk skin, and raven eyes. And it is."

"This is ridiculous," Marjeta began.

"But you are like one of the forest ponies—"

Marjeta laughed. "Yes, I can see how ponies turn the heads of men."

"Hush and listen. You're powerful, and you're fast, and you have a wildness to you that some men will find attractive. Whether you see it or not, whether you like the idea or not."

"Well, I don't like it." Marjeta pushed her half-eaten meal away and picked up her wine instead. It washed away some of the prickling fear. "Why are you telling me this?"

"Because I'm not an idiot, and neither are you. Devan is one of those men, and he will look at you and see the wild thing and want to own it. Men always do. They might not understand themselves, but it doesn't change the story."

"I am not responsible for Sir Devan's thoughts," Marjeta said. "And I will be wed in less than a year."

"Oh please, as if that has ever stopped a man. Or any woman who wanted him. You must be careful that you don't make a cuckold of the duke before he is even married."

"I would do no such thing!" Where did Areya get the idea that Marjeta would run off and bed some stripling boy because he wanted to tame her. It made both of them sound like grunting fools. "You overstep your place."

"I do nothing of the sort," Areya said. "I am your friend. And I know what it is to fall in love. You will feel it move like a river in you. And I would be a fool and a useless companion if I did not know you would rather have a handsome boy still strong and new and full of promise, than a duke more than twenty years your senior, who has no interest in you as anything other than a broodmare."

"You shouldn't talk like this." The strange sickness was fading, and in its place was a black heaviness, a knowledge that what Areya said was true. Devan was handsome and young, and he paid her attention as though she were something more than just an unfortunate replacement for two dead women.

"What — tell you the truth? Someone has to, before you walk yourself straight into a trial and a pyre. The duke does not care for you, but that does not mean he will let another have you. And already that bitch Lilika whispers about your witchery and your tainted blood. It will only take a little misstep to lead you to The Penitent's Tower. Brother Milos would love to see you burn. I think it would be the only pleasure the man gets in life, the only women's screams he would want to hear."

Areya was right. Other than the occasional strained conversation during the times Marjeta was expected to attend the high table for meals, the duke had no more interest in her. After all, he had his daughter to fawn over, to hold up as some precious symbol of his great lost love, and he had Lilika to warm him at nights. She knew well enough that Calvai only wanted two things from her — a powerful link to the Eastern Border Forts, and a viable heir to the duchy throne. *Or perhaps*, the thought flickered small and uncatchable as a midge, *a throne far grander*. "It's not fair," Marjeta whispered, her fists clenched in her lap.

"It never is." Areya sighed deeply and refilled their wine glasses.

Marjeta barely remembered draining the first, but her head did feel heavy and slow. She sipped at her new drink, tasting pale apples and ice brown rivers and lies.

"We must talk carefully."

"What do you mean, carefully? What is there to talk about? You've opened my eyes. I'll not go near Devan. I'm not interested in whatever punishments Brother Milos digs out of his holy book." Even the Three — as much as they were on the side of women — had strict laws against women who cuckolded their husbands. Marjeta frowned at the realisation. All the punishments were for the women, as though no man ever committed a sin by lighting his wick in different oil. She glanced at the statues on their house altar, and down to the empty trencher Tarkis had abandoned before returning to the flames. "I'll stay far from him," she whispered. "I'll stop the weekly rides."

"Oh, girl," Areya said. "You're young, and the river will run deep and black, and you'll be caught in it, I promise."

"What's that supposed to mean?"

"It means that I can make sure that when you do go swim in that water, no one need know."

Marjeta blinked as she worked out Areya's meaning. "Spells to hide infidelity?"

Areya inclined her head in a slow nod. "And to stop a child forming."

Marjeta went scarlet. "I think you presume—"

"I presume nothing," Areya snapped. "I'm not that many years older than you, and I know just how strong desire can be." Of course she did. Areya went off at nights to meet with her own beau. A sudden surge of curiosity ran through Marjeta, followed sharply on its heels by confusion and guilt. She was not a barnyard cat, given to rutting simply because it was the season for it, she told herself. But at the same time, she thought of Devan, of how he had grown taller, how hunting and policing the wooded borders against the forest boys had made him strong, his muscles compact, his skin honey sweetened. The warmth spread through her again, catching in her pelvis like a candle flame.

"I can help you."

"Why would you?" Marjeta turned sharply, her brow creased. Areya might be the only friend who came from her own lands, her mother's last gift to a traded daughter, but she owed her no loyalty as deep and twisted as this.

"Because we Hanevas have always been the Petrell duchess's cloaks."

"The what?" The Hanevas family were a minor one, and not particularly noted for doing anything more than running farmlands, keeping the borders quiet, and having an excess of daughters. They were not lauded for witchery or social power or political intrigue. On the other hand, Areya had turned out to be a witch, and her mother had sent the woman to be her friend at court, to be her intimate and confidante. And her mother was many things, but careless and stupid were not any of them. "I'm afraid I don't quite understand," Marjeta said, her stare intent. "You'll have to explain this to me."

"Oh, I think you've worked it out right enough, whether you want to admit it to yourself or no," Areya said. "But if you need it spoken plain, I can do that for you." She crossed her hands in her lap and looked down for a moment, gathering her thoughts. A wisp of her dark-blonde hair fell loose as she thought, curving across her cheek and leaving an inky shadow that cut bloodlessly across her face. A corpse wound. "You know well enough that I'm a witch, and your mother sent me to you as protection. In my family, the name is passed down through the women, and the men marry into our lineage."

That was impossible. Surely Marjeta would have heard of something so unusual.

"There's a reason the Hanevas family has only a minor house on the borders. We are far from interesting, you see. We make sure of it. We were granted the right to descend the line back when all the houses were little more than clans fighting among themselves, and the king was just another word for a warchief whose house was bigger than all the others. Times changed, and the Great King united the warchiefs, that's true enough even if it reads like legend today. And the Great King fell, and the kingdom was ripped apart again. And now we have a host of minor dukes and barons."

"I don't need a history lesson," Marjeta said drily. "I need *your* history lesson. Tell me more about the Hanevas women and what they have to do with my family."

"You're a rude and forward little thing when you put your mind to it, which seems to be fair often," said Areya, impatience snapping in her voice. "But, yes, you've read these stories, I suppose. Our history isn't written. What's important is that for as long as I know, as long as our family can remember, there has always been a woman of the Hanevas in the service of the Duchess Petrell. My aunt Lisi is part of your mother's entourage, though I wonder if you remember her at all."

Marjeta had paid little attention to her mother's flock of chattering women. They'd all seemed much the same to her — a gaggle of women with their gossip and their pointed tongues, their laughter and their needles. It had been nothing that she'd wanted for herself, and she'd dismissed them out of hand. "I confess—"

"Of course you don't." Areya dismissed her excuse with a wave of her hand. "And you were never meant to. It's harder for me here, of course, since you go out of your way to not build a circle around you." She sighed. "When you do get it through your skull that there is power and safety for us in numbers, I have some names you might consider," she added in a pointed aside. "The duchesses need freedom, and it is our job to give it to them."

"How?" Marjeta pressed her fist against her belly as though to still a pit of vipers. She didn't need to ask Areya about freedom from what. A duchess had a duty. She was a wife, to be sure, but her marriage was a political one decided for her by a council of land holders, by maps and tokens and the need to strengthen this boundary or ensure this trade route provided better deals. It was a marriage in the same way a fortress was a house. So, the Hanevas gave the Petrell wives freedom from their marriages.

By magic? It was the most obvious answer, and it explained why Areya in particular had been sent. She was a witch, and she was secretive about it. Perhaps that was a requirement of all their women, that they practised their spells in shadows, that they kept a smiling pleasant face while their hands wove secrets. "You use your magic," Marjeta said, "to help the duchesses. When they have affairs," she stumbled over the word, "of the heart, you use magic to help them keep their secrets."

Areya tipped her wine glass, swirling the last dregs as though she could divine the future from the pale liquid before draining it and setting it down. "We do not take chances. We merely..." She frowned. "We grease the wheels that are already turning."

"What happens if you are caught?"

"We are never caught," Areya said. "My family has been doing this for hundreds of years. You have never heard of this contract before, even though you lived right in the centre of the nest. We are not fools."

"And every duchess—" she began.

Areya stood and took up a small loaf of honey-bread. "No." She walked the room, pacing the length of the rug. It seemed she needed to keep herself busy, tearing the loaf in small pieces and laying them out on the trencher in front of the three. "Not all duchesses need our assistance, though we are always in their service, whether they know of us or not." She dusted the last crumbs from her fingers. "It's not that all marriages are loveless. Even arrangements can turn into sweetness. So yes, there have been women of Petrell who have not wanted our help, and we have kept our tongues still and wished them well, woven charms to ensure happiness, embroidered peace and fertility into their nightgowns, with them always none the wiser." She took a deep breath and closed her eyes, staying silent for a few moments. When she opened them again, she looked nervous, just a little, as though she were confessing her crimes before a silent judge. "We are not here to cause suffering."

"I know that," Marjeta said softly. Her brain had been whirring as she listened, the clicking of tiny wheels, of the elegant points of clock hands, of the press of fingers against rosined horse hair, the swift sweep of sound. Memories of being in her mother's halls, and the sound of music filling the spaces between the women's laughter and talk. "There was a musician," she said slowly.

Areya blinked. "Yes. He was your mother's and my aunt did what she could to hide them. Your mother was careless though. There is only so much we can cover. Aunt Lisi has spoken to her. Not long after you left, the musician was sent away, exchanged with another duchy for a harpist." She returned to the table for the oil jar. "So here then. An offering, and a warning. I can help you with this, should you pursue it. I will always help, and I will offer no judgement. But you must do as I say. If I tell you to step off a dangerous path, do so. I am not limitless in my power to save you." She poured the oil over the bread and mouthed a quick soundless prayer.

"I see." Marjeta's hands were cold, almost throbbing with it, an icy pain as though she'd clung to handfuls of snow. She shivered, recognizing a spell take root, even if she had no idea what it was. Marjeta lurched to her feet, knocking her own wine glass to the floor, where the spilled wine soaked into the wool. She held her hands out before her as though they were horrifying appendages that did not belong to her. "What have you done?" she whispered. The cold was moving up her arms, numbing them. She felt the icy pain hit her elbows, crawl up to her shoulders. The more of her body it covered the faster it moved, until her skin was stinging with frost bitten pain.

"Hush," Areya said. "It will pass."

"What is it?"

"A binding of silence," Areya told her. "I will protect you, but I'd be a fool to not protect myself."

"You don't trust me?"

"It's not that." Areya stepped forward to take Marjeta's upper arms and hold them fast. It felt almost as though she was about to shake sense into her like a wayward puppy, but she did nothing of the sort. Instead, she leaned in closer, so her breath puffed against Marjeta's face. It smelled of ash and something licorice-sweet, as though she'd been chewing on fennel seeds. "I trust you as much as I trust my sisters and my mother. You're all I have of home here." She gripped tighter. "Yes," she said at Marjeta's expression. "You think I don't feel friendless here?"

"But — but you go out nights, and—"

"I have a stable hand who keeps me warm and makes me laugh and shares apples with me, because he thinks apples are the way to a girl's heart." This time she did give Marjeta a single shake for emphasis. "But friends? No. I have you. And as much as I like you, I miss those I've lost and left behind me. You can understand that."

Mari nodded. Of course she could. It wasn't just Val, and the dreams of how Val used to be; it was Mother and even Father, distant and bluff. It was Sir Tev and his wooden toe, it was Olaga who had nursed her and smelled of comfort and warm porridge and powders and lanolin. It was even the portraits along the hallways, those familiar faces with their repeated motifs — here a nose, there a look, a chin, a sweep of a brow. People that Marjeta had never met and yet had seen repeated in the features of those she loved and who loved her.

What was here for either of them? The loneliness was the slow death of a sapling uprooted and replanted in ill soil. "I can," she whispered. "But then what makes you think—"

"You'll be surprised at the secrets people tell when they have to." Areya released her tense grip on Marjeta's shoulders, and she stumbled back in relief. "You have an honesty that even being here around people like Milos," she spat the name, "hasn't scraped out of you." She tossed her head and stared past Marjeta, at some past remembrance. "We all start out with the best of intentions, little hen. But someone will come whose every deed and word are like a whetstone to your skin. They will grind the goodness out of you, smooth you into the shape they want. And I need to protect myself against that, even as I protect you against the talk and chatter of women and servants with nothing better to do."

It was better not to argue, Marjeta thought. "I understand." It didn't matter if she swore over and over that she would never betray Areya, her ladywitch needed peace of mind. And the spell would give it to her.

Marjeta knew plenty of ways to unknit a spell. This one was deep into her as a burr worked into a dog's tail, but like that burr, it could be prised free — though it would take time and care. Or cut free, but that was never a good way to get rid of a spell. It left marks on a soul.

But whether or not Areya had spells that could keep her safe, perhaps it would be best for all of them if she turned her head from temptation. It would be better to spend more time with Silviana for a while. Marjeta sometimes found it hard to think of her as a child. She had the world weariness of any prisoner. She went through her days with resigned determination. The games of skip and catch and hare and foxes played seldom now, given way instead to Silviana's latest hobby — acquired after Calvai had gifted her with a set of pigments imported from the east. While the girl had initially painted only the most primitive, childish blobs, her skill had grown rapidly with practice, and now she'd moved on to small religious images copied from Caneth's stacks.

Milos approved, just barely.

Marjeta glanced to her wall where a board painted in thin egg yolk glazes now hung. It was one of the few Silviana had painted that wasn't an image of Furis and his bull horns, or his black hole where his human heart had once been. This was a luminescent flower — a rose of the deepest yellow, painted from a study of a bunch Marjeta had brought in with her from the castle gardens. Each petal swept from a pale yellow — almost white — at the base and blushed golden toward the petal's edge. Marjeta had been impressed as she'd watched Silviana layer glaze after glaze to build up the deep jewel rich colours, the emeralds of the leaves and sepals. It had been like watching a spell being cast — Silviana's own version of witchcraft. A subtle and beautiful art.

And Silviana had given it to her as a birthday present. Not at the formal party held in Calvai's hall with visiting border lords, farmers and merchants and important people of the town. She'd been handed this gift on her birthday morning by a girl smiling with the sweet and unblemished joy of someone giving something they were proud of to someone they loved.

The memory of it made warmth rush through Marjeta. She'd spent too much time with Devan. What had started off as a once-a-week excursion was now happening twice a week. Time with Devan was eclipsing the moments she used to spend with Silviana.

And the girl could do nothing but look through her windows down to the small private gardens that had once been her mother's. And now she suffered from a fever. And Marjeta had made an excuse — pretended illness — and run off to enjoy freedoms that Silviana could never have.

She pushed away thoughts of Devan, and Areya's spells. "I'm going to visit with Silviana," Marjeta said, and turned away from the painting. "Where is the small box my mother sent, the one with the leaping hare carved on the lid? Perhaps I can cheer her a little the way Val cheered me."

The Three

"And what are you doing here?" Lilika blocked the entrance to Silviana's rooms. Exhaustion had cut deep lines into her forehead and around her eyes. She smelled sour, musty. Like the sick and the near dead. "You can't come in here, she's sick enough, and you will only make her worse."

"I was not ill," Marjeta said. "I lied so that I might spend some time with my pony Dust. She is old, and I was lonely for something of home."

The half-truth seemed to catch Lilika off guard, for she stepped back, her expression clouded and nervous. "Then come in. She's been asking for you, after all."

"Why did you not send me a message?" Marjeta brushed past her, catching the woman's awkward flush. "Never mind, I'm here now." She took a deep breath and held the small, carved chest closer to her breast, the satiny wood heavy and solid. It held memory. She stepped past Lilika into the grand reception room, and through to the girl's bed chamber.

Silviana lay in the centre of her vast bed. Blankets and comforters of silk and wool and embroidered linen were all bunched up around her. Even as a serving maid straightened a cover, Silviana thrashed, twisting them out of true again. "My lady," the woman said as she noticed Marjeta's entrance. "I had not—"

"It's all well," Marjeta said softly. "Is she awake?"

The maid shook her head, then nodded. "She sleeps and wakes — and makes no sense."

"A fever." Marjeta glanced at Areya, who had said as much to her earlier. "And she's been taking the tonic Areya made?"

The maid flushed. "Well, your Lady, we wasn't quite sure—"

Marjeta turned sharply with a fierce exhalation of frustration. "Can you make more?"

Areya nodded and left in a swirl of skirts and judgemental silence.

"While the Lady Areya makes up another fever tonic — which has nothing more exciting in it than elder and mint, and the smallest grating of white ginger — I will sit with Lady Silviana." She nodded to the doorway where Lilika was watching with hooded eyes. "I think some quiet would be best. Perhaps you have something you should be doing elsewhere." It was no question, and anger had made Marjeta fiery and calm and powerful. That the idiots hadn't even let the girl take a simple tonic for fever because they believed the Petrell homeland rotten with witchery. It was infuriating. "Lilika," she snapped, and the woman drew herself upright, blinking rapidly. "Go and find Lord Devan, and tell him that Lady Silviana requests him here, with his violin."

There was a momentary silence as Lilika considered Marjeta's command. Then she dipped her head a fraction and schooled any betraying emotion from her wan face. "What an excellent idea, Lady Marjeta. The music of her beloved cousin would soothe her greatly, I am sure."

"Before you go, what surgeon or sawbones has seen her?"

"None as yet, my lady. We thought the illness nothing more than seasonal ague."

"You will also bring the duke's doctor here. On my orders, if he asks. Lady Silviana suffers more than just a child's cold, and the duke would be most unhappy to hear of such negligence toward his most cherished daughter."

Lilika's face turned an alarming shade of puce, but she kept whatever she wished to spit at Marjeta inside, and merely turned on the ball of her foot, her skirts snapping in her haste to leave.

They were finally alone, and Marjeta paused, felt herself deflating a little. The rush of power had passed, leaving her feeling light headed.

Silvi twisted onto her back, moaning softly in childish pain.

There was sweat beaded on her brow, making her skin shine.

"Oh, lamb," Marjeta whispered and reached out to touch her fingers lightly against the girl's cheek. Normally she was pale as new fallen snow, but her illness had flushed her cheeks a deep red. The heat radiated off her, she was as hot as Tarkis risen fresh from the fire.

She'd been like this herself, once, as a young child. How close she had come to death that year. Sometimes she wondered if she hadn't died and if the dream bear had brought her back from those dark lands, that deep and cold water, and returned her to life. Marjeta opened up the chest and felt inside for the soft remains of the woollen charm-hare her own mother had tucked under her pillow so many years ago. The box kept childhood trinkets, and though this was not the one she had intended to give Silviana today, it would do just as well.

The charm had kept, hidden away in this warren of memories, though the place where Marjeta split the stitches was still open, and Marjeta carefully tucked back in the ancient, dried remains of peppercorns, rosemary, and juniper leaves. She drew a needle and thread from the pockets of her skirt and pricked her thumb hard enough for a large bead of bright blood to well up against the flesh like a fruiting mushroom. She ran her thumb along the thread, anointing it with her blood. Embroidery blood, Val had called it. Good enough, even if it didn't come from the heart or the moon. Quickly she stitched the old charm back together, and snapped the thread clean with her teeth.

"The hare," she said as she tucked it under Silviana's pillow, "has always been the sign of women's love. I suppose it's not something Milos would want you to know or allow Lilika to teach you. There is too much of the Three in hares. The meadow-dancer is love for mother and daughter, for sister and friend. The hare is the symbol of women."

Silviana did not answer, though her breathing stilled and she opened her black eyes. The two stared silently at each other, and a knowing passed through them that required no words or explanations. Finally, Silviana spoke, though her voice was rough and soft, and sounded as though each word pained her. "I thought you weren't going to come."

"I'm here now." Even though she'd not been aware that Silviana was this ill, it was still no excuse to have left the child alone, suffering. Silvi had Lilika, of course, but her version of comfort probably consisted of praying over her and calling on Furis. Marjeta brushed a strand of sweat plastered hair from Silviana's brow and the girl tried to focus enough to follow the movement of her hand, but her pupils were black and wide. A steady flow of tears pooled in the hollows of her eyes, as though some irritant kept her crying. "Do your eyes hurt?"

Silviana nodded once. "So hard to see."

This was strange. Marjeta remembered nothing similar from her own illness. She'd had fevers, yes, but the sickness had sat deep in her lungs, making every breath a saw edge, clamping her ribs in a crushing vice. Air had rattled in her chest, a bright pebble in a hollow jar. But Silviana wasn't drowning on dry land, trapped under ice only she could see.

Carefully, Marjeta drew back the thin coverlet the last maid had pulled over Silviana's shoulders. The girl's night dress was already soaked grey with sweat, and Marjeta eased the girl's hands toward her. First one and then the other, uncurling the fingers and checking the damp wrists for any wounds. Nothing. Her pulse fluttered in pale blue lines and her skin was almost translucent, but there were no marks on her arms. "Has anything bitten you?"

"Bitten?" The word came out in croaks.

"Yes. An animal — a rat or some creature..." Marjeta looked around the room. No beast ever came into Silviana's cage. No tomcat or hound, no whistling bird for company. "Even perhaps some insect or spider?"

"No."

That was how Val had died. Turned and twisted by Sasha's infected bite. A sour rush pushed into Marjeta's throat and she swallowed it down. Whatever Silviana suffered — it was neither illness that had struck the Petrell sisters.

There was no need to fear death just yet.

The door to the bedchamber opened, and Marjeta glanced back to see Areya standing there with a tray bearing post and a cup.

The smell of bright, sharp mint overpowered the other scents, but Marjeta could pick up the sweet elder, the fiery hint of ginger and pepper, and honey to make the tonic palatable. She motioned Areya closer.

"Can you sit up, pet?" Marjeta cooed, and gently helped Silvi into a sitting position, her back resting against a mound of cushions. The girl was wan and sweaty, her black hair loose around her shoulders like a burned-out, fallen star. Even the slight movement made her shiver as though her bones were reeds in a spring storm. "Areya has made you a tonic for the fever. I will hold the cup for you."

She was slow, deliberate in her movements. Silviana's eyes were still unfocused, and Marjeta swore that they were hazed with a strange nocturnal blue. Marjeta blinked, but the haze was visible only at certain angles, for a moment. It was a trick of the light.

The girl drank in tiny sips, and by the time she had finished the cup, Lilika had returned, crow-watchful as though Silviana were almost a corpse and at any moment Lilika could tear her belly open and spread her entrails across the silken bed. She scowled at the tray of herbal pots but made no comment about them.

"Your cousin Lord Devan will be here soon," Lilika said to her charge. "He had heard you were ill but had no idea whether it would be safe to see you. I told him that his presence would make you feel far better, that his music would soothe you."

"You are so kind, Lee," Silviana said. Her voice sounded a little clearer, and some of the high colour. had faded a little from her hot cheeks.

"And I've sent for your father's personal doctor. He will bring medicines suitable for a duke's daughter. Hedgerow magics are for peasants." Lilika smiled thinly. "And I will read to you from the Book of Troubles Past—"

"Please don't," Silviana said weakly, and laughed once. "Just for today, I would prefer cheer."

Marjeta flicked a sidelong glance at Lilika, then drew her box back onto her lap. "Do you like puppetry?"

Silviana cocked her head, curious.

"My sister made these for me when I was too ill to leave my bed,"

Marjeta continued as she drew out the three little harlequin hares, patchwork puppets made from scraps. *Oddment, Threadment*, and *Endment*. "I was young too, and bored. And my sister sat at the foot of my bed and kept me company, playing out whole stories to me where these little knaves went on adventures through the duchies of my blankets and coverlets." She smiled distantly as she slipped one onto her finger and made the little hare knight bow and skip and twitch.

Silviana leaned forward to get a better look, then shook her head. "Can't see them."

Marjeta slipped the hare free and placed all three in Silviana's cupped palms. "You will see them properly soon, but until then, you can enjoy how they feel. Their ears are velvet inside — a crushed rose, and each of them has a head of linen dyed grey or white or brown. They wear cloaks and raiment of silks from the eastern lands. Scraps of turquoise, crimson, saffron and emerald, and their eyes are ebony buttons. Their paws are black leather snipped into tiny fingers, and their tails are made from felted wool from my father's flocks, wool my sister plucked from teasel and wooden fence."

"I can feel them all," Silviana said, as she ran her fingers along the empty little hares.

"They fought terrible battles," Marjeta told her. "Valerija gave them embroidery needle swords, and great courage."

"And what did you give them?"

"Nothing," Marjeta said. "But I give them to you. They brought me joy when I lay sickly, and I wish only the same for you."

Silviana tightened her grip on the hares, then released it as suddenly, and pushed them back. "I'm tired," she said. "I have no need for children's toys."

Spellwork

Eventually the meddling witch girl left to go to her own rooms and routines, and Lilika breathed out a fierce rush of anger that had been tamped down for far too long. Lord Devan had arrived earlier, and he played soft lilting tunes, mournful sweet sounds that filled the rooms with wraiths and echoes.

The duke's own doctor had also come, and been most alarmed by Silviana's fever, her half blindness and the weakness that sapped the strength from her limbs. He'd tutted and cursed the slatterns who tended the good duke's daughter, though he'd allowed the fever-drink that the witchgirl's servant had made was likely to do little harm. Even though he'd sniffed it and dismissed it as nothing more than a midwife's concoction, he'd agreed with Marjeta that he would not stop the Lady Silviana from consuming the tonic. "The warmth of it will do her some good, if nothing else," he'd said. "And fluids while ill are necessary. If she won't take weak wine, then this ... potion ... will suffice in its place."

But the doctor was gone, and now only the Lord Devan still remained at Silviana's bedside. Not long after he'd arrived, Marjeta had excused herself, muttering some nonsense about how too many people in the room would only make young Silviana feel worse. At least Lilika hadn't had to make a scene and force the girl to go. She wasn't exactly sure who would have won a battle. Only a month ago, Lilika had known these rooms to be her own kingdom, but something had shifted, the land had changed, and she hadn't even noticed.

Lilika drew her velvet cloak around her shoulders and snapped at a serving maid who was clearing away the pots and glasses brought in for Silviana and her guests. Most of the food had remained untouched: no one had wanted to eat while Silviana barely pecked at her meal like a dying bird. "Leave those. Tend to the fire first, girl. Your mistress must sweat out her fever if she is to gain her health. You may clear the tables once the fires are high."

Devan paused at his playing and he lowered his bow, looking down the length of his fiddle to Lilika. "You are tired, nanny."

Irritated by the name, but aware that she could never show it to the man who was one day to marry her charge, and if Calvai's plans went well, wear the crown of a new kingdom, Lilika lowered her head. "I apologize for speaking so roughly in your and the lady's presence," she said, her voice carefully modulated. "I have a great many things on my mind, and all of them ill. I have fears that worry at my thoughts like dogs at an ewe."

Devan looked over to where Silviana lay sleeping. The worst of the fever flush had sunk from her skin. Still, she shivered and sweated in turns, though not as fearsomely as she had done in the hours before. Her eyelids fluttered, and she made a soft sound, recognition or fright, that passed into murmured dreamspeech. He set his bow and fiddle into their velvet-lined case, careful with the instrument as though it were a sleeping baby, and the slightest bump could wake it to screaming. "We are all worried," he said. "Talk, perhaps there is something I can do to allay your fears."

He spoke to her like a lord to a simpleton, Lilika thought. As though he were not a stripling boy who had barely learned to shave in the last few years. She remembered the boy he'd been when he'd arrived from his father's duchy — gangly legged, knees like swollen galls, and ears too big for his bony face. He'd been a stumbling, foolish creature, but Calvai had shaped him. The colt was now a hunter's stallion, and perhaps, one day, would be a war horse. He was graceful and strong, and kind enough that Lilika almost did not hate that he would marry Silviana.

He would be a good ruler once she'd made him understand that he was merely the crown on Silviana's head, and that it would be her words he spoke, her commands he gave.

That Silviana would say and do what Lilika whispered was her own affair. Furis would guide them both, and Furis wanted the duchies.

She bowed her head. "I think someone has done this to Silviana," she whispered. "But if I speak, Lord Devan, I fear that I would turn you against me."

"Against you? No. Silviana trusts you — you are like her own mother. If you know of someone that would harm her, I would have you tell me, whatever consequences you fear."

Of course he would. Lilika plucked at the folds of her skirt and took a deep breath before making the protective sign of the horns over her lap, and in the direction of her beloved charge. All she did was for Silviana's sake, and the girl would understand that, but not now. Furis would show her as he'd shown Lilika.

It was always easiest to speak the truth, Lilika knew. Webs of lies were too easy to trap yourself in. "I fear," she said, and lowered her voice. "I fear that this illness of Silviana's has no natural cause."

Devan drew back, frowning, then leaned in again. "What do you mean — speak plain, nanny."

Nanny. The impudent little upstart. Hunt a few rogue boys down in a forest, and suddenly the child thought he was truly a man. She cleared her throat. "There has been no one near her with any illness, and Brother Milos would never allow anyone past his threshold were they showing signs of disease. My lady's rooms are kept clean of fleas and lice — we use fleabane, and we sweep and wash daily." Indeed, Silviana's rooms were almost startling in their cleanliness — floors scrubbed with lye water, the air sweetened with herbs. Even her bedding was boiled and beaten as often as possible. "And there are no animals that can come to these rooms — no chance of some plague spreading on teeth and claw."

"So, what brought this illness on, do you believe?"

"Witchcraft," Lilika hissed. "Spellwork. A curse."

Devan's eyes narrowed, his thick dark brows drawn together. "In my uncle's duchy?" The words were drawn out slow, fighting disbelief. "That is unlikely. His is not a law that looks kindly on witches."

"Then perhaps that is why witches do not look kindly on the duke's law. Nor on his blood and issue," Lilika said. "Your uncle

— you must know — he is an ambitious man, and men with great visions draw to them enemies like a lodestone will draw iron filings. There are those who know the duke's weakness is his daughter, the treasure he can never replace."

"What are you saying — that my uncle has enemies within his walls?"

"Within and without." She shrugged. "Don't all great men?"

"He is a good leader, his men follow him — trust him. They would die for him and they have done."

"As you say," said Lilika, and began to busy herself with small tasks — folding clothes, straightening the sleeping Silviana's bed covers. "His men."

Devan watched her in silence, his eyes narrowed.

Lilika pulled Silviana's pillow neater, and as she did so something rough and brown was dislodged from under it. She stepped back, at first thinking it was some large spider that had crawled up the high walls and decided Silviana's rooms were a safe dry haven in which to make itself a new home. The thing didn't move, and Lilika cautiously leaned forward to pluck it between forefinger and thumb, as though it were a dead mouse.

"What is that?"

Lilika squinted at the dead thing, then down at Silviana's face, calm and slack in deep sleep, her fever seemingly passed. "It is a curse," she said, as she fought to keep the delight from her voice. Furis truly shone down on her like a sun. He had known, he had guided the witch-girl so that she would work her spells in Lilika's favour. "An ill wish."

"It cannot be." Devan stood, and moved round to take the thing from her unresisting hand. "Ah — it's nothing more than a rabbit. A toy." He squeezed it, and inside the little woollen creature dried herbs were crushed, their smell faint, but still pungent.

"A toy filled with herbs," Lilika said mockingly. "And not with down or wool? Unlikely."

"So?" Devan tossed the scrap back to her and Lilika caught it in her palms, cradling it there as though it were some small beast that she had trapped. "The cooks use herbs when they make soup, or roast pigs and cattle. Are you telling me that they're all witches too?"

Lilika stroked the hare, fingernails scraping at the threads binding its belly closed. "There is blood on this," She held it up to her face and sniffed deeply. "New blood." When she looked up at Devan one corner of her mouth was crooked in a snarling smile. "Blood and herbs, and a hidden witch-charm under a sickbed pillow, and still you want to pretend. No." She shook her head. "Your uncle's men all trust and love him, but this enemy is not a man."

"It's nothing but a luck token," Devan said, and he gathered his fiddle case. "She's sleeping now, and she looks better for it. Perhaps this was not what made her ill but what healed her."

"Perhaps," Lilika said. "And perhaps it wasn't. We should be vigilant," she told him. "You can hunt all the wild men of the forest, fight armies alongside your good uncle, but Silviana needs a knight protector closer to her side."

"And you think it should be me?"

"Are you not supposed to be her husband one day?"

Devan looked somewhat stunned, as though it was a notion he had looked at only sidelong and in darkness, had never truly considered to be a fact. "She is still a child."

"And all the more in need of protection then." Lilika took the hare and tossed it into the massive fire where it crackled into flame with a smell of burning hair, sending spirals of choking smoke up the flue. "I will do what I can, but I am only one woman. If the lady Silviana has enemies who can cast spells, we will need to work together to keep her safe."

"So we shall," Devan agreed. "We will speak of this to no one else."

"Naturally." She dipped her head in a show of servility. "You have my word, Lord Devan. And I love the lady Silviana as if she were my own child. I will do anything to ensure her future on the Jurie throne."

*

She was alone again. Just the flames and shadows, the faintest silken rasp of sleeping breath. Lilika brushed one hand down Silvi's cheek. Definitely cooler than she'd been earlier — the worst had come and gone.

With her chest tight, Lilika folded her hands in her lap and bowed her head. She pushed her mind into that place in her imagination that resembled Calvai's new built temple — the place where she had first spoken to Furis. It felt real; hard ground underfoot, the faint smell of mushrooms and smoke from outside, the eerie whistle of the autumn winds in the arched rafters. And there on the wall, the man-god himself, his bloody chest and missing heart, his sweeping horns.

"I did as you told me," she said, but came no closer to the painted figure.

The mural shimmered, shifted, and Furis stepped from one dimension to another, growing form and solidity. He walked up to her, the faint sound of dripping blood following his soft footfalls. The temple room filled with a barnyard smell. A comforting sweet and rich smell. It spoke of industry and wealth. Of humanity. Furis was a god for men who had put down hard stone roots and knew their place. Not like the Three who seemed to care more for field and forest, who thought a mouse as important as man, a hart worthy as a hunter.

His voice was rough and deep, a voice of the good-tilled earth, a black voice, a loamy voice. Rich and ripe as harvest wheat. "You have done well, daughter."

Despite her unease, Lilika felt herself breathe a little easier, a coil of guilt loosening its knotted grip on her ribs. It emboldened her. "She will not be hurt?"

"Of course not. But together you and I mould a queen who will wear my cloak and crown, and she will be the first of her name. No king comes to his rule without sacrifice, and it is the same for my daughter Silviana. She will not be unrewarded."

"Ah, I worried," Lilika confessed. "I have never wanted to harm her."

"It is a little sacrifice. Nothing she cannot bear. The Queen Silviana must bow to the wisdom of her advisers. She must trust only you, and this is how it will happen."

Lilika kept her head bowed, not speaking. A small part of her remained unconvinced, but to say that now after her god had spoken to her in his true form, had commanded her not to worry, to believe and trust him, well, it seemed worse than foolish. And Lilika had no small amount of practice in biting her tongue. She risked a glance up from under her lashes to the great black and gleaming head of the bull, its eyes glassy-glossy, the horns vast and sharp as spear tips.

It was as though Furis sensed her last dregs of distress, and his human hand settled on her shoulder, slid down and caught her hand in his. Slackly, Lilika allowed the god to move her like a child's poppet.

He raised her hand to the gaping hole in his chest, pushing it inside the empty space. Hot blood slicked her to the wrist. She could feel the bellow and heave of his lungs, the splintered edges of bone, the slippery wetness of moving flesh. But more than that, she felt peace.

The last of Lilika's worries drifted to the floor. She was a bride at her nuptials, her gown falling from her shoulders. There was no fear, no pain, only the tremor of want. A need that filled her every hollow space, that ran between the lines of her veins, that took the shape of her lungs, her womb, followed the threads of sinews and sparked down her hair and from her eyelashes.

When she opened her eyes, Furis was gone. Lilika sat alongside Silviana's bed, her hands clean, her heart peaceful.

With a soft murmur, she drew a small glass tube on a leather cord free from her dress and anointed her fingertips with the fluid inside. Still singing her hymn to Furis, she brushed her fingers across Silviana's eyelids, and set the last spell in place.

Furis would forgive her this little bit of witchcraft because it was what he wanted. He was a god who could turn all things to his own use, and Lilika knew that very soon she would finally be absolved. She might have been responsible for the death of Belind, but she would make her daughter a true queen and their debt would be settled. Furis would keep his word. She would be made pure again.

The Way Back From Death

Silviana was lost. She spun this way and that, and on every side of her trees grew tall and black, as close together as stacked firewood furred with lichen and thick with vines, filled with ghosts and scuttling things.

"Hallo?" she cried.

It was night. Moonless and cold. And she wore nothing but a sleep gown that buttoned too tight at the throat and was so long she kept tripping over the hem. It was sweat stained, ripped in places, smeared with mulch and streaks of mud and moss. Her feet were numb and filthy, and her teeth clattered against each other.

No one answered Silviana's cry. She had no idea how she had got here. One minute she'd been fast asleep in her own bed, fire warmed and silk wrapped, and the next she'd woke to this strangeness. This inconceivable strangeness. She was outside the castle. Outside the arms and corridors of her father's palace and in some nightmare place. It was too wild, too dark, too cold. "Is anyone here?" Her voice was thin, weak, and was lost in the slender branches.

A night bird called high and eager back to her, and Silviana cried, wrapping her arms around herself for protection.

A shriek sounded in the distance — a woman's desperate cry for help – and Silviana's heart stuttered. The cry came again, and she let herself breathe. "It's nothing but a vixen," she told herself. "Even from your room you've heard such before."

There was nothing here to scare her. No wolves hunted in her father's lands, and the wild boys of the forest had been quiet now for months. Her father's men had hunted them down, sent them running and hiding. Wherever she was now, however she had gotten here, it had to be close to the castle still. "Calm yourself," she said. "You behave like a child."

To her right, the leaves in the dark mass of undergrowth rustled, and Silviana slowly turned to face the sound.

A long face stared back at her, topped with two long, black-tipped ears. The nose twitched, and the entire animal vibrated in an ecstasy of fear. It was nothing more than a hare. Silviana had one that was a life-like puppet, and she had seen enough dead ones. She'd seen them partitioned, stripped of fur, jugged, chewed down to the gristled bones. "You cannot scare me," she whispered.

The hare stood up, stretching its body higher, front paws tucked against its chest. It cocked its head, then turned and loped off.

Silviana stepped after it without thinking.

The hare paused again. And looked back at her patiently. It stood on a narrow track that wound between the sentinel trees. A safe passage between the slender thorny arms of the brambles that still clung to the last of their leaves. What else was there to do, Silviana thought. She could stand alone screaming for rescuers that never came, or she could follow the hare's path. At the very least, it might lead her to an open space where she could get better bearings. The trees here loomed too high and too close, as though they were watchers and spies who waited to see what she would do, and if she were to make a wrong move, bury her. Silviana hitched her night shift higher and pattered after the hare. Its tail flashed like a guide light ahead of her, and the girl lost herself in the mesmer of that white flicker, following it for hours or minutes, she couldn't tell.

She stepped out into a small clearing and the hare turned to smoke. It was a foetid smell, like burning blankets. Silviana blinked her searing eyes, and the smoke grew thicker, darker, rounded in on itself and took form. It grew bigger, thicker, formed a snout as heavy as a fighting dog's, four great lumbering legs tipped with long claws.

Come, said the smoke bear. It turned its haunches to her and lumbered away.

I'm dreaming, Silviana thought. She had to be. The knowledge that she walked ghostwise through a dream-forest and that she was actually under blankets safely in bed made her calm. She would follow the bear. After all — it could not harm her. If it turned on her, she would simply wake.

Now that the dream was revealed, the world melted, bending to the rules of its own. The trees shifted as the bear walked, making a space for it to pass through the forest, and for Silviana to follow.

"Who are you?" Silviana asked the bear.

Urshke, it said. The smoke was trailing from its back in silver-black ribbons, and it grew more solid with each step. *Sky and Sea and Earth.*

"I've never heard of you."

No? The bear laughed, a huffing growling noise that did not frighten Silviana. *I have not heard of you either. Nor does it matter. I am the One Who Shows the Way.*

"The way where?" Silviana walked closer to it and rested her hand on the thick fur. The bear glowed softly with an inner light, and its fur was dark golden brown, richer than honey. The fur smelled musky, and heat flowed up from the softness under Silviana's fingers, pushing away the cold that had numbed her skin and set her teeth rattling. She relaxed. Her eyes itched, she noticed. She had been too cold and scared to notice it before. She rubbed at them, but the itching only grew worse, and tears rolled uncontrollably down her cheeks. "Bear? Where are we going?"

Back, it said. *Always back.*

The bear Urshke would answer no more questions, and Silviana eventually gave up, following it instead through the dream forest, her eyes weeping silver. She stumbled on until Urshke halted, and when she looked up, she found that they were in a little meadow secreted between the trees. The grass was starred with flowers out of season — yellow crocuses like fallen suns, and the last bowed and beaded heads of snowdrops. In the shadow of a stand of gnarled trees was a wood and stone cottage. It looked like it had grown out from the earth rather than been built, its walls whorled and pitted, its roof thatched in branches and reeds and skins and mud.

"Where am I?" she asked.

The bear stood so that it towered over Silviana. *Home*, it said, and bent its head to lick at her left eye.

*

Silviana woke to a haze of grey and black. She was wearing a sweat drenched night shift, and her blankets were twisted around her legs. In the giant hearth the last of a fire crackled softly to itself, coals glowing red and welcome. Lilika, darling, familiar Lilika, lay slumped in a chair alongside the bed with her head pillowed on her arms.

Silviana blinked in the darkness, but her vision stayed gummy and incomplete, and to her left was nothing at all. Just a hollow, hungry blackness. "Lilika!"

Her nursemaid and oldest servant snapped awake, and with a look of panicked relief, swept Silviana in her arms, pulling her tightly against her bird like chest. "Oh, my sweet one," Lilika said. "You are well, you are well. All praise be to Furis. He has healed you."

Out of the corner of her left eye, Silviana saw a shape flitter. It grew in the blackness, and Urshke bared her teeth, before she disappeared.

"We will find who did this to you," Lilika whispered. "And they will pay for it."

Trial by Fire

Silviana's illness and long, slow recovery had demanded the palace's attention, and while all the servants and knights and ladies had been engaged, Marjeta's eighteenth birthday had slipped past, unnoticed. Marjeta had spoken of it to no one, though Areya had offered her a small gift of a riding hood that she had been working on in secret — russet and gold and rich with autumn magic. But she had also understood why Marjeta had not spoken up, or reminded the world that she existed, and the gift was handed to her in secret, and no mention made of it. The way her birthday had been forgotten gave Marjeta a twisted hope that, somehow, she would get a reprieve from the sentence that hung over her. She did not speak it aloud, as though putting her hopes into words would break the spell.

Weeks had passed since Silviana's sudden illness, and though the girl had come through her fevers and was well again, the unknown disease had left its mark. Silviana was paler than ever. She was still black haired, but she was already sporting threads of silver. She would be grey by her second decad, Marjeta guessed. The illness had sucked the marrow from Silviana's bones and the colour from her body.

Her hair was not the only thing changed. Whatever illness had infected her eyes, only the right one had survived it. The left had turned a milky pearl, the iris lost under a clouded sea. Silviana could see nothing out of it but darkness.

And shades, the girl had insisted at first. But Marjeta and Lilika both dismissed these as the nightmares brought on by her semi-blindness. Much as Marjeta hated that she agreed on anything with her smiling enemy, she was certain that the drifting shapes Silviana claimed she could sometimes see out of her left eye were no more than the brain compensating for the darkness — trying to form memories of vision. At least, she hoped that was all.

"Why do you not believe me?" Silviana said. They were in her rooms, playing a quiet game of Seven-Hand. Silviana sat with her left side turned to the wall, her chair scooted into the corner. She had been like this since she'd risen from her sickbed — always protecting her vulnerable side. "If I say I see ghosts, then why not agree that I do — why tell me that it is some nonsense vapour my mind has made up?"

"Would you rather it be ghosts?" Marjeta asked drily and sifted through the fan of cards in her hand. It was a paltry mismatch of suits, hardly worth fighting with. She pulled her fur-trimmed cloak tighter around her arms; even with the fires roaring, the chill of winter slithered through the stone, digging deep into bones and meat. "Even if it were, I would say to pretend otherwise."

"Why?" Silviana's face was marred with scowling, and she was so pale now that Marjeta had to wonder if the maiden of bloodied snow and crow black war had turned to salt and ice instead. If Marjeta could lean forward and flick at Silviana's arm, the girl would crack and crumble, leaving no sign that flesh and blood had sat opposite.

"Why — because—" Marjeta shuffled her cards uselessly and took the moment to glance surreptitiously about. Lilika was on the far side of the room, her three ivory needles clacking as she knit new winter stockings for Silviana. She chattered with several other women of Silviana's court — Genivia and Areya among them. Between them and the sound of the small group of musicians that Marjeta requested play to soothe the company, they would surely drown out any overheard word. "Because you do not want the likes of Brother Milos thinking you are a witch."

Silviana folded her fan of cards and looked intently at Marjeta with her one dark eye. As the girl grew older, she had begun to look more like herself and less like a cheap copy of Valerija, and the mismatched eyes and greying hair only accentuated the difference.

It also made her look even more like a witch than Valerija had, an amusing twist, if one was amused by the prospect of a painful death. "Do witches see spirits then?"

"Some of them. There are those who can raise the dead and talk to them." With a sigh, Marjeta picked the best hand she could out of her sorry collection and set down three twos. "I fear I will lose this round."

"Of course you will. What's the point? What does one say to the dead? I would have more exciting conversations with Grandmama, and she is only nearly dead."

Marjeta shuddered at this mention of the old woman who had cursed her. "Ah, well, you can ask them questions about the past, or the future. They don't exist in the same time we do, shades can walk forward and back. They can see your enemies, or your friends. Kings in the past would ask the dead for counsel before going to war."

Silviana put down a fourth two to complete Marjeta's set, then followed it with a court spread. The Duke, Duchess, Knight and Priest stared blankly up. "So perhaps I can see my enemies, likewise."

"If this was a war, I see I am surely defeated. I claim the first privilege." Marjeta took three new cards from the waiting deck. "Perhaps you can," she said softly. "But, pet, I would not speak of it. And certainly not where those who love Furis can hear."

"And what of you?"

Marjeta met the girl's burning gaze, that single black eye. "What of me?"

"Do you not love Furis?"

Marjeta looked at her three new cards. All as useless as the ones she held already. She folded the hand and placed the discarded sets on the little card table between them. "I think Furis does not care if I love him or no, and I think I have lost this game. I humbly declare myself defeated before your superior wit and hand."

Silviana blinked, slow as a contemplative cat. "That is no—"

Whatever she had been about to accuse Marjeta of, the words were drowned out in the sudden thunder of mailed fists on wood, and the loud bark of a commanding knight who slammed into the suite without giving the women a moment of decency. Brother Milos shadowed him, the horn symbol of Furis painted in black across his brow for protection. An icy wind from the passage followed them in, nipping at the women, and making the flames spit and gutter.

Marjeta recognized the first man as Sir Provas, Calvai's personal knight, and the retinue with him as being other men close to the duke. She stood, as did all the other women in the room except for Silviana, who sat like a tiny deity in her delicate chair, her face a cold mask. The women curtsied, and Marjeta saw Lilika smile once as she dipped her head. It was a smile that flitted away like a goldcrest diving into gorse.

"What is this?" Silviana drawled from her seat. "Why do my father's men intrude so raucously in my rooms?"

Sir Provas cleared his throat and bowed, his court armour making him stiff and out of place inside the games rooms and parlours. "Your pardon, good my lady. It is your father who bids us come here and unsettle your peace with our presence."

Marjeta rolled her eyes. Sir Provas loved the sound of his own voice and fancied himself a poet; a lover and noble warrior combined.

"I am suitably unsettled," Silviana said.

"A witness has come to your father, accusing one of your trusted women of cursing you." He held up his hand before Silviana could interrupt. "Your father's doctor and priest both agree that your illness came from no natural causes. It was an ill-wish as made by witches that almost killed you and cost you your eye."

"This is not an amusing jest, Sir Provas."

"No jest. An ill-wish was seen in your bed, and several women — servant and ladies alike — have heard the accused hint at her own powers, or converse with foreign idols when she believes herself alone."

Marjeta stayed still, her breathing gone shallow. All around her the room dilated and constricted. Perhaps it was no oversight that the castle had seemingly forgotten that she was now of age to be married.

"This cannot be. Someone accuses one of my own women of

trying to harm me, and of using witchcraft to do it. This is cruel. Lies and untruths spread by some jealous spider. Who do they accuse, and what wretch makes the accusation?"

Marjeta swallowed around the sickness in her throat and stepped forward, her knees shaking beneath her gowns. So, Brother Milos and Lilika had played their hand — played it before she had even thought to check her own. She'd believed she had time still. That they would see their duke wed and a suitable heir incubated in her before they disposed of the unwanted womb. It seemed she was wrong. Her skin was ice, her hearing drifted, her thoughts blackened.

"Lilika Satvika." Sir Provas nodded toward her, and the woman dipped in a low curtsey in return. "She accuses the Lady Areya Havenas of the Duchy of Petrell, of being a foreign witch who has used her arts in ways most evil, to work towards the death of the Duke of Jurie's only daughter, in order to undermine the bond between the courts of Jurie and Petrell. She is a witch, and a traitor."

*

It was a nightmare. It was being drowned, being dead, being trapped under lake ice. But this time there was no bear come to break the barrier and lead her back home again. Marjeta stood in stunned and broken silence as the men led her dearest friend away between them. They had not even time to exchange a word.

I will save you, Marjeta promised, and clenched her fists in the folds of her skirts.

"Did you know this?" Silviana asked her coolly, when the men had left.

Marjeta shook her head. "I did not, because it is not true." She shot Lilika a look of such fury that she was surprised the bird-woman did not simply combust and go shrieking to Furis's black hall of pain then and there. "Areya would no more harm you than she would me, or a lamb or a bee. She is honourable."

"But she is a witch."

Marjeta pressed her lips tight together. "If she is a witch," she said loud enough for every ear in the room to hear, once the anger had stilled enough to let her speak, "then we should all burn. We maidens and mothers, we future crones. Every one of us is a witch to some or other man."

"Brother Milos would agree with you," Silviana said. "But I mean it truly — does she have powers, can she cast spells?"

"She can do no more nor less than half the women in the eight duchies, my lady. And now I beg you to excuse me. I would plead the case of my country woman and friend before your father. The duke must hear reason even while snakes whisper loving venom in his ear."

She did not wait to hear Silviana's answer, but flew from the room, ignoring the whispers and hisses of the women she left behind.

The palace walls closed in around her, and to Marjeta it seemed that the passageways and rooms were rearranging themselves to stall her and lead her astray, but she came to the duke's public hall to find a large crowd gathered already. Apparently rumours that a witch was to be brought before the duke for trial in the attempted murder of his daughter had spread faster than fleas before a fire.

Marjeta pushed through the throng until she came to where Calvai sat at his great table; advisers, knights, scholars and priests around him as jury. Before them was Areya, her hair loosed from under her cap, her outer robes stripped. She stood within a crude warding circle.

"Do you fear her?" Marjeta shouted and walked forward to stand alongside her friend.

The talk in the crowd dimmed to silence, and the men at the table leaned toward each other and whispered. Only the duke stared impassively, saying nothing, doing nothing.

Marjeta scraped her foot through the salt, breaking the pathetic warding. "Is this the kind of thing Brother Milos swears will keep you safe?" She scoffed. "Salt and prayers. She is no more a witch than I am. And look, this little circle will not hold us because we are not what you think we are." A sudden fierce loathing rose in her. If she had her way, she'd burn Milos. There was no-one more deserving. This adder who pointed his forked tongue at every woman he did not like, or think he could control.

"You care for your lady," Calvai said, and the men around him ceased their muttering. They watched him, stoat still, waiting to see what he would do to discipline this insolent little girl, this wife-to-be who had forgotten her place and how to hold her tongue. "That is honourable. It is the sign of a good heart, and I am glad that my bride has such mercy in her breast. It is the duty of women to feel these soft, gentle things. To forgive and to mend."

Marjeta held herself still, tried to stop the shiver that set her skin vibrating. She took Areya's hand in her own, felt icy damp sweat, felt her own tremor, and her heart sank as the man she was to marry in a matter of months continued to speak.

"And just as it is your place to hold these fragile ideals safe, so it is mine to protect my land, my people, my family. Where you do not want to see the truth because it hurts you, I will look clearly. I will be cold for you, my love. I will be the sword so that you can stay unblemished—"

"She is not a witch," Marjeta screamed.

"The evidence brought to me was plain." Calvai shook his head. "I do not do this to hurt you. But if this hag can turn on a child, how long before she turns on you likewise?"

"Mari," Areya said softly. "Stop, you will make it worse for yourself."

"I do not care," she hissed back, then louder: "The Lady Areya has done nothing—"

"The Lady Areya Hanevas has been accused of witchcraft, and the items of her crafting have been brought before us." Calvai gestured at a small collection of goods on the table that Marjeta only noticed then: canisters of herbs, a spell book that had once belonged to Valerija, three broken idols, their faces scratched. A cracked trencher stained dark with years of oil.

"Those are mine!" Marjeta screamed again. "You are fools. They are nothing — just words and little statues. There is nothing powerful in them."

"The lady is distraught," Areya said. "She speaks so only because I have spelled it."

Marjeta froze, numb with horror. "What—"

"She confesses to idol worship and to curse work because I made it so. I control her with this." Areya pulled her hand free from Marjeta's grip and grabbed at the amulet Marjeta wore instead. "I gave her this token as a gift, but it was meant only to blind her to what I was. She knew nothing. She is a child."

"The witch confesses," said Calvai, his voice low and sonorous. "Take her to the Penitent's tower. In three days, we will burn her in full view of the people, that all of Jurie will see the judgement meted out to those who walk the paths of ancient evil and who stray from the loving hand of Furis."

*

Marjeta moved numbly. She was in her rooms, stripped now of small familiar things. The Three and their offering trencher confiscated as fuel for a fire of lies. She was not alone. The Lady Genivia had accompanied her back to her suite. Marjeta wanted to punch the woman's bland face, make her scream, make her admit that what was happening was barbarous, insane.

More than that, she wanted to return to Silviana's wing and strip the skin off Lilika's body, reveal the maggoty truth of her, the evil that lay under her pretty, delicate frame. The woman looked like a little sparrow, wore her prayers like copper feathers, but she was more worm than bird.

Instead, Marjeta took a seat on the corner of her bed, not wanting to move. All around her were little things belonging to Areya — a silk handkerchief abandoned on a small round table, a riding cloak still with a small splatter of pale red mud dried onto a corner, a ceramic thimble. How could all these things still exist, Marjeta thought, and the person they belonged to be sentenced to death? All these normal little symbols of a normal life.

She wept silently, the tears burning raw tracks across her cheeks, anointing her mouth with salt. It was impossible. Only this morning they had been doing the same stupid things they did every day, and now, with a single serpent's bite, everything had changed.

And Areya's confession had sealed her doom.

She confessed because of you. The accusing voice whispered in her head, cold and true and clear. If Marjeta had not rushed to defend her friend in such a stupid childish fashion, if she had waited and gone to beg help from someone like Caneth, or Devan, or asked an audience with her future husband alone and used magic as Areya had shown her, her friend would be safe. It would all have turned out to be misunderstanding, or perhaps Areya might merely have been banished back to Petrell. But now her confession and fate had been heard by a court full of men and women, and there would be no going against it. The duke would never allow himself to look as though he'd been cowed by his future bride.

"Where will they take her now?" Marjeta asked. The words came out hoarse and harsh, her throat too closed up with weeping. She sounded nothing like herself. Grief had turned her into a crone.

Genivia stood. She'd been sitting quiet and watchful on a corner stool, as though uncertain what to do now that she was placed in the rooms of her enemy. It was clear that Lilika meant her to replace Areya, but all happened so fast, that even the pieces Lilika moved into place seemed struck by the sudden changes. "Tonight, they will hold her in the palace cells."

"I don't even know where those are," Marjeta admitted. The palace was a maze of interconnected architecture of varying ages and styles, and with the surrounding support buildings, almost a miniature city itself.

"Below ground." Genivia poured a glass of red wine from an open carafe and pressed the glass into Marjeta's hands. "This..." she paused, frowned, and seemed to rethink whatever she'd been about to say. "Drink this, it will help."

"I don't want the help of wine," Marjeta said, but drank anyway. Perhaps it would black out the day, and she would wake to find it all some drink ravaged nightmare. She thought of Areya underground. "It will be cold," she whispered to herself. As if that were the most pressing thing now. But to go to the dark and the cold to wait for death seemed an added torture.

"My lady—"

"I am not your Lady," Marjeta said with a harsh laugh. "We all know that, let us not pretend who you serve."

Genivia swallowed and nodded. "It is true I have been no friend to you here," she said softly. "But this was ill done."

The wine was almost black, strong and sharp as a destrier's kick. Marjeta drank deeply and wiped her mouth with the back of her hand. She tasted salt tears and sour berries, smoke and blood. She laughed out loud, a bitter, ugly sound. "Oh, was it now?"

"We are not kindly to each other, I know this," Genivia said, "but I have never desired for the game to go so far."

"A game." Marjeta choked. "My friend is to die, and you still believe we play."

"I never thought that Lady Lilika would go so far in her dislike. Always, the battle was simply amusements to us," she admitted. "You were an outsider, and so the game was set against you, but I did not believe she would do this. The Lady Areya has always been kind to me."

"How lucky for her that her kindness is so well repaid."

"She helped me when — it matters not, it was a private issue, and she did not judge me or mock me, but counselled and aided. I know that you think all of us are enemies, but I had no knowledge that Lilika would accuse her of witchcraft before the duke and temple." She lowered her voice. "Mistress, I cannot save your friend, but I can bear her a message."

Marjeta finished the wine. "What good is a message? Will it help her burn faster?"

"They will move her in the morning, my lady, and once she is in the Penitent's Tower there will be no way for me to reach her. The duke will not permit simply anyone to talk with a traitor witch. Especially one with such close ties to yourself."

"How long will they keep her in the tower, before — before the execution?" The words came out, though Marjeta did not know how she managed to say them. It was some other voice that used her tongue.

"It will take a day at least to build the pyre, and for word to spread to the nearby villages. Not tomorrow, but the day after, at the soonest."

So soon. Marjeta began to shiver at the enormity of what they were discussing. The woman who had been her constant friend, her guide and teacher since she came to this hostile country, was going to die. "What can I possibly say?" she whispered. "What message can I give her to make this end sweeter? There is nothing. No comfort."

Genivia was silent a long time, the question hanging heavy as shrouds in the air. "Is there nothing you could give her?" she finally asked.

Marjeta's head shot up, and she stared at the invader in her room. "Give her?" she echoed.

Genivia flushed. "Something that would dull the pain or make her insensible to it."

It was a trap disguised as kindness. Marjeta bared her teeth in a snarl. "Do you mean to make a witch of me too, and go running with proof to your mistress? Perhaps the people of Jurie would like a larger bonfire. Perhaps I should raise a storm and douse the fire with snow. It matters not that it's winter, it would be my witchcraft that did it, no doubt."

Instead of responding with an attack, Genivia stepped back and shook her head. "You misunderstand me, Lady. I am on the side of witches, though I will never say it outside these walls and in front of anyone but you."

"You mean to twist some confession out of me by pretending sympathy." Marjeta stood and walked over to where the trencher and idols had once sat, an innocent throwback to her childhood home, a ritual she had no more believed in than the prayers she offered to Furis — and look where they had led. She ran her palms over the empty space, conjuring the memory of them, of Areya pouring the libations. "Let me speak plain, then. Whatever else you and that vile mistress of yours have whispered in the ears of others, there is one thing I am most definitely not. My sister Valerija was a witch, my Oma Zoli was a witch. There is witch blood running through the Petrell lines, it webs through all the families of my father's duchy, but that does not make me a witch." She turned to face the blond woman, who was watching her with an expression that could almost be sympathetic, if Marjeta believed that her enemies could feel anything so soft. "I am not a witch. Whatever powers you think I have, they are nothing compared to true magic. If I were a witch, I would not have allowed myself to sit in this palace waiting to marry a man who does not see me, waiting to bear a son who will not be mine, waiting to watch a friend burn on a pyre that was intended for me." She spat the last words out, the figure before her blurry now with hot tears. She did not want to cry again, not in front of this woman who would merely gleefully report back to Lilika how well they'd broken the girl, the pretender. Areya's death meant nothing to them.

It didn't matter what Marjeta wanted. As all things, her body was determined to betray her. The tears came fierce and burning raw. Marjeta pressed her knuckles into her eye sockets, gouging at the soft jelly. Perhaps it would be better to be blinded, to see ghosts, to see nothing.

"What would you have done?" The question came soft, after a long moment punctuated only by Marjeta's sobbing.

She dragged her hands down her face, wiping the snot and tears away with her sleeves. "What?"

Genivia held out a hand, palm up, a question. "What would you have done?" She repeated. "If you were ... like your sister?"

It struck her with all the force of a horse's kick to the belly, unexpected and dizzying. "Run," she said, before she could stop herself. "Turned into the wind and gone to the woods. Turned bear-maiden, turned wild."

"Ah." Genivia sat down and folded her hands in her lap. "I do not think you would have. You are not as brave as you like to think you are." The words were harsh, but delivered like feathers, falling lazily through the air, soft spinning. "Even a peasant girl without money or magic will run if she needs to."

"You think to judge me." Her voice was cracked with grief.

"No." Genivia shook her head. "Not at all. We judge each other. You think I want to see you hurt, and I think you are not as strong as you wish. You wanted plainness. Truth. Here it is."

Marjeta coughed, clearing phlegm from her throat. Her words were weighed down with thickness. "Insults."

"No. Practicalities. I cannot and will not go openly against Lilika, but nor will I let Areya suffer. So again, if you know a potion or brew that will save her from the pain, make it, and I will take it to her." Her voice was firm, cool and practical. "I will go to her tonight with blankets — the guards will allow me — and I will conceal something in them for you."

"You mean it."

"I do."

A wave of despair rose in Marjeta's throat. "I — do not. Areya might have known, but now..." The madness of the situation was incomprehensible, too big to think on. It could not be true.

"There is nothing that you can remember from home, perhaps?" Genivia finally began to look worried, as though the composure she wore was being eaten away by maggots of doubt.

"No — I—" Marjeta paused. She had put the dying out of their misery before. "There is something I could do. But I will need you to lie for me. Will the duke expect me to accompany him to — to this thing?"

"He will."

"Then I will need you to find a way to have me called away from his side before the fires are lit. Can you do as much?"

Genivia frowned. "Between us, we can think of something. If you drink a little black thistle in water beforehand it will make you vomit — and I can escort you from his side. The duke has never liked illness of any kind around him. And then what would you need?"

"Good." The plan was simple. Cold. It was better to not think on anything but logic and hard facts, as though Areya were not a person, not a friend, but merely a piece to be removed from the board with as little fuss as possible. "I'll need high ground, and a clear shot."

"Oh." Genivia's face hardened as she understood. "The duke will not be pleased with you."

"I'll weather it," Marjeta said. And hadn't her bow and arrows been truer, crueller friends than magic ever had. Perhaps her father was right, and she was a cursed thing, best sent far away. She started laughing; a hollow, awful laugh that frightened even herself and made her enemy-friend look at her with unconcealed distaste. Let Genivia judge her. She had no understanding of what happened to those Marjeta loved. They died on the points of arrows or the claws of illness, but always, always, because of her.

The old dowager duchess had been right when she'd called her a thief and a murderer. Her magic was nothing more than borrowed; the deaths she brought were her own.

She poured herself another glass of the sour dark wine and felt it burn all the way down her throat and fill her stomach like acid. She would drink until she threw up all of the flayed remnants of the girl that had once been Marjeta Petrell. After this murder she was about to commit, she could never go back. Never pretend any kind of innocence ever again. She would drink until it didn't matter anymore. "There are worse things waiting for me," Marjeta told her new lady's maid. "I will be judged, someday."

Part Three

The Bear and the Maiden Fair

People looked at Marjeta differently after Areya's burning.

Some, obviously, thought that she had to be a witch too, that somehow, she had slipped out of her punishment and made Areya suffer for it instead. They were only too quick to believe that she had blinded the Lady Silviana with spells and near killed her for her own mad purposes. Their gossip was fuelled by Lilika's whispers, by Brother Milos's unconcealed venom when he preached about the evils of women. They made the sign of the horns, and fell silent, staring, when she passed.

Marjeta hated them with a fierceness that was almost pleasant. It felt good to stoke her rage and let it burn out all the weakness. She let it billow through her, could feel it spark through her blood and sear her insides. She could taste ash, smell smoke and burned skin.

There were others who looked at her with a strange respect; Caneth, while he said nothing, never turned her away from his libraries or gave any indication that he thought her some creature of evil and darkness. Of course, Marjeta thought, it was always simply possible that deep in his dungeon rooms, in his stacks, surrounded by dead words and fading ink, that he never heard the living whisper.

But it wasn't just him. Devan looked at her in a new way. Hunter to hunter. He had murdered. Perhaps he understood the casual empathy that put a bolt through a brain, that slit a throat rather than leave a human to scream and suffer slow.

Areya was dead, either way. All Marjeta had done was speed the

end. After she'd loosed that final arrow and it had gone straight
and true, punching through Areya's eye socket with a thud loud
enough to be heard over the waiting crowd and the crackling
flames, the duke's men had come. She'd let them take her; mute,
dry eyed, head held high.

They had not jailed her. As such. She'd been confined to her
rooms and Marjeta had waited, pacing bear-wise, wandering
when Calvai would send for her and what he would do. Surely,
he would not sentence her to the flames. He wanted to keep her
father happy, and he would not be keen to go looking for another
suitable wife with the right ties, and in the right age group to bear
him a healthy heir.

For once, being who she was stood in her favour.

For several days she'd seen only Genivia and the same sallow
faced little maid who was sent to tend her hearth and her toilet,
to bring her food and clear away the empty dishes. Neither the
girl nor Genivia brought news, and Marjeta refused to ask for any.
But within a matter of weeks Marjeta was slipped back into the
industry of the palace as though she had never been gone from it.
The lacuna in the shape of Areya was never mentioned.

Now the palace seemed determined to smooth over this tear
in its fabric as though it had never been, and they made up for it
with an increased humming of activity. Like the world outside, the
palace was waking from its long nights and readying to face a new
round of seasons.

The winter had not been a terribly harsh one and the land had
stayed green, the trees still wearing their cloaks of ivy even while
their crowns were bare and cold. Only a few snow flurries had
fallen near the palace, and faint drifts of crisp blue-white snow
gathered in the shadows of farm walls and on the distant mountain
peaks, but already the rain was turning the hard ground to mud,
and the air was warming. It would be an early spring after a mild
winter. With the bowed heads of the snowdrops would come one
more milestone in Marjeta's long journey.

Her marriage to the Duke Calvai would be a reality and she
would wear the diadem of the duchess. In preparation, the duke
had engaged a new dance master for Silviana. The wedding was

to be her first formal appearance outside her tower, and privately Marjeta wondered who it was he truly intended to have as the bride.

The door to her rooms opened slowly, and Genivia peered in. "I came to remind you that you are meant to be with Lady Silviana—"

"Dance. I know." The Master from Pelissia had finally arrived, and the first of Lady Silviana's new instructions to begin. "I shall need to change." And prepare. It was the first time she was going to Lady Silviana's rooms since ... since what had happened.

She poured herself a small glass of watered wine, and drank it while Genivia sorted through robes, laying out something suitable for the day. Marjeta did not care what the woman chose, she would wear it like a horse saddled for war. The charger does not argue with the groom over saddle and bridle and the trappings of battle. I could be braver, she thought, and laughed into her glass.

"My lady?"

"It's nothing." Marjeta set her emptied glass down and contemplated pouring another. It would help to have a barrier between herself and Lilika and Silviana, however flimsy that barrier might be. But wine would also make her dull and slow, and Marjeta, as much as she wanted to be numb, could not risk being an easy target around her enemy. "If only there was a wine that dulled the pain, and not the senses," she said softly.

"If there were, my lady, and you could make it, then you would command a king's fortune." Genivia held up a dress of forest green with a delicate trim of bracken fronds and star-pointed flowers. "What of this one?"

Areya had embroidered these, Marjeta remembered, and her heart thudded in her throat. She felt ill. "It — it will do."

*

It was not only Silviana and the new dance master waiting for her. Marjeta raised her eyebrows in surprise at the sight of Devan lounging on a long couch, one leg swinging. He looked so unlike the boy she went riding with that for a moment Marjeta didn't know who he was. He wore an azure split-coat and dancing trousers of pale ivory tucked into long supple boots of soft red leather. Against his dark hair and olive skin, he looked like something out of the witch-tales her mother's court had spun to amuse themselves.

He was not the huntsman and horse rider she'd met every week. He was a moth turned butterfly, caught in a wine glass to show off to a lady. His face was troubled, his eyes dark, but he spoke lightly, as though he were simply amused to be there.

"Marjeta." Devan stood to offer her a low bow. "It seems we are all to study together with the esteemed Master Fris." He gestured at the sprightly man next to him, who bowed equally deeply. The man was in his fifties, but muscled and lean, his grey beard was trimmed neatly against his jaw line, and his curls like the wool of an old ram. Marjeta half-expected to see horns coiled against his head, and his legs to end in cloven hooves.

She curtsied in return. "A pleasure to meet you, Master Fris." The words were rote. Did this foreign man know that the last dance master had left because it was whispered that he refused to teach a witch and murderess? And what did it matter if he did? She smiled haughtily and kept her head high. *Think what you like.* The rage burned brighter.

She could not look on this reminder that things had changed so sharply, nor on Devan who had become something else while she wasn't paying attention. She couldn't look on Lilika and not want to strangle the woman. "Lady Silviana," she said. "I see you have recovered in full from your illness." The last time they had spoken, Areya had been accused of witchcraft and sentenced to death. Though it was not Silviana's fault, Marjeta felt the prickling return of her rage.

The girl, now drawing nearer to womanhood, inclined her head. The milky eye stared vacantly. Streaks of grey lay like frost over her dark hair, and the girl looked almost ethereal. A ghost girl. "I am well enough to dance," she said. "Though I don't trust my cousin to not stand on my toes. You shall have him," she flicked her fingers. "Train him to put his feet in the right place."

Marjeta clenched her jaw and kept smiling. "I would be delighted to dance with your noble cousin," she said. "Shall we begin, Master Fris?" She cocked her head, lowered her lashes. She felt like an echo of her mother, had seen her move just like this, a thousand times a thousand, when she had wanted to subtly steer the conversation to less dangerous waters.

"Ah indeed." Master Fris clapped his hands and beckoned the musician who stood at the wall. He was a jug-eared man, stout where Fris was lean, and round faced and sweet. When Gerrard played on his fiddle, the whole world danced when it stood still before. There were whispers that under moonlight, if he played, the very stones of the palace would shift and strain, trying to match his song.

"We will begin with something simple, I think," said Master Fris. "One of the local tunes, one you know well." He smiled at Marjeta with little fox teeth. "In my country we know it as The Dream of Sunny Morgan, but here it is called The Bear and the Maiden Fair."

Marjeta started. A summer song, a lilting whirling dance of a song, a breathless headlong tumble through sun dappled woods. And Val's song, her *no-one-can-catch-me* song.

"I will play the bear, and instruct the fair Lady Silviana," Master Fris said. "Lady Marjeta will partner with the Lord Devan and follow us." He bowed to Silviana and offered his hand, who took it, her dark eye bright and fixed. "One, two three."

Gerrard began playing, and Marjeta found herself opposite Devan, his hand warm in hers, the other curled around her back in a copy of Master Fris. The steps were simple; a stamping one-two-three, a swirl, a turn, and again from the start. It was, in its own way, hypnotic, following the skirl of the tune, which slowed and deepened, ascended and accelerated into a dizzy rush, before the fall and the reversal. It took Marjeta only a few stumbled steps before she caught the rhythm of it and she and Devan danced together, her forest green skirts whispering around them both with every turn.

It was a dance that prickled with magic. Marjeta felt it under her skin like a blossoming bruise, starting at the point where her palm pressed against Devan's, a conjoining of pulses and patterns and futures. She tilted her head and caught Devan's gaze, eyes dark and grey green, like the great lake under ice. It was too personal. She concentrated only on her rage. It had been Devan who had come with the guards to lead her away from the tower wall. Who had taken her bow from her unresisting fingers.

Heat spread from her palm, igniting fine pathways down her wrist and from her elbow, spreading like the copper wires of a magic spell, but fainter, faster.

"You're not paying attention," Devan said softly, his voice puffing against her ear and neck, the faint exhalation sending sparks jittering along her nerves.

"I barely need to," she hissed back. "I have taken dance lessons before. I know the basics."

Their feet moved as though someone else guided them, like puppets tiptoeing in unison. The stone floor felt suddenly very far away, unreal. Marjeta closed her eyes and imagined them dancing on ice, on brittle layers of glass, and far beneath them in black cold waters moved monsters.

The dance ended and Marjeta drew back from her partner like a child recoiling from a heated furnace, fingers scorched. Her chest had been crushed by a blacksmith's hammer, ribs reduced to cracked fragments, every breath splintered.

In Devan's storm eyes, she saw an echo of that same unexpected feeling.

"We should dance more often," he said. "It seems to wake my blood."

And that was not a good thing, Marjeta thought. She gave him a cold, polite smile, careful to turn away and wait for Master Fris's next instruction.

"We should talk," Devan said as the new dance started.

"Should we? About what?"

"You cannot pretend," Devan said against her neck. "You cannot think by not talking about it, that it never happened."

"And I am to confess myself to you, and that will make everything better?" She spun away from him in time with music, then let herself be drawn back, following the pattern like a clockwork doll. His hands were hot. One burning her palm, one branding her hip.

"It will help," he said simply. "And that's all I offer."

*

The offer had wormed into her head, repeating itself like the ticking of a clock. And perhaps Devan was right. Perhaps all it would do to make her feel like herself again would be to speak of what had happened, instead of continuing this grim farce where everyone went on as normal, and no one mentioned what had happened, or said the name of a woman who no longer existed. It made Marjeta feel as though perhaps she'd dreamed it all, that she'd gone mad and everyone around her had lived in a different reality.

Or perhaps she'd been slipped from one world to another, and here she could do whatever she pleased because she barely existed. She was the bear-girl walking through the woods. She was the ghost in the temple bell, the snake in the wheat. In a matter of weeks she would be married, and after that everything turned black.

Moving quietly so as not to wake Genivia who slept in the small adjoining room, Marjeta pulled a child's cloak out from one of the bench seats. It settled over her shoulders like a capelet, and the old magic woke, fluttering and grey. She breathed it in. Valerija's. Something she had not wanted to touch for years. And why not? Because the magic stitched into it was too much her sister's.

I am not Marjeta. I am Urshke. Bear-girl and witch, she thought. *It does not matter what I do, it never did.* She had no Duchess's Cloak to protect her from herself — that offer had died in flames — but she had this last remnant of her childhood. She had Valerija's faded magic of shadows and silences, and a hood she'd had since a little girl. Relics of childhood would be her protection as she walked into adulthood.

No one stirred or stopped her as she snuck from her rooms, through the winding routes of the palace. When Marjeta came to the far suite of rooms on the third floor, the guards fell back, yawning, they opened doors for her even though she wasn't there, they left spaces through which she could slip. Marjeta walked dreamwise into Devan's rooms and stopped as the door to the bedchamber swung shut silently behind her.

Marjeta closed her eyes and pressed her palms lightly over the sockets, counting down from sixty. When she opened them again the room was washed in greys and charcoals, in deep navy shadows and the cold silver of starshine falling through leadlight.

In front of her was a large four poster bed, ornate as her own, but with deeper, darker covers. The gilded cheerfulness of her own rooms contrasted against this melancholy richness. It too suffered from an excess of gold in the Jurie style, but in this room, it was oppressive and crushing.

She shivered. This was not a room Devan would have chosen for himself. But the room smelled of him, his faint sweat, the wildness and musk of him. She breathed deep and there was no doubt that the sleeping figure curled up on the left side of the immense bed was Devan.

Marjeta stepped carefully, quietly, but any footfall was lost in plush carpet. Her feet sank deep into the tufted wool. She dropped her sister's cape from her shoulders and felt herself become real again. The magic faded, and a faint pang of sadness clenched in her chest, before the rage burned it down.

Asleep, Devan looked younger, more like the boy she'd met years ago. But there was no denying the way his face had lengthened and shifted with time, as though he had regrown his face to fit his ears. "Devan?"

He stirred, frowned in his sleep, turning over so that the curve of his spine faced her and all Marjeta could see was a tangle of dark curls. "Devan," she said, louder. She sank down on the edge of the bed and placed one palm gently on his shoulder, felt the thrill of heat rush up through her veins, just as it had when they had danced earlier.

Devan would not say no, if she woke him. Marjeta leaned forward and whispered against his neck, breathing in the scent of his nape, the faint earthiness of skin and hair. "Wake up, Devan Sevari."

At the sound of his name the sleeping man shuddered and turned, his eyes wide, and stared at a face only inches from his own. Before Marjeta could pull away, a knife point kissed the base of her throat. She should have expected it, she thought, and swallowed against the blade point pressed almost hard enough to break skin. "Hush," she said. "It's me, Marjeta."

Recognition swept across his features, but the blade stayed where it was. "Witchcraft," he said. "Who are you really?"

"Marjeta of Petrell." She drew back, but the blade did not follow her. "You can see it's me, Devan. You know me, you know my voice. We ride together, we shoot together, and as of today, we dance together." The flames burned higher, and she let them. Rage and lust were both fires. She could use them. She could feel something and what she felt wouldn't matter. Wouldn't hurt her.

Devan sat up, the knife still held tight, the blade unwavering. "How did you come here?"

"I walked." It was true enough.

"Through the whole palace, past my men, past the duke's man, past servants, and not one stopped you?" He squinted. "I can't believe that."

Marjeta shrugged. "You don't have to, but I did. Please." She motioned to the knife, and raised one brow.

Devan flicked his chin toward the table. "Bring that candle," he said. "I'd like a better look."

After a few moments, the furrows dropped from Devan's expression. He gestured for her to set the candle down. "You're remarkable," he said finally. "Or there's something you're not telling me."

"Of course."

"Which is it?"

Marjeta tilted her head. "It's a trick," she said finally. "Something my sister taught me. We used it to sneak out the castle and go where we shouldn't." She shrugged. "I wanted to see you. After today. You said we should talk." She glanced sidelong, gauging his reaction. If she'd misjudged him totally and read everything wrong, then what was there to stop him from simply marching her to Brother Milos and declaring her a witch, a heathen whore, anything he wanted to.

Men would do that, if they were scared or disgusted. They didn't mind witchcraft when it suited them, though.

"Talk, yes." He swallowed. "About—"

"About something else," Marjeta said. "I cannot face it. I want you to distract me, make me think of anything but the things I do not want to remember."

"You cannot run from what you did. It will get into your head if you let it, fester and sicken," Devan said. "Trust me, it's better to face it."

"One day," Marjeta said. "But not yet. Please." She'd begged twice now. A third time, and she would know to leave.

Devan sighed softly.

She reached out before he could try to persuade her again, skimmed her fingertips across the shadow of stubble on his jaw. The touch was so slight, so close to a whisper that she could almost pretend this wasn't her. "Would you like me to leave?"

He swallowed and set the knife down on the white linen, before reaching out with that same hand to take her wrist gently. "No."

Marjeta felt the last vestiges of her childhood leave her, burned out like sap from a greenstick on a bonfire. She smiled and leaned forward.

The Wedding

The seamstresses had outdone themselves on the dress. It was the palest green of snow with the promise of moss beneath, it was the bellcurve of a snow drop, the sleeves and chest threaded with pale gold smocking. The cuffs and trailing hem had been embroidered with thread almost as white, so that milky suns bloomed over fronds of snail-curled snowbracken, and creamy grey wrens flitted their tiny wings like delicate moths. The designs were ones Marjeta herself had worked on, and it was such a strange thing to see her own stitches so delicate and beautiful. Valerija would have laughed. For little obstinate Mari to have finally learned to wield a needle instead of a kitchen knife pretending to be a sword. To have lowered her bow, nocked magic, and strung spells.

Marjeta kept her face in a neat approximation of a smile and held the dress against her breast as she turned. It was far too short, and the colour would never have suited her. It was a dress made for a bride, but not for her. This was Silviana's.

"It will look beautiful," Lilika said. Her little teeth showed as she spoke, each word gritted out. The women had learned to pretend a new layer of civility. They spoke past each other, directing their opinions to the air, or to Silviana. "The women have worked their fingers to the bones to make something so fine."

"It is quite an event," Genivia agreed. She played at her harp, watching Marjeta with the dress, and sparing the rest of her concentration for the dance of fingers across strings. "Lords and ladies have come all the way up from the border forts, and the Petrells will be arriving soon."

Marjeta paused, and gently shook the dress and hung it up. "You've had word?"

"Scouts came from Verrel to say the caravan was drawing near. By midday, at least, I think."

It was an odd sensation. That evening Marjeta would marry. There would be feasting all through the night, and her parents would watch as she was bound to the Jurie lands, the two duchies wedded. She hadn't seen them in years, and they had become unreal in the interim. Occasional letters and gifts were exchanged, but Marjeta found she could not recall her father's face or her mother's voice. "I shall have to change to meet them," she said. It would not do to greet visiting powers in unsuitable outfits.

"First, we must do the final fitting for your dress," Genivia said. Her hands stilled and the trickle of music died. "I'm not happy with the adjustments. Belind was taller than you, and the fitting seems off to me."

Marjeta felt herself darken. The dress had fitted perfectly only a few weeks back, but now it seemed too tight across her chest, as though it meant to crush the air out of her.

"Nothing a few quick darts won't fix," Lilika said brightly. "Silviana," she turned to her charge, who was sitting on her throne-chair watching the women and the dresses with stony interest. "Come, you've said nothing. Do you not like your dress?"

"It is very fine," Silviana said.

"Are you nervous?" Marjeta asked.

Silviana turned her head slowly so that she could fix her one good eye on Marjeta. "Should I not be asking you that?"

Marjeta shrugged one shoulder in acknowledgement. "I have seen weddings before and sat through many long feasts and entertainments. This will be the first time you leave these rooms." She let the false smile drop a little. "If you are frightened, we would not judge you for it."

"Lady Silviana does not fear a glorified party," Lilika said. "I think we must hurry this day along." She clapped her hands together. "Heated water for bathing, and something light for the Lady Silviana to eat." At her command, several servants who had been hovering in the shadows and trying to look busy dashed from the rooms.

"My lady." Genivia stood and set her harp carefully under silks. "The Lady Lilika calls it well, we should do the same." She curtsied toward Silviana, and the two women left. They hurried down the corridors, their feet shushing the stones. The palace echoed with more noise than usual as below in the kitchens and courtyards and ballrooms and feasting halls the men and women prepared for the second marriage of Duke Calvai Jurie, and for the inaugural presentation of his esteemed daughter to the nobles of Vestiarik.

"I'm almost surprised my parents are coming to this," Marjeta said. "I feel like an afterthought."

"Best keep that observation to yourself," Genivia said. "Today is Lilika's day, and she will watch that you do not ruin it for her. Silviana is her glory, the diadem she wears. Tonight, she shows the nobles who truly sits beside the duke."

"I know." She sighed. "And I am to be on my best behaviour for the whole court will be looking at me and wondering if I truly am a witch."

"Do not let them think it. Be grace and dignity." They came to the doors of Marjeta's suite, and a lone guard nodded at them as they entered.

"I am sick of grace and dignity," Marjeta said. She broke a few grapes off from a bunch on the table and tossed them at the fire place. The salamander hidden in the ashes shook himself awake and snapped at the treats. "I am sick of yellow dresses that belong to a dead woman." She glared at the wedding gown that hung on its stand like someone had skinned the sun and left the remains in her rooms.

"What would Areya say to you now?" Genivia said softly. "What words of comfort?"

Marjeta stared glumly at the fireplace, and though she hated the sound of Areya's name, she recalled her, her rolled eyes at something idiotic Marjeta had said, her mocking laugh, her fierce, loyal whispers. A mixture of hate and love pierced her — a swift hatred for Genivia for forcing her to remember what she did not want to, and love, for the same. Areya would take one look at her and know what the problem was. Of course, Areya would never have let the problem take root. "She would tell me to eat something."

"Then eat something," Genivia said. "No one cares what you think today. They care only that you look the part."

Marjeta began to laugh, then pressed her hands to her face for a moment. "Good, good," she said. "I like that you don't bother to speak soft lies to me."

"It would be a waste of time," Genivia said. "Yours and mine. I will call a servant to come fill your bath and bring you something to eat. No one will expect to see you before nightfall. You may take some time to rest."

"I have a headache," Marjeta told her. "Have the kitchens send willow steeped in wine."

Genivia did not call her out on her lie, merely smiled tightly and nodded. "I will do so. Go rest, my lady. The day ahead is long, and you do not wish to be tired when you make your vows."

"No, just drunk," Marjeta said under her breath, but she went to lie down as instructed. There was little chance that she would sleep, but perhaps, once she'd had a few glasses of the willow-wine she would not mind as much. She pressed her face into her pillow and breathed in the smell of perfumes and dust, thyme-oil and the human scent of her own hair. Today was Valerija's wedding day, late, perhaps, but never escaped.

"My name was Marjeta Petrell," she said to the pillow. "Tonight, I become no one."

*

Marjeta had never danced in the Duchess's Halls before. The rooms which had once been the realm of the Duchess Belind, where she had thrown her glamour and light over the Jurie people, had been closed up after her death. They had been reopened for Silviana's entrance into the world. For this greatest of weddings.

Lights and lanterns, oil burners, candles, torches filled the vast space. More lights than people so that a slice of daylight was transferred into this night time palace, a million suns shining on the gathered throng in their glittering finery. Their currant and daffodil dresses, their crocus coats and beetle boots, the dew strings of diamonds and pearls that hung from throats and ear lobes, that wove through coiled braids.

Marjeta stood at the entrance doors, as the crowd sighed and muttered, waiting for her to be drawn down to the duke where he waited by the ivy-wreathed font of Furis, where Brother Milos waited, his dark red face gleaming under the flickering light. Among the butterfly brights of the wedding colours, Milos squatted, a narrow toad pushed gulping and blinking out from under his rock.

Tonight was a night for all the hidden things to come creeping out, or to be put on display. Here, a toadying god-man, in the crowd, the Dowager Duchess Sannette, wheeled out from her shadow court, surrounded by old woman with sunken mouths, who whispered together in a language no one understood. The dowager duchess looked older than time, her hair cobweb thin, her hands gnarled like rotten wood carved into a grip that never let go. She did not smile as she watched the wedding of her only son. Perhaps she did not even know why she had been wheeled out from her rooms. A bowed lady-in-waiting wiped a trickle of drool from her mistress's slack lips.

Her curses are dust and nothingness, like her, Marjeta thought.

And at her grandmother's side, regal and ancient before her time, the tiny figure of Silviana, pale as snow, her one dark eye watching her father's union, the other milk white one full of ghosts and shadows that only Silviana could see.

Marjeta shuddered, and on either side of her hands tightened their grip. She was only distantly aware of the figures that bracketed her. Mother and Father. They were strangers who no longer resembled the people she'd left in Petrell. They had shrunk and twisted, turned small and soft. Marjeta let them guide her body forward. She was dimly aware of how her feet had to step one in front of the other, of the swish of the borrowed yellow gown against her legs, the heavy weight of her hair piece and net of jewels that pushed her head down.

The space that separated her from the waiting duke grew smaller, and Marjeta found herself standing beside him as the wedding ceremony rushed forward, enveloping her, she heard herself speaking the rote repetition.

Her skin was damp and cold. Her voice echoed distantly.

Marjeta swayed, and a sudden hand propped her up in the small of her back. She was vaguely aware that Genivia stood to her left, and that the woman's stern presence was all that kept her upright. On the duke's right Genivia was mirrored by Sir Provas, but the duke merely looked annoyed, slightly bored, as though he wished this dreary incident over so that he could continue with his day. He had no need for some servant-friend to prop him up.

Dimly, Marjeta heard the words of binding.

Her mouth shaped words of agreement, and her neck dipped as Brother Milos placed the diadem of the duchess of Jurie on her head. For a moment she thought she'd be unable to raise her head again. The weight of all the women who had worn this before was crushing her. Her breathing grew faster, and all she could hear was the rush of blood in her ears, the crack of the bones in her neck.

Her hand was placed in the duke's. It was warm and hard, like wood that had been left in the sun. The mottled piece of fabric with the prayer of Furis written down in the original eastern script was bound about both their wrists, then released. It fluttered to the ground and lay there in a shed snake skin coil

It was over.

Marjeta spun away, and Genivia righted her gently, and pushed her back to her husband, who pressed a dry bearded kiss against her mouth. A lightning prickle that Marjeta was sure would leave stippled bruises.

Music began.

The wedding was over, and the celebrations took over from the rote ceremony. Marjeta's new husband led his wife to the grand table for the wedding feast. The crowds took their seats for the food and the festivities. The noise of chatter filled Marjeta's head, and she could barely put more than a few slivers of tasteless food into her mouth and force herself to chew them into a mush she was able to swallow. Her mother spoke to her, and Marjeta tried to concentrate, but it seemed she spoke to some girl who wasn't there, to another Marjeta. One who had drowned years ago.

Eventually people stopped talking to her, and the buzz and flow of conversation made space for her silence.

Cold relief coated her skin, and Marjeta watched the night as though she were a bird perched high above a stage filled with gaudy players. Watched the food come and go, the servants clearing courses, pouring wines and meads and ales and cold liquors from the north. When the dancing began, she stepped in the right spots, let her husband lead her through the motions, let him transfer her to a waiting crowd of men. To her father, Sir Provas, a million men whose names she did not know, whose faces blurred into each other. At one point she found herself facing Caneth, and the librarian managed to break through the sheath of ice.

"You are sad," he said to her. "You should not show it so easily."

It was a sharp reminder, and Marjeta remembered the muscles that pulled her mouth into the right shape and smiled. "Not sad," she said, and let a bright brittle laugh shape in her throat. It tore her palate but sounded right. "Merely overwhelmed. I never truly dreamed this day would come." And she knew that under the million lights, in the dress as bright as the sun, with the diadem on her brow, she looked like the duchess that the people of Jurie wanted. Nausea rose in her throat, and she swallowed it down. If she were to be ill on the dance floor, the rumours would flow fast as rivers.

Caneth relinquished her, and Marjeta spun to face her next dance partner.

"May I?" Devan bowed, and for a moment Marjeta remembered that there were bears, that there were wild places, and that she belonged in them.

"I should dance with my husb—" She twisted to look for the duke, but he had a partner. A girl, slight and solemn, a straight -backed wraith in a snowdrop dress, her greying hair silver under the midnight suns. Calvai gazed down at his daughter with devotion, his eyes soft, the smile disguising the weak chin. He looked younger for a moment, his mane threaded chestnut, virile and earthy. If his first wife had been the sun, and if his second was the shadow of the sun, then here was the moon. His own perfect satellite.

Marjeta snorted and turned back to Devan, "It would be my pleasure," she said, and when his hands met her skin, it was the first time that day she found herself back inside herself, her own bones and muscles pivoting her through the room. In her head, the bear-girl laughed harsh and bitter, and Marjeta danced to the spring time notes of the song Valerija had sung to her as a child.

*

The wedding night was the wedding morning by the time the duke and his new duchess crossed the threshold of the duke's official chambers. Marjeta still moved in a daze, outside of herself, watching with detached repulsion as she was undressed, entered, and discarded.

It was less pleasant than her times with Devan, who was funny and bumbling and fierce and shy, but it was not unendurable. Marjeta lay still and waited for the consummation to finish, for her husband to dress and leave. She sat up when he was gone and looked blankly around her. She still wore her undershift, hiked up around her hips, and she drew it down over her thighs and wondered if Calvai had gone down to his private rooms where he met Lilika. She found she did not care. She'd rather he spend most of his time with the other woman. They did love each other, she had to assume, and wasn't that better than this empty coupling all for the sake of a child born with the right to sit on his father's throne? It was pointless and ugly, but Marjeta was just one small voice in the darkness, and she was never going to change the world.

That sort of thing was for the powerful. And the powerful made targets of themselves.

There came a soft tapping from the door, and Marjeta jerked. She was certain that she should wear a brighter expression, but she hadn't the energy for it. Genivia peered around the door frame, and Marjeta nodded at her to enter.

She carried a pitcher of steaming water and folded towels — a small concession to what had happened, though neither mentioned it. "Are you tired, my lady?"

Marjeta shook her head. She was exhausted, and her exhaustion had pushed her past a state where she could sleep, into a realm where her skin itched as though it were not her own, and her mind felt both too small and too large for her. She was minute, and yet she could not be contained. "Thank you." She stood and made her way to a discreet screen and cleaned herself as best she could. When she emerged, Genivia held out a long robe of emerald linen, and matching slippers were placed before the fires. "If you would dress," she said. "I will take you to your new rooms."

Once again, without a say in the matter, Marjeta had been rehomed. She'd known long in advance, and already some of her belongings had been transferred, in the weeks before the wedding, to the Duchess Suite, but Marjeta had tried not to think on it. She let Genivia shepherd her down the hallway, a combination of tiredness and self-loathing and useless anger making it feel as though she waded through a nightmare world where every step was echoed by an immense, invisible monster that would tear out her throat if she looked back.

The Duchess Rooms were much finer than her previous suite, and more than rivalled Silviana's rooms. Belind had decorated with an excess of saps and apricots, blushes of rose and gold and primrose and spring green. Everything was layered in ivory, or gilded, or mirrored. It was a box to keep a flame in. Even dead, Belind still flickered across the walls, was reflected in mottled silver and on the waxed furniture.

Marjeta stared at the huge hearth, almost as tall as she was. She could see no comforting shift of embers and charcoal that meant Tarkis was hiding there. Still, it meant nothing. The salamander was a creature of magic and air and fire and was not limited to this world. He would find her, he always did.

"You are very quiet," Genivia said.

It was hard to talk, and Marjeta spent a few moments trying to dredge up a memory of words and sounds. "They are very nice rooms," she said. A large Book of Furis sat on a small, scrolled table, open to an illuminated page. Marjeta glanced at the capitals, the swirl of words and horned gods and tried to drag some meaning from them.

She scowled. Of course it was open to the passage where Furis addressed the whores of the city of Atayon, and told them the duties of a good woman and a good wife. After that, he'd had the women hanged from the city walls. Most tended to skip that part, but Marjeta had come to Furis's readings as an outsider, and she did not find it easy to blindly gloss over the parts that made her heart seize with cold fear.

Brother Milos had left her a message.

Marjeta bit her tongue until she tasted blood, then swallowed, and turned back to the life she'd been given. "The Lady Silviana had a most entertaining evening, I trust?" Marjeta walked through the rooms, observing the grandeur, the similarities and differences to her previous suite. In the centre was a grand parlour that reminded her strongly of her mother's solarium where as a child she'd had to sit with the women and stitch. At the time she'd thought it a nuisance — a bunch of prattling idiots gossiping to each other as their needles clicked and their hands darted. It had been a shadow court that hid all it did under polite smiles and painted words. "She certainly seemed to enjoy the dancing."

"She did," Genivia replied as she tugged at a woven bell pull. "It was about time her father gave her room to breathe."

Marjeta glanced sharply at her. "Careful where you say that."

"I am always careful." Genivia turned to examine the young maid who had just entered the room, her eyes beaten black from the late hour. "The duchess requires something warm and sweet — a drink of milk and honey thickened with bread, I think." She looked to Marjeta. "Will that suit, my lady?"

It sounded childish and sweet, like something you would give a fretful toddler after a fever. It sounded perfect. "That will do, yes," she whispered. It was good to have someone take care of her for a moment, even if that care were distant, hesitant. Areya would have plied her with bitter cacao from her jealously guarded stores and sung her spells to send her to dreamless sleep. Tears gathered in hot sparks behind her eyes, and she blinked them away.

Bitter cacao or milk and honey, it was all to the same end. Genivia had her own witchery, simple as it was.

The Ghosts of Warnings

It was a dream, Silviana thought. She walked through her father's palace, her fingertips brushing the wall on her left side. Sinister side. Side of blindness and ghosts. Behind her the women walked on silken slippers, their skirts hushing the stones, their whispers rushing water. It was a dream and, when she woke up, she would be back in her rooms, unable to leave. Just like the cages full of birds Nanna Sannette had left her.

Nanna who had passed away like a whisper after the wedding. Her ghost was in the walls now, finally freed from her wheeled chair.

"You are very quiet this morning, my lamb," Lilika said. She was walking just a step behind Silviana's right, a sparrow following a bread crumb trail. "Is something troubling you?"

Silviana shook her head. It was a new ritual of hers, this walk through the passages she'd never seen, only imagined. Now she mapped them over and over, tracing new routes, calculating which were fastest where, which avoided which places, and what passages led her to things she wanted to see.

She had danced with her father at his wedding, in a room where her dead mother had thrown party after party. She had watched her new stepmother wed her father in robes Lilika told her had once been her mother's own wedding gown, altered to fit an impostor.

"She is trying to replace your mother," Lilika had said.

Was she? Perhaps. Silviana's fingernails scraped gently against the stone skin of the sleeping palace, an affectionate skritch. This was hers. This was her palace, built from roots as old as an emperor's dreams, grown piece by piece, stone by stone, tile by tile, until it had become a city in its own right. The fort that had seeded it was ancient, and like all ancient things, it remembered.

She could hear it muttering in its sleep. See shades passing her, border lords and ladies long dead, their forms eaten away by time.

"If there is something I can do," Lilika said, "you have only to ask me, you know that."

"I know." Silviana's voice sounded strange to her these days. It carried whispers that were not hers, the voices of the dead. She shook the thought away. She was going mad, thinking on such nonsense. Her illness had left her weak, left her damaged, and at nights Silviana worried that it had affected her brain too. Changed it in some terrible way that left her not herself, but a muddy replica. "You would do anything for me," she said. "You have told me that so many times." She came to the great blue doors of the Duchess's Suite and glanced at Lilika. "Why is that?"

Lilika blinked her black eyes. "Why, I would do anything — because I love you like my own heart, like my own child."

"But I am neither," Silviana said. She nodded to the servant who waited at the door. "Inform the duchess that I am here." It was the first time she had accepted Marjeta's invitation to come join her in her new territory, though she'd had the run of the palace for several weeks now. She had first wanted to learn the shape of the land before coming here. And she had wanted her own army at her back. The women Lilika had gathered, all eager to press their young ward between them like a flower in the pages of a book. What would they do when Marjeta gave birth to a son? Perhaps then they would flock to his side instead. After all, the heir would stay and become the ruler of a vast duchy — perhaps even more than that.

And she would marry Devan, who one day would hold the duchy of Coriast, but by that time he might be no more than duke under a king. A warlord sworn to her father's service. Silviana was not stupid. She listened, and now she saw more than most realised, and heard voices that others did not. Her father did not need to confide in her. The walls did that.

And Devan was already mostly her father's. The years growing up here had done that to him, shifted his alliances so subtly that he probably didn't even notice it himself.

Silviana and her retinue were led into the grand apartments, and she made note of the brightness, the golds and yellows and sunlight cleanness. These had been her mother's rooms. She breathed in deep, wondering if she would catch some faint lingering scent of a woman dead almost thirteen years. She could smell only the herbs in their baskets, the high sour note of apple wine, the musk and perfumes of her stepmother's coterie of servants and ladies and musicians.

And Devan, sprawled in a chair among the ladies, like a hound in a basket of a kittens. He stood as she entered and bowed deeply to her.

"I did not expect you here," she said.

The musicians slowed their song, fell to silence, and Marjeta stood from her own seat where she worked on the hem of some stupid shirt she prepared for the spring feast. Always, always stitching, as though she had nothing else to do. She was growing fat.

"I invited him," said Marjeta, "in the hopes that you would accept my invitation, and we could all be together." She looked past Silviana as she said this.

Silviana squinted her good eye, trying to hold the figure of this woman she'd known now for years, and yet could not understand at all. There were filaments of gold and silver dancing around her, like the comet trails of dust motes. She shook her head and the image passed. "How thoughtful of you."

"Lord Devan tells me that you enjoyed your first event so much, we should throw another ball, this time with yourself as the honoured guest, rather than simply being a bridesmaid to an old woman." Marjeta winked. "You should have been presented at your decad, but we can throw you a most wonderful thirteenth year party. I am sure the lady Lilika would help me. We both want only your happiness."

So it seemed. The idea of a ball thrown purely for her honour was a strange one. Thrilling, and also terrifying. It had been one thing to be the daughter of the duke at his wedding, clad in finery and thrillingly important, but at the same time, not the very heart of the event. For her birthday, all eyes would be on her. She drew herself a little straighter, and watched the shadows ghosting about the women. Was one of them her mother? She had died in these rooms, Silviana thought. Not this one, of course, not even in the room where Marjeta now slept, laid her head on pillows that had once cradled her mother's brow. But in that little antechamber just off the bedroom, where the duchess would have retired to birth. The last room she had been alive in, and the first room Silviana had drawn breath in. She wondered what Marjeta would say if she asked to see it.

The ghosts sighed and danced, shaking their billowing heads and Silviana wished she could clap a hand to her dead eye and stop seeing these things, but she knew it made no difference. It was best to pretend not to see them. Instead, she focused on the strange eddies of molten dust that followed Marjeta about, settling on her shoulders like pollen. There was more similar dust spiralling up from the dead hearth. It was too warm now for daylight fires. Silviana frowned. The ash was moving. Impossible to tell any more what was real and what was her imagination.

"What is that?" she said in a fierce whisper, as a golden head burst out of the ashes and stared at her, reptilian eyes blinking lazily.

Marjeta cocked her head and smiled. It sat false on her. Silviana had seen her real smiles before, faint and infrequent as they were. This was an abomination she had cultivated. Blank and wide and empty. "It's a salamander."

"Ah, like the Petrell herald?" Silviana asked.

"Just so. This one came with me from my family lands when I moved here. They need heat to survive." She gestured at the hearth. "Hence, the fires."

The salamander waddled out of the fireplace, shaking ash from its head, before skittering under Marjeta's skirts to coil around her ankles so that only its sly golden head peered out from under her hem.

Silviana found herself smiling. "It's a pet?"

"It is."

She crouched to bring her face closer to the beast's.

"Not so close, it may bite," Lilika said.

"It will not bite." Marjeta looked up and focused on Lilika as though she'd only just realised the woman was actually there. "Salamanders only bite if they're afraid — and that would never happen here, I am quite sure." She gestured to Silviana. "You can stroke his head, he'll do nothing."

The salamander's scaled skin was dry and hot, the saw-tooth edges a faint pleasurable roughness against her finger tips. He blinked, his throat gulping softly as Silviana scratched her finger nails along his head and around his spikes.

"Does the duke know you keep a magical creature in your rooms?" Lilika asked, her voice dripping honey.

The salamander hissed a soft warning, and Silviana quickly withdrew her hand.

"He does," Marjeta said. "I believe he found it amusing."

"The salamander's not a true magical creature," Devan pointed out. "It's hardly a fire breathing dragon."

Lilika's pained expression only looked worse with a smile twitching over it.

"Come, Silvi," Marjeta said, and patted the seat between hers and Devan's. "Tell us what kind of a celebration you would like. After all, in this palace, it's the only magic we get." She gestured at her musicians to begin playing, and the sound came humming softly back, a counterpoint to the babble of conversations that restarted.

Lilika, who was forced to sit at the far end of the circle of women, kept her grimace in place. It was strange, Silviana thought. Perhaps it was a trick of the light, but all around Lilika danced the fiery motes that spun likewise around Marjeta. It was as though each woman wore an invisible halo and cloak, and only Silviana could see the faintest traces of them.

It was too much like the first days after waking from her illness, when everything she had seen out of her left eye had been a nightmarish vision, and Lilika had worn a black horned mask, and stared at her with eyeless pits of fire, the empty hole in her chest dripping blood onto the carpet. Where Marjeta had grinned at her with bear fangs and worn a dress of golden-brown fur, and her eyes had shone green as fireflies in the darkness.

At last, now they both looked almost like themselves again. Whatever the fever had done to her mind, Silviana could not shake these vestigial visions. She glanced back to Marjeta to see if the patterns were still there, but there was something else now, a shadow that loomed over Marjeta's chair, a shadow that held her shoulders, and looked down at her with sympathy and hatred in equal measure. A stench of abattoirs filled the room, and Silviana heard screaming — a high pitched gasping wail that pierced her eardrums. She clapped her hands to her head.

"What is it?" Marjeta leaned to her and placed one hand softly on her knee. Her brow was furrowed in concern. Everything stank of blood, of the coppery-salt reek of menses and death. The wail continued, faltered, and died. It was the sound of birth. Of an infant taking its first and final breaths. The shadow over Marjeta's chair let go and disappeared, her foretelling done.

Silviana blinked. "It— No. It was nothing, just a silly turn," she whispered as she lowered her hands. She shook her head, and thought of balls and dancing, thought of the stories that Lilika had told her about her mother, and how the Duchess Belind had made the world fall in love with her. She would do the same, she decided. She would make all of them love her, and she would dance, and never go back to her rooms and hear the keys turn in the locks.

*

That evening, as Lilika helped Silviana undress and prepare for bed, Silvi made her startling observation. "The duchess is pregnant."

Lilika was unpinning Silviana's hair, and she paused, before continuing to run her fingers through the untwisted curls, so she could brush them out and rebraid them for evening. "What makes you certain?"

"Nothing." She shrugged. "It's just a feeling. She holds herself differently."

"Does she?" Lilika mused. "I thought that simply her childish pride at her new status." She flipped the hair across Silviana's back and reached for the ivory-handled boar brush. "If she is pregnant, there's no telling who or what it will look like."

Silviana gasped and twisted to look back at Lilika. "You cannot say such things about my father's wife!"

"Not to anyone but you," Lilika said. "But you are not a child to be lied to. There are rumours about what the duchess does when she goes hunting in the forests with Lord Devan—"

"My Devan? That cannot be, they have escorts."

"And no one can watch a man and woman every hour of the day and night." Lilika gently turned Silviana's head back and began to stroke the brush firmly from crown to tip. "It is well known that the duchess keeps magical artefacts and has a way to leave the palace unseen. There are those who say they've seen a woman dressed in furs running through the forests at night. That she sheds her skin and becomes a beast — she hunts with wolves and goes on all fours for bears and dogs."

"You speak most foul. This is gossip and the prattling of bored servants."

"We servants see much. And you are old enough to hear the truth. The duchess tries to woo you with balls and music and her little court, but she is not to be trusted. Brother Milos and I both believe she cursed you, that time when you were so ill that we thought you would die. It was only his prayers that saved you. It was Furis who fought off the evil of that woman's magic."

"You do not know that."

"I know more than you realise. I know what she is capable of, and I swore always to protect you from all harm. What kind of a mother would I be if I hid the truth from you because it was ugly?"

Silviana stayed silent, letting Lilika drag the brush through her hair, over and over. It was a soothing monotony, and a mantle of calm settled over her shoulders. The things Lilika said were ugly and could be untrue. But they could also be ... something else. She was certain she'd seen Marjeta smile at Devan more than once, that looks had fluttered between them, soft and windswept as early butterflies. "Perhaps I am mistaken," she said softly.

"And perhaps you are not. Furis speaks to us in strange ways. He tells us things for a reason."

"And what reason would he have for telling me that my stepmother is pregnant?"

The brush scraped Silviana's scalp, caught in a snarl of hair, and Silviana winced but made no sound as Lilika jerked the brush free. "Perhaps he gives you time to prepare yourself. If it is a son, then everything we have here changes."

"We?"

"Everything you have," Lilika said. "And am I not yours?"

Silviana pondered that. "Perhaps," she said finally.

Milk, Honey, Poison

Lilika went to her bed troubled. She held wisps of Silviana's silver hair, tangled them around her fingers, and wondered how the girl had known. It was clear, perhaps, now that it was pointed out, that the newly wed duchess had fallen pregnant. The girl had always looked rawboned and harsh, feral under her silks and diamonds, but a mantle of softness had settled on her body.

Calvai had bedded her, of course. But however much the girl tried to hide it, there were looks cast between herself and the duke's nephew, and while she had not the proof of it, Lilika was certain that the budding child was more Sevari than Jurie.

"I should poison her," Lilika said to herself. "It would be a kindness to Calvai, before he ends up raising a traitor's child as his own heir." Her rooms were small, little more than a sleep chamber and privy, but unlike most servants, Lilika had a certain power and privacy. She could bolt the door between herself and Silviana, if she wished it, and she had space enough for her own secrets.

She lay on the covers of her bed, the canopies drawn around her, like a room within a room, and she closed her eyes, one hand held in the sign of the horn over heart. "Hear me," she whispered to the night air.

The room grew very still, so that Lilika could hear only her own slight breathing stirring the air, the delicate thundering of her blood in her body, her skin pulsing in time with each beat of her heart.

Furis's heart, she knew. The brothers liked to say that Furis had hidden his heart away so that he might be immortal, and they made all kinds of stories about where it might be hidden, but Lilika thought them all fools. Furis had hidden his heart a thousand times over, seeding it in human chests, so that when it beat, it beat for him, and the blood that moved through their veins was his.

Hear me, her heart, his heart said.

Lilika opened her eyes, and the dark spun around her in motes of grey and silver and black, threading together to form the looming figure of her god, his wide horns spread to touch the carved ceiling. His eyes were candle lights, flickering, watching her, seeing through her skin and between her bones, into the desires traced in secret designs within her flesh.

Why do you call me?

Because the usurper carries a child, and it is not Calvai's, she wanted to say, but her throat was dry, her lips cracking. But her god would know her thoughts. He would see what she saw, and he would tell her what she needed to do.

What does a good wife do when there are rats in her kitchen?

The question was strange, and Lilika frowned. Furis did not speak to her in riddles, he told her the way to walk. Perhaps he expected more of her this time. Perhaps he had grown bored of guiding her.

"Am I a good wife?" she asked.

You are. Good wife, good mother, good heart. The shadowy god reached out and brushed long fingers over hers, still curled in the sign of the horn, Silviana's silver hair wound around them. He pressed his fingers through her skin, through the plane of her breastbone and stroked her heart like it was a frightened rabbit, being soothed before the butcher's blow.

The feeling was like being lit up by the rare lightning storms that sometimes touched the borderlands, like being on fire and freezing at the same time. Lilika gasped and reached out, and the god was gone. The silver strands turned to dust and disappeared.

She sat up slowly, shaking her head to clear the strange sparking inside it. That had been Furis himself who had touched her, and no trick of the Three. She knew what she should do. Calvai might be married to Marjeta, but she was not his wife. Lilika was. A good wife set traps for rats and burned the nests where she found them. She lit candles, and pulled out her desk drawers, reaching deep into the back to look for items she had not used in more than a decade. There — dust furred, but unbroken, a little vial.

And in packets of paper, covered with wax, herbs that had once been fresh and deadly, but now had dried to dust. Their potency would be much reduced, but they might still work. She slit open the packet and found the herbs had been crushed to a fine gold powder. Like this, they would cause little agony for the mother, but they would twist the thing inside her.

Perhaps kill it, perhaps not. If it was Calvai's it would be strong, and it would survive. And if it were not...

To make it stronger, the herbs would need to be boiled in white wine, but she had no need of such a concoction yet. The dust would do, sprinkled into warm milk, the bitterness disguised with honey.

It would be an easy thing to do. Midwives often used goldenseed pollen in strengthening draughts for the mother-to-be. Lilika could give Marjeta this poison, and not even attempt to hide it. No casual observer would be able to tell the difference, and if ever the words poison were whispered, no one would ever think that the poisoner would be so bold as to do it in full view of everyone.

Carefully, Lilika tipped some of the powder into a small, enamelled box, and screwed the lid on tightly. The rest she packed away. Perhaps there would come a time when she needed it again, but for now, this would be enough.

A Once and Future Son

Marjeta laced and unlaced her fingers over her stomach. Her cape lay discarded on a bench in Devan's rooms, and her layers of dresses and petticoats and chemises were a soft snow drift on the deep blue carpet.

"You're sad."

She looked up from her tapping fingers, and at his worried frown instead. "Am I?"

"You were sad the year you arrived, and you've grown sadder and smaller every day."

There was no arguing that. She couldn't even bring herself to respond. What was she to say that wasn't a list of the dead that had followed her here? Unless she pushed her thoughts away and drowned them under apple wine and mint-and-juniper water, then she would see their faces: sister, hound, friend. One by one she had destroyed them. And now this.

"You whip yourself," Devan said.

Marjeta shivered. If she did, the wounds left were invisible. "I do no such thing." She turned around, showing off unblemished skin, slow as shadows in the candle light.

"I don't mean that you flagellate yourself like one of the brothers, you know that." Devan stood and walked barefoot to the table to pour himself and Marjeta two small black glasses of sweet wine. He wore only a night gown loose over his shoulders. It was dyed crimson so dark that it pooled darkness down his back and sides. The rest of him was a moonlit contrast. Bone against blood. "You punish yourself with guilt and hatred, and it kills me to see you do it."

"I don't know what you mean." She took the offered glass. "But even if you're right, don't I deserve it?" She sipped. It was rich and heavy, spiced with something salty that offset the sweetness in a pleasing way. "At the very least, I have made a cuckold of the duke."

"Who has done the same to you, before and after your wedding." Devan ran one hand through the mess of his hair. "Look. He is my uncle, and for that I have love and loyalty, but he is also a man, and I can see his flaws as well as I can see anyone else's. I want you to be happy, Mar. I want to see you smile and know that it's yours, and not some falsehood you wear to please the people around you."

"You see more of the real me than most." Marjeta sat back down on the bed. The cold was creeping up her legs and she wanted a little warmth again before she pulled her clothes back on and wrapped herself in her stolen magic and ran back to her rooms. She breathed in deep and tasted musk and sweat and the perfumes of men and women mingled. While she tried so hard to keep herself locked up, to feel nothing and give in to no one, there was something about being alone and naked in Devan's rooms with him that made her trace the edges of love, and wonder if she should risk it. "You see skin, and magic."

"I'm glad you trust me enough about the magic, at least," he said. "And you know I will never turn against you for that."

"Even if Lilika tells you I tried to murder Silviana?" She raised a brow and watched his reaction.

Devan set down his wine and rubbed at his face. "I know you did not," he said, his voice slightly muffled. "Only a fool would believe it. You love her, even if you hate yourself for loving her."

"How astute. You murder my pride as easily as you murder boys in a forest."

"At least I don't have to mount your pride on a spike for all the city to see."

Marjeta laughed bitterly. "There's that. And yes, fine, I love Silviana. I wanted her to be my sister, and I would never do anything that would cause her harm. But what about those I hate? Surely I could have used these evil witchcrafts of mine to destroy my enemies and grind them to dust?"

"Then Lilika would be dead a thousand times," Devan said. "I'm not an idiot. You aren't a killer."

"Areya would argue that point." Marjeta was proud of herself for not choking on the name. If she could say it often enough it would lose all meaning, become dull and useless.

"No. That was mercy. You do not murder." He leaned over and took Marjeta's hands in his, the warmth enfolding them and sending rivers of lightning down her veins. "Something else is worrying you," he said softly, dark eyes serious.

"I'm pregnant," Marjeta said. And held his hands so he would not be able to pull them away, though she didn't have to. "Probably. Most likely."

"Ah. An heir for the duke."

"Yes." She held tighter, her fingers desperate. "And if it is a son, then the worst of my duties are over, I can ... create myself again. Do you understand?"

"What are you saying?"

Marjeta took a deep breath and wished she were drunker. Truth was always easier to pull out of her when she could wash the lies away first. "If I have a son, there will be a wetnurse and tutors and servants for him, and my share of his life will be over. You and I — we can leave."

"I'm meant to marry Silviana."

"Do you want to?"

Devan pulled free and rolled away to get to his feet. He paced the room, brow furrowed. Occasionally he looked over at Marjeta. "I do not," he said after a long while. "You call her sister, and so do I. But, to leave? To simply run away like beggar-thieves — what honour is there in that?"

"What honour is there in this?" Marjeta waved one hand to encompass the room, the bed, the crumpled clothes, the wine and the soft folds of magic that had led her there. "We don't even know if this child would be yours or his. So don't preach to me about honour. I hear enough of that nonsense from Brother Milos and his band of sanctimonious, sour little men." She sat up. "I want the forest. I want the hunt and the wild, and we are both content to live without the comforts of palaces. We can run and become something else. I don't need to be a duchess any more than you need to be a petty king's border lord dancing to the tune of his daughter's wetnurse. You want a ship instead of a horse, then let's go find an ocean."

"And you would leave your child here, just like that?"

Marjeta shrugged. "He will not be mine."

*

It did not take many more weeks before the news of Marjeta's new state spread through the palace on a muttering river. She told the duke herself, of course, and he was delighted. For the first time since she had ever met him and tried to weakly ensnare him in her little wisps of borrowed magic, Marjeta saw something like joy on his face.

The services in the temple were devoted to family, to tradition, to sons and strength, and Marjeta stared over Brother Milos's sour, chanting head, at the horned god that took up the whole of the wall and dreamed about how far she would run from this land. She pretended faintness and closed her eyes to the painted walls, and imagined herself in fur cloak and leather boots, with bow and dagger and travel cutlery and thimbles, mounted on Dust, with a hunting hound at her heel, while behind her Devan steered a ship of plaited willow through an ocean of bracken and oak. They would leave Jurie and cut through the lamb-lands and the forests, not into Sevari — which would be too obvious — but perhaps to the tiny Duchy of Drias, so small it seemed always forgotten. They could lose themselves there, or catch a trade ship further west, or even south to the strange red lands where neither Furis nor the Three walked.

In a matter of months. In less than a year, and until then she had time to make plans and say goodbyes that did not look like goodbyes. Her back and breasts ached and she felt heavy and awkward, though there was barely any change to see.

Brother Milos' words spilled over, meaningless, endless, and Marjeta smiled.

"Soon you will have a brother," she told Silviana later, when

the women's court was gathered together in the room that was
so like her mother's solarium, and the musicians played while the
women laughed and sang and made crafts or teased one another.
The rooms were filled with bird song, the cages full of finches and
canaries green, black and white magpies who called the names of
serving girls, cages trembling with life as the birds fluttered from
perch to perch. "And your father an heir."

"You can't be sure of that," Silviana said. They were playing an
elaborate game of cards. The deck had been printed and painted
in Sevari and sent as a gift by Devan's mother for Silvi's decad,
and were dog eared and faded. Games of Hare and Foxes were
for children, and even Silviana no longer pretended at childhood
or bothered with amber beads and black stones. People were her
game pieces now. "I could very well have a sister."

"No." Marjeta shook her head. It was impossible to explain, but
the knowledge was in her bones, deep and thick. "It's a boy, I am
sure of it." Though she had become very good at feeling nothing,
there was a brief twinge where she wondered what it would be like
to love a child of her own, until she reminded herself that the child
was no more hers than Silviana was. It was a symbol, and symbols
were not easy things to love. They did not love back.

"Of course it will be a son," Lilika said. She had sent servants
to bring her an assortment of herbs and spices and creamed honey
and boiled goat milk, and she stood now at the table mixing a pot
of sweetened milk and spices together. "A mother knows these
things. I knew."

"You had a son?" Marjeta found herself asking, before she could
stop herself.

"Once." Lilika tipped a spoonful of golden powder into the
milk pot and stirred, clucking her tongue. "He was born too early,
and he never drew breath." She took the little milk pot to Marjeta
and held it out. "You will drink this every morning, it will help the
baby knit strong."

"I did not know," Marjeta said. "I'm sorry to hear it."

"It does not matter. It was long ago, and I am blessed. Furis
gave me another life to live."

"What is in this?" Though the two women now stayed courteous around each other, and Lilika had brewed her concoction before the entirety of Marjeta's little court, it was still hard to bring herself to trust Silviana's nursemaid.

"Nothing ill." Lilika showed her little teeth. "It is a drink the midwives of Jurie have known for hundreds of years. It is good for mothers and babies both."

For the first time, Marjeta considered that when she left, this would be the woman who raised her son as her own. Perhaps it was fitting then that Lilika had also lost a son and Marjeta would be the one to replace him for her. She took the milk pot and drank. It was sweet, thick as cream, spiced with cinnamons and cardamoms, and other bitterstrange and delicate spices. She'd tasted these same things in feast food both here and in Petrell. Whatever game Lilika played now, it seemed she had no wish to harm the heir that Marjeta grew for Calvai.

The Coming Storm

Her new freedom was not truly freedom, Silviana acknowledged to herself. Her cage was simply bigger — extended from the walls of her suite to the walls of the palace. Outside, the woods and wild things were still off limits. While her father was home, there was no chance of asking to go beyond her cage. She waited for him to go back to war, and then waited still longer so that her bid for freedom would not be seen for what it was. She waited for spring to shed its skin, to dawdle into summer. For summer to begin turning.

She waited for a day that filled the halls with the smell of outside, the floral sweetness, the greenness beckoning, the heat indoors too stale to be comfortable. She did not ask to go far or go alone. And she watched how the ghosts of the palace smiled around her, watchful and intent as if they knew some secret that she was yet to discover. At first, Lilika had demurred, but the women of the court were fractious, bored. They too wanted out. There was no danger in the nearby woods.

The first time Silviana set foot outside the palace walls, she saw the dead.

It was an arranged picnic, rich with women. Servants carried rugs and blankets, pillows, picnic foods, silk tents and all manner of comforts. The women were dressed in finery that pretended comfort: split skirts heavy with embroidery, fur slippers, long coats in deep jewel colours. with wide, impossible sleeves and high mantles. Even the Duchess Marjeta with her protruding stomach waddled with the other women.

It was ostensibly for her benefit and pleasure that the outing had been arranged. The company of women and servants walked over grass kept neat as moss, the turf springy under foot, and above them the sky was limitless cerulean, no clouds to mar its perfect heaven. Silviana walked with one hand clutching Lilika's. Although she was no longer a child, a vicious terrifying urge to scream and run kept pushing at her head. The sky was too vast, the trees taller than towers, draped in cloaks of ivy and old man's beard, alive with tiny, feathered monsters that rippled through the undergrowth. The air was thick and drowsy but turned sharp on a breath. There was no perfect stillness. The world was a maelstrom of infinitesimal change.

The smells were overwhelming. No longer limited to the dried herbs and the pine on the hearth, or the perfumes of musk and ambergris and pressed flowers in oils, rich red wine and sour white. There were those traces, certainly, but they were stale and small outside the stone rooms. What Silviana had once thought rich and heady turned out to be dust and pot pourri. The air was too big for her lungs. It threatened to suffocate her. So much air. So much sound. The whisperings of women and the crackle and whirl of rosined bow against taut gut, the melancholic drone of the pipes — they were nothing compared to the shattering bird song, the distant cries of workers in the fields, the rustle of leaves and the trill of rivers and burns.

Silviana's hand grew sweat-slick in Lilika's grip, and her blind eye flashed golden and white pulses like elfshot into her brain. With her right eye she saw green and yellow and blue in endless intensity, and in her left, instead of the shadows of figures moving toward her, their clawed hands outstretched, she saw the sun. It would burn her alive.

"Nervous?" whispered Lilika, and at Silviana's stilted nod, said, "Do not be. I'm with you. Always. And I will protect you. Always."

"And you are certain my father will not hear of this?" she whispered back. She'd had the run of the palace for many months now, but even then, she'd never even considered leaving. The world outside was too big. Too ugly. It had killed her mother, it took her father away to war, and every time she wondered if he'd return. Had both longed for it and feared it. The world changed on its axis when her father was in the summer palace.

Lilika said nothing. "We will not go far," she murmured, finally. They had come to the wide gates that led onto a small wood. The same wood Silviana could see from her rooms. If she looked up behind her she could see her own windows, glinting down blind and narrow and cold. An urge to run back to the palace doors and up the whirled stairways and back into the safety of her suite shook her bones. She bit the inside of her cheek and forced herself to keep moving. There, ahead, Marjeta laughed with Genivia over some foolish chatter and gossip. The woman was as large as a cow. If she could lumber out of the confines of the palace and into the sunshine with no care that someone might hunt her down, then Silviana should not fear.

The thick high walls arched overhead as they passed the entry portcullis, where the sentries watched silent, their gleaming long-nosed guns another sign of the changing world. Her father had brought these back from an Eastern trading meeting, and all the border forts now had trained riflemen. *The king returns*, the rifles whispered in lead and powder voices. Soon the duchies will stand together. The king returns.

On the outer walls hung three iron cages. Silviana stopped short, her hand slipping from Lilika's grip. "What?" But whatever else she wanted to ask could not come clear from her throat. The words caught there, choked in a wire noose like a hare. Strangled slow.

"Your father's punishment," Lilika said. "Don't look at them, it is enough to know that your father will always protect you."

"Who were they?" Despite Lilika's instruction, Silviana found she could not turn away. They had been people, once. One of them still had clumps of ragged hair attached to his skull, scraps of clothing binding his ribs and joints together. The other two had been taken apart by the rooks. One rook still sat, pewter-beaked, pecking at the remnants of a knee. It seemed bored, passing time. The rest of the bones littered the ground beneath the cages. "What did they do to deserve this?"

"You know of the forest men, the wild boys of the glens?"

Lilika made to grab her hand and drag her on after the party, who were moving away up ahead. "There was a ring of smugglers and traders, they were stealing wools and moving them down to the Sevari coast to sell to the western isles and the southern reds. It was your cousin who caught them. These men confessed, and for their confessions they were punished."

Silviana tore her gaze away and looked down at her feet instead. "Not an incentive to confess," she said.

"Ah, but you do not see what happened to those whose guilt stayed quiet," Lilika said. "Their suffering was unimaginable."

A sudden illness rose in Silviana's throat, and she swallowed it down. "Is my father a cruel man?"

"Not to his friends," Lilika said. "Not to his family."

Family. They had passed now into the small woods where the trees shaded bracken and fallen logs, and the servants had begun to set out rugs and erect gentle tents. They unfolded silk and wood chairs and small tables. Others set out glass and porcelain and filled the bowls with fruits and wines. Within moments, they had recreated a women's lounge in the middle of the forest. The walls were wood and black ivy and the ceiling was sky and arching branch, but still the musicians were the same, and the women danced their same rapturous dances, feet flying over familiar carpets. The first leaves were turning yellow, high in the branches.

"What will happen to me when the boy is born?" Silviana whispered. She took a seat in a long chair opposite where Marjeta reclined, one hand resting on the bulge of her belly. She looked like a bladder blown to bursting point. Despite that she seemed ... pleased, almost happy. It was unusual to see Marjeta looking so relaxed and joyful. She shone under the late summer sun, the light that fell through the green boughs catching on foxfur undertones in her dark hair, washing her face soft.

"Nothing, my lamb," Lilika said. "Do not worry."

But the words were hollow, meaningless. Silviana could do nothing but worry. Now that there was a real heir on the way, perhaps her father no longer feared for her safety. She shook her head. No. He would simply acknowledge that she was no longer a baby to be coddled and petted and kept out of every draft and wrapped in lambswool in case she broke. She was becoming an adult, and it was only proper that she was given the freedoms of one.

So why did her stomach churn, and why did she hate it when her beloved cousin joined them in Marjeta's rooms, and danced with them and played games, and called her Starling like he always had? It should have made her happy to be here in this realm that had always been his and never hers. Silviana clenched her fists and stared through her blind eye at the white-brightness, at the emptiness, and wished she could see shadows again. At least the shadows told her something, even if she wasn't sure what they were.

"Lee?"

"Yes, my sweet?" While the other maids had taken to dancing giddily arm in arm, their laughter swirling around them, Lilika had mirrored the seated duchess, though she had taken out a complicated shawl of saffron wool to work on, and it spilled over her lap like threads of sunlight.

"Do you ever have..." How to put it that it would not sound like something Brother Milos would condemn? "Dreams, or feelings about what might come?"

"Visions of the future?" Lilika's needles snipped against each other, precise little clicks that sliced the seconds apart. "Furis frowns on augury."

"Does he?" Silviana looked down at her feet, at the basket of waiting wools and threads. She'd rather dance, but dancing felt like giving in. She would do nothing. "Brother Milos talks of prophets."

"That's different," Lilika said. "A prophet is sent by Furis to speak of his glory. Dabbling in augury is a selfish thing — men and women do it only to see their own fortunes."

There was no way to explain the shadows, Silviana thought. How to tell Lilika that she saw a black shadow that clung to Lilika's back, that aped her every move like a hobgoblin. That she saw other shadows dance between the occasional servant or maid, like ill thoughts that had taken life. How to explain that even though Marjeta glowed under the sunshine, content as a brown cow in the field, that there were shadows that swirled over her distended belly. Tiny wreaths of storm clouds that surged and dissolved and reappeared.

"Do you think you see portents?" Lilika whispered, soft enough that the click of her needles almost drowned them out.

"No." Silviana shook her head. *I think I see magic.* And what a confession that would be. Could it truly be magic she saw? And if so, why did it cling to Lilika who hated magic, and why did it eddy around her father's head in a black crown, and why did it curl between Devan and Marjeta as though it had knit them together in a shroud. "The wind has turned."

"So it has." Lilika set down her needles and cocked her head toward the darkening sky. Soon the heavy winds of autumn would be stronger, as the seasons turned. But this was more like a winter storm, black and frost-jawed. Clouds were coming in rapidly from the northern mountains, sweeping down their flanks towards the summer palace. The woods grew emerald and jade, as the sky bruised overhead. A cold wind had flung its hands toward them, ripping healthy leaves straight from the branches and scattering them, laughing in the sudden madness.

Marjeta's face darkened, and she frowned.

"This is out of season," Lilika said. "Come, we must get you back to the palace." Even as she spoke the sky turned black, slammed down a white fist of lightning and split a nearby tree in half. Everyone leaped to their feet or staggered out of their swirling dance. The air shook, and the rain fell hard and cold and sudden.

Genivia and Devan were helping Marjeta to her feet, and the servants hurried about like ants in a kicked-open ant nest, scurrying for tents and cushions and glasses as the wind ripped and tore the little outdoor court to shreds.

The black miasma that swirled around Marjeta darkened, and for a moment she was lost to Silviana's vision. Her good eye still saw the duchess — pale and sweating and clutching at her belly — but her blind eye saw only a pillar of black smoke where Marjeta had been.

Another lightning strike split the air, and the women screamed again. Small pack donkeys were calling abrasively, and the birds were gone. No more singing and music, just thunder and screeching. It sounded like the end of a nightmare. Silviana found herself tugged away from the frenzy of humans and covered with a woollen cloak and hood against the pelting rain. Lilika kept a firm grip on her, hustling her back toward the palace at speed. "What of Marjeta?"

"Do not worry yourself. She has Genivia and her servants." Lilika tugged. "Faster, child. I don't need you catching sick again."

"But she's—"

"Not my concern. You are."

The path underfoot was rapidly turning to thick mud, and the rain fell harder, soaking her down to the bone, while the mud splattered across her skirts and bodice and cloak. They passed under the iron cages, where the human remains were being hammered by silver and ice, where the bones were lost under churning mud, and into the safety of the palace walls. Though they were not yet indoors, the high walls gave some shelter, and Lilika led her charge on a convoluted route back to the great stairs and the main entrance, where servants were already rushing out holding canopies to protect their young charge.

Silviana looked back, but there was no sign yet of the rest of the party. Somewhere out in the howling maelstrom of wind and rain and lightning, Marjeta was slowly being moved toward home. It was not as if the woman could run. She was not yet due, but she'd grown to a size that hobbled her and there was no way she would be fleet footed now, and certainly not with the wind lashing at her.

"Come, come, we must get you dry." Lilika had grabbed a thick woven blanket and was bundling her up tightly in it, scrubbing at her wet hair and cheeks even as she marched Silviana into the halls. The rain ceased, leaving only the torrential sound against stone and tile.

*

Silviana did not see Marjeta after that. She was left alone in her rooms with only Lilika and a scattering of bored ladies-in-waiting for company. She stalked her suite, feeling caged, nervous. She could leave her rooms, but a buzzing ran along her skin, making her edgy. She had no desire to talk to anyone. All around her eddies and flickers of magic moved. A maelstrom of imaginary dust that she could not mention. In their cages, her grandmother's birds flew back and forth, terrified by the storm. She motioned for the women to cover their cages with the indigo silks. And under the sudden darkness, the birds stilled. If only she could so easily calm her own visions, hide them away under silks and send them to sleep.

Lilika had very quickly shut down any conversation that turned toward her visions, and she was hardly going to start a discussion about it with the other women. They had all been there when her father had ordered the lady-in-waiting Areya burned as a witch. Silviana had heard only snippets and rumours — enough to know that her stepmother had shot her own servant, sent an arrow through her eye rather than leave her condemned to suffer through the flames.

It had made her father rage, Silviana remembered. He'd gone south to raise more armies, to convince more dukes to fall under his banner to show a united front against the coming war from the east, and the anger had been let from him like sour blood from a sick man on his return. Still, it had not been a pleasant time. Silviana shivered and pulled her fur-lined cloak firmly around her shoulders as she watched the rain hammer silver down on the private gardens below, the ones that had once been her mother's.

Why had Marjeta not come to join her on her return? It was possible that she'd been left exhausted by the sudden return journey and the unexpected storm that still lashed the distant trees and turned the sky black and purple.

She turned away from the window at the sound of a servant entering the room, her feet pattering on the thick carpet, her breath coming in soft gasps. The girl looked like she'd run a race from one end of the palace to the other, her pale cheeks flushed clay red.

"What is it?" Lilika snapped, getting to her feet.

The darkness swirled around the girl too, faint veils that slowly dissipated as she tried to get her breath back. Silviana pressed a palm to her blind eye and shut out the vision. It was just a breathless servant, with some message or other.

"My lady. My ladies," the girl corrected and half-collapsed in a curtsy. She was only vaguely familiar. Silviana thought perhaps she'd seen her in Marjeta's rooms, filling the hearth with fresh wood or clearing away a meal. "Please, it's the duchess."

"What of her?" Silviana asked before Lilika could. "What has happened?"

"It's coming, your grace. The baby. The storm's brought her birthing on early."

"Early," Lilika scoffed half under her breath, but still loud enough for both Silviana and the nameless servant to hear. "Or in perfect time, who can say?" She began to gather her baskets and called for a cloak. "Has the midwife been sent for?"

The servant nodded. "And word sent to the duke. Until his return, we thought to come tell you." This time it was clear she spoke to Lilika, and Silviana frowned.

"I'll go to her," Lilika said. She smiled sweetly at Silviana. "Do not fret, little one. We've been expecting this day, haven't we? Soon you shall have a brother. Stay here and have something to eat. Lexia will help you change for bed, and I'll be back as soon as I can."

"Why must you go?" What did Lilika have to do with this new and unwanted child, this interloper? "I'll come with you."

But Lilika shook her head. "It'll be a long and tedious night, stay. You can do nothing now but pray to Furis for the safe birth of your new brother."

No mention made of the safety of his dam, of course, and Silviana smiled sourly. "Pray?" She clenched her fists. "If that's all the help I can be."

"You'd be surprised at how powerful prayer truly is," Lilika said. "And what Furis will tell you if you listen to him." There was no time for further argument; the door was closing and Silviana was left alone with the handful of ladies and the muted crackle and roar of the fire. A log popped, and something shifted in the hearth. Silviana walked over to the flames but she could see nothing in the fire but the dancing pattern of black and blue and orange and white gold. "Salamander," she whispered, and immediately felt like a fool. "If you're there, and you can hear me, let me know if all is well with the duchess." The fire flickered toward her, but no creature emerged, and she backed away.

There was no point in following Lilika to Marjeta's rooms, and Silviana knew she was angry because she was powerless. Her world was going to change now, for ill or worse. It was hardly unheard of for mother or babe to die. Everything hung in a delicate balance and she had no way to know which direction the world would spin now.

Silviana looked at the concerned faces of the women gathered, watching her in expectation. Whatever she did or said now, they would talk, and the talk would spread to the rest of the palace, and to Brother Furis and his men. It was something she had not even realised until she'd finally been allowed to leave her rooms. Nothing she did went unnoticed, unremarked. She took a deep breath. "Come," she said and held out her hands. "The lady Lilika is right, we should pray for the safety of our duchess, and for my father's new heir. May Furis bless us all." The words tasted like bile and rot.

Wolf Child

The storm had shaken the thing inside her loose. Marjeta bowed over her stomach, panting her way through the arching pain that seemed determined to split her in two. She'd had her share of false pains throughout her pregnancy, but they'd barely prepared her for how bad the labour was going to be.

For a moment the pain receded, and the taut muscles of her stomach softened. She drew breath, felt it tear bloody through her lungs and throat. The sheets around her were soaked, and she let herself be maneuvered so that new dry bedding could be pressed under her. Genivia's face swam into her vision, her brow furrowed. She wiped at Marjeta's brow and cheeks with a dampened cloth, cooling away the rivulets of sweat and tears. Marjeta leaned into the careful touch.

"There, there." Genivia put the cloth down and held a glass of honeyed wine to Marjeta's lips. It was sour and disgusting, but cold, and Marjeta sipped gratefully. "The midwife is on her way," Genivia whispered. "Everything will be well."

Marjeta managed to nod, just as another contraction built up its tearing agony, and she leaned forward, squatting over the nest of blankets and sheets, her thighs trembling, hands clenched against Genivia's supporting arms.

There were several women in the tiny birth chamber — more than Marjeta wanted — but she had no power to speak, to shoo them away, and a dim animal part of her was relieved that they were there. Surrounding her like a pack, and, she their leader.

When the contraction passed, Marjeta managed to ask a

question, pushing Genivia's hand and the glass of wine away. "The duke?"

"Messengers have been sent to Fort Verrin," Genivia said. The unspoken truth was it was no short journey to the capital and the stronghold. It could be days before Calvai returned. Weeks.

"Devan," Marjeta said. He'd not gone with the duke this time — having been left to safeguard the palace and command the small army that protected it from any attack.

Genivia frowned. "Hush, my love, breathe deeply."

After that, Marjeta lost time. Everything narrowed down to the breaths between pain, the immense shoving sensation in her lower body, the blood and beat. She was vaguely aware when the midwife arrived and crouched before her to feel at her entrance to see how far along she was, and dazed when the midwife guided her on hand down to feel the wrinkled scalp that waited between her legs.

"Near done," the midwife said, her voice matter-of-fact and soothing. "The worst will be over soon."

Marjeta felt the child shoot from her in a surge of relief and fluid and grunted as the creature slipped from one watery world to a new one filled with air and earth and pain.

There was silence around her, and she felt the midwife working at the child, clearing mucus away from its mouth.

"Is it a boy?" she asked through cracked lips, an aching throat. That was all she needed. A son. Then she could also slip into another world. Take her beloved Dust, take Devan's hand, and run far away from the ceaseless greed of dukes and future kings.

The midwife turned from her, quickly bundling the infant in light cloths.

"A son?" Marjeta repeated.

It was Genivia who answered her. "Yes," she said. "You — you must rest."

"Why does he not cry?" Marjeta struggled into a better position. The child was still connected to her, cord pulsing as the next stage of her labour began. "Show me my son."

"It would do you no good," the midwife said. "He was born dead."

"Show him to me." The world turned black around Marjeta, blood pouring from her, pooling around her, magic at its ripest. The words held command in them, and the midwife turned, startled, her arms rising to pass the child to its mother.

The child was still, wizened and wrinkled and furred with vernix. He looked like a carving covered in wet white moss. But there was more to him than crouched and twisted limbs and silence and womb fluid. He was slicked with fine dark hairs from head to foot. A small wolf-creature with a human face and an animal pelt. "What — what is this?"

Marjeta took the child, ignoring the echoed pains of the placenta being delivered, looking only at the strange wood-carving face and dark fur of the little creature that had been born without ever having life. It was not possible. She'd felt him stir and kick and turn all through the months. Had seen her stomach shift as he'd pressed a fist or a foot against the inside of his prison, jammed a limb under a rib, danced in his eagerness to be free. And now. And now. Nothing.

"Why?"

The midwife had begun to twist a string about the cord. A life line that passed on no life. A pointless chain connecting mother and baby. "We do not understand the ways of gods," she said.

"Furis has judged."

Marjeta looked up from the tiny face and into the bird-black eyes of Lilika. She had not even heard the woman enter. But she stood there now, a trace of a smile hooked at one corner of her mouth, her victory evident in her pious head tilt, her clasped hands. "The son of a king needs to be noble of body," she continued. "Pure; his blood free of witchery and curses."

The women began to mutter and hiss among themselves.

"Calvai is not a king," Marjeta said. She could taste blood from her split lip, could feel nothing but emptiness, deflated aching. She had been hollowed out, all her hope torn from her with this birth.

"But he will be," Lilika said. She motioned for the midwife to take the baby from Marjeta, but Marjeta pulled the dead child to her chest and shook her head.

"Give her some time," the midwife said, "for the grieving, you ken."

It seemed that even Lilika could allow that, now that the stillbirth of Calvai's son kept her place secure. She nodded, dipping her head and quickly rounding up the women. "Come," she said. "The duke will soon be home, and we must ready the palace for him."

They left Marjeta alone, with only the midwife, who was clearing the worst of the bloodied mess away, and Genivia, who was mixing herbs into another glass of wine. She held this out to Marjeta, who shook her head.

"It will help stop the bleeding, and dry up milk," Genivia said. "I had a sister lose a child," she explained softly. "I've not come to take him away from you, keep him as long as you need, but drink this."

Reluctantly, Marjeta reached one hand out for the glass, and drank it deeply, though it was sour and bitter and rancid in a way that no amount of honey could disguise. She shuddered. It was practical to dry up her milk, to begin the process to rebuild her body as though no child had ever existed within it. The boy — the small nameless creature — would be buried, and after a time, Marjeta would be expected to resume her duties as duchess again. She choked. She could not. She would not. She would never go through this again. She pressed the wolf-child closer to her aching breasts and swallowed away the salt-thickness in her throat.

She would bury her son. And then she would leave.

The Truth

A winter pall hung over the summer palace. The myriad servants and workers and grooms and women and men who kept the little city running with boisterous efficiency had been quietened. Made pale, voiceless puppets of themselves.

The duke had not yet returned from a skirmish with southern boatmen on the Misk. It would be less than a day, Silviana thought. By now he would be approaching the city of Verrin, his horse sweat-dark, his men grim and bloodied. It had taken a few weeks for the armies in their war-dimmed panoply to follow the great river path back north to Jurie. And he would return with the news that his first-born son had never breathed, had died before he could live.

Silviana pitied the messenger who'd had to deliver that particular missive to her father. While she wanted to believe he would not take his disappointment and rage out on a servant for the ill luck of simply bearing bad tidings, she had begun to see that her father was not the shining king-to-be she'd believed him when she was still his precious bird. His caged starling in her room of gold.

There had been the bodies she'd seen on the outer walls, and other news that came to her now that she could roam the palace freely. Before, everything she'd heard had been filtered through the ladies-in-waiting, catching all the worst and giving her only what they deemed suitable. Even their gossip and whispered news had been filtered through the fine silk of their sleeves and sweetened for her ears.

There were no such barriers now.

Silviana heard things. True and false. And she watched the words flitter from mouth to ear, her blind eye steady and curious, able to pick up the trails the words left in the air like mica and sand. Some truths were easy to spot — they were gold bright, motes of tiny suns that danced joyous through the air. Just like some lies were coal dust spun lazy and slow. But it was rarely that simple: fact and fiction interwove in a glittering pageant of light and dark, rainbow hues threaded with smoke.

The room she was in, so familiar from childhood, had taken on strange fugue-like dimensions since her illness. Even now, with fires banked against the cold, the room seemed to exist in an icy netherworld; a half-hell. Each time Silviana thought she was adapting to these visions and hallucinations, they seemed to worsen. She learned to say nothing of them, which meant she learned to say very little.

She heard more, though. She heard how people thought she'd been witch-tainted by her brush with death, that a spell had been cast on her, and she was no longer the duke's true child, but some kind of poppet made in her image and controlled by wicked forces.

She watched Lilika's mouth moving, a slow, slick popping. The women were huddled together, their heads bent close enough that their whispers eddied around them in dull constellations. Silviana could pick up a word here and there, but she already knew what they were saying.

It had been a repeated refrain since her half-brother's death all those weeks ago.

Witch.

Slut.

It had fur, just like a beast—

It wasn't born dead, I heard it howl once, before the midwife smothered it.

Abomination.

She must have lain with wolves to breed such a monstrosity.

How—

Witches can shift their form, I've heard—

Please, you sound like you've drunk the afternoon wine for breakfast—

No, it's true.
I heard—
I heard-
And I heard—
And I heard her sister—
Her sister was a witch.
And I heard—
She poisoned her—
Poisoned the duke's daughter too.
You hear lots of things.
No, but this is true.
I heard she killed it herself, that the midwife tried to stop her—

One of the women paused to look over her shoulder at Silviana, and others followed suit. Their voices dropped, and Lilika scowled from where she presided over them in her black throne.

Silviana pressed her hands to her ears and closed her eyes to stop the assault of half-truths. Every grain of truth spun around a sun of lies. Or was it the other way around? It was so hard to tell.

A hand shook her gently by the shoulder. "Lamb, what is wrong — do you sicken?" Lilika, concerned, motherly.

It was the one rock in the shifting world. Surely whatever Lilika said had to be the truth. Silviana opened her eyes, stared up into slantwise brown, into her golden face, the long coils of her hair, threaded now with a few fine strands of silver.

"No." Silviana shook her head but raised her hand to stop Lilika from leaving. Her fingers met cloth, and for a moment she was relieved that she grasped something firm. Someone real. It was tiresome, this world of ghosts and shadows. "My father returns today," she said, and Lilika nodded. "I would like to see Marjeta before he does."

Deep lines cut Lilika's face. "I do not think it wise," she said. "The lady is not herself."

"She is grieving," Silviana said. A pang shot through her. Grieving for a child she never knew, just as Silviana had grieved for a mother she'd not had the chance to meet. Perhaps there was some shared suffering between them they could bridge. "Of course, she is not herself."

"No, that's not what I meant."

Silviana stood. She had made the decision. "Take me to her," she said. "Perhaps there is some comfort I can give her that others could not."

"She does not look for comfort," Lilika said. "She feels nothing. She is like a stone in a field. She does not weep, she does not care. You can go to her doors and beat them till your fists turn bloody. She has no time for visitors. The only one she speaks to is Devan."

"Devan?" Silviana stuttered over the name, squinting at the trails of gold and black and purple and yellow that danced through Lilika's words. "Why—?"

"Oh, my lamb," Lilika said with a sigh. She took her, held her close and whispered against her neck. "It is too obvious for either of us to deny it. The duchess and your cousin are lovers."

Silviana wrenched out of Lilika's embrace, staggering back. Between them, Lilika's last pronouncement fell in a showering veil of sparkling light.

Truth.

And truth.

And condemning truth.

*

Silviana still wanted to see her. Maybe the truth was only what someone believed, and not fact. She clasped her hands in front of her. She stood small before the door that led to the Duchess Suite, the rooms that had once been her mother's, and took deep cold breaths.

She'd run after Lilika had told her. Turned like a hare and raced through the trails and tracks of old stone until she'd reached this door. And now that she was here, she was too ... something ... to raise her fist and knock. Not scared. Though maybe that was it. She felt as though she stood on a window ledge with the stars screaming in the dark above, and below her only the waiting ground like ink and secrets. The temptation to drop. To fall endless and forever through nothing.

But the drop was never endless. Silviana had pushed enough

pigeon eggs off window ledges to know that.

The door swung open, the hinges oiled silent. A red-headed woman Silviana knew stood on the other side. She squinted. Genivia. One of Lilika's coterie who had flown (or been pushed from the window ledge) from her side to land next to Marjeta after the death of the witch servant. Silviana blinked. She knew nothing about her, beyond her talent for the harp, her face a cluttered field of freckles, and the pinched way her heavy brows knitted together in permanent concentration. She was just another of the massed women who had been her captors, and comforters in captivity.

"Lady Silviana." Genivia dropped into a curtsy, and as she straightened, Silviana could see the tiredness that sunk under skin in green-grey shadows, the tightness of her mouth and the hollows under her cheek bones. "May I inquire—"

"I've come to see Marjeta," Silviana told her, walking forward.

Genivia did not move out her way. "The duchess is not accepting visitors," she began, when Silviana simply thrust past her, ducking under arms and racing into the golden rooms.

She darted from doorway to doorway, past the great hearths that lined the myriad rooms, until she burst into the bedroom.

The first thing she saw was Marjeta. Not lying ill in bed as the whispers went. But standing at the foot of it, dressed in leathers and high-collar jacket, her wide split skirts folded and tucked into leather boots. Her hair was drawn back and pinned out of the way, the golden salamander was crouched on one shoulder, his tail curling across her chest, and she was packing saddle bags as though she were about to set out on a long journey.

It was not this that stunned Silviana into silence, but the man who sat on the long couch along one wall, under the mullioned window, his dark clothes and dark hair and dark skin like a stone in the heart of the peach gold room.

"What are you doing?" Silviana said. And then on the next breath, before Marjeta could answer, "And do not lie to me."

Marjeta looked at her with a strange dull calm. "I would not," she said finally. "I wish to leave before your father returns."

"Leave," Silviana repeated dully, as the words fell in sundrops.

"Yes." Marjeta continued to pack, her hands steady. The last few items were placed reverently on the top of the saddle bag — a mirror wrapped in silk, and an amber bear older than the Summer Palace. Marjeta hesitated momentarily, her hand hovering over the bag, the bear clutched tight. She turned to face Silviana. "I don't do this to hurt you," she said. "Any of this. I wanted to be your sister, your friend, anything you wished from me, but the world turns in ways we can't control."

Devan stood, his eyes flat, empty. "Mari," he said softly. "It's a sign, this — now is not the time."

"And you." Silviana whirled on him. "You are a traitor to my father."

"My uncle," Devan said.

"And your king," Silviana hissed.

"Not king yet," Marjeta said, still mild and calm. She spoke over Silviana. "We should leave now."

"I—" Devan hesitated, and Silviana pushed against the shadows that gathered around him.

"Is it true," she whispered, "that you are under her spell?"

Marjeta laughed like a barking fox.

Devan stood grim and silent.

"I had thought the whispers just jealous rumours that bored servants made up to pass the time, that ladies who read too much made up to make their lives more interesting, but it's true. It is as Lilika always said. You are a witch, and you have enspelled my future husband in this witch web." Although Silviana had meant the accusations as manipulation, as she spoke them the tears clogged her throat, and the realisation that everything was once again being taken from her — the friend she'd believed she'd had, the beloved cousin who she was meant to wed.

"If I am a witch," Marjeta said, "I am a very poor one." She clicked her tongue, and the salamander leaped from her shoulder down to the bed, bouncing there, its wide eyes watchful. "And a poor sister," she added.

"We can't leave," Devan said.

"We must."

"If you go," Siliviana said, and her fists clenched at her sides, "I will tell my father everything I know, and he will hunt you down like dogs, and he will put you in cages on the walls and the crows and rooks will eat your eyes while you are still alive."

From outside, a bugling trumpet call sounded, and Marjeta sat down on the bed, her legs crumpling beneath her. "I have left it too late," she whispered.

Silviana smiled. It was the sound of the heralds announcing her father's return. They could not run now. And she would make sure that Marjeta never ran again. "If you promise never to leave this palace," she whispered, "I will say nothing to my father. I will say nothing to Brother Milos and his men."

Marjeta's mouth twisted. "Will you lock me in my suite?" she asked. "Are we to exchange places, little starling?"

"Yes." Silviana pressed her hands to her ears at the strange howling that echoed inside her head. "Yes." It was not fair that Marjeta thought she could simply leave. She must learn her place like all the mothers who had come before her. The heralds sounded their trumpets again, and Silviana gave the couple one last contemptuous look before she ran from the rooms to greet her father.

Marriage Proposals

Calvai had gone and returned a hundred times. And always Lilika had waited for him. She had been a mistress for so long that sometimes she forgot she was not a wife. It took all her strength to contain her smiles, to rein in her desire to touch the duke's hands, his face. It was not the time, not the place.

He looked tired.

Angry.

Lost.

Under his beard was the mien of a boy who had lost his favourite hound. Broken a favourite toy. It was the look of someone who cannot quite believe the world has gone against him again.

The soldiers were tired, filthy, and limping, and their banners hung, dripping rain. Border wars and scuffles had worn men and flags ragged, and for Calvai it was not just swords but wits he had to parry. He fought on battlefields and in duchy halls, regimenting the dukes into new alliances. Or old ones, perhaps. Older than myths.

Although it was not Lilika's place, she slipped past the waiting men and women to stand by his horse's head as he dismounted. One hand caught in the bridle, the other free that she could touch him as quickly as the briefest brush of a dandelion seed blown past. He managed a grim twitch of his mouth when he saw her, but there was no time now for happiness.

His son was dead.

If that even had been his son, which Lilika had her doubts about. The Duchess Marjeta had not her skill when it came to keeping her truths screwed deep into her heart. She looked too long on Devan. She crowned him with her eyes.

"My king," Lilika said, "it pains me that you return to such news."

"King," he said, and his mouth twisted in black humour. "Almost, but not yet. Where is it?"

"She — the lady Marjeta buried it in the yellow garden." Where the Duchess Belind had spent too much of her time — private gardens overgrown with sunlit roses, with daffodils and gorse and every yellow flower she could cajole from the cold mud. Where Belind herself had been planted after she bled herself dry.

Now the corpse of the smallest Jurie lay next to her, between the Mother and the Grandmother that were not his. Perhaps it was best that Calvai never got to see the beast. Hideous and furred, its face more of a snout, eyes white and lidless. It would have broken him to see his hopes so cruelly formed.

The men were loud and tired, and there were feasts waiting for them. Stable boys and servants passed, leading horses off to be brushed and fed and stables, tack taken to be cleaned and oiled. Porters hefted goods and gear to their places, and a kitchen servant had brought out clay mugs of black beer for the men to wet their throats. Lilika handed Calvai his, and their fingers met as he took it. His touch was firm, filled with intent, and he nodded at Lilika.

They had been together so long that they did not need words. Lilika would come to him that evening, to the private rooms that only his most loyal men know of and would be his love and his comfort. *As I have always been.*

"Where is Silviana?" he asked. "I do not see her."

Lilika stepped back. "She will come down to greet you in the hall, when the feast begins." She didn't want to say anything to upset the duke, but Silviana was turning strange. Fey and wild. She looked like a creature from old women's tales, born out of cobwebs and moonlight. She looked nothing like Belind or Calvai. Perhaps the magic that Lilika had prayed for all those years back had made of her a new creature. Something old and evil. "She has been waiting for your return." If the girl truly were evil, Furis would not have wanted her protected, surely, Lilika told herself.

Or perhaps it was not that Furis had wanted the girl protected, but instead for Lilika to see the error in what she had done. To see this child she had loved as a daughter turn sour and strange, and to know that she had caused it with her magic. To pay her dues in guilt and suffering.

She would have to pray to Furis. Seek guidance.

"Bring her to me now," he said. "There are arrangements I must make." A grim cast appeared on his face — an expression that in fourteen years, even Lilika had never seen. It made him look like a stranger.

*

They met in the duke's war rooms and not in their private bedroom. Sir Provas stood, armoured and reeking, in attendance along with the retinue of duke's wolves, and Brother Milos. Calvai and Milos were in deep conversation, their heads pressed close, their whispers low, when Lilika drew Silviana into the room. They were very nearly late, because the girl had been determined to not wear shoes, wanting to appear before her father barefoot and bareheaded like a beggar. Finally, Lilika had convinced her to wear a pair of leather slippers embroidered with bright salamanders that the duchess had made for her and had braided her hair back and pinned a net of little red stones in place. It did nothing to cover the silver or to disguise how cursed the girl now looked, but it was better than she'd been before, tangle haired and stare-eyed, her feet ashy with dried mud.

Lilika curtsied deeply, her neck bent, and made the sign of the horns. Brother Milos nodded. His thin sunken face grew more and more skeletal with each year. Sometimes Lilika wondered if he carried a canker inside him, but why would Furis curse one he so loved? It was age that wore him thin. Like it ground them all down.

The duke stared grimly at his daughter. "I'd heard," he said. "But I had not realised that she had spoiled so." He spoke as though Silviana were witless, mute, deaf. As though she did not exist. "My brother-in-law has sent news that he must with regret cancel the engagement of my daughter and his son." There was no change in his tone, but Lilika, long practised, could see the fine tremble of anger that lay under his calm words. "It seems I cannot even trust those bound to me by family," he said. "Treachery on every side. In the forests, the fields, and in the palaces themselves." He smiled then, but it was bright and false as the evening star.

Silviana said nothing, she simply stared blankly ahead of her as though she saw things that were not there.

Her father did not notice but kept talking. "While at the time it seemed best to keep the bonds between Jurie and Sevari tight, I see now that Furis moves in ways that are impossible for us mere mortals to divine." He glanced at Milos, who nodded once, almost in encouragement. "I have been assured that this too was part of Furis' plan for me, and that greater ones would come. We have made much progress uniting the duchies. Many of the border lords swear fealty to me, and already proclaim me king. In a matter of months, the Grand Gathering will take place and this decad it is to be held in the fort at Verrin." Calvai's eyes glittered. "I am assured that most of the dukes are willing to bend their knee and declare me their high king, as it was in the elder days. The few who are undecided will see that I mean no harm, only that I want our lands protected from all threats. From the sea, the northern lands, the eastern empires."

Lilika fidgeted, unsure why she and Silviana had been called here for these insights to Calvai's plans. While it was true most of his goals were whispered knowledge, and hardly secrets, it was not like him to spew his plans before mistresses, daughters and wives. It would make more sense if he held forth with his kingsmen. She risked a quick glance to her charge. Silviana still kept her blank stare, but she was frowning now, her mouth moving, shaping silent words. She looked madder than ever.

Suddenly, her silent whispers stopped, and she drew herself straighter. Lilika fought the urge to grab Silviana's sleeve and hush her before she said something foolish and dangerous.

"Father?" Silviana sounded confused, almost unsure of where she was and who she spoke with. "Is this you?"

"Of course, my dear," Calvai said, though he shot a glance at

Milos again, who shook his head very subtly. "What would make you think otherwise? I know," he laughed, though it sounded reed-hollow, "I have come straight from the horse and road. I swear that under this stink and grime, I am your duke and father."

"The boy is dead," Silviana said. "Hurrying back would make no difference."

The room went silent, and Lilika clenched her fists, waiting for Calvai to strike. He was an even-tempered man, for the most part, until pushed. And then he reacted with a cat fast rage. Claws and spit. But there was no blow. "I did not return for the boy," he said. "Dead is dead."

"Oh?" Silviana's face cleared, and she looked upon her father, her good eye gleaming, her dead eye pale as a grub.

"I came for you," he said. "I have arranged your marriage to the Emperor in the East."

The men did not react — obviously, this was news they already knew — but Lilika felt ice strike right to her heart. She gasped, trying to catch breath that would not come, to voice her disbelief, her displeasure, her shock and rage.

Silviana blinked once, very slowly. "Marriage? To our distant enemy?"

"All men were enemies once," said Calvai. "But they do not need to be. The emperor will take you as a second wife. After the marriage, the Empire and the eight duchies will be at peace."

"And I am the price of this friendship," Silviana said, drawing the words out as though they were garnets on a chain, and she a jeweller considering them for flaw and beauty. "I see. How convenient then that he has agreed to this match. And his good wife, likewise."

"Convenient, indeed."

"What of my cousin?" Silviana asked. "Now that we are not engaged?"

Calvai laughed. "I will settle that with my sister, you've no need to worry your head about such things. Your place is to trust me." The words were a final end to any argument. Calvai wiped a hand over his face and turned to his kings-men. "I will not be at the feasting," he said. "Have servants bring me food." He was dismissing them all, even Silviana, but he said to Lilika. "And you, stay with me. We will talk."

The cold horror that overwhelmed her now was nothing to the previous shock. This was a slow twist of the knife in a gut and not a killing slice. Of course, Sir Provas and the kings-men knew she was Calvai's mistress, but it had been a secret grown away from Silviana. Always, she had wanted her surrogate daughter to see her father the same way Lilika saw Furis. Bigger than humans, above the sweat and pettiness of debauchery and greed. She'd wanted the girl to see him as noble, and not as a man.

And perhaps, more so, she'd wanted Silviana to see her as a priestess. A mother-figure. Not a treacherous slattern who bedded a duke and smiled at his wives and held his daughter.

She wanted to grab on to Silviana and explain everything, to say that she gave the duke comfort that only a woman could, that she had for years, and that she hurt no one, that what did it matter since the duchess herself had a lover, but Silviana was already turning away. Her back was stiff and shaking.

Brother Milos passed the sign of the horns over them, then departed behind her. The door closed, and Calvai and Lilika were alone in the war rooms.

"You cannot do this," Lilika pleaded.

"Cannot? But I must. Even when I have all of the Eight united under my banner, the emperor still has greater lands and armies."

"And why would he trouble us now? There is little happening on the Petrell border that is greater than robbery and minor skirmishes. The trade between us is too rich to jostle with battle."

"You talk of things you do not understand," Calvai said. "You have not seen outside the borders of this duchy and yet you would try tell me how I must reign? You should stick to prattling over tapestry. The girl must be wed, and no one of rank in the duchies will take her. Word has spread too far."

"But not far enough," Lilika realised sadly. "And after the marriage — when he finds that she is ... troubled? What happens to her then?"

The duke sat down, almost collapsing into his chair at the great map table. "I cannot tell. These foreign men have strange appetites, perhaps he will find her illness amusing rather than insulting. I've heard it said his first wife has a palsy that strikes on occasion, though it has not stopped her from bearing him a son. He will not care that my daughter looks to have been cursed with madness as long as she at least can give him what he wants."

"This is a cruel thing you do," Lilika said.

"And it is my choice. You knew she would marry eventually. She is not your daughter, and you never had a claim on her. I gave both of you too long a rein. I thought I protected her, but perhaps I have only ruined her."

"Too much freedom?" Lilika nearly choked. "You kept her locked away for years."

"And even then, she was still not safe."

Lilika bit down on her lip and fought the trembling in her limbs. "And what now? With no son, surely you could rather make Silviana your heir and pass the Duchy on through her? It would be better done than sending her to the east, to these madmen and their evil magics."

"You question Furis?"

"I — I do not. I question only other options."

"No." Calvai shook his head. "I have considered all. Marjeta may yet give me a living son, she is ripe still for ploughing. If she does not, there are other women. But I have only one daughter. She will understand. She was bred to."

"This crown has changed you," Lilika said, before she could think to stop herself. She had fallen in love with a man bright and beautiful, had hidden her love as best she could, had twisted it, yes, with magic, but she had repented for that love. And now — now she looked at him anew, and the veil of love had grown thin. It was hard to pretend that Calvai was still that young man. His cruelty had grown, slow as a worm in a rotten branch, hidden away, but Lilika could not pretend to be blind to it now.

"I wear no crown," he said.

"You wear Furis' crown, all the same."

Calvai bowed his head as though exhausted by the weight, but Lilika found that she had no pity. It was one thing to send her daughter to Coriast to be a duchess-wife to a man who loved her

only as a sister, but it was another thing altogether to send her far
from the safety of her countrymen and -women, and into a foreign
land with ways that were dark and strange and evil. Furis could not
have commanded this.

Would not have. She bit her tongue and prayed, tasting blood.
Sacrifice. *What must I do?*

Starling's Flight

A man from her father's army escorted Silviana back to her rooms. They passed the Duchess Suite, and for a moment Silviana paused before the bright blue wood and considered throwing open the doors and pointing out the false mother and false cousin, and all they did together, betraying them as they betrayed her. But she did not. Her father had not asked after his wife, had barely bothered to acknowledge that he had, however briefly, had a son. He had summoned his daughter to tell her future, then kept Lilika at his side.

The maids and ladies in her rooms looked troubled, gathered together like hens after the fox has been. She ignored them. All except one who would perhaps speak truth if Silviana asked.

"Lady Genivia," she said, and the curvy woman craned her neck. "Attend me, the rest of you will leave."

She waited grim faced as the gaggle of women gathered their tapestries and books, their half-sewn shirts and hymnals, and left walking on whispers.

"What is it, my lady?" Genivia asked. "How may I serve you?" There were no truths or untruths in the questions, just showers of words that fell like grains of sand blown by a string summer breeze.

Silviana sat down in her chair and breathed slowly, trying to pull ghosts and shadows apart, trying to think clearly. It was hard. Her father's words had wound serpent coils about her throat, and the knowledge that Lilika went to him like a wife sliced at her wrists. "I would know," she said, and the words were choked and small. "How long you kept the truth from me."

Genivia frowned.

"About my cousin, and Marjeta."

The silence was profound, and Silviana felt her world spin again. She was alone. "Leave me," she commanded.

"My lady—" Genivia grew uncertain, her hands twisting. "I know they meant to leave, but—"

"You knew. Of course you did. For how many months. No, do not answer." The blackness whirled in on Silviana from all sides and she stood at the centre of her own private storm, her vision darkened by fear and rage. Everyone had known the truth. Marjeta full of magic and lies, Lilika warming her father's bed, Devan entwined with Marjeta and making a cuckold of her father. Genivia, stolid, solid Genivia, who looked like no falsehood could take root on her tongue — she had kept secrets from Silviana. "Did everyone know that my nursemaid was my father's whore, and my stepmother lay with my cousin? Did you all look at me and laugh behind your hands? Did you think me simple?"

"Not simple," Genivia said. "We did not want to hurt you."

"Get. Out." Silviana spat each word like a stone. She stood, rage stiffening her spine as she watched Genivia curtsy regretfully and leave.

Leave.

That's what everyone in this palace did. They left in coffins, or they left on horses, or on beds of lies. Silviana held her hands out before her face and concentrated. What had she dreamed of, so long ago when she'd first fallen ill? Of hares and bears and forests.

She would not stay. Her cage was open, and there was nothing worth staying for. Certainly not to be married off to some distant emperor, so that she could be a second wife, always a shadow, always a girl in a cage.

Like Nanna's birds, who had been passed down to her, convicts in their own little hells of wire and wood. "You too," Silviana said to them. "You are reminders, and you are warnings." The birds whistled and chirped, buzzing from perch to perch in scatterings of song and seed. Silviana went to the first cage and opened it, and the second and third. All down the room full of birds she went, releasing the captives. Some waited longer in their cages, but others flew straight out, until the room was filled with flying bodies, testing the limits of their new world.

Most of the windows were great frames that held the mullioned glass, but there were smaller windows that could be opened with hinged framework, and Silviana struggled one of these open, letting out the miasma of perfume and wine and feathers, letting in autumn, red as fox fur, cold as first ice.

The birds flew.

*

Perhaps it was magic, or perhaps her dead eye simply showed her the right path to walk, but Silviana saw not another soul as she left the palace. They had dissolved like mud men under rain. She walked with one hand tracing the cold grey stones. The strength of her resolve had reduced them to their atoms. All she saw around her were the birds, dark guiding stars, yellow breasted, red capped, their songs leaving trails of truth like marsh-lights through the shadowing sky

She went wrapped in the scatter dark of visions, between thought and dream. The twilit sky in green and gold, the sounds of herded animals headed home tolling from the distant fields. The faint murmur of speech, but no words. The river rushing in the gorge below the palace. The distant yip of foxes as she passed the empty hanging cages that crowned the High Gate. The cages moved in the wind, but there was no meat, and so no ravens, no crows, no pewter-beak rooks or mocking jackdaws. They had left to hunt carrion pickings in the fields and forest.

She left Crow-Hill road and turned down a dirt track that cut between the fields of high grasses, meadows that edged the forests. "Starling," Silviana said her name to the empty sky, its underwater near-light, its flicker promise of coming stars. With a caw like a startled bird, she flew her stone cage and followed the deer trails though jaggy brambles that prickle-stained her with their blood and hers. The birds had gone, flown further than she could ever hope to follow.

A shadow-hare ran into the gloaming, and Silviana followed.

She left the roads of men, and went deep into the forests, following badger trails and deer paths through the dying bracken and nettles.

She ran until she lost her leather slippers, until her dress was torn to rags and her net of jewels ripped from her hair to garland some sprightly birch, slender as a wand. She ran until she fell to her knees in a clearing, her breath tearing in her chest.

She felt rather than heard the arrow. It thudded into the ground before her face, shaft quivering, flights crow black and shining.

"What have we here?"

Silviana looked up to see a ring of young faces. Boys and almost-men worn rough and raw and scabbed and hard. She knew what they were: thieves and murderers, wildling orphans who made the forest their kingdom, who bowed to no throne but the mountain, and respected no borders but the rivers and streams. As soon as they realised who she was, she was dead. All they saw now was a maiden who was ancient before her time. Half-blind, thin as a winter rabbit, with bare and bleeding feet, a face scratched, a dress that was no longer fine. They would not see the daughter of a duke.

"Starling," Silviana said.

"You're a funny looking sort of bird," said the boy, and he stepped out from the shadows of the trees, his bow held with a casual grace that Silviana recognized from Marjeta. He would pin her as surely as Marjeta would hit the painted circle of a target from a hundred paces. "Where do you come from then, Starling?"

Silviana shook her head and swallowed the pooled saliva in her mouth. "From nowhere. I have no home. I have no hearth. I have no sister nor brother. I have no mother," she said, "I have no father."

"What do you have?"

Silviana tore her knotted necklace free from under her shift. Lilika had given it to her back when Marjeta had first arrived in the palace. A witch stone for protection on a leather thong. It had proven itself useless. "This."

The boys laughed, but they did not kill her.

Passion Play

"You should eat." Lilika gestured at the food the servants had brought for the duke, but he merely grunted. Exhaustion rolled off him, palpable as a stench.

"I'm not hungry," he snapped.

"Then bathe," she said. The water in the wooden tub still steamed, scented with dried flowers and oils. "I will wash you." She'd done that before, so many times. She had a lifetime of washing babes, even as they grew, and what was a man but another child. Calvai did not argue this time, and she helped him out of his leathers and breeches, bundling the rank cloth for the laundry maids. She soaped his shoulders and back, running her hands down skin piebald with sun, rinsing his knotted hair clean and smoothing it with more oils.

And while she washed him, her hands moving in unconscious patterns she had repeated a hundred times, she thought of what she would do.

It was Furis who had to lead her. Lilika closed her eyes and squeezed her hands along the ridges of muscle, massaging the journey from Calvai's shoulders. She prayed, while her hands were consumed by other tasks.

Show me, she begged, over and over. I am lost, I do not know the way. In her mind, she saw the flicker of a bright tail and long ears as a hare leaped past, then disappeared. She could smell the rank musk of bear pelts and she squeezed her eyes tighter still. *Not you, never you.* She had long since left the Three. Furis would show her. This time she would do right.

After a while, lulled by the gentle slap of water and the repeated curve of her own hands, the hares and bears were drowned under as a red light filled her skull. The air smelled now of heart-ease and pine wood, it smelled of burning and blood.

The shadows of the great horns passed over, twin points that trapped her, stilled her and Lilika listened to her god speak in the spaces between her heart beats.

She moved dreamwise, drying the duke, dressing him carefully, kissing the skin of his chest and fingers.

"You're different tonight," he remarked. "Quiet."

"I am thinking," she said, still lost in her instructions.

Calvai laughed, a little of his regular good humour restored. "It doesn't do to think," he said, "could get a woman into trouble."

Lilika smiled blankly. "Sit," she said as she steered him to the table. "I will feed you." She sat on his lap and fed him fragments of bread and meat from her fingers. She filled his wine glass and drank from it between each sip. Calvai, sated and calmed, ran his hands along her hips and breasts, and Lilika allowed him this, as one allows a condemned man his final joys.

When he was spent, Lilika slipped away to clean herself. She gathered her clothes and as she dressed, found a small vial in the very bottom of one of her deep pockets. She had once intended to use this in the drink she'd given Marjeta while she was pregnant, but Furis had stayed her hand. She had forgotten where the vial had gone, had no memory of putting it in this skirt pocket, and surely it would have been found by laundry maids, or crushed? She held it up — small and round as a coin, the blue glass stoppered and waxed. A drop could send a man into a coma. Three drops would fell him. She slid it back into her pocket and went to make her duke a dessert of sliced apples and cheeses.

She had to be careful about this, Lilika thought. Too much, and she was dead, too little, and she was dead anyway, hanged or burned or quartered. Poison was not a game she played, and if she wanted her accusations to hold against Marjeta, she would need to suffer. It was no easy thing, coming back from the dead.

She held out the plate of apple slices. "Eat, my love," she said, and after he had taken one slice, she took her own, swallowing down the sour taste of her fear. The apples were red as fallen blood, their flesh sweet and white and crisp, but Lilika could not taste anything but bile. She made her final meal last, while Calvai ate until his mouth began to foam.

The pain started in her chest under her ribs, small as a baby's fist, and it spread up her throat and choked her. The pain grew with each ravaged breath, and Lilika felt the tears and blood pressing out from under eyelids and running down her cheeks. Her mouth filled with copper. Lilika stared into Calvai's bulging eyes and clenched his hands in hers as they fell to the ground. He convulsed under her and she shuddered likewise, a mummers' pantomime of coupling; a little death.

Lilika's last sight was not Calvai's death. It was the great bull head of Furis, and her heart was his, and her knowledge was this: There would be no king uniting the duchies.

But there would be a queen.

And a witch would burn.

An Empty Cage

"We shouldn't have waited so long," Marjeta said after Silviana had left her rooms. Her hands were shaking, and she couldn't understand why. What did it matter that the girl knew, that she would feel betrayed? Silviana was not a sister, not a daughter. Barely even a friend. They were simply two girls who had been thrown into the same cage by circumstance. Each of them had to make a meal of the bones they were given.

"I thought it would still be a day or so before my uncle reached here," Devan said. "The armies will have camped and taken refuge in the Verrin barracks and fort, and it would have been a hard day's ride from there to reach the summer palace so quickly." He sounded tired, doubtful. "He should not be here."

"And now?" Marjeta sat down on the edge of her bed and stared at her half-packed bags. The plan had been simple enough. Devan would leave on his hunter that day, ostensibly to go meet his duke; but would veer off to follow a path he and Marjeta had agreed on. She would wait till nightfall and go down to the paddocks where the older horses grazed, feral and heavy-coated, and call Dust to her. They would slip away under spellwork, and the pair would be gone from Calvai's lands before the duke entered the palace. They were both hunters, they had coin and small treasure enough between them. Two riders could travel fast and untracked and live off the autumn land long enough to get to safety. Winter was at the borders, restless, but they could find shelter before the first snowfalls.

All that was gone. "We should have left sooner," Marjeta

whispered to her clenched hands. She kept her head down, looking at her lap, at her white and red knuckles. Her head beat mercilessly. The duke had not called for her, even though he had returned and must surely have rested and eaten by now. What was going on? Had some whisper of her infidelity reached his ears? That serpent Lilika had hissed in his ear long enough that he would find a reason to have the marriage ended. There was little chance that would go well for Marjeta, accused of being a cuckolding witch. Lilika would be happy enough to see her dance in the flames below the Penitent's Tower, and she could only hope for the blessing of a friendly arrow through her eye.

"There is still time." Devan got to his feet. "We must leave tonight." He crossed to her and knelt, taking her folded hands in his and warming them, callous to callous. "Whether or not my uncle knows now, I cannot stay longer. I cannot see you so unhappy. You kill yourself each day, your flame grows smaller and colder. We will run."

"And you will give up everything," Marjeta said. It was an argument they'd had many times. It was worn, safe and comfortable as an old woollen dress.

"I told you, I would rather a ship than a crown, a horse than a throne. And I would rather be with the woman I love than married to a queen who feels like a little sister."

"You never were one for ambition," Marjeta said, and pulled one hand free from his grasp to stroke at his head, to curl her fingers through the dark hair that fell across his forehead.

"I know," he said. "I'm terribly disappointing." He smiled at her, awkward, but honest. "Come." Devan pulled her to her feet. "Perhaps he will not call you tonight. I will leave now — make some excuse, and you will use your magic to slip out tonight. Nothing has to change, perhaps it's better that Silviana knows the truth. She will not pine for something she hates."

A rapid knock sounded at the door, and Marjeta frowned as she got to her feet. That had been Genivia's sharp tattoo of warning, and she stood, weaponless but ready for whatever came her way now.

It was Genivia alone, but the woman was flustered, her freckled skin flushed as though she had burned under a summer sun, her red hair in tangled disarray. She looked as though she had run from one end of the palace to the other — an unlikely thing, Genivia was more musician than athlete.

"What is it?"

"The lady Silviana," Genivia panted. She pressed one hand to her side. "Oh, Furis damn my ribs."

"What, what has happened?" Marjeta felt her heart rise, her throat close. Surely the girl could not have been so upset that she had leapt from a window or done something equally foolish and permanent. But she'd always been a strange and emotional thing, and only more so after her illness. "Please, Genny, tell me quickly."

"She's gone."

"Gone?" Devan and Marjeta spoke simultaneously, then Marjeta asked, softer, one hand held out to Devan to still him. "What does that mean, gone? She hasn't, she hasn't—" The words would not come, the thought too big and dark.

"Oh no." Genny shook her head, then said, "Or at least, I think not. I hope not. I mean to say she has fled the palace. She's disappeared and I cannot find her."

"Does her father know?" Devan asked harshly.

"Not yet. Only myself and you two know. I thought I'd come straight here, before you left. Word will get out soon enough. Maid servants will notice. Her bed is empty, and she's missing a travel sack. I think she has run away."

Running away, Marjeta thought, was what they seemed to do. But she could survive well enough. She'd grown up half in the Petrell forests, and in her family the women had been as able to churn butter as they could sew seam. They could shoot and ride and work a loom. The Jurie manner seemed to have kept Silviana powerless and pretty. The girl would die. She would starve, or trip and break her neck in the woods.

Or be shot down by the wild ones who hunted the woods, who would not think twice about killing the duke's only daughter in revenge for those bodies that had lined the palace walls every year.

"You must find her." Marjeta turned to Devan. "Quickly, before it's too late. Go now and hunt her down. If she's run to the woods, she will be dead by moonrise."

Devan nodded. He was already rushing to the door when he paused. "And you?"

"I will stay here," Marjeta said. "We can do nothing until Silviana is safely returned. My conscience will not allow it."

When he was gone Marjeta took a deep breath, smoothed her hair back and ran her hands down the front of her clothes. It was clear these were not palace fineries, but travel clothes, riding clothes. It hardly mattered. The truth was all worming its way out of the corpse of her marriage. "I will inform the duke and tell him that Devan has already gone to search out his cousin."

"Is that wise?" Genivia said.

"Probably not. Would you rather it be you who bears this news?" She tried to smile, to make light of it, but Marjeta knew that there would be questions, and that the duke would have his answers somehow. *It is my fault she ran. I should have been truthful with her from the beginning.* "It doesn't matter," Marjeta said, dully. "In the end." She forced a long-toothed grin. "Perhaps I'll write her a letter explaining everything when they lock me in the Penitent's Tower."

"Do not joke so," Genivia scolded.

"I do not."

"I know." Genivia reached out and grasped one hand. "I will come with you."

"No." Marjeta shook her head. "You keep looking. Perhaps the girl has simply hidden herself somewhere in the palace just to frighten us. If she means to do something foolish and permanent, I need you to stop her. I will deal with whatever Calvai does."

The women left Marjeta's rooms together, and it was with a sinking heart that Marjeta closed her doors and walked past the bustling men and women of the palace. They knew nothing yet, and servants curtsied or bowed as she passed. A few quick questions and it became clear that the duke had gone straight to his usual official chambers. No one thought it strange that Marjeta went to him. She was his wife, after all. The mother of his child, even if that child had not been mothered long.

She climbed the stairs, her thighs aching with each step, her heart slowing. There was no spell that could save her from cold anger, and she had long ago given up trying to bind Calvai to her. Those had been Areya's spells and look what they had done.

Marjeta paused before the door, frowning. Where was the man who should be guarding here? She pushed the heavy door and it opened easily, unbarred. There was no sound from within. Her skin prickled, heart thrumming. Perhaps he had departed. Someone else may have noticed Silviana's disappearance and already informed the duke. "Hello?" she called softly, but there was no answer. She moved quickly through the adjoining rooms, until she came to the private inner chambers where Duke Calvai Jurie had eaten his last meal.

Mirror, Mirror

The table was set for feasting. Meat gone cold, bread gone hard. The fruits were still glowing softly under the flickering candles, and the air smelled of beeswax and apple wine.

Marjeta stood very still, as though any movement, any breath, would disturb the strange scene laid out before her. The chairs had been kicked over, the carpets rumpled, a plate shattered, a glass of wine spilled. The wine soaked into thick wool, and shards of glass glittered green from the thick plush. Nothing moved. The air was frigid, as though winter had taken root here and begun unfurling, spreading out from the duke's room like a frozen canker.

If she were fanciful, Marjeta would have compared the scene to one of those buttery rich oil paintings from the south, where the artists were so keen on painting the ordinary with jewel like luminosity. The artists that Silviana had loved so before her vision was ruined. Artists who made petals and curled leaves, the feathers of dead cock pheasants and the dew on a ripened peach look more real than reality itself. Artists who made you taste and feel, fall into a world they built themselves. Perhaps, if she did not blink, this would be one of those paintings. More real than real, but not real at all.

The bodies were pale, golden shadows from the fire the only flickering movement across their skin. Calvai with spumey froth around his blue tinged lips, his eyes rimmed with blood. As though he were a child who had festooned himself with cosmetic graces, but not known quite how to do it.

And beneath him, cradling him, Lilika, her features slack and old, her jaw hanging open, imbecilic. One hand was curled loosely around a small bone-handled knife, and Marjeta crouched to free it. There was no blood on it, though the point was sharp as a pin. This close she could smell the apple mulch on Lilika's tongue — faint fruit, a sweeter, stranger rot.

Though who would come into Calvai's private chambers to poison the duke and his mistress?

The bodies were still. Gently, Marjeta pressed one hand to her husband's face, covering his nose and mouth. There was no breath stirring against her palm, no final flicker of life. She'd hardly expected it. Marjeta chewed at her lip. In a few hours it would be daylight and the men would find their duke dead, bitter froth on his face, his cheeks purpled, his eyes weeping cold blood. Even a halfwit would be able to say "poison" and look at the witch-wife who'd poisoned her own sister in order to marry well.

Stories didn't have to be true in order to break you.

And what of Lilika? She caressed the woman's face. Her cheek was still warm, but perhaps she was too soon dead to tell. Her breath, if it was there, was too fine to feel against Marjeta's frozen fingers.

It didn't matter.

They would say she killed them both, Marjeta knew. Poisoned them with apples and bitter wine. She looked over at the half-eaten fruit. Calvai had eaten sliced golden apples, crunched his way through them like a horse, almost unthinking. Marjeta frowned and went to get a better look at the gleaming fruit. Lilika's apples. And she had eaten also. Her half-eaten apple had rolled to one side, the white flesh losing its crispness, already browning under the flickering light of the candles. Marjeta held the paring knife that had cut into it. Lilika had used this to cut herself off only a slice, a little moon sickle of white flesh. Just enough. There, among the debris on the floor was a tiny vial, blue and empty. Marjeta scooped it up gingerly between finger and thumb and held it closer to her right eye. Not empty. A faint trace of fluid still coated the inner glass.

She'd poisoned herself. On purpose. But even Lilika was not suicidal. She'd meant to look as though she was a victim. "I should finish your work for you," Marjeta said and held the knife tighter. Smother her with a pillow. Cut her throat. Force the last of the apple down her unresisting throat. "And make myself a murderer in truth." She palmed the knife, feeling her want heat it from handle to blade tip. "But no. You win. And I lose. But you will not set yourself on the duke's dais and think to rule after my death in Silviana's absence. What did you plan?" she asked the sleeping woman as she gathered an apple small and yellow as a little sun and placed it in her skirt pocket along with the paring knife and the vial, stoppered with a piece of wax. "Did you think you could latch on to the next duke they found to replace Calvai? Did Furis tell you it would be so?" Marjeta snorted. "I will not kill you, sister. You can ruin my name, but you cannot make me into what you say I am."

She left the sleeping dead, making her way back to where her packed bags were waiting for her. Genivia also waited, ringing her broad hands.

"What has happened? You look so grim."

"It is nothing," Marjeta said. "The duke—" She choked. What lie to say? "He has asked me to do something," she settled on. "Witchcraft."

"The duke?"" Genivia's look of surprise almost made Marjeta laugh. "So, he knows?"

"I told him." Marjeta opened the saddle bags that lay on her bed of blood and broken things. In a moment she had her childhood cloak, the embroidery stitches tacky and dull with age, the cloak no better than a capelet now. She threw it over her shoulders and knotted the laces with hands that did not tremble.

Marjeta unwrapped her mirror from its soft and yellowed silk and stared into her reflection. The last time she'd looked into this hoping to find someone she'd lost, it had shown her nothingness, blackness. But then, Valerija had been dead and no longer of this world. Perhaps, once again, it would show her nothing she wanted to see. Silviana was gone into the forests, and like any small and helpless thing she could have already died.

"I am a fool," Marjeta said as she cut her thumb open.

Blood dribbled, then gushed out onto the mirror surface.

Enough blood to cast a spell even if magic was weak and thin, and Marjeta hardly a witch at all.

"Mirror, mirror, take my soul, show me the thing which makes me whole," she whispered to the blood, and she did not think of her baby, dead and buried in a black and lonely grave, or her sister white and seeing ghosts, or her hunting hound with her stomach full of maggots. She concentrated on a girl with hair like starling's wings, her skin like snow, her mouth bloodied, one eye dark as oncoming storms, the other cold as bones.

In the mirror the blood began to swirl, and from it a bare black forest grew around a clearing, a log and stone cabin covered in dying vines and moss; a bolt hole for wild things. It shimmered with distance. However far it was, the mirror would lead her there, but the Three only knew how long it would take to bring Silviana home.

By the time she returned, Lilika would most likely have woken from her self-induced slumber and told the whole palace her story.

"Forget them all," Marjeta said. She should erase this life from her skin, walk out into the world and disappear. Who was she to care what happened to Silviana? Devan would surely find her eventually. He could still come back and take his place.

"What will you do?" Marjeta asked the mirror. "If I leave you to your wild ones?"

The blood washed away the forest and in its place was a field of fallen dead, the skulls white, picked clean by rooks and ravens. There was the Penitent's Tower, and below it the great flickering fires and a figure that danced in its charring skin.

"And if I bring you back?"

A girl reflected back at Marjeta, a girl of black and white and red. Simple colours, complex colours. She wore a diadem of holly and she carried a sword in one hand, a wooden sceptre in the other. Behind her the men stood with flags and pistols. They would die too, some of them.

But not all.

"I am a fool," Marjeta said. "But I have never been a traitor."

*

Caped, and with the mirror held before her like a dowsing rod, Marjeta ran from the castle into the deepening night. She did not bother with going to the stables, she had no need of tack and explanations and saddlebags. She ran leather booted, with her skirts tucked in tightly, her hair pulled back from her angular face.

Marjeta made her way through the outer complex of palace buildings, past the well road and the curved dungeons and the minor barracks, past kennels and privies and abandoned dovecotes and herb spirals and potagers scraggly with the last harvest of ripening fruit and gourds, and through the narrow side gates. A guard only nodded at her as she left. The news still lay undiscovered.

Marjeta crossed tussocky fields to where a handful of older horses and ponies were pastured, their coats already growing thick and rough with the changing seasons. Behind them the forest rose, tall as mountains. The great beeches and chestnuts had shed their fiery leaves, and they wore faded gowns of ivy, their feet buried in thick, ancient loam. Marjeta stood at the split wood fence and whistled, and from the little knot of a herd, an ancient sway backed pony trotted, her face sunken, her teeth long, her coat staring.

"My beauty," Marjeta said. "Will you carry me this one last time?"

Dust whickered softly, and lipped at her mistress's hands and face, her muzzle like velvet and steam. Marjeta climbed the fence to mount her old pony, and bridleless and saddleless they moved together to leave the curiously watching herd and take the rough trails into the forest, already black now with shadow and nightfall.

Poisoned Apples

With one hand tangled in Dust's thick mane, and the other holding the mirror tightly, Marjeta followed the path the blood and silver pointed out for her. At first the mirror was easy enough to understand; it darkened when she went the wrong way and grew clearer as she drew nearer to the path Silviana had taken. At her back, and wrapped about her neck, Tarkis was a solid comfort, the heat of the salamander reminding her that she was real, that she had not passed into a nightmare

Once Marjeta reached a hollowrode that led from the palace through part of the wood, she also noticed other small clues that let her know that both Silviana and Devan had come this way: a broken twig hanging listless, a tangle of pale hair glinting in the last of the silver shrivelight, the curved impression of hooves in the thick dark soil. Devan had taken the deer path at reckless speed, judging from the depth of the prints, and the space of the gait. Marjeta clicked her tongue and squeezed Dust's flanks firmly, urging her on. Devan might be able to gallop blindly through woodland without fear, but Marjeta had seen too many animals killed on hunts from a misstep and snapped bones to take the risk with Dust. They would outpace the girl. She was on foot, tired, half blind.

Marjeta slipped the mirror into her skirt pocket and with both hands keeping her balanced, urged the little mare on. "Before the last of the moonlight is gone, my sweet."

Dust pricked her ears forward, and shifted, moving faster through the narrow pathway, sure footed as any mountain pony.

The moon was descending already, and though it was fat as a milk fed baby, the light only barely pierced the thick branches. As they drew deeper into the forest, there would be none at all.

The path would be harder to follow, it would be easier to trip over a root, snap a leg in an animal's hollow.

And harder to see enemies.

The deep woods were dangerous. Devan and his band of hunters may have cleared the forest near the palace of blackguards and thieves, however much Marjeta hated their methods, but the wild forest boys were still eking out an existence in the heart of the greenwood.

The pathways branched, and Marjeta commanded Dust to slow. The pony stood, flanks gently trembling, while Marjeta felt in her deep skirt pockets for the mirror.

Vial, apple, sharpened blade wrapped in a handkerchief.

But no mirror.

Marjeta's heart froze. She lifted Tarkis from her shoulders and set him before her on the pony's withers. She glanced back, but all that lay behind her was darkness, and the crackled whispers of night animals.

She closed her eyes. Why had she not felt it fall from her pocket — and how was she to go on without it? She would have to dismount and lead Dust back while they looked for the fallen hand mirror. The ground here beneath the trees was spongey with leaf litter and decay, so there was a good chance it had not broken, but even so, a great pall of disappointed rage sank over Marjeta. She should have held it fast and kept watching it, and sacrificed speed for surety.

She tipped her head back and said aloud to the forest: "I am not a believer."

The forest *hssshed* back at her, the tree tops conferring uneasily. Tarkis rattled his long spines; a gentle warning.

"I tried," Marjeta said, her voice growing stronger. "It would have been so much easier if I had faith like my mother. Even Areya believed. All I know is that there were three little statues who never ate the sacrifices we gave them. I fed your offerings to the salamander. If you answered prayers, they were never mine."

The trees stilled, and the rustling of the undergrowth dropped away. No nightbirds called. The silence was as impenetrable as a filled grave. Her breath misted before her face.

"So, hear me now," she continued. "If the Three still have power, then show me where Silviana went. If you care at all for the future she will bring."

She snapped her mouth shut, waiting, but not expecting much. Magic and myths had never come easily to her. She had the blood, but not the power. She could draw a bow, ride a horse at hunt, gut and skin a rabbit. She knew what roots and mushrooms to eat if she was far from home, and these days she could sew a seam and weave wool on the little tapestry loom she'd always hated as a child. But prayer and magic were mysteries.

The air warmed, almost imperceptibly, though the unnatural silence lingered.

"Is that it?" Marjeta shouted, and her sudden noise caused a flurry of movement from a nearby curl of thick brown bracken.

A hare stared back at her. It stood on its hind legs, nose twitching furiously, black eyes glassy. It was barely more than a silhouette.

"Ah," Marjeta breathed, and put one hand to her chest. "Starting at hares, like a child who has never left the village."

A second hare popped up alongside the first, and moments later, a third joined them. They stared back at her like three statuettes.

Then the first cocked its head, and — *one, two, three* — the hares shot off, their white tails leading the way like ghost lamps.

Marjeta followed them. They were slow, constantly stopping to watch her, make certain that Dust could follow their signals. Marjeta clenched her hands tight against the coarse hairs at the ponies withers, and felt her heart seize in a rapture of fright and disbelief.

The three hares drew up to where the path widened and spilled out into a small clearing. One side had been formed by a tree that had fallen down. Its roots were still half buried, and the downed tree had thrown narrow twigs skyward along its length, as though it had grown itself a miniature forest along it back.

The hares scattered, running off in three directions and leaving Marjeta alone in the clearing.

Or not alone. On the other side of the fallen tree lay a large form. Marjeta could smell horse manure, sweat, blood and the sour reek of vomit. She edged her pony round the fallen tree, and found Devan's horse, its belly slashed, arrows jutting from its thick neck. Dust snorted nervously, dancing back away from the terrible sight.

Crushed beneath the beast was a familiar body. Devan, still as one of the statues of Furis that haunted the recesses of the summer palace. Grey and moonwashed. She slipped down from Dust and edged forward, her heart hammering. The arrows were enough. The wild boys had been here, and they had killed the one she loved. In revenge, most likely, for he had killed so many of them himself. Perhaps Silviana was likewise dead, her throat flowering shaft and feathers.

Her face was wet with tears, though Marjeta made no noise. Curse the Three who had filled her with hope just minutes ago, she thought, and placed one hand gently against the pale corpse.

He moaned, and she drew her hand back. The wounds he'd taken had stained his clothes black, but he was still alive. Without thinking, Marjeta pulled her split skirts from her boots and used the little paring knife to tear long strips of material. It took all her strength to pull Devan free from his dead horse, and though he stayed unconscious, he kept breathing, kept moaning in distant pain.

Marjeta bandaged him as best she could, and she was knotting a strip of linen tight about his chest when his eyes opened.

"Goddess?"

Marjeta snorted, but her voice was thick. "You're not dead yet, fool, though not for lack of trying. Can you stand?"

She helped him to his feet, though he swayed and staggered and clutched at her for support. "Wild boys," he said. "They took her, unharmed."

"You're certain?"

"I heard them talk while they thought me dead. I can't go on," he said, and his voice cracked. He was defeated. For all that had happened between the three of them, Devan loved his cousin dearly. "I must try." He lurched toward Dust, as though ready to clamber back astride and continue his hunt.

"No. You need a healer, and sooner would be better." Marjeta made her decision quickly and she kissed his cheek, feeling the stubble scrape at her mouth, and wiped her tears away against his shoulder. The hares had led her here, and they would lead her further. "Mount Dust, and I will tie you securely. She knows the way back and she will bear you, though she will not be fast."

"And you?"

Marjeta felt the blood moving through her heart, as though tying her to her path. She looked down at the torn remnants of her skirts that hung jagged at her knees, and at her supple riding boots. They were not meant for walking, but they would do well enough. Dust would take Devan back, but she would not be alone. At her feet, the golden salamander waited, resting his head on her meagre pack of food and water. "I will find Silviana, and I will bring her back."

*

The night was deep and cold by the time Marjeta had seen to Devan and helped him mount Dust. It was a risk sending him back on a bareback pony, but it was the best Marjeta could think of in the situation. It was clear now that the wild boys of the woods had taken Silviana, though whether she was still alive, Marjeta didn't know.

Her chest ached. If she'd not lost the mirror, she could try once again for a vision of the girl.

And what if it showed black? What then? Would you turn back and go to the waiting fires? Marjeta pulled her cloak firmer around her shoulders and held the furred hood closed against her chin. The wind hissing through the trees was sharp and wintry, iced from the northern mountains. At least without the mirror, she had a kind of hope to hold on to. There was no confirmation of Silviana's death.

She watched as Dust disappeared into the shadowed trail, Devan hunched over her back, swaying slightly with each plodding step. Dust was wise, and she'd be careful. She knew Devan, and she'd listen to his commands, even if she'd whickered nervously when

Marjeta had rubbed her long grey nose in goodbye, and held her neck, pressing into the sturdy warmth, the comforting scent of her. "You take him home," she'd whispered, soft enough that only the pony and her own heart would hear it. She couldn't burden Devan with her fear now. He had already assured her that he would make it back to the palace and gather men to hunt down the wildling boys and find Silviana.

Marjeta had said nothing of the duke's death. It was too much to explain, too much in too little time. He would find out for himself.

When the last flicker of grey disappeared from her sight, Marjeta took a deep calming breath. Her skin still tingled, but not with cold. She recognized it — had been around it enough as a child. She was in an old place now, and old places had eddies where the magic caught and stayed. "Show me," she said again. "Like you led me here, lead me to Silviana." The command was swallowed up by the stillness of the ancient forest, muffled by moss.

A branch snapped, and Marjeta started, looking back to see if Devan was returning, but all she saw was a humped shape, a blackness in the blackness. "Do you come to guide me?" she asked.

The shape stood upright, peeling itself away from the shadows and staring down at her.

Marjeta's heart hammered. This was no leap of hares, or a guiding benevolent spirit. The musky reek hit her as the wind shifted, curling the stink around her. Carrion and sweetness, fur and ice.

She was trembling. There was no point in running, if she even could. She swayed, dizzy, soft and weak as a foal. The magic welled up between her and the bear, strong enough to make it feel as though the air between them vibrated like a swarm of summer midges, and then the bear huffed, and dropped back to four feet and padded over to her. It walked past her, even as Marjeta stayed breathless and unmoving, too scared to blink. It stood higher at the shoulder than her own pony, had jaws bigger and stronger than any mastiffs. If it chose, it could eat her alive, snap her bones and pull out her innards like coils of stuffing from a child's poppet.

The bear paused and huffed again as it looked back at her.

As though to say *come along, little furless cub* and the spell of immobility was broken. In wordless wonder, Marjeta followed the bear. In a moment of giddy shock, she hummed the first few bars of Valerija's favourite song, the one she would sing as she worked, the one Mother had taught them in their cradles.

The bear flicked one ear, but did not pause, and in a cracked voice, unused to singing, Marjeta whispered the refrain, "Oh, the bear will dance with the maiden fair, and take her into the woods, oh, and there they will wed and a crown she'll wear, all in the summer woods, oh!"

They walked on, wrapped in magic, and Marjeta, for the first time since her sister's death, felt almost happy, a strange deliriousness that felt almost like falling in love, like falling, like falling and never landing.

The bear and Marjeta walked together through the forest, the miles falling away underfoot, until the sun began to pink the darkness to a pale silver, and the birds around them woke in a sleepy, querulous clamour. Marjeta stood on the edge of a large open clearing, almost a meadow, and next to her, the bear turned to shadows and nothingness, and faded away.

In the clearing was a wood and stone bothy, its sides packed with mud and moss, its slanted roof overgrown with flowers and leaves. The grass around it was high and golden, ripe with seeds, and the sky was cold and clear and pale blue. The house stood alone, and Marjeta pressed herself against a tree trunk, and watched.

Her stomach ached, and her throat was dry, but she ate only a little crust of bread, and wet her mouth with dew. She shared her meagre breakfast with Tarkis, and the salamander grumbled at the food, before wrapping his sinuous body about her feet and settling in to sleep. She pondered on how she would get Silviana to return home, quietly, calmly. They had no time to waste in argument, and Marjeta did not want the girl rousing her captors with her stubbornness, or her hatred of Marjeta.

After a while, several men and boys emerged from the bothy, yawning and talking in slow, sleepy grunts. As they woke, the conversation picked up, and Marjeta listened to the snatches of it ring around her, though she could follow no words. Eventually, the wild boys melted away into the forest, one even passing her where she sat and seeing nothing, and the clearing fell silent again.

Marjeta got to her feet and waded through the golden lake of grass, Tarkis scrambling alongside her. She knocked on the wooden door. Before anyone could answer, she placed the golden apple on the threshold stone, and dropped a single drop from the vial onto the wrinkled skin.

*

Marjeta was waiting at the tree line with her salamander curled across her shoulders and her cape pulled over her head, crouched against a trunk, when the door finally swung inward a crack, and a thin, familiar face peered out. Her hair had gone greyer in the intervening night, so that the girl looked like a tiny crone from this distance. One hand twisted against her side in indecision.

Pick it up. The thought was no more a spell than any empty prayer was, but it worked. After a few more seconds of nervous deliberation, the girl swooped down to grab the little golden apple. Perhaps she thought it a gift left by her captors. Or rescuers. Whichever she believed them to be. What had they even fed her out here in these wild places? Boiled roots and charred lean meat? The girl was used to feasts piled upon feasts. Even if Silviana had never considered that she might be spoiled, a few days away from the plenty of the palace would have shown her how wrong she was.

Marjeta was rewarded. Silviana ate the apple there on the threshold, right down to the very core, and even that she chewed almost to the stalk, spitting the pips out into the meadow grasses.

The poison Lilika had used to kill the duke and put herself into a death-like sleep worked far quicker than Marjeta had expected. When Silviana grasped at her throat, eyes bulging, Marjeta shot to her feet and ran across the open field, pulling back the hood from her hair. Tarkis dug his claws in deep through the linen of her shirt, hard enough to break skin and make her blood flow down her shoulders and back. The faint, weakened spells that Valerija had threaded into the cloth so many years ago could not hold, and Silviana shouted as she saw Marjeta appear before her, before she crumpled to the ground, her limbs thrashing, eyes rolled up into white, wet marble.

Marjeta knelt beside her stepdaughter, one hand against the girl's side as Silviana shuddered and went limp. A terrible fear rose in her, but the girl still breathed, though it was an almost imperceptible motion. Already her skin grew chill. It would be easy to mistake her for dead, just as people would be doing to Lilika now. Unless the woman was already awake and swearing to the sons of Furis that she'd been poisoned by the dreaded witch, and that Marjeta was a murderer and would be murderer three times over.

She grimaced. "What am I supposed to do?" she said to the unanswering woods around her.

Tarkis hissed softly against her ear, as though offering advice. He was all she needed, surely. Devan — Devan was a love she had locked carefully into a small box, and Silviana she'd learned to keep always at a distance. Who did she owe loyalty and compassion to, but the symbol of her family that had come with her from home, had comforted her when there was no one else to comfort her? She knew what she should do — run, leave the girl, leave Devan. She was far from the palace, and she knew how to cover her trail and how to survive the deep woods. It would not be pleasant and winter was too close for comfort, but she could do it. It was not a certain death, at any rate.

Marjeta snorted in self-loathing. Should was all very well. But she was a Petrell, and she was not afraid of death. She would carry guilt in her far worse if she left the girl to her fate here in the woods. Silviana would only survive so long once the wild boys discovered what it was they had in their home. She would pay for her father's sins, and Marjeta could not allow that. With a deep sigh, she lifted the girl. She was thin as a willow sapling and lighter than Marjeta had expected.

With Silviana held in her arms, Marjeta began the long trek back through the woods, this time with no bear to guide her, and no dear Dust to bear her home. Her belly cramped, and she grew weaker and more bloodless with every step.

It took a very long time before she found a familiar trail, and her arms were aching, the muscles torn and useless. Although Silviana was light for her age, she was still a burden, and one that wore on Marjeta with every step. The girl was dead weight. Only the faintest flush at her cheeks let Marjeta know she lived.

They were about four miles out from the palace when the duke's knights surrounded them.

The Burning

Lilika's recovery took longer than Silviana's. She looked ... thin.
Like dough stretched between a cook's fingers, she was tearing
apart. When Silviana came to her sick bed, she held out her arms
for the girl. "You'll not break me, lamb," Lilika said gently. "Your
old Lee-Lee is stronger than that."

"My father is dead," Silviana said. "And Marjeta brought me
home."

Lilika lowered her arms, resting her palms flat against the wool
covers, stroking them. "What did Brother Milos tell you?" she
asked finally.

"Milos? Nothing." Silviana dismissed the idea of the priest.
He was no more than an annoying midge. "I care not for what
brothers of Furis have to say."

"You walk on treacherous ice. Furis sees all."

"Does he?" Silviana cocked her head, the blank eye seeing right
through Lilika as though she had turned to blown glass. "Furis is
just a man pretending to be a god. I see things too."

"Hush now, lamb. Your father's passing has shocked you, I
understand."

"It has," she agreed.

"You must not say such things. It is only by Furis' truth that
the witch responsible for his death — and nearly for mine — is
trapped in the tower now. It is Furis who has saved you, and Furis
who will make her suffer in fire for all her wrongs. She will pay for
everything she has done to you."

"That she will."

A sudden crack made them both start and turn just in time to see a bird, broken necked, fall down from the window. It left a comet trail of black feathers swirling behind it, then that too was gone. "So brief," Silviana whispered.

"Birds?"

"Life." Silviana looked back at her and saw the truth of Lilika fall across her face in a shadow, dark as sorrow. "But yes, birds too. They are brief. They live their little lives, caged or free, but in the end they all stop flying."

Lilika shivered. "You are safe now," she said. "Your father's funeral will pass, the traitor will die, and eventually there will be a wedding feast to celebrate the good fellowship between your family and Devan's. Life may be brief, but it does go on."

"It does," Silviana echoed. She smiled, a sudden, vicious slip that was gone almost as quickly as it arrived. "Tell me the truth, Lee-lee."

"Always, lamb."

"How did my father die?"

*

Silviana watched the two figures burn from the window of the Penitent's Tower. The first time the wood refused to catch, still too damp and rotten from the long autumn, the deep and heavy rains. Finally, one of the guardsmen brought a large pitcher of oil and doused the lower branches and logs of the pyre, pouring golden in the slight sun.

The next try the branches caught, licking hungrily, breathing out great black rolling plumes of smoke.

Through it all the Duchess Marjeta had stayed silent, watching from her seat in the stands, her face expressionless. Almost calm. She had only once shown anything, when Brother Milos had kicked at the branches, as though he could fight his way free from this ending Silviana had chosen for him, and Marjeta's mouth had twitched, as though she were amused. It happened so quickly, so small a movement that Silviana was half convinced that it had only been a flicker of dust, a dream of her own.

The witch who had killed her mother and father had died before the flames came to her feet, slumped in her bonds of rope and smoke.

A small mercy, Silviana thought. And her heart ached. Love was not an easy thing to burn. It caught slow and smouldered. It dragged out its agony.

There had been no such mercy for her Brother Milos, whose guttural screams for Furis to save him had reminded Silviana of a mating fox. A wild shriek of animal pain, all the eerier for being out of place in the smoky courtyard.

"What would you have us do with the ashes, Lady Silviana?" It was the servant woman Genivia, come to join her in this room where Marjeta had spent the few last hours before this execution. Sewing at shirts, if that was to be believed, though the pile of clothing folded neatly on the table spoke to the truth of it.

A small scrap of paper on top had been left as final instructions. Silviana had read them, hoping for some truth that would make her feel better about this first act of hers as her father's heir. It had simply been instructions to Genivia as to which village families the shirts were to go to.

"The ashes," Silviana said slowly, and fingered one of the shirt sleeves, pulling it free from the pile. The stitches were tiny and delicate, small enough to have been worked at by mice. Perhaps Marjeta had conjured a furry army of tailors to do her work while she waited in her prison. She shifted the sleeve, trying to push it back into place, when her fingers made contact with something hard and thin inside the bundle of newly sewn shirts. "You've gathered them?"

"All that we could," Genivia said. "It's mostly — mostly ... human." She sat down on the stool by the empty hearth and stirred the dead ashes at the edge with the tip of her boot. "In the old days, the best way to make certain that an evil was cleansed from the land was to take the ashes of the villain to sea, and there cast them away."

"Is that something from your three goddesses?" Silviana asked.

Genivia swallowed. "Most likely."

"And what would Good Furis have us do, I wonder... It would

be more fitting, after all. They were his people."

"I — I shall find out, my lady."

Silviana pressed her fingers deeper into the pile, glad for the moment that her hands were out of Genivia's sight. It was a letter, the paper crisp and tempting. Slowly, she caught the letter between her fingers and eased it out, slipping it up her sleeve without looking at it. "These shirts need to be distributed," she said at last.

"And the ashes? I can ask the brothers of Furis what to do with them — send them to the coastal abbey, if necessary—"

"No," Silviana said. "Leave them in my rooms."

She needed, after all, to say goodbye to this false mother of hers. This false brother. Silviana watched the truth fall like ash around her.

"It has been a trying day for you, my lady." Genivia stood. "I will arrange food and drinks for you in your rooms, and leave the ashes there as instructed." She curtsied before leaving.

Silviana leaned her elbow on the table and looked at the white shirts. The Duchy of Jurie had changed, like a coin that had landed on its edge. Her father's soldier's, her cousin's armies, even the distant knights of Petrell were still waiting for a king to lead them on.

There was no king.

And with the armies of the west and the east massing at the borders of Vestiarik, the eight duchies were too split and small to do much more than be slowly crushed between them, like little almonds between the pincers of a vice.

There needed to be a marriage, and there needed to be a force to lead them. Her father's armies waited, as did the plans he'd laid in place. He'd meant to make of himself a king to stand high in Verrin Fort, with its massive walls and its five towers, but Silviana supposed a queen would do in his place. She sighed, and felt for the letter in her sleeve. She would have to move fast while the duchies were still reeling, still biding their time. All of the Eastern duchies still belonged to the Three, even if the dukes pretended to follow Furis.

She did not need the dukes.

She needed their people. It was time to make some changes,

but first she would see her stepmother raised to the throne, and her cousin wed. A queen would come from Jurie, but it would not be Silviana.

She turned to look one last time at the scorch marks far below. It could so easily have been Marjeta who had died there. Lilika had spun her webs well. But she had not thought that Silviana would ever go against her. A brown widow who had loved a fly grub and kept it bound in silk and fed on carrion, only to find she'd raised a wasp instead.

"Good bye, Lilika," Silviana whispered to the open window. "I will thank you for one thing only, and that was the truth."

From the blackened remnants of the pyre, a shadow slipped free. Then a second and third. The trio of ghost hares raised their ears once in salute, then leapt through the cinders and bone dust, and disappeared.

———

Acknowledgments

Cast Long Shadows began as a simple retelling of Snow White. I was tired of the trope of Evil Stepmother, and decided to rewrite the most famous of those with the idea that she was nothing more than a human caught in circumstances she couldn't quite control.

Over the years it warped and grew, until it was finally the story that it needed to be.

My deep thanks go to Francesca T. Barbini who snapped my novel out of the Luna Press slush, and between her and Shona Kinsella, beat the story into shape. It was such a pleasure to work with a team who have such faith in their writers.

I have a small army of first readers, fellow writers, and supportive pals who have helped me with my novels, including this one. Thank you to all the Musers, and to Nerine Dorman and Elizabeth Retief for their eyes and thoughts.

A special thanks to my daughters Tanith and Noa for being cool humans, and to my family for supporting me in my writing.

Cat Hellisen, 2022

Lightning Source UK Ltd.
Milton Keynes UK
UKHW040916100322
399856UK00001B/37